THE SHINING DAY

FRANK ROSS

FAWCETT CREST · NEW YORK

A Fawcett Crest Book
Published by Ballantine Books

Copyright © 1981 by Literary Holdings (Gibraltar) Limited

Library of Congress Catalog Card Number: 80-69394

ISBN 0-449-20376-x

This edition published by arrangement with Atheneum

Printed in Canada

First Ballantine Books Edition: October 1983

FOR
JOHN GREATHEAD
in gratitude, affection and respect

CONTENTS

BOOK ONE
1939

Wilhelm Sommer shaved moodily, conscious that had he not taken a cold shower he would still have an erection. He had dreamed all night of Lotte Hansa, the Lower Secunda tutor, a rawboned Valkyrian blonde with whom he had never exchanged more than a polite "good morning" in five years, and the frustration still showed in his face.

He glared at his reflection in the steamed glass. Exhaustion glared back. And tension. And guilt. He pushed back a strand of fine gold hair and patted it in place. During the past few weeks he had taken to parting his hair in the middle to hide the deep arrowheads of baldness opening up on either side of his skull. The effect took years off his age, but it was a fruitless kind of camouflage. He pulled down the loose skin under his blue eyes and hissed despairingly at the crazing of blood vessels on the whites. No youth left there. None.

Else shouted something to the maid from the dining room and he flinched involuntarily. He must compose himself before going in to breakfast; compose the blood, the guilt in his face. She would pretend, as always, to be occupied but she missed nothing.

He splashed water on his face, toweled it vigorously, chafing blood into his pale cheeks, and went back to his bedroom to put on his tie and jacket. Why she persisted in treating him as if he were an irresponsible rake and she his devoted and vulnerable lover mystified him. They had not slept in the same room, let alone the same bed, since Kurt was conceived nearly eleven years ago.

He stepped into the hall and saw her at the table, her dark, neatly bunned head bent over the *Berliner Volkszeitung*. He pushed open the door to the children's room and Kurt looked up eagerly.

"Good morning, Father."

"Kurt, Willy." He waited for his elder son to acknowledge him.

Willy raised his eyes briefly. "Morning." He was sixteen

3

years old and already shaving. He had inherited his father's classic Nordic face and coloring, but he was Else's son in every other respect. It wouldn't be long now before Willy rejected him entirely, but there would be no wrench in the final separation.

"You'll be at the rally tomorrow?" Sommer asked awkwardly.

Kurt's small face ballooned with pleasure. "I'm marching," he said excitedly. He snatched a cautionary glance at his brother. "Herr Fulke said I'll be a standard-bearer."

"That's very good. And you, Willy?"

The older boy looked up again with studied irritation. "No!" He had the shoulders, the arms and hands of a wrestler—and the temperament of a butcher, Sommer thought.

"Why not?"

"Because we have better things to do than march with kids."

They eyed each other militantly for the space of three seconds. Sommer was the first to yield. "Well . . ." He fidgeted at the door. "I'll talk to you. . . ." Willy went back to his breakfast.

"Will you come to see me, Father?" Kurt asked.

"Yes, of course." It was a lie; there was no possibility of his being able to leave the examination board meeting to watch a parade at three in the afternoon, but Kurt would have no way of knowing that. "Tomorrow, then." He left them quickly.

Else lifted her head to him as he bent to kiss her hair but she did not take her eyes from the *Volkszeitung*.

"Did you sleep well?"

He sat down. "Yes. You?"

"Thank you."

He breathed a sigh of relief. No inspection this morning. She seemed preoccupied.

He buttered some black bread, spooned a generous layer of Belgian *confiture* across one corner, and opened the *Lokal Anzeiger*. They kept religiously to their own newspapers at breakfast—Else to the *Volkszeitung* because it espoused the official Party line, Sommer to the *Lokal Anzeiger* for the arts criticism it carried. Else regarded his cultural indulgences as thoroughly decadent at this point in Germany's political development, but although the paper had declined sadly since '33 he refused to give it up. There were limits to conforming.

He bent his head, pretending to be absorbed, but shot an exploratory glance at the opened letters beside her plate. One, half folded, bore the unmistakable letterhead of Friedrich Wilhelm University. Else had been made coordinator of the National Socialist Action Group there in 1931, a task she had pursued with such vitality that two years ago she had been elected to the Party's loftiest local cabal, the Berlin Advisory Committee.

He felt her eyes on him and retreated guiltily to his paper. He had learned not to pry into her mail.

She took up the letter. "Do you have an appointment for lunch?"

"Well, nothing important. Heini Wassermann wants to talk about the summer curriculum. Why?"

She passed the paper across the table.

"My dear Frau Doktor Sommer. How kind of you to write, and with such dispatch. I shall, of course, be delighted to meet your husband, my respected former student Dr. Wilhelm Sommer. I suggest the hour of two o'clock on Thursday in my office at the university. I am indebted to you. Heil Hitler." It was signed, Friedrich Meinecke, Professor.

Sommer found it hard to conceal his elation. Meinecke had been his teacher-father at Friedrich Wilhelm, a pillar of the history faculty who, although now retired, still exercised enormous influence in university affairs. Meinecke would undoubtedly be consulted on appointments from the habilitations list, the roll of Berlin teachers whose status and experience qualified them for consideration as university lecturers. Sommer had been admitted to the list less than six months before.

"What's this?" he asked offhandedly.

"Isn't it self-explanatory?"

"You wrote to him about me?"

"Yes."

"You could have told me."

She shook her head. "No, I couldn't."

"Don't be childish. Why not?"

"I can't tell you that either."

He rarely allowed himself to be angry with her; she never

6

succumbed to embarrassment and her coldness under attack was utterly implacable.

He said gruffly, "Is it about the habilitations list?"

She furled her napkin neatly and slipped a pewter ring over it. "Why don't you ask him?"

"I disapprove of backstairs bargaining, you know that. Why couldn't he write to *me*?"

It sounded petulant. She sighed crossly. "Don't be pompous, *Liebchen*. It doesn't suit you."

He watched her gather up the rest of her letters, fold them into the *Volkszeitung*, and fit the package into her briefcase. She got to her feet briskly and he turned in his chair as she started to leave.

"I have the right to be consulted about my own career," he protested weakly. "I refuse to submit to—"

"Go or don't go," she interrupted. "You must do as you think best. After all, the only thing at stake is my reputation."

She had a way of closing a door quietly that gave it the seismic significance of an earthquake.

He heard her call to Willy and Kurt, dragoon them into their coats and caps, and sweep them to the outer landing in front of her. She walked them to their gymnasium each day before taking the underground to the university, where, as a paid Party official, she now had an office of her own. Her duty, she said. If they had owned a dog, walking it would also have been a duty.

He pushed away his plate and poured some coffee. The fifteen minutes of privacy he snatched each morning before leaving for work were increasingly important to him, the truth being, when he was prepared to face it, that at no other time could he consider himself master in his own home. His eye caught the third place setting and his feeling of contentment dissolved.

He swung in his chair. "Gerda!"

The old maid slopped in on slippered feet from the kitchen, and he stabbed a finger at the unused cutlery. "How many times do I have to tell you, woman?"

She scuttled round the table and scooped up the offending silverware nervously. "I'm sorry, Herr Doktor. I just . . . it's so hard to remember he's gone."

"Get out!"

He sat back and lit a cigarette. His father had occupied that chair for fifty of his sixty-three years, obscuring the view into the single paved courtyard below, dominating the table, the household, the lives of everyone in it. He had tried to dominate Else, too, of course, but only at the beginning, and more out of habit than hope of conquest.

It was characteristic of his hold over everything that happened in the apartment in the Dortmunderstrasse, that Gerda still set a place for his ghost five months after his death.

After the funeral last November, Sommer had deluded himself, for perhaps as much as an hour, that he was free of him; that he could talk and act and think from that moment according to his own lights, but it was a fallacy. Karl Wilhelm Sommer was as omnipresent in death as he had been in life; his spark had come to reside in Else, and Else had nursed it to an eternal flame. "We owe him everything we are," she was fond of saying.

Karl had left them his home, his money, his furniture, a comfortable middle-class position in an elite society of professionals. He had also left behind a son who wanted none of it.

Wilhelm sucked hungrily at his cigarette, reveling in the knowledge that both Karl and Else would have forbidden the disgusting habit of smoking at table. To hell with them both!

He hated the apartment. He had been born here in the spring of 1901, in the bed to which Else no longer welcomed him, here in the Neue Hansa Viertel, hard by the river Spree and the Tiergarten, the womb of Berlin's respectability. The Dortmunderstrasse was not as grand as the Speer-baroque Tiergartenstrasse but, as Karl had always said with such fine contempt, "I'm a lawyer, not a sucking leech of diplomacy."

Karl had felt a loathing for diplomats and Weimar functionaries that resisted rational understanding, but he never discussed it. His beliefs and ideals were his own, passionate and irresistible, and Wilhelm had been required to accept them faithfully, as a priest accepts the burden of his vows. "Nobility is an end in itself—not a fortune and a palace in the Tiergartenstrasse. What counts is what you as a German inherited from me: a keen eye, an enduring spirit, a healthy mind."

You, a German. The inheritance was flawed.

At the height of his powers, on the very brink of manhood, Karl had made a mistake that dogged his conscience throughout his life: he had fallen in love. As a struggling young lawyer, he had taken business as it came; one day it brought him Edward Penny, an Englishman representing a Birmingham brass foundry in Berlin. Penny's business was profitable and Karl had cultivated the fool against his deepest prejudices. One soft June evening, he was invited to join the Pennys at dinner; their daughter Rose had, only that day, come out from England. Karl proposed a month later and, in his towering infatuation, even agreed to be married at the British Embassy.

When he came to his senses the union was a year old and Wilhelm an embryonic reality. Karl made the best—and the worst—of it. He insisted the child be bilingual, because, although the slurred impurities of English were a constant irritant, he reasoned shrewdly that language was also a weapon. And to protect the boy, he denied him the petty indulgences of mother love. Rose was forbidden to coddle the child, embrace him, kiss him, bathe or dress him. A good German nurse was engaged and firmly instructed on how to conduct herself. Karl was a giant in those days: six feet three inches tall, strong as a lion, his curled and waxed mustaches more frightening than his unswerving gray eyes. "You will not tell your mother what we have discussed today," he would say after one of his dissertations in the nursery, and Wilhelm, round-eyed, would give his word. There was no doubt in his mind, even at the age of four, that execution was a punishment well within his father's power.

But excluding his mother from his private world was not, after all, so difficult. She had been a sickly woman from the day of his birth, given to fainting fits—real or imagined— high blood pressure and pains in the chest, anemia and headaches and fits of forgetfulness. When Wilhelm was packed off to kindergarten at the age of five she took the opportunity to withdraw from his life with what little grace she had left. The only memories he retained of her were of dark winter afternoons by a blazing drawing-room fire, he cross-legged on the floor at her feet, she wrapped in a black lace shawl and propped up with pillows on a leather couch. She would read passages of Chaucer and Congreve, Pope and Dickens, and he would recite his recollection of them in his own words. By the time he was ten she was too ill for even these exertions and his English lessons were taken over by Miss Ernestine Phipps, a governess at the British Embassy.

Frau Rose Sommer died on an April afternoon in 1913. Neither Karl nor Wilhelm cried at her funeral. When it was over, Karl returned to his office and Wilhelm to his gymnasium. They never spoke her name again.

In 1914, Karl volunteered, at the age of thirty-seven, to fight for the Fatherland in the Great War. Those were the words he used: "fight for the Fatherland." It came as no surprise to Wilhelm; he was already fully prepared for the new era of sacrifice. In the summer of 1913, at the age of twelve, he'd been dispatched to the Hohe Meissner, a mountain south of Kassel, for the inaugural gathering of a new youth organization, the Wandervögel—the Birds of Passage. It was, ostensibly, a hiking fraternity, a fact that had terrified Wilhelm when Karl informed him he was to join. Having been born with a congenital malformation of the ankle, long-distance walking was the least of his accomplishments. As it turned out, he needn't have worried. The leaders of the Wandervögel, though devoted to hardness of body, were far more interested in cultivating intractable minds. They demanded unconditional obedience, preached the iron ideals of Aryan superiority and eternal readiness against the enemy, and excluded the racially unclean, particularly Jews.

He met Else there.

She was a spindly, flaxen-haired little vixen of eleven, but after only two days she had won a place in the leadership cadre. Why she singled him out he never knew; the camp was filled with blond athletic giants, all of whom recognized in her a passion for service that vastly outweighed their own, but she rejected their overtures with a disdain that was almost regal. Her intensity scared him. She forced him, by sheer weight of personality, to strive to attain her standards, and she refused to countenance failure. He suffered unendurable agonies of body and spirit. But it was just the beginning.

When Wilhelm returned from the mountain Else insisted on accompanying him home. Karl's horror at this by-product of a fortnight of warrior training lasted a full hour. He could hardly be blamed. Else advised him without a trace of embarrassment of her interest in Wilhelm. A bond of comradeship, she said. Then she related in stark detail why she believed Herr Sommer might be opposed to any further contact between her and his son.

Her mother, she explained, was only sixteen years her

senior, a Friesian peasant who had come to Berlin in 1903 to find work. Within six months she was dispensing her favors on the Friedrichstrasse. By the time she discovered she was pregnant, it was far too late to do anything about it. Else was born in a hospice on a bag of straw. "Frau" Koenig was unable to supply the name of the father.

To this day, Wilhelm could not recall the scene without torment, even physical pain. Else in her Wandervögel beret, shirt, and skirt, ramrod stiff, as if giving evidence to a tribunal; Karl, mouth open, astounded and disbelieving; Wilhelm himself, scarlet-faced, ashamed.

When she finished—on the admission that she and her mother were living in a disgraceful tenement in the east of the city—Karl was at a loss for words. Else made it no easier for him. "Do you wish me to leave now, Herr Sommer?" she asked politely. Her honesty was breathtaking, her confidence in it unshakable. Karl's immediate reaction was to order Wilhelm to leave the room.

Outside, ear pressed to the keyhole, he'd listened as best he could to their talk—a zealot of thirty-seven and an unformed child. He found it incomprehensible. The Spartans at Thermopylae; the Romans at Cannae; lyric heroism; the Fuehrer prinzip; earth, blood, fire, and steel; the purity of conquest. Else left the apartment at ten o'clock that night with an invitation to return the next day.

Karl was away for four years during the war. He rarely wrote, but there was no sense of separation. Else was Karl in everything but stature. She strengthened Wilhelm's body and opened his mind, encouraged him to lean on her. Later, she programmed his reading and introduced him to Hugo Schildberger's bookshop under the railway bridge near Bellevue Station where they were allowed to browse for hours. She made him read Herman Hesse's *Demian* and *Steppenwolf* as examples of the besetting sin of intellectual cowardice, and for courage she fed him Spengler's *Untergang des Abendlandes*, Stefan George's totalitarian lyrics, and Walter Flex's *Wanderer Between Two Worlds*. And in his Upper Prima year, she coached him for his final examination; he passed with the most exemplary grade.

Karl's return had significance only for Else. His first words were to her. "I survived, child." And she nodded gravely; no smile. "Only the strong can withstand the storm, Herr Sommer."

Marriage was inevitable; Karl had probably promised her that in private. The old man and the girl had by then fused their ambitions and fathomless energies. Their goal was historic. Their yoke was Wilhelm.

From that moment, they threw themselves into the new conservative movement. Karl had spent his war service at the side of Ernst Juenger, a visionary and an activist, winner of Germany's highest honor, the *Pour le Mérite*. His war diary, *In Stahlgewittern*—"Thunder and Steel"—made him a living martyr and Karl became his disciple. Throughout the twenties, as Wilhelm and Else grew and Germany suffocated under the blanket of the Weimar Republic, Karl spent most of his evenings in Juenger's attic in the Barbarossastrasse, talking loudly with the rest of the Fascist coterie of blood and steel and a resurgence of Teutonic nobility and purpose. Else was occasionally permitted to sit at their feet.

Wilhelm's future was by then firmly established. Else and Karl determined the path he should take. History, they decreed; the teaching of history would be a sacramental task in the years to come. Wilhelm did not complain; he preferred history to law, the fate he assumed Karl had in mind for him, and considered himself lucky to have escaped it. It was all quite painless.

He was now a master at his old gymnasium, the Friedrich Werdersches, a respected member of an honored profession and firmly installed on the habilitations-list; better than that, perhaps, after the meeting with Meinecke this afternoon.

No, he really had no grounds for complaint. After all, what had Karl and Else inflicted on him other than themselves? Nothing he would not have chosen himself, given the freedom to act. Love in some form would have been a comfort, but neither of them had been equipped to love, except in the patriotic sense.

The cigarette had burned to nothing in the ashtray. He stood up and glanced down from the window to the neat paved courtyard below. Hyacinths bloomed in hooped tubs. It was a good spring, benign, bursting with early life.

He left the gymnasium a little after eleven thirty—ridiculously early, but it relieved him of the necessity of apologizing to

Heini Wassermann for missing their lunch. He took the underground to the Stettin station, came up into dazzling sunshine, and decided to walk the rest of the way.

He loved this quarter of the city with its teeming, transitory population of young people, the entertainments and beer cellars and cafes they inhabited, the gaunt four-story houses. When he was a student himself he had lived at home, but it was said there were 9,000 students in residence here, living in rooming houses run by landladies with 9,000 daughters warming 9,000 beds. He had never experienced the fleshy truth of it himself, but he had no doubt it was true.

At a quarter to two, he crossed the main courtyard of the university and entered the one place on earth he now wanted to be. Friedrich Wilhelm University was the intellectual centerpoint of all Germany; not an aristocratic ghetto-cum-dueling fraternity like Bonn, but hallowed academic ground. There was a magic about it—layered tradition polished by practice that in its day had caught the imagination even of foreigners. Mark Twain had been captivated by the sight of a class of Berlin students raising their sabers and stamping their feet to honor the entrance of a historian of the Roman Republic. The sabers were no longer required, but the spirit and authoritarian disciplines were unchanged. To be a Herr Doktor of history in this place . . .

Professor Friedrich Meinecke was waiting for him in his study, but he was not alone. The stranger was tall, amply domed, pear-shaped; probably in his mid-fifties. His manner and bearing marked him as a schoolmaster, but his soft-featured benevolent face wore the faded threat of a military mustache and small severe spectacles, as if to instill a degree of gravity. The niceties were performed quickly. "So then, Dr. Sommer"—a measuring glance at his silent companion—"let me introduce my colleague, Dr. Praetorius."

The name meant nothing to Sommer, but he shook hands with a required stiffening of the body and a neat click of the heels. The stranger waved him to a chair and took charge immediately. He opened a green folder on his lap and studied it for a moment. "Your name is on the habilitations list for consideration I see, Herr Doktor." A confiding tone, half-admiring.

"Yes, sir."

"You have expectations here?"

"It would be a privilege to—"

"Of course, of course." A plump black-and-gold fountain pen made a pretense of writing. "Your record as a student here and"—he flicked over a page—"as a teacher at the Friedrich Werdersches Gymnasium is quite impeccable. You are a member of the Party?"

"Since 1928."

"Ah yes," as if he had only just found the appropriate reference in the file. "You were at Hohe Meissner in 1913? the Wandervögel?"

"Yes."

"Halcyon days, Herr Doktor. You were one of the lucky ones. You have two sons."

"Willy is sixteen. Kurt is ten."

"And they take after their father, I understand." More sifting of pages. "It wouldn't do to tell him, of course, but your boy Kurt has passed the Pimpf tests with honor. He will be promoted to the Jungvolk next month."

A purposeful indication of the range of his authority? No matter. Thank heaven for Kurt's sake. The Pimpf was the most junior of the Nazi youth movements, designed for boys from six to ten, and a vastly more demanding venture than the old Wandervögel. Its most famous printed slogan, framed on the wall of Kurt's bedroom, was "Clench your teeth. Endure." The Pimpf learned history without textbooks and gorged on fables of bravery under fire, courage under pressure, and the Fuehrer prinzip in Nature (a leader must be obeyed, as in the case of ants and bees; soldiering is the most honored of all professions in the eternal struggle for life; strength vanquishes weakness).

Kurt had learned by heart a poem that ended with the lines:

"Please, begged the victim, let me go, for I am such
a little foe."
"No," said the victor, "not at all, for I am big and
you are small."

The Pimpf test involved question-and-answer routines aimed at pointing the lessons of racial purity, most devastatingly against America the melting pot, where undesirables went to mingle blood with Jews and Negroes. Parents were required to coach their sons in preparation for it. What is democracy? Wilhelm would intone, reading from the text written by Dr. Rust, the education minister. Rich Jews, Kurt would respond swiftly. What does it lead to? Time wasting and crime and corruption. What is Franklin D. Roosevelt's real name? Rosenfeld the Jew. What will happen to him? He will be defeated by the Fuehrer.

Dr. Praetorius had been scouring the page in front of him for several minutes. He said suddenly, "In the event of war, your age would be a strike against you."

"I think . . ." Sommer began carefully, but the visitor waved him to silence.

"You at thirty-eight and I at fifty-four." Praetorius beamed philosophically. "War is for young men. Like your son Willy."

Willy was the product of two leadership schools of the Hitler Youth and this summer was to be barracked at the General Ludendorff Jugendheim in Demmin-in-Mecklenburg for instruction in gliding and flying. He had already studied the chemistry of explosives, the geography of potential war target countries, and the mathematics of artillery trajectory and bombing angles. He had emerged among the top fifty boys of his age group and was certain to gain entry to the special academy at Brunswick for the elite. Beyond that a military career was assured.

Sommer cleared his throat. "My son Willy—"

"Speaks excellent English. But not quite as good as yours."

The remark seemed to be on an unnecessarily wide tangent. "When he has had a little more time to practice—"

"At his age you were word perfect. Tonally pure, according to your Upper Tertia report from the gymnasium that year. At sixteen. How . . ." He leaned back in his chair. "How would you account for that, Herr Doktor?"

What possible interest could it be to Praetorius how he had acquired his English accent? "My father believed English essential for anyone aspiring to—"

"Ah, your father. He encouraged you?"

"Yes."

"He taught you?" Praetorius ran his finger down the page as if searching for a remembered passage.

"No, my mother did initially."

"Of course. She was English, I believe. Still living, I trust?"

"She died in 1913."

"My condolences." The small spectacles flashed. "Your English instruction did not end there, I presume?"

"My father engaged a private tutor. A governess at the British Embassy here in Berlin."

"Of course." Dr. Praetorius broke into English. "It is—ah—unnormal for us Germans so completely to break the patterns of our speech."

Sommer's response was quick and fluent. "It's what the English would describe as a knack, sir. No more than that. Practice and a great deal of reading."

"You enjoyed the reading?" In German again. "What did you read?"

"My mother preferred the classics—Chaucer, Shakespeare, Congreve, Sheridan. Then the nineteenth-century writers: Galsworthy, Dickens. And English history, of course."

"But nothing beyond that?"

"Miss Phipps, the governess, had a secret vice—a working-class appreciation for what are called penny dreadfuls."

"Which proved useful to you?"

"In terms of colloquial usage, yes."

"You could be said to be perfectly fluent, then?"

"It depends, Herr Doktor. In Berlin, yes. In London . . ." He shrugged. "I haven't spoken English in London since 1930."

"When you conducted a party of students around England."

"Yes."

"With your wife accompanying you."

"Yes."

Dr. Praetorius appeared to be deeply affected. He said, with unmistakable admiration, "Frau Doktor Sommer is highly regarded in the Party."

Sommer bowed his head. "My wife is a source of inspiration to—all of us."

"Hmph." Dr. Praetorius studied his polished boots, his head rocking rhythmically. "Indeed, indeed. We must be grateful to her."

"In what regard, precisely?"

Praetorius smiled thinly. "In every regard, Herr Doktor. Perhaps for—the English have a saying, do they not?—adding a string to your bow?" He half closed his eyes. "A man who aspires to the elite . . ." He snapped the green file shut. ". . . and is too old to fight is wise to cultivate all his assets and talents. Against the day the Fuehrer calls upon them."

MARCH 6, 1939

He heard nothing for four days; indeed, as he told Else over dinner that same evening, he expected nothing from such an interview. She cross-examined him minutely, as she always did on matters of importance to her, and demanded a verbatim report of the conversation. Again she refused to say why she had written to Meinecke in the first place, and her curt refusal to discuss the matter in a civilized way led to anger, argument, and an icy silence as they went to their respective beds. By the second day Sommer was sufficiently himself to cajole her into a more accommodating frame of mind and by Sunday morning had convinced her he had forgotten the whole affair.

It was almost true. They had been toying with him, he was sure; and perhaps with a dozen other young hopefuls, separating the wheat from the chaff in preparation for a more official interview. In which case . . . But he did not have long to wait and hope. At three fifteen on Monday afternoon, as he was taking coffee in the Senior Common Room, the porter came to say that a Herr Doktor Scholz wished to see him and was waiting in the Lower Secunda lecture room.

Dr. Scholz was cast in the same physical mold as Dr. Praetorius, but the air of joviality he projected lacked warmth and his smile fitted almost as badly as his shapeless gray serge. He handed Sommer an envelope of stiff white vellum. The letter inside bore the seal of the Foreign Office and an indecipherable signature.

It began, without prefix: "You will, forthwith, accompany the bearer of this letter, Dr. Scholz, to the destination he indicates. You will do so without question, without further contact with your superiors at the gymnasium, with fellow members of staff, with your wife and children, or personal friends. You will require no clothes or luggage, no personal effects or toiletries. You need attend to no obligations, professional or domestic. This order is issued under my hand on the instruction of the Fuehrer.''

His first reaction was anxiety. He was due to meet Else at the university at four o'clock for one of Joseph Goebbels' ritual addresses to the Action Group. His absence would not be taken lightly. He examined the Foreign Office seal again. There was no arguing with *that*. He had no doubt what Else would advise.

Clench your teeth. Endure. He clicked his heels stiffly and bowed. Scholz responded.

A Mercedes was waiting for them outside and the driver set off as soon as they were seated. For the moment, *where* they were going was less important than *why*, but he was astonished when they turned into the wide gates of Tempelhof and felt a surge of horror as the car drove straight to a waiting Heinkel 111 parked on the southern perimeter. Four men in Luftwaffe flying jackets separated as the car glided to a halt and a good-looking fellow with a square soldier's face, blue eyes, and silver-splashed hair came to shake Scholz's hand. He introduced himself as Hauptmann Edmund Gartenfeld and invited them to board immediately. One of the crewmen buckled them into the steel-frame webbing seats.

Dr. Scholz promptly closed his eyes and went to sleep.

Wilhelm Sommer learned his first lesson on the nature of terror when he climbed down the ladder to the ground at Hamburg (he had no doubt where he was; he had traveled there often). He was ushered into another Mercedes. The rear compartment was separated from the driver's seat by a glass partition and every window was curtained. Dr. Scholz bared a pacifying smile but offered no explanations.

Logic dictated he had no cause for fear. He was a respected citizen, professionally valued; his background and publicly declared beliefs were in perfect accord with the tenets of the Third Reich. He was not a Jew; there were no lurking impurities in his bloodline, and his wife and children were impeccably "new German."

A misunderstanding then. It had happened before; many,

many times before. The Gestapo, the SS, the SD—independently spinning cogs in the remorseless machine of state security—had arrested honest Germans often enough on grounds of unfounded suspicion and ludicrously tangled facts. When Else discovered what they'd done, he would be freed instantly.

The Mercedes slowed to a crawl and traffic noises broke in on them. He could hear pavement voices, street cries, the steel-shod rattle of a hand cart in a gutter, automobile horns. Then the car stopped.

They were in a side street, old, narrow, in the flaking heart of the city not far from the docks. The smell of sullied tidal water was strong in the air, braced with the odors of oil and grain and unweathered timber.

Scholz led the way across the pavement, through double oak doors and into a yellow-painted corridor with a high vaulted ceiling. A young man in the uniform of the Hamburg police shot to his feet from a stool in the lobby and half raised the Erma submachine gun slung at his hip, but Scholz flicked dismissive fingers at him and the policeman subsided.

At the end of the corridor was a white-painted door, unmarked. Scholz threw it open and stood back to let Sommer enter. The offensive odor of formaldehyde assailed him, and when he saw the marble-topped dissecting table and the banked walls of steel cabinets his stomach heaved. Scholz affected not to notice his discomfort. He turned to a white-coated functionary at a cluttered desk in the far corner and said "Price" as if it were an order. Then he addressed his companion.

"It is safe to talk now, Herr Doktor. I apologize for the limitations of the airplane."

Sommer shrugged. "Duty is rarely comfortable, Dr. Scholz." He was proud of the coolness he brought to that statement and Scholz's shallow deference instantly gave way to respect.

The functionary unlocked a cabinet on the second level. Sommer refused to let his eyes be drawn to it.

"I must apologize, also, for the inconvenience." Scholz's gloved hand climbed up and over his lightly fluffed skull. "But as you'll see in due course, there was no other way." He swung on his heel as the cabinet rolled open. "Ah!"

The face was perhaps seven or eight days dead. The eyes had sunk deep into embracing sockets, the cheeks and tem-

ples were hollowed, and the lips slightly parted in a skeletal
grin. Sommer, staring down at it, felt his heart pound.

"Who is he?" He barely got out the words.

Dr. Scholz's gloved hands came together under his chin in
an attitude of prayer.

"You recognize him?"

Waxy white features loomed up at him. The nostrils flared
perceptibly wider, the skin around the eyes was more deeply
striated, but over all, from a distance of a meter or so, the
face was his own.

Uncanny. He reached down and touched it . . . him . . .
himself, and then felt very sick indeed. He turned away.

"You are surprised, I judge, Herr Doktor?"

"Is this why you brought me here?"

"You see yourself?"

"Yes." It would have been foolish to deny it.

Scholz plucked a clipboard from the attendant's hand.

"Allow me to introduce Dr. Thomas Arthur Leslie Price,
late of the . . ." He smiled crookedly. "Shall we say for the
moment that he taught at a local realgymnasium here in
Hamburg until his death last week. You would have shared
something in common, I imagine. His subjects were English
and pre-Renaissance European history."

"He's English?" Nature's little jokes knew no boundaries.

"Of Welsh extraction."

"He died accidentally?"

"Death from heart failure," Scholz read from the clipboard,
"induced by an attack of asthma leading to emphysema." He
patted the curiously faded yellow hair of the corpse. "Like
you, Herr Doktor, our friend Price suffered with asthma from
childhood."

"You say he *taught* here?"

That was unusual; within the terms of reference laid down
by Minister Rust, positively unthinkable. History taught in
German schools—even in the less favored, science-oriented
realgymnasia—stopped short at 1870 and was required to
display a strong Aryan bias. An Englishman, reared on an
academic diet of objective analysis, would hardly be seen as
an acceptable molder of young German minds.

"For seven years."

"He was a member of the Party?"

"He was not."

"Then I fail to see . . ."

Scholz displayed his teeth.

"Dr. Price"—he patted the cold hard shoulder—"was not invited to join the Party. I don't pretend to understand why myself, but you can take it as a fact. In every other respect he was perfectly acceptable to the gauleiter's committee here."

"In what sense *acceptable*?"

"Politically, academically. I can't say socially; there seems to be some doubt that he had a friend to his name. A lone wolf, friend Price. He came to Hamburg from England in 1931. A remarkably well-qualified teacher with an enviable record of achievement in his own country."

Sommer glanced down briefly at the lifeless face. In spite of himself he was morbidly fascinated. "A *successful* teacher wouldn't leave his own country, surely."

"Ah." Scholz stared at the clipboard. "Well, there I can't help you, Herr Doktor. We can speculate, of course. His colleagues at—ah—the realgymnasium found him withdrawn, rather shy, reclusive. His next-door neighbor, for instance, couldn't remember exchanging one word with him in eight years. Not a language problem, of course. Price's German was faultless."

"I still can't understand why he was allowed to teach here—particularly after 1933."

"Well, he got his job under the Weimar cretins, naturally. He'd been here a year, then, trying to write some grandiose historical treatise apparently. He never finished it. His money ran out, I imagine. The realgymnasium accepted him and their choice seems to have been well judged. He was reexamined by the gauleiter's committee in '33 and allowed to continue his work." Scholz offered the clipboard. "Perhaps you'd care to study his clinical data card."

Same height: five feet ten. Same coloring: fair hair and blue eyes (the card described them as turquoise). Same weight: 75 kilos. Same disabilities: asthma and a limp (right foot, though, not left, and the result of childhood poliomyelitis). Other essential differences: Dr. Price had larger feet—two English sizes—was a year younger, and would have been a great deal lighter without his paunch (according to the pathologist). A lung section revealed Price's addiction to heavy smoking, insane in view of his asthmatic condition, and his liver was enlarged. A drinker, a smoker, a cripple; unfit, lonely, probably disillusioned. A weak man.

"What has this to do with me, Dr. Scholz?"

"Later, Herr Doktor."

Dr. Scholz retrieved the clipboard, returned it to the attendant, and led the way back to the waiting car.

The Phoenix Hotel was a gray-white building that strained toward grandeur but achieved only provincial pretentiousness. There was a restaurant at street level and a pastry shop with lace-curtained windows, but neither seemed to be heavily patronized when Scholz led the way inside. There was no fuss, no signing of registers. Scholz called over the proprietor, introduced him as Herr Harbeck and Sommer as "Herr Krohle."

"Is everything ready?"

"Of course, Herr Doktor." The proprietor gestured to a framed hotel registration sheet behind his reservation desk. "The Fuehrer's room, as you ordered."

Sommer leaned across the counter. The coveted memento, dated March 1929, carried the names and signatures of Rudolf Hess, Hermann Goering, and Adolf Hitler. Hitler's room was shown as number 101.

It was a small room and its two windows, heavily curtained, admitted virtually no light. Scholz went to each of them in turn and drew the curtains even tighter. He gestured to the bulging brown-leather suitcase on the drab green coverlet of the three-quarter bed.

"I'd like you to change into those clothes. Everything's been laundered, of course. I think you'll find they fit. We can have any necessary alterations made later. I shall be back to fetch you in an hour—no, let's say eight thirty. Herr Harbeck is always on duty at the desk—correct, Herr Harbeck?"

The little man bobbed dutifully.

"Call him if you want anything to eat or drink. Coffee, that is. I suggest you avoid beer or spirits, at least for the time being."

"May I talk to you privately?"

"Of course." Scholz swept the proprietor from the room with fluttering fingers. "Well?"

"Am I now permitted to telephone my wife?"

"You have no telephone at your apartment, surely?"

"She will be at the university."

"I see." The gloved hands explored his chin. "No, Herr Doktor. I think not. You have something important you wish to tell her?"

"She will be worried." He stumbled over the word, knowing it to be untrue. "I should have been at the university at four."

Scholz's hand came down firmly on his shoulder. He was very much taller than first impressions suggested—well over six feet. "Your restraint is admirable, Doktor. I commend you for it. But I fear I'm not empowered to permit telephone calls. However, I do assure you your wife will be kept informed. She is, I'm told, a woman of considerable strength and resource. A Party official, is she not?"

He nodded.

"Well, there you are." Scholz brought his gloves together with a perfunctory slap. "Until eight thirty, then."

It would have been almost comforting to feel as afraid as he had at the aerodrome, but something far more sinister had come to haunt him—his suspicions about why he had been shown the corpse of Thomas Arthur Leslie Price. Surely they didn't expect him to replace this man at a damnable real-gymnasium in Hamburg? To teach history to grease monkeys and aspiring mechanics? If that was the case, he would resist every step of the way.

He sat down on the bed and released the catches of the suitcase. The earthly possessions of Dr. Thomas Price lay inside, neatly packed in white paper laundry bags. Three suits, badly tailored and much worn; a half-dozen shirts, all white with stripes and frayed cuffs; a dozen detached shirt collars, heavily starched. Handkerchiefs, ties of funereal hue, balloon underpants, and thick cotton vests. Heavy woolen socks—all gray and all darned. Cheap cufflinks, cheap tiepin, cheap belt, cheaper braces. The toilet bag decorated in blue squares was soiled and its lining torn; it contained a small Gillette razor of great antiquity, a hairbrush backed with mother-of-pearl, a shaving brush—still unaccountably damp— and an antiseptic stick in a tortoiseshell tube for doctoring cuts. There were no books, no papers, no bric-a-brac of the kind that even the loneliest, most disillusioned outcast might be expected to keep about him in memory of his lost world. Perhaps Scholz had those.

He stretched out on the bed, one leg draped carelessly over

the open case. What *they*—Praetorius? Scholz?—intended for him obviously depended on who *they* were. Not SS. Not SD. Both arms loved the panoply of their uniforms too much to sacrifice them in the cause of confusing a doctor of history. Gestapo? Possibly. Although Praetorius fitted no Gestapo type Wilhelm Sommer had ever encountered. Aside from the popular image—large-brimmed soft hats and leather coats—he knew them only as blunt instruments, an abusing, abusive vanguard of the new social order. Jew beaters, strong arms, thugs. He was more familiar with the SS, as every Berliner was; their black uniforms were visible at every "demonstration" in the Jewish quarter, in every parade, at every rally and weekend camp. But again they were types: fish-eyed intellectuals like the racist ideologue Walther Darré and the gimp-legged Goebbels; manipulators like Himmler and his lieutenant Reinhard Heydrich, with their pinched mouths and narrow-spaced eyes; or round-faced, jolly, thigh-slapping, shaven-skulled, thick-necked, and gross—like Julius Streicher, Sepp Dietrich, and the now discredited Ernst Roehm.

He caught himself; even silent reflection on that theme was dangerous. Besides, he did not really feel that way about Hitler's Praetorian Guard. They had their place. It was not fitting, moreover, for a doctor of history, protected from the clamor by his calling and intellectually divorced from it by an Olympian view of human experience, to criticize the means when he so eagerly espoused the ends.

He stripped and washed himself in the hand basin and donned Thomas Price's clothes. The shirt was a tent and the trousers slopped over his hips; everything was of German manufacture—which meant Jewish manufacture, he thought obscurely—and too cheaply tailored to be smart. Price had taken no interest in his appearance and, on this evidence, had had no taste whatsoever.

Scholz arrived promptly at eight thirty and they climbed again into the still-curtained limousine. But this time, when the car stopped in front of a watchmaker's shop, Sommer got his bearings at once; they were in the Grosse Burstah, behind the city hall. Narrow stairs led from the street to a landing and a glass-partitioned door with the black-painted legend "Stegemann and Company, Importers and Exporters."

A homely woman in spectacles sat typing at a desk in the

sparsely furnished front room. She looked up with a start when they entered, as if she was unaccustomed to visitors.

Scholz angled his head stiffly. "Fräulein Kammer."

"Will you go in, Herr Doktor?"

The inner sanctum carried its pretense of commercial activity with even less conviction than the outer office. The desk supported the only light in the room, an ancient hinged lamp flooding down on a green blotter. The man behind the desk rose and stretched out his hand.

"Herr Doktor Sommer. What a pleasure to meet you again."

Dr. Praetorius really seemed to mean it.

He looked up again at the clock flickering away the seconds with its purposeful red electric hand: ten forty-five. Sweat saturated Thomas Price's blue-striped shirt and voluminous underwear.

Scholz had taken refuge long ago in a padded swivel chair in one corner, but Praetorius sat as he had for the entire two hours—stiff-backed, calm, apologetic, but firm.

"With respect, Doktor, you cannot retreat from a position you have not reconnoitered," he said gently.

"The question of retreat . . ." They were mad, both of them. "I've reconnoitered *myself.* I'm thirty-eight years old and—"

"Price's age," Scholz interposed inaccurately from the corner.

"I know my limitations!"

"Ah. Limitations." Praetorius was visibly aggravated. "We come back again to limitations, Herr Doktor. And I answer you again as I did a few moments ago. You grew to manhood with the ideals of your remarkable father; you support the theories and ambitions of the Party; you encourage your wife in her great work and commit your sons to the most challenging frontiers of achievement. Yet you talk of limitations." He closed his eyes.

Sommer rubbed his sweating hands on his knees. They *were* mad. He had to make them understand.

"Dr. Praetorius, I *give* myself to the cause. Heart and soul. In any capacity. All I beg you to consider is the effect—the disastrous effect—of forcing me to reach for something beyond my grasp."

"There is no question of force," Praetorius corrected him severely.

"And nothing is beyond the grasp of a German with the will to succeed," Scholz growled from his chair.

"Masquerading as Thomas Price is beyond my capacity."

"A soldier's duty is to fight! Not to question his orders," Scholz roared suddenly.

"A soldier is himself. He wears his own face."

"You already wear the face," Scholz fumed. "What's so difficult about wearing his mind?"

"*My* mind is the difficulty. My instincts. My feelings as a patriot, a German. You ask me to adopt the character of a man who hates this country. You expect me to persuade the English that I have lived and worked here with the sole object of learning enough to be useful to them in a war." He shook his head firmly. "Oh, no, gentlemen. Ask me to show courage, and I'll try. But don't ask me to spit on my country's name."

"Spit on your . . . ?" Scholz spluttered disbelievingly.

"Please!" Praetorius glared his underling into submission. "Dr. Sommer, I really think you must allow me to be the judge of the moral aspects of spying."

"I'm sorry. I merely—"

"No! Apologies are unnecessary. Let me explain myself again. Six days ago, a man of whom I previously had no knowledge died in an attic here in Hamburg. An Englishman. The deaths of aliens are automatically reported to—to my office so, next morning, there he was—Thomas Arthur Leslie Price, thirty-seven, professor of history, teacher at a real-gymnasium—there in front of me on my desk."

He took off his spectacles and began to clean them with a handkerchief. His eyes bulged shortsightedly; Sommer doubted if he could see beyond the table.

He fitted the spectacles over his ears. "Inspiration is a state of grace, Doktor. I was inspired. Suppose, somewhere in Germany, I asked myself, there was a man who in face, form, and qualifications was the doppelgänger of Thomas Arthur Leslie Price. My superiors, I might say, thought I was mad. However, there was only one way to prove my point: to comb every German gymnasium and university, every institution, every diplomatic and government department. A tall order. Security, of course, was all-important. No one must know, even if this gem was there to be found, why he was important to me. I needed an army of researchers and they could only be highly trusted Party officials. Men and women of impeccable commitment.''

Else. He felt no surprise, no outrage. She was too intelligent to believe that in pointing the finger at him she was merely assisting the Party in some obscure academic appointment.

"So." Dr. Praetorius laid his hands palms up on the table. "We performed the impossible. I suspended dear Dr. Price between the deathbed and the grave and my inspiration was rewarded. Now, I'm a very simple man, Dr. Sommer. Here you are, an unassailable candidate. You have Price's face. You suffer his incapacities. You are a historian. You are unique. Irreplaceable. But there is more.''

He consulted the typescript under his hand.

"I confess none of this would have occurred to me without . . .'' He held up a sheet of paper with two letters pinned to it. "Without this. Two months ago Dr. Price applied to the history department of University College, London, for a teaching post. I assume he had seen an advertisement for it somewhere. He duly received an application form which''—he flapped the papers again—''he was methodical enough to copy. He then received this letter''—he tapped a small letterhead—''to which he replied at once. Again, he made a copy. The letter from London invited him to present himself for interview for the position on a date convenient to him; his reply nominated last Monday, two days before he died. Now, my dear Sommer, it's highly unlikely that in the course of a severe, protracted illness, Dr. Price gave thought to canceling that appointment. In fact, I have it on good authority he was unable to leave his bed. So last week I had a letter dispatched to London in Price's name apologizing for his—ah—incapacity and promising to appear rather belatedly in April.''

"Next month!''

"Yes.''

"But you couldn't know . . .''

"That we'd find you. Of course not. But the gamble was worth the price of a stamp, wouldn't you say, Herr Doktor?''

"Dr. Praetorius, how can I convince you that inspiration is not in itself enough? I'd be exposed in hours. Here—yes, my English is good. But in the closed community of an English university . . .''

"Detail. Dr. Price has lived in Germany for eight years. His own accent was colored by German vowel sounds, I understand."

"I'm sorry." He made it firm, unequivocal. "I can't do it."

"You *must* do it!" Scholz erupted. "You're a historian, aren't you? Look at what's happening. The Anschluss, Sudetenland, Munich, diplomatic victories based on German strength. Strength breeds fear and fear breeds reprisal. That's what we face now—reprisal. From the British, from the French, from the Poles. God Almighty, man, this isn't a game. We're not proposing some damned intellectual exercise. We're being pushed into a war. Do you want 1918 all over again? Versailles and the Weimar puppets?"

"We already have agents in England," Praetorius said urgently. "We shall train more. But saboteurs and field observers are not natural infiltrators. The true infiltrator is born, not made, Sommer."

"Will you please *listen* to me!"

Praetorius leaned further across his desk. "When the time comes, we shall strike at our enemies swiftly and without hesitation. Our plans for the invasion of southern England are fully realized. *Fully* realized. A year, Dr. Sommer. One year."

"No." Sweat slid from his hair into his eyes. "I know my—"

"Limitations," Praetorius finished for him. He sighed and picked up one of the telephones. "The Sommer call, please," he said into the mouthpiece. He waited, his eyes on Sommer's streaming face, then: "Ah, I'm sorry to keep you waiting. I shall pass you to him now. No—I'm afraid he hasn't."

Sommer took the extended phone.

Else said, "Is it true? You refuse to cooperate?"

He tried to shield the instrument with his hand. "You don't understand what—"

"There's nothing to understand." She sounded farther away than Berlin. "You've been given an opportunity to serve and you refuse."

"If you'll give me a moment to explain, I'll—"

"I don't want explanations, Wilhelm. Not from you. I want a promise that you'll do exactly as they ask."

"Else, it isn't a matter of—"

"For me and the boys—if you need a reason. We have our duty and you have yours. If you fail us—"

"Damn you!"

For the first time in seventeen years of marriage he robbed her of the last word.

MARCH 12, 1939

The first few days had been given over to a tactical appreciation, as Scholz termed it, of Dr. Thomas Price, deceased. Posing as Gestapo investigators, Sommer and Scholz talked to the Englishman's former colleagues at the realgymnasium. Sommer deduced two things from these cross-examinations: that men were prepared to agree black was white to win the approval of the secret police, and that Price had made no friends, revealed nothing of himself, and left no clues to his true personality.

His dingy fourth-floor garret, thoroughly searched by a team of Abwehr specialists from the Knockenhauerstrasse, yielded only three books—*Hereward the Wake*, Robert Louis Stevenson's *Treasure Island*, and a handsomely bound volume of Arabian erotica. The University College correspondence had been found in an old school exercise book. His passport, work permit, and Ministry of Education registration card were the sole documents of identity he possessed.

"So you see, Herr Doktor, you have nothing to worry about," Scholz placated him.

Sommer did not rise to the bait. One thing was already abundantly clear. Praetorius was prepared to back his inspiration against all the realities of the situation and nothing was to be allowed to deflect him. He was a planner in a community of professional opportunists preparing for war; his status was determined by the imaginative sweep of his ideas.

Praetorius had declared himself on the third day; he was chief of the Economic Intelligence section of the Hamburg Abwehr, the foreign arm of the German secret service. Control was vested in the Berlin headquarters in the Tirpitzufer, where the fabled Admiral Wilhelm Canaris held court, but it

was a tradition of the service that powerful field offices like
Hamburg exercised great independence in their activities.

"We're particularly proud here," Praetorius confided
expansively, "of our networks in Britain, America, and the
Iberian Peninsula. Naval and air intelligence is our forte. I
would go so far as to say that in the coming war, the
Hamburg office will prove to be as irreplaceable as yourself."

There were too many such compliments, and they unnerved
Sommer. Far too much was being taken for granted. His own
assessment of Price should have damned the operation from
the start. The Englishman had taught at two eminent British
public schools, was a graduate of Oxford, and apparently
unmarried (although Sommer was not prepared to dismiss the
idea that an unhappy marriage had driven him to Hamburg in
1931). But there was no documentary proof of his academic
background, no clue to his standing, no information on his
parentage or family connections, and the curriculum vitae he
had sent to London was skeletal at best.

Praetorius dismissed these objections.

"We must not allow ourselves to be bound by minutiae,
Sommer. You will find that bold broad strokes characterize
the best work in this field."

On the sixth day they plucked him from the Fuehrer's room
at the Pheonix Hotel and installed him in the Abwehr communications center at Hamburg-Wohldorf.

MARCH 20, 1939

Sessler screamed in his ear, "Come on now—knees up,
up, *up*!" and they sprinted the last hundred meters to the big
old sycamore that marked the finish of their morning run.

Sommer sprawled on the grass in its shadow, panting hard,
but Sessler continued running on the spot for another half
minute, back straight, head up, legs pumping like pistons. He
was a vast slab of a man—six feet three and fifty inches
round the chest. He had the beginnings of a beer drinker's
belly which bounced as he ran, but it was encased in steel-
hard muscle. He stopped, hands on hips, and breathed deeply.

"On your front!" He flipped Sommer on his stomach as if he were weightless, knelt down beside him, and began to massage legs, ankles, and feet. He had done wonders with the malformed ankle.

Sommer cushioned his chin on his forearms and stared across the manicured lawns to the old house in its frame of ancient elms. The communications center at Wohldorf boasted an elysian setting. The park was a landscape gardener's dream: rolling lawns, extravagant flower beds, avenues of Lombardy poplar, and towering copses of sycamore and elm that screened the house on all sides. The mansion itself sat on a slight rise, its high-pitched mansard roof spiky with radio aerials, the open windows of its semicircular central tower emitting the clack of busy typewriters and the occasional scrape of chairs.

Dr. Praetorius had driven out from the Knockenhauerstrasse that morning to take breakfast with them and was now sunning himself in a deck chair on the terrace. He seemed loath to leave.

"Why's he here, do you know?" Sommer's words came out in a string of staccato gulps as Sessler moved up to pound his back and shoulders.

"Can't leave you alone, can he? Like a cat with a mouse."

"Thanks."

Sessler performed a drumroll along Sommer's spine with the sides of his hands. "Same as the rest of us, Praetorius. Feeling his way in the dark."

"With me?"

"With the whole thing." Sessler leaned back on his heels and turned his face to the sun, eyes closed.

"Would you mind expanding on that?"

"Huh!" Sessler, too impatient a personality to stay still for long, broke into a vigorous arm-and-shoulder exercise.

Sommer tried again. "What are they trying to do with me?"

"Don't ask me, Willy."

"Willy?" he flashed back at once.

"Sorry. Tom."

Sessler shook with silent laughter. From the moment he arrived at Wohldorf, Wilhelm Sommer had been required to answer only to the name Tom Price. Every member of the training team had been instructed to test him on this as often and as indiscriminately as they chose. Only Sessler continued to see the funny side of it.

Sommer now began each day with a triple incantation on his lips: "My name is Tom Price. I hold the passport of Tom Price. I am Tom Price." It gave him no comfort but Dr. Praetorius was signally impressed. "Good, Dr. Price. Very good," he would murmur in his fractured music-hall English. All instructors on the Gimlet Project, as it was now called, were required to address him in English.

"Scholz says he's trained a dozen agents this way."

Sessler made an explosive rasping sound with his mouth. "Scholz, my ass."

"Do you tell him that to his face?"

"Herr Doktor Scholz? Matter of fact, I do. He's no more a doktor than I am. Just a lieutenant like me. Less than me." Sessler was afraid of no one. No walls in his domain had ears. He stretched out on the velvety turf. "Get something straight, Willy—*Tom*. As far as this bunch is concerned, believe half what you see and nothing you hear. You won't go far wrong."

"Is that supposed to be a joke?"

"I don't joke about something this serious. Listen. I know about bodies. How to build them up, how to make them work. I trade in muscle and bone and I know what I'm talking about. But I'm no spymaster. Wein, Trautmann, Baruth and Koehn are first-class wireless men because they learned the trade as civilians. But they're not spies, either. The rest"—he flung a contemptuous arm toward the house—"are amateurs. Amateur soldiers for a start; never fired in anger. Amateur spies, too. There isn't a man on the staff who's ever worked in the field. Not one."

"But—"

"Something else." Sessler studied the rippling bulge of muscle on his forearm. "Praetorius had a bright idea; that's why you're sitting in the stewpot with an apple in your teeth. Not because he researched the thing. In this business you stay at the top as long as you keep hatching schemes. It's the scheme that counts, not the result. The more agents a controller runs, the bigger his reputation. You're just another notch on Praetorius's gun. A big notch if it works out, but only one of several."

"You think I should walk out?"

"Huh!" There was no mistaking the sarcasm. "Nobody walks away from this, particularly you. No—I'm just offering some friendly advice. You've got a brain in your head, so use it. Don't rely on this bunch or you'll be six feet under before you've had a chance to turn around."

He pushed himself up and bounced impatiently on the balls of his feet. "All right, Price. Shower first, then back to the blackboard." He poked his charge playfully in the ribs. "At least you'll be fit when you leave here."

MARCH 26, 1939

He took the sleeping pill and lay flat on his back, staring at the weaving tracery of tree branches on the ceiling. The pill was an essential now; he could not sleep without it. His insomnia sprang not so much from fear, although he was rarely free of it, as from the realization that, for the first time in his life, his natural flair for absorbing facts had deserted him.

The source of his torment was the wireless room and its denizens: Major Trautmann, the senior communications officer, Lieutenant Richard Wein, his personal radio instructor, and the operators Baruth and Koehn.

They were tolerant men, infinitely painstaking, and the relationship had started out well; Sommer had managed to memorize the Morse alphabet swiftly and passed Trautmann's written examinations with ease. Encoding and decoding, the second stage, also posed no problems for him. But at that point he ran into a brick wall of incomprehension. The practical side of wireless telegraphy eluded him; it was as though his finger gave up all contact with his brain the moment he sat down at the Morse key.

This evening, after six hours of soul-destroying practice, Richard Wein had sent him to bed in what for him was a rare fit of despair.

"It's no good, Tom. You've got to master it. Unless you can hit that key smoothly and without hesitation, you're lost. A transmission must have *flow*, rhythm—like music. Dum-tata-dum-tata-dum dum dum. Rhythm. That's what differentiates your 'send' from anyone else's; it's what we call your handwriting, your signature. If you can't send smoothly, there's no signature to look for; no fingerprint."

"I'm sorry, I'll try again in the morning."

"It's not laziness, man. You try hard enough as it is. Maybe you're concentrating *too* hard, but you've got to get it right. I can't let you leave here without it."

"I know."

"I hope you do. Unless you develop a signature we won't be able to identify you when you transmit. And you know what that means."

"If I'm captured, the English could send messages in my name."

Wein yawned widely. The dark, slightly protuberant eyes in his sharp face were liquid with exhaustion. "And we'd never know—one way or the other. It could cripple us."

Cripple them! It was crippling him, all of it. With the radio men he was at least conscious of his own shortcomings. With the others, all but Sessler, he was becoming more and more convinced that their shortcomings dwarfed his own.

Praetorius appeared every other day, usually at mealtimes, to lecture his changeling in a low mellifluous monotone on the metaphysics of misrepresentation and solitary survival. Sessler claimed he had no qualifications at all for doing this outside his own preference for social isolation, and it was not hard to believe. He was an ex-schoolmaster, ex-civil servant, who had drifted into the Abwehr in 1934 as a clerk.

Scholz was senior instructor in fieldcraft and methodology, but he was hopeless without a textbook. He dodged any question falling outside the Abwehr training manual and relied on written and oral tests to keep his pupil occupied.

The "mechanics of tradecraft" came from the horses' mouths: an ill-assorted gang of professional agents sent out from the Knockenhauerstrasse or from the Tirpitzufer in Berlin. They were poor advertisements for the profession of espionage and wholly incompetent as tutors. If they had anything of value to pass on, they displayed great reluctance to part with it; they found greater scope for their talents in recounting personal exploits in the field, all bizarre and outrageously exaggerated. None of them had worked under cover in England. The agents were also responsible for introducing him to the handling of explosives and small arms. He proved disastrously inept at both.

He turned wearily on his side. The hard silver finger of a searchlight beam swung momentarily across the window, crawled through the branches of the sycamore on the terrace, and slid away. He might as well be in prison. They wouldn't let him set foot outside the house on his own, even to sit on the terrace; he was forbidden to eat alone; a Wehrmacht sergeant stood guard outside his door all night, every night; all communication was *verboten*. A week after he arrived, he'd written a short note to Kurt, quite innocent, and given it to Praetorius to read and post. Sessler told him a day later it had been burned and he was not to write another.

The pill took hold and he closed his eyes, floating down into an ocean of turbulence—then a hand shook his arm and he woke with his heart in his mouth.

"Easy there, Dr. Price." The guard sergeant grinned comfortingly in the darkness. "Downstairs. Scholz wants you."

He dressed slowly, head swimming. His watch showed four fifteen. On his way down he realized he'd put his sweater on back-to-front.

Scholz was in the officer's mess, a vision in pajamas and Chinese dragon robe, bleary-eyed and testy. Beside him, in a chair before the unlit fire, sat a slight, rather effete man swathed in a long traveling coat.

"Ah, here you are, Dr. Price." Scholz dropped a proprietorial hand on his shoulder. "Allow me to present a fellow countryman of yours, Mr. William Joyce. He's come rather a long way to meet you."

"So. *You're* Price, are you?" The tone was patronizing and wrapped in an accent that rang oddly in Sommer's ears: dry, flat-voweled.

"Mr. Joyce." He offered his hand. It was ignored.

"I'll leave you. We'll meet at breakfast, no doubt." Scholz narrowed his eyes warningly at Sommer as he withdrew.

"Bloody cold here." The visitor got to his feet and buttoned his coat. "Warmer outside, I'd say, wouldn't you?"

"I've just got out of bed."

"Take a stroll, shall we? May as well be hung for a sheep as a lamb."

"Unless the guards gave you clearance, we probably shall be hung."

Joyce's lipless mouth quivered. "Figure of speech, old man. After you."

They stepped onto the terrace. A helmeted sentry appeared as if by magic from the shadows at the bottom of the steps. Another trotted out from under a tree, a Dobermann Pinscher straining ahead of him on a check chain. Joyce shouted in English, "It's all right." Sommer added quickly in German, "We're just taking a walk." The sentries backed away.

Joyce sat on the lichened stone coping of the terrace wall. "Be up a gum tree without you, would I?" He made no attempt to hide the note of challenge in the remark.

"You would. They're very protective."

"Shouldn't wonder. Devil take the hindmost."

Sommer smiled, almost laughed aloud. So that was it. Another test. English speech form and diction.

"It might upset the applecart."

The visitor frowned. "Born in England, were you?"

"Carlisle."

"Oh, yes. That's just south of Mansfield, isn't it? Shropshire."

"You're in the right country, Mr. Joyce—but only just. Mansfield is in Nottinghamshire, and it's southeast of Carlisle."

"Let's walk," Joyce said abruptly and led the way down to the lawn. Their feet squelched in the soft ground. "Been raining," he grumbled.

Sommer felt quite light-headed; the pill was still doing its work.

"Cats and dogs. Just before dinner." He sensed Joyce's eyes on him but did not turn his head. He felt a juvenile urge to offend this silly little man. He said, "Curious. I wonder why we talk about being right as rain when we can't stand getting wet. Colloquial prejudice, I suppose." He glanced slyly at his companion. "Figure of speech, old man?"

They walked for two hours, round and round, crossing and criss-crossing the park, occasionally disturbing nervous sentries hiding preposterously behind bushes and trees, and, just before six thirty, came within a hairbreadth of being run down on a blind bend of the driveway by Sergeant Baruth on his motorcycle.

Sommer was frozen to the marrow when the sun rose at last from a protective bank of purple stormcloud and Joyce was tired and angry. The interview had not gone his way. He seemed to believe his role was to fail the pupil, not judge his competence, and Sommer played on the fact with deliberate animosity. He applied the coup de grace at the end of a petty cross-examination on English place-names.

"Have you ever been to Happisburgh?" he said conversationally.

"Happisburgh?" Joyce tasted the word, echoing Sommer's pronunciation. "No, why?"

"Because if you had, you'd know it was pronounced Haisb'ro. Norfolk dialect."

William Joyce halted; his face drained and his small fists bunched. "You think you're so bloody clever, don't you!" He swung on his heel and marched back to the house.

MARCH 30, 1939

Dr. Kahler turned from the blackboard and placed the stick of chalk on his desk with immaculate precision.

"I think that's enough for this afternoon, Dr. Price. Tomorrow we shall examine the interplay of British economic forces and their significance in a wartime productive machine."

He turned to the window, dusting his hands to remove the chalk dust, a slight disturbing little man wholly bound up in himself and his work. Everyone at Wohldorf, even Praetorius, deferred to Kahler. He never attended group discussions, never mixed socially with the staff, and took all his meals in his room. He had arrived unannounced a fortnight ago to assume responsibility for Gimlet's instruction in "tactical recognition"—sources of industrial production and technology, evaluation of primary targets, assessment of coastal defense installations, docks and shipping systems—and his impact on the project had been little short of traumatic. He was far and away the finest lecturer Wohldorf had ever seen: fluent, elegant, precise, immensely authoritative. And he was unchallengeable. He had Berlin in his pocket, said Sessler. The gossip was that he had personal access to Canaris.

As a distant rumble rolled over the elms from the south, Kahler crossed to the window and glanced up at the sky.

"Thunder." The storm had settled in at dawn; now, sunlight shafted down through a break in the cloud and turned the spiteful rain to chips of gold. "I suggest, Dr. Price, that you read your notes tonight on—" He got no further. A concussive *whuuuump*! rattled the windows in their frames and, as he ducked, a deafening round of submachine-gun fire raked the lawns. Sommer leaped instinctively for the window but Kahler intercepted him two-handed and slammed him back against the wall. "Down, man! Get down!"

Sommer dropped. A dull roar shook the floor. Then another erupted twenty yards from the house, and his ears popped. Kahler was shouting at him but he couldn't hear, then his ears popped painfully again and the roar engulfed him; two machine guns on the terrace, a hellish fusillade from the driveway, shouting. The lower half of the window suddenly shattered inwards and spat tinkling shards at Kahler's back. Sommer scrabbled furiously across the floor on hands and knees.

"Where are you going?" Kahler grabbed at him and missed. "Dr. Price!"

"Get out of here! Upstairs. We'll have more—"

The surviving upper half of the window erupted inward with a heart-stopping crash and something solid struck the wall above the blackboard and bounced into a corner. It burst with the hollow popping sound of a large balloon and the room filled instantly with dense white smoke.

Kahler vaulted Sommer's legs and pulled open the door into the hall; the smoke rushed after him. Sommer staggered to his feet, coughing and choking, tears streaming, and ran blindly after him, blundering headfirst into a wall of half-dressed bodies. The hall was thick with smoke, and from somewhere to his left, above his head, probably on the stairs, he heard Georg Sessler shout above the din, "Open the armory! The armory! Who's got the goddam key to the armory!" Then the main doors thundered inward and the smoke fled up the staircase on a squall of rain and wind from outside.

"*Achtung! Achtung!*" The voice came from the open doorway.

Sommer flung himself to the floor and wriggled under a solid refectory table by the wall. Bile rose in his throat. From behind the house came more firing, ragged and hesitant, then another window shattered.

"You will lay down your arms! You are surrounded and your position is hopeless! Lay down your arms!"

The smoke began to clear and a solid phalanx of gargoyles in long-peaked forage caps and black overalls swarmed into the hall. Choking sentries and clerks were pushed face first against the walls. Sommer heard a bull roar from Sessler, then the unmistakable clunk of steel chopping bone. A steel-capped ammunition boot kicked him in the hip. "You too, Dr. Price. On your feet, face the wall."

The beat of his heart was thunderous; it shook him from head to foot. His hands, arms, and legs were uncontrollable, his knees drained of strength. His face plopped forward on the mahogany paneling and capable hands patted his clothes, felt under his arms, swept along the insides of his legs and thighs, touched his genitals, his backside.

The voice at the door ranted, "You're all finished, under-stand me? You're dead, every last man!"

Wilhelm Sommer's knees gave under him and he vomited. Then he fainted.

He came to in his room, stretched out on the bed, an insensitive hand slapping him rhythmically across the face.

"Are you all right?"

A black forage cap rode squarely on the blackened face above his. The eyes were a startling gray and at the corners the creased skin showed dazzling white. Black scarf at the throat, black overalls. Some kind of machine gun.

"Who . . . ? Yes, I'm all right."

"Here." The intruder slopped water from a jug into the hand basin. "Wash up. Where do you keep your shirts?"

"Ah . . ." He swung his feet to the floor. "In the top drawer."

He stripped, washed, and pulled on a clean shirt and Price's hideous Fairisle pullover. Before he could look for a tie, the intruder grabbed his arm and shoved him out to the staircase.

The hall was a shambles. A half-dozen men in black were lounging in the open door facing the terrace, weapons slung casually at their shoulders. None of them spared him more than a questioning glance. They seemed to be amused.

"In here." He was propelled into the mess. The door slammed loudly at his back.

"Ah! Dr. Sommer." He knew the voice—it had accompanied him into unconsciousness in the hall. A short, powerfully built man with vigorous brown hair brushed back like porcupine quills stood roasting his backside at the fire, a miniature Goering with a sagging beltline and mud-spattered boots. He wore the uniform of a Luftwaffe major. "Come in, come in, come in."

Sommer advanced hesitantly. Don't *crawl!* Shout, scream, accuse. "I think someone owes me an explanation," he said lamely.

"Explanation!" The major slapped his ample thigh. "My dear Sommer, we owe you an *apology*. Come—allow me to present myself. Major Nikolaus Ritter, head of Luftwaffe Intelligence." He clicked his heels and bowed.

"You were responsible for this?"

"Oh, very much so, my friend. And I want you to witness the rest of it. Your privilege, Sommer. Perhaps you'll be good enough to join me, will you? Here." He opened the door into the hall and stood aside with a little flourish to let Sommer pass. They walked together to the terrace doors.

Twenty or thirty men were drawn up in a wide semi-circle facing them, their backs to the terrace wall, rain slapping on their already drenched clothing—the whole staff, as far as he could judge. Scholz, Sessler—his head swathed in a bandage—Trautmann, Wein, Baruth, Koehn, Hauptmann Lenz and his guard platoon, the drivers, the off-duty wireless operators, the cooks, the company clerks; everyone but Dr. Kahler.

Major Ritter stepped into the rain and swaggered once along the line from left to right, challenging them to look at him. None of them did. He stepped back into the shelter of the open door.

"Kalsmann!"

"Sir." The man who had fetched Sommer appeared at the major's side.

"Casualty list."

"None on our side, sir. Two Wohldorf sentries wounded, not seriously. A few cuts and bruises." He grinned at Sessler.

"Two wounded. A few cuts and bruises." Major Ritter's lip curled. "Did you hear that, Trautmann, Wein, Scholz?" He raised his voice. "The most sensitive Abwehr installation in Germany is attacked by a handful of men *and not one of you is dead!*'' He surveyed them, hands on hips. "You hold the key to the most successful penetration operation in the history of this service''—he gestured at Sommer—''and you let an enemy walk in and pluck him from your hands.'' He turned away, marched a few paces into the hallway, paused, and came back.

His voice dropped to a whisper, barely audible over the swish of rain on stone. "You are dis-gusting, incompetent, ignorant, lazy *swine*! A few thunderclaps, a dozen rounds of machine-gun fire, a smoke grenade, and you're shivering in corners like old *women*. If I had my way—'' He touched a gloved hand to his jaw, savoring the thought, "I'd execute every last man, here and now. But that would deny me the pleasure of reporting your cowardice personally to Admiral Canaris.'' He swung on Hauptmann Kalsmann. "Where's Praetorius?''

"On his way from the Knockenhauerstrasse, Herr Major.''

"I want to see him the moment he arrives.'' Ritter marched to within a foot of Scholz's sodden bulk and raised a finger under his nose. "If this—exercise—had been the real thing, this man,'' he leveled his finger at Sommer, "would be dead. Lost to us. I shan't forget that. And I promise you faithfully, every one of you, that if you fail me again—fail him—you'll spend the rest of your lives regretting it.'' He sighed heavily and turned to Sommer. "Shall we give them another chance, Sommer? Can we risk letting these baboons—'' He whirled on Scholz in sudden passion. "Apologize, you bumbling ape! Apologize to Dr. Sommer!''

Scholz closed his eyes. "I apologize,'' he whispered.

"I am a coward and a worm and I apologize with all my heart! Say it! Say it!''

Scholz said it. Sommer looked at Sessler. He had his eyes closed, too.

"Get them out of my sight, Kalsmann.'' Ritter strode to Sommer's side, took his arm and drew him back into the house. In the mess, he tossed his cap onto a chair and straddled the rug, backside to the flames. "I embarrassed you, Sommer. I apologize.'' He inflated his chest and beamed with sudden pleasure. "Good for them. Remember that, eh? Fear can make a man strong—and only the strong can withstand the storm.''

APRIL 17, 1939

"Ritter's a damned clown."

Georg Sessler relaxed on the cushioned back seat of the Mercedes as the driver slowed down behind a farm tractor. The peasant at the wheel wrenched around to squint into their headlights, pulled over, and waved them on. The driver accelerated.

"I don't draw much comfort from that," Sommer grunted. "When he turned up that afternoon . . ."

"He could've killed someone, the stupid little prick."

"He's killing me. If he doesn't leave me alone for the next forty-eight hours . . ."

Sessler pressed a button on the arm of his seat and the glass partition at the driver's back closed noiselessly.

"Watch it, Tom. He's got half the station tittle-tattling to him."

"I can't move an inch without him. He eats with me, he sits in on every lecture. He can't stop talking! Do you know what he told me last night?"

"Don't tell me."

"He said an SS colonel, Franz Six, has been appointed to take command in England after the invasion and he thought it was a bad choice. He said, 'When we land in England, I shall be with the first wave on the beaches and I intend to be the first officer to reach London. The summit of my career, Sommer.' He thinks Hitler's going to make him Reichsfuehrer in London. He said to me, 'Your success will be my success. The Fuehrer can't refuse me London when the time comes.'"

"He's a clown," Sessler repeated warmly. "But he's also a game player. Every fat-gutted bastard in the Tirpitzufer's a game player. Look at Canaris. He nearly had a fit when Hitler gave half the intelligence operation to Himmler, but you wouldn't know it to watch him in action. He thinks the Security Service is a nest of vipers and he knows that if Reinhard Heydrich gets a chance to cut his throat, he'll take it. So what happens? Canaris plays croquet with the bastard,

41

invites him to his house to play his bloody violin with Frau Canaris's string ensemble. They're vicious, double-crossing shitheads, Tom. You can't trust them or anyone around them. Ritter's up to his neck in people like that.''

"And you tell me not to worry!"

Sessler gave his arm a comradely squeeze. "I said don't worry, friend, because the sooner you're over there the better off you'll be. Out of sight, out of danger."

"Convince me."

"You'll be your own man, making your own decisions. You're no fool, Tom. Forget the bullshit they give you here. If you can make a go of it in London, well and good. If you can't, duck. That's my advice."

"It's easy to say that when you know you'll be sitting over here."

"I'm here because I don't have your talents."

"I don't *have* any talents. I just have a face that fits."

Sessler slapped a huge black-haired paw around his shoulders. "The only thing that matters tonight is whether your cock fits. Because twenty minutes from now you're going to be bedding the juiciest tart in Hamburg. She comes with my personal recommendation."

Sommer stared at him incredulously. "You said . . ."

"I said we had a special appointment in town and I couldn't tell you who with."

"Damnit, you might have asked me first. I'm not a—" A sudden thought paralyzed him. "What does Ritter think I'm doing?"

"I told him I'd worked out a night surveillance exercise. Teach you how to chase a tail. You'll be chasing tail all right."

"But I don't want a . . ."

"I've never seen a man in my life who needed it more. Call it a going-away present. Don't worry. You don't have to talk to her. She thinks you're Gestapo. If that doesn't guarantee you a night to remember, nothing will."

APRIL 18, 1939

He was still floating when Ritter got him out of bed at six thirty, two hours after Sessler had smuggled him into it, but he had no feeling of tiredness, only a slight concussion of the libido. The girl had been . . . There were no words for it. Else, in comparison, was . . . There were no comparisons.

He dressed and shaved in the fitful dawn light, avoiding the temptation to switch on the lamp because it would have disturbed the intimacy of the memory. He experienced a surge of almost superhuman power. There were minute pricking sensations in his skin, his breathing was deep and clear, and a wonderful aching pulsed in his loins.

So none of it had been his fault—the fumbling disasters in their first year of marriage. Else as still as a corpse under him, her mouth stretched tight—with disgust, he'd told himself—her body submitting but never yielding. Two or three nights a week in the first month, then less often, then not at all until they decided (she decided) to have Willy.

A formal mating. Else had informed Karl quite openly what they were about to do and Karl had gone to sit in a pastry shop for the evening to give them privacy. When he left the apartment, Else produced a half dozen newly laundered bath towels, spread four on the bed, and left the others within easy reach of her hand. "Stay in the living room till I call you," she ordered, and she bathed and changed and lay down for an hour to rest and prepare herself.

He was a bag of nerves, shuddering with tension and impotence, by the time she called him in. The light was out and he undressed clumsily in the dark while she sighed heavily at his lack of finesse. At the last moment she sent him to the bathroom to fill a bowl with hot water, and he set it on a chest of drawers beside the bed.

She would not touch him when he lay down on the towels at her side. He was limp with indifference but she wouldn't touch him. He turned away from her in the darkness and

43

coaxed his flaccid penis to erection. "Tell me when you're ready," she said calmly.

He muttered, "Ready," and she spread her legs; he forced entry through that dust-dry gateway and summoned concentration till the veins stood out on his temples. When finally something triggered inside him—no heat, no passion, no sense of release—she pushed him away, took a hand towel from the bedside table, and tied it between her legs like a baby's diaper; then she raised her knees to her chest and held the position for several minutes while she bathed her body where he had lain. Her eyes were wide, her expression intense, the way it looked when she was marking examination papers.

"You can go now," she said when she had dried herself, and he got up and left the room. The next time she allowed him in was five years later, very nearly to the day. She had decided to have Kurt. It took four and a half hours to achieve a satisfactory fusion. Karl came home in the middle of it.

He paused in the process of tying his tie. He could think of her, of Willy and Kurt, and feel nothing. Not a tremor of remorse. No guilt. He went down to join Ritter in the breakfast room.

They ate in silence, but Ritter's face was working as though he were rehearsing a speech. When he had drained the last of his coffee, he cracked a grin as wide as the Cheshire cat's.

"Two days, Herr Doktor. You must be very excited."

He had learned to deal with Ritter as he would a disturbed child. There was nothing to be gained by telling him the truth. "Yes, sir."

"Then"—the smile grew broader—"what would you like to do today?"

"I'm in your hands, of course, Herr Major."

"Excellent!" Major Ritter roared with delight at his little joke. "Then I think we'll take a little trip." He paused tantalizingly. "To Berlin."

For perhaps ten minutes after boarding the Heinkel, Sommer deluded himself that he was to be taken to see Else and the boys; it was the kind of magnanimous gesture Ritter might envisage as a fitting farewell for a hero. But he dismissed the thought when Hauptmann Edmund Gartenfeld came back after takeoff to confer with Ritter. The pilot confided he would be joining them "on the trip to headquarters." A final briefing, Sommer decided.

They were met at Tempelhof by a motorcycle guard of six outriders and a Mercedes staff car flying two pennants. They roared into the city at a furious pace, straight to the Tirpitzufer.

Wilhelm Canaris was a riveting figure, not tall but strongly built, superbly controlled, and spectacular in a naval dress uniform encrusted with decorations and banded braid. His square tanned face displayed none of the weaknesses Sessler accused him of; his mouth was firm but generous, silver brows ran raggedly over dark, intelligent eyes, and his voice was deep and melodious. He inspired in Sommer a momentous panic.

Canaris showed no interest in Sommer's training and, in fact, dismissed Ritter as soon as the formal introductions were completed. He then led his guest to an airy reception room adjoining his office, where three Luftwaffe stewards stood rigidly to attention around a table sparkling with napery and ornate silver. He apologized for the inconvenience of the early-morning flight and offered Sommer an excellent fino sherry, a personal gift from his old friend General Franco in Madrid. An hors d'oeuvre trolley was wheeled in and they sat down to eat.

They were about to tackle an elaborate *caneton à l'orange* when the guard-strewn corridor outside rang with booted feet and a chorus of Heil Hitlers. Canaris rose expectantly and motioned Sommer to do the same. The door swung wide.

Adolf Hitler was smaller than Sommer would have believed possible.

From beginning to end the episode could have spanned no more than twenty minutes, but Sommer lost track of time as he lost track of everything else. The shock robbed him of coordination, speech, and—afterwards—recollection of all but the vaguest details. The Fuehrer shook hands with him, that much he recalled, but he knew he must have looked and reacted like a peasant.

Hitler sat down; some salad preparation was placed in front of him but he did not touch it, nor did he take wine. He addressed himself to Canaris initially, ignoring Sommer completely, and seemed preoccupied with a small pillbox he clutched in one hand. He took three white tablets, drinking sparingly after each one from a glass of Vichy water, and then, a few minutes later, two yellow ones. Sommer was mesmerized by his hands; he registered nothing of the Fuehrer's exchange with the admiral.

At length, Hitler turned to him. Sommer tried later, many times, to remember what he had said, but his only abiding recollection was the sound of Hitler's voice. Canaris said afterwards that it was the most compelling, beautifully composed thesis on Germany's destiny as the leader of a world of nations he had ever heard, a tour de force, but for Sommer it remained simply a hypnotic orchestration of sound.

What he did remember, would never forget, were the Fuehrer's parting words, spoken at the open door as he prepared to leave, his hand coiled limply around Sommer's fingers.

"Remember, Herr Doktor. Where you are, Germany is."

He was on the plane again two hours later, returning to Hamburg with Ritter fulminating his envy in the seat across the aisle, when the acute irony of the remark struck him. Unwittingly—no, with wry insight, he was sure—Hitler had quoted the words of the liberal anti-Nazi novelist Thomas Mann, who had focused the observation on himself when he fled from Germany to sanctuary in America.

"Where I am, Germany is."

When they arrived back at Wohldorf, he went straight to his room. He wanted to be alone, at least until the next morning. Somewhere deep inside him he knew that what he had experienced was a masterly piece of psychological trompe l'oeil. In the cold light of day he would see it for what it was; a carefully judged exercise to boost his confidence and reinforce his resolve.

But for the moment he was happy to be its victim. No amount of intellectualizing could change what he had felt at that table. It was frightening, irrational, illogical, but he had been . . . inspired. His father's zeal, the Wandervögel training, his own reading, Else's fervent idealizing—embodied in the fluttering hands of that spare, perversely emotional man, it all suddenly made sense, seemed possible.

Whatever happened now, whatever the harsh realities of tomorrow revealed to him, he knew he would do what they asked without question. He would do it for a classic myth come alive, for the Teutonic godspell of earth and blood made flesh.

APRIL 19, 1939

The last hours were electrified with paranoia—his and theirs.

Trautmann and Richard Wein ran through the transmission disciplines and timings, wireless maintenance and servicing and emergency procedures, but they could not hide their distress; he was still as far from achieving a Morse "signature" as he had been when he began.

Trautmann had opted for a bigrammatic substitution cipher for Sommer's personal use, a system that substituted code letters for the original text, but in pairs rather than single letters. Figures were also transmitted as letters to add to the density of the encipherment. Since this form of polyalphabetism required memorizing a bewildering range of associated letters and symbols, Trautmann had designed a series of daily cipher keys which could be repeated indefinitely with minor modifications.

He had overcome the problem of how to record these keys by persuading Tom Price's bank, the German-Dresdner, to print a special checkbook in which the normal backing color of mottled cerulean blue was omitted. He then had the color overprinted by Tirpitzufer specialists in Berlin. The blue mottling appeared conventionally on the checks, but on the stubs the letter blocks of the daily keys were printed in microscopic type in the overprint color. Without a powerful magnifying lens they were quite illegible.

Wein set the seal on their neurosis about his signature. "We've decided to delay your first transmission till May 20. That gives you a whole month to settle in, find somewhere to install the set, and get your bearings. Now, that means you'll have time to practice your keying. Don't let me down. Every spare minute you've got—practice, practice."

He knew they saw the relief in his face.

"That first send will be an 'in-place' message," Trautmann added. "It's a simple number-substitution code. The number will be the date 5-20-39. Nothing else. Use the Day One key stub.''

"And remember," said Wein, "site your wireless set as high as you can—the top floor of a house at least. High. And after the in-place send, never break the transmission sequence."

"I know, eleven forty-five on Monday night of the first week, same time Tuesday of the second week, then Wednesday of the third week and so on. But what happens if they get a triangulation fix on my transmission site?"

Trautmann placed a fatherly hand on his shoulder. "I've told you, Tom. They're not equipped to pick up every piece of wireless traffic in the country. You'll be instructed from here when I decide it's time for a change of venue. Trust me."

But he could not trust them, any of them.

Scholz's hysterical question-and-answer session in the main lecture hall nearly brought them to blows. Scholz conveyed the impression that he regarded his last-minute effort as utterly futile. Ritter stepped in as peacemaker, but even his ham-fisted ebullience was visibly in decline.

Georg Sessler was more philosophical. They walked together in the grounds before the final briefing at midday.

"I said it once, I'll say it again. If it doesn't work, get your head down. Forget Ritter and Praetorius. Forget Canaris." He stole an inquisitive glance at Sommer from the corner of his eye. "Forget your friend at lunch yesterday."

"That won't work and you know it."

"It will if it's what you want." They flopped down under a tree, and Sessler said heavily. "I'm not going over my side of things again. If you haven't learned by now, you never will. Just keep one thing in mind: trust no one, not even us. Stay suspicious and you'll stay alive. That goes double when we start sending in more agents."

"When's that?"

Sessler shrugged. "Praetorius is already recruiting. God knows what he'll turn up. Berlin's planning to put in a couple of dozen saboteurs and observers. My bet is, they'll wait till the invasion date's set. Next year sometime, the way things are going."

* * *

"But, of course, Dr. Price, you're far too important to put at risk. You'll have no contact with other agents," Praetorius said smoothly. "You'll function in isolation. Any agent I—" He glanced apologetically at Ritter "—*we* send in, will know nothing of your existence."

They had finished lunch and were conferring over their coffee. Scholz sat silent and immobile, Wein and Trautmann were suffering guilt pangs for their earlier defeatism, and Dr. Kahler, his brief résumé over, had lapsed into a dream. Sessler broached a bottle of schnapps to break the tension and was delighted when his pupil declined to join them.

Sommer needed that drink badly but refused it because he knew how much faith the Abwehr placed in appearances. *Clench your teeth. Endure.* Ritter had announced his intention of accompanying Sommer personally to the Hook of Holland ferry. They were to catch the 3:20 express from Hamburg to Amsterdam, where a car would be waiting to carry them on the last stage.

"Naturally!" boomed Ritter. "You'll soon be in a position of great trust in London, Sommer." The major was now the only member of the team who consistently broke the rule that the pupil be referred to exclusively as Tom Price. "Nothing must be allowed to jeopardize that. Dr. Praetorius—ah—under my guidance—will supply relevant information on agent status, as and when required, but only as a guide to strategic intent. As Dr. Kahler has told you, your brief is to penetrate, not to pursue aggressive actions."

"Your safety, Dr. Price," Praetorius broke in smoothly, "lies in your *conviction*. Your name is Thomas Price. You hold the passport of Thomas Price. You *are* Thomas Price. I've told you many times: live a normal life, Dr. Price's normal life. Aspire, as he would aspire. Stay in his skin, think and act as he would."

"What happens to my wife and children?"

The question momentarily shocked them. Scholz glared at him malevolently.

Praetorius recovered first. "The question is superfluous. Your wife and children will receive your—ah—income. Diverted through the Ministry of Education, I think, to avoid unwelcome inquiries."

"And I, personally," said Ritter grandly, "intend to keep an eye on your boys. My privilege, Sommer. My duty."

*   *   *

Scholz laid out the equipment and "provisions": the compact Wehrmacht wireless set, crystal-tuned to a fixed frequency, and its headphones and Morse key; the cipher-key checkbook; £1,000 in English currency—five packets of suspiciously new five-pound notes bound in Barclays Bank wrappers; a vial of invisible ink; a Swiss multipurpose pocketknife; a mapmaker's pen; a Luger P-O8 automatic and one hundred rounds of ammunition. The wireless and its accessories fitted innocently into the polished rosewood casing of an old English HMV gramophone.

"What's *this*!" Ritter held the Luger by its trigger between thumb and forefinger. "And this?" He pushed contemptuously at the Swiss knife.

"A German officer—" began Scholz.

"Dr. Price is not a German officer—can't you get that through your thick skull! Get rid of them, you dunderhead!"

Ritter swept the pistol and ammunition and the knife to one side. He glared again at Scholz. "Haven't you forgotten something, Scholz?"

Sessler stretched accommodatingly across the table and flicked a slim, quarter-inch lozenge from behind the wireless set with his finger. Sommer looked at it without comprehending.

Ritter picked it up and held it under his nose.

"A cyanide pill, Sommer. You won't need it, of course—except in the supreme emergency."

The train was late, its corridors packed. Ritter drew down the blinds in their reserved compartment and talked without interruption all the way to Amsterdam. He appeared to take Sommer's silence as a mark of his fortitude and, as they rode through the Apollolaan on the way to the Hook, he chuckled, "You're a cool one, Sommer. My God, you're cool."

They reached the ferry terminal just after six o'clock, an hour and a half early, but Ritter insisted on walking him to the departure shed to "see you on your way." An absurd figure in shoulder-draped camel's hair coat, his wide-brimmed soft hat turned up roguishly, he stood to one side as Sommer handed over his ticket. Then he threw an arm around his shoulder, enveloping him in camel's hair, and drew him aside. The passengers waiting in line at the desk eyed this act of familiarity with icy disapproval, but Ritter was impervious to outside influences; he was a man possessed.

"Sommer." He breathed urgently in Wilhelm's ear, deeply moved. "We're bound together, you and I. You feel this, I can sense it."

Sommer averted his head from the odor of stale garlic sausage on Ritter's breath. "Of course—ah—"

"Bound together. We shall meet in London. You believe that?"

"I'm sure we—"

"You have a right to know. I can't deny you. The invasion of southern England is code-named Sea Lion. The fall of London"—his fingers tightened, drawing Sommer's face so close he could see the broken capillaries on the whites of the major's small bright eyes—"will be signaled to the Fuehrer personally in Berlin. On his birthday. Three words. The Shining Day."

Sommer felt the color rising in his face. The Shining Day; Goebbels' ringing phrase of celebration for Hitler's birthday— "the Shining Day, the day of blinding destiny." Or some such rabble-rousing drivel. It was tomorrow, of course: April 20. What the devil was he trying to say?

"A year from now, Sommer. You and I in London. The Shining Day. Yours and mine." He stepped back with a finger to his lips and thrust his arms into the sleeves of his coat. "Bound together, my friend."

Then he tugged the brim of his ridiculous hat and strode away, his coat billowing behind him like a ritual lionskin.

APRIL 20, 1939

The mist parted and sunshine splashed the streaming decks. As it broke through the condensation on the windows of the first-class saloon, a raucous cheer went up from inside and there was a concentrated rush for the doors. Sommer, hunched comfortably on the rail, squinted into the far west over the flat silken sea; a smudge of gray-blue coastline, speckled with pinpoints of reflected light, showed fine on the starboard bow. England, he thought, and tensed himself for nervous reaction. None came. No sensation of panic, no fluttering of the heart. Just another place, then. Home.

My name is Tom Price. I hold the passport of Tom Price. I *am* Tom Price.

The deck below the companionway flooded with children and he studied them thoughtfully as they scampered to the rail to point excitedly at the shore. The Danzig children, as everyone had known them since midnight last night: the reason for the passengers' ten-hour wait. A group of children due to arrive by bus from Danzig had met with unavoidable delays along the way, the Hook authorities had announced over the public address system. The inconvenience was regretted but port officials refused to permit the ferry to sail without them. Curiously, the information seemed to anger the crowds rather than console them and the Danzig children became a focus of universal irritability, tiredness and discomfort. When they finally turned up at four thirty in the morning, they were met with hostile stares and whispered reproaches.

Eighty of them. He bent over the angle of the rail for closer inspection. The youngest ones could barely walk; three or four years old at best, near-circular bundles in woolly coats and curious bonnets. The eldest were ten or eleven, he judged, round-shouldered, skin and bone draped in ill-fitting gray or black; the girls hand in hand, expressionless as dolls, the boys agitated, heads shaved to the whites of their skulls. Jews, as everyone knew the moment they appeared. The vermin of Hitler's Europe, scuttling to freedom.

There was another stampede from the first-class saloon and an army of tweed ulsters and scented furs jostled for position at the rail. The red-haired Englishman Price had met at the bar appeared at his shoulder and he pulled back to let him in.

It had happened shortly after the ferry buffeted across the bar into the open sea. He'd decided to remain on deck throughout the voyage—not a question of insecurity, he simply felt the need to be alone. But it was cold, the sea mist had gone straight to his throat and chest, and a drink, a sensible schnapps, seemed the obvious medicament. He'd gone inside, taken a stool at the bar, and settled down to husband the liquid—a sip at a time, slowly, drinking for the stomach, not the head—when the red-haired young man clambered onto the adjoining stool and knocked his elbow. "I say, I'm most awfully sorry.'' The English did that sort of thing so well. ''Not at all,'' said Dr. Thomas Arthur Leslie Price generously. No further communication, of course; they had not been formally introduced. But ten minutes later, the fellow asked the barman if he knew the result of the English Cup Final and the barman replied that it hadn't yet been played. A discussion followed on the putative claims of the two teams, Wolverhampton Wanderers and Portsmouth, and at *that* point Price had been unable to restrain an urge to air his knowledge. Wolverhampton, he offered learnedly, were caught up in a controversy involving the injection of monkey glands into the bodies of their Cup team. An unheard-of break with sporting tradition.

As he'd known it would, the revelation started a rare debate. He withdrew to the rail before he got out of his depth, but the exchange gave him new confidence. The men at Wohldorf knew what they were doing after all. Georg Sessler had drilled him relentlessly on all aspects of English sport, convinced that a man could converse for a whole year in London without once leaving the triumvirate of football, cricket, and rugby.

Now the young man grinned down at him in the most friendly way. He was extremely tall, one of those classic public school types who cling to gawky adolescence well into maturity. Lean, broad-shouldered, stomach flat as a board. His strength seemed to be concentrated in hands and feet and knobbly joints. He would never possess grace, but he'd probably been a force to reckon with on the playing fields.

He threw back the swatch of hair hanging in his green eyes with a nervous jerk of the head. His manner matched his construction: awkward, unsure. ''Do you make this trip often?'' he asked. The English did *that* sort of thing so badly.

''No, thank heaven. You?''

''About the tenth time this year. I usually spend the trip hanging over the rail.'' He grinned boyishly and rubbed his nonexistent stomach with a large knob-knuckled hand. ''Mal-de-thing. It's a treat to get a smooth passage for once. Is that why you stayed on deck?''

Trust no one!

''I feel better out than in.'' He laughed. It sounded natural.

''Been on holiday?''

It was not easy to keep the grin intact. "No, working. You?"

"Working. Wine and spirits. Import, export. I've been buying wine—or trying to. Market's in a hell of a state at the moment. At this rate there won't be a wine industry at all in France in a year."

"Rumor of war."

"Shakespeare!" the young man said impulsively.

"The last resort of the inarticulate. I'm a teacher."

The young man wiped his hand down the seam of his trousers and held it out. "Curzon. Paul Curzon."

He took it. The grasp was firm.

"I'm Tom Price."

The undistinguished, soot-blackened building across the street from St. James's Park underground station would not have held the attention of the most aimless passerby for more than seconds. Broadway Buildings was, nevertheless, a temple of its kind. As headquarters of the Secret Intelligence Service, it housed three hundred and sixty ill-paid, ill-assorted functionaries of what had been, twenty years earlier, the most potent espionage system in the world. For more than fifty years the security of an empire embracing half the civilized world had been forged there in an atmosphere of lofty self-assurance and privilege so impenetrable that even prime ministers had been excluded. In the vocabulary of the trade it was known as the Buildings and the machine it housed as Six—a clubby diminutive of the service's official designation, MI6 —but both were simplifications.

Since the Great War, British Intelligence had suffered from an embarrassment of civil service intervention and a long-running battle, only recently won, with the meddling mandarins of the Foreign Office. The fight for superiority had left it weak and vulnerable. Naval, Air, and Army Intelligence services lived and had their being in jealous separation, linked by the umbilical of the Joint Intelligence sub-Committee of the chiefs of staff.

The world of the Buildings had a language of its own, arbitrary as schoolboy slang and quite as opaque; initials proliferated and a code name was the holy grail of every hardheaded young operative in Section F. But Six was growing up and, since the rise of Hitler, growing more and more complex behind its shabby facade.

Technical advances in wireless interception, pioneered with astonishing success during the World War by the legendary geniuses of Admiralty's Room 40 staff, had spawned a motley brood of independent units and the modern art of Sigint—Signal Intelligence. Codes and ciphers, devised not long after man first put stylus to parchment, were now a machine science. Sydney Cotton, a nerveless Australian pilot, had only a month before initiated the incredibly dangerous game of vertical aerial photography by flying reconnaissance missions over Germany and the Mediterranean. Economic Intelligence was another fashionable mouth to be fed, and a new breed had been born: the diviners, interpreters of mystic trends in industrial development and investment.

The Buildings, once a simple cell, broke down under pressure of change into dozens of self-interested specialist groups who took themselves off to isolated country houses at St. Albans, Maidenhead, Portsmouth, and Southampton to ply their chosen crafts. Secrecy is expensive; before the ink was dry on the SIS estimates for 1939–40, its £700,000 budget had been wildly overspent.

The old soldiers of espionage—control executives and case officers who had won their spurs in the hand-to-hand school of spying—despaired of this new age of enlightenment; the service was spread thinnest where they considered bread-and-butter espionage mattered most—in the potential battlegrounds of Europe. The monitors, the experts in wireless telegraphy, were taking over from the Toms, the alleycats of field espionage. Strategic forecasting was the new evangelism, mechanical eavesdropping the new order.

Stuart Menzies, deputy chief of SIS—DCSS in the vernacular—who had joined the service by way of a career commission in the Household Cavalry, was a founding member of the old school whose brief now was to impose the disciplines of the twentieth century. He fixed the red-haired young giant in the visitor's chair across his desk with a glare of accusation.

"So you aborted the mission?"

Paul Curzon crossed his legs uncomfortably. "I decided the best thing to do was to focus on Ritter."

"Why?"

Why indeed? He could hardly repeat to the man's face what

everyone in the service celebrated as the prize spy story of them all. According to legend, the British Joint Intelligence coordinators had called, in the summer of 1916, for the death or kidnapping of a certain Leutnant Wilhelm Canaris of the German Secret Service, an efficient and disruptive spy then making a nuisance of himself in the Mediterranean. The setting for the coup was to be the Spanish port of Cartagena. The British agent selected for the task was Lieutenant Stuart Menzies. The coup failed. Canaris escaped with his life, and Menzies never forgave himself. Twenty-three years later, they faced each other once again in labyrinthine endeavor, but now from the pinnacles of their profession. The slightest hint of Canaris's personal intervention anywhere became, for Menzies, a cause célèbre. Major Nikolaus Ritter was widely known to be immediately responsible to Canaris.

"There were just the Dutchman and me to cover Wohldorf, the Stegemann offices in the Grosse Burstah, the HQ in the Knockenhauerstrasse, and Ritter. He made straight for Wohldorf so I concentrated the effort there. Ritter was at Wohldorf for three weeks, as far as I can make out. Anyway, the Dutchman was watching the place when Ritter came out in a car yesterday and drove to the Central Station. If the train hadn't been late I wouldn't have made it."

"This fellow Price was with him?"

"Well, they were together on the train, I think, and Ritter was all over him like a rash at the Hook. That's why I decided to take a chance and follow him."

"Hmmmm." Menzies stared into space. "What then?"

"I met Price briefly at the bar on board—he was traveling first class. I kept it casual; asked him if he knew the Cup Final result."

Menzies' taut mouth relaxed. "Did he?"

"Game hasn't happened yet. He knew that—and everything else I might have asked. Too damn smart by half. We met again on the boat deck as we came in."

"Did he seem suspicious?"

"Not at all. Relieved, I thought."

Menzies compressed his lips doubtfully. "You're sure he hadn't rumbled you?"

"Pretty sure."

"Accent?"

"Not a trace. I threw in a couple of phrases—the kind of

slang you wouldn't expect a Hun to know—but he didn't miss a trick. Couldn't fault him. Perfect. I'd say too perfect, but I might be kidding myself.''

"You might indeed."

Menzies examined Paul Curzon dispassionately. At twenty-nine, he looked ridiculously young and innocent for his years and experience. But when war came, this choirboy would merit automatic promotion to section leader, a manipulator of human resources. And unless they had all been wrong about him, Paul Curzon would send men to do the impossible in war with that same engaging grin and endearing green-eyed honesty.

"What then?"

"I said I was taking the London train and he said he was too, so we came up together. Around Ipswich he began telling me about the job he was going for as a lecturer at London University, and about having taught in Hamburg."

Menzies glanced down at Curzon's notes on the blotter in front of him. "Do you think he was lying about that?"

"I'd take a sizable wager he wasn't."

"And at Liverpool Street you took a cab and dropped him off in Victoria Street?"

"That was my idea. He had nowhere to go—said he didn't know London well. I suggested he take a room at the Mendip."

"What's that? A hotel?"

Curzon grinned disarmingly. "Sort of commercial traveler's rooming house."

"Why there?"

"He said he was pretty strapped for cash. All he had was his last month's pay. Wouldn't run to a suite at the Ritz."

"I see. And you agreed to look him up for a drink. When?"

"I didn't want to press it too hard, sir. I sort of left it up in the air."

"Did he react to that?"

Curzon twisted his mouth sheepishly. "Grabbed at it. I think he took a shine to me."

"Hmmm."

There were no precedents for Dr. Tom Price. As far as Menzies was aware, Hamburg-Wohldorf was simply a wireless station for transmitting and receiving intelligence. It had no espionage training capacity, and, if MI5 were to be believed, there had been no recently detected attempts by the Abwehr to plant spies in London. They had had their subagents in place since the mid-thirties; down-at-heels mid-European nationals, Spaniards, the odd discontented British blueblood—but they had yet to send in one properly trained professional. If Price was a trail blazer, there was rather more in the wind than the Joint Intelligence sub-Committee was being told. But the handmaidens—the counterespionage bloodhounds of the Security Service, MI5—were notoriously reluctant about sharing secrets. The opinion of the security trade was that "Five plus Six equals Nein."

"You'll talk to no one about this," Menzies said. "Your report stays here in my office. If anyone asks you what you've been up to, lie to them. Understand?"

"Yes, sir." Curzon looked quite incapable of lying.

"Come and see me again tomorrow. Four thirty. I'll have this fellow Price processed by Home Office."

Curzon rose.

"Get some sleep. I'm temporarily co-opting you to G staff. As far as you're concerned, your only interest—until I tell you otherwise—is Price. Now get yourself home to bed, man."

APRIL 21, 1939

It was an unnaturally early hour for lunch in London's clubland, but the seven men who made their way independently to the fine old house in St. James's Street were inured to untimely gatherings. In a sense they were themselves members of a very exclusive club. One by one they filed through the black, brass-knockered door and climbed thickly carpeted stairs to the third floor.

A policeman, rolling by on slow dependable feet, was taken aback to see Winston Churchill squeeze from a cab and pay his fare. The bobby threw up a salute and the old man acknowledged it.

William Stephenson greeted his guests at the door to the executive dining room. By twelve fifteen they had all arrived:

Churchill; Brendan Bracken, his close parliamentary ally and disciple; Admiral of the Fleet Sir Roger Keyes, MP; Alfred Duff Cooper, who had been First Lord of the Admiralty until he resigned in anger over Munich; Colonel Colin McVeagh Gubbins, ostensibly a serving officer in the Royal Artillery; Admiral Sir Reginald "Blinker" Hall, pivotal figure of the old Roman 40 and the lion of British Intelligence in the twenties; and Major Desmond Morton, one of Winston's euphemistically titled "special assistants."

The atmosphere was relaxed; the guests grouped and re-grouped with the easy assurance of social equals, but the purpose of their gathering was far from social. In a nation officially at peace with the world and striving to preserve that peace, they were energetically planning for war.

Stephenson was not tall, neither stubby nor slim, but his sober black suiting and stiff white collar concealed a boxer's build and poise. Fair, short-clipped hair started high on his broad forehead, and blue eyes, deep as the Canadian lakes that bred him, could switch from arctic coldness to Caribbean warmth without a flicker of the narrow mouth or the dimpled jaw. In Britain he was still virtually unknown, but by the late thirties he and Churchill had created their own unofficial secret service. "Churchill's Activists" were not merely unofficial; their existence was a contemptuous challenge to Prime Minister Neville Chamberlain's authority and his poli-tics of appeasement. Winston Churchill had no parliamentary power, no formal status; he was again, as he had been many times before, in the political wasteland, castigated as a war-monger whose day was over; yet secretly, inadmissibly, he numbered King George VI among his sympathizers, and the American president, Franklin D. Roosevelt.

Lunches such as this one were rare, for absolute security was essential to the Activists' collusion. Public disclosure of their activities would have "melted the ice cap," as Bracken once put it. Churchill would certainly have gone to his politi-cal grave, Bracken as always at his side, and Desmond Morton and Duff Cooper, recruiting officers for the Activists' covert committees like Focus, Electra, and XYZ, would have led the procession to the Tower of London. Not least among those who would have perished were the officers of the Secret Intelligence Service who voluntarily cooperated in their endeavors.

Stephenson tapped the table. "Gentlemen, shall we . . . ?"

They sat down; lunch was served and the idle conversation continued. Forty minutes later, with the dishes removed and coffee and brandy circulating, Stephenson cleared his throat. "Can we get down to cases? I don't imagine any of us has much time."

Desmond Morton got in first. "I think we should all be aware of a new development. I had word last night from Stuart Menzies. He's picked up a possible Peeping Tom."

"German?" Stephenson craned down the table.

"English, as far as he can tell. At least, English passport, English accent, English background. Teacher of history. Came over from the Hook to Harwich yesterday. One of Menzies' young men followed him from Hamburg."

"Hamburg?" Blinker Hall shook his head as if waking from a long sleep. "Not one of Dr. Praetorius's radio people?"

"We don't know. Menzies is checking up on him now. For the moment the fellow's under surveillance, but there's no telling what his game is or why he's been sent over here. He's almost certain to be equipped with wireless, though. If he *is* one of theirs, that is. Man could be perfectly legitimate. But Menzies agrees we can't take chances. And—ah"—he looked around the table—"for the moment he'd prefer Five weren't brought into it. His operation ran the chap to ground and he'd like to hang on to him till we all know where we are."

"He's right," drawled Gubbins.

"What does Menzies propose?" Churchill boomed.

"A joint venture—with us. For the time being. This chap claims he's been teaching in Hamburg; came back, he says, for an interview at London University. History department, University College. He's applied for a post there, he says. Menzies' contacts there aren't good, but he knows yours are, Blinker. He thought you might like to arrange a . . . welcoming committee."

Blinker Hall closed his eyes. "Pepper." He repeated the name. "Professor Something Pepper. Yes, I know him. Little chap. How welcoming are we supposed to be?"

"Very!" Churchill pushed his empty brandy balloon aside decisively. "Whoever and whatever he is, this man's welcome to London will be exemplary. Desmond, tell Menzies Blinker will make all necessary arrangements. And tell him, too, that I shall expect a personal report the moment he's established the fellow's bona fides. Or not. Particularly if *not*. When is this—what's the man's name?''

"Price. Dr. Thomas Price."

"When's he expected to turn up for interview?"

"We don't know, sir," said Morton. "At this stage we don't really know anything at all."

Thomas Price.

It sounded provincial; looked curiously uninspiring when he signed it in the hotel register. There was a certain comfort in that, he thought, as he ate eggs and bacon in the Mendip's gloomy breakfast room.

Live a normal life, Praetorius had said. Dr. Price's normal life. But what had Price considered normal? All they knew about him was that he avoided the company of his colleagues, drank excessively and probably in private, had an addiction to tobacco and an unhealthy preoccupation with erotic literature. But that was the Hamburg Price. He might have been quite another man on home soil.

He left the hotel, bought some cigarettes at a tobacconist's nearby, and strolled down Victoria Street to Parliament Square. It was good to be among people who had no thought for anything but their own affairs. Come to think of it, the real Price would probably have done no more than this himself on his first morning in London—testing the ground, sniffing the air, finding his balance. Eight years in Germany was bound to have sapped his confidence and, if Scholz was right, he would have been like a cat on hot coals at the prospect of an interview at the university.

The interview. He slipped the letter from his pocket and stood in the shadow of Big Ben to read it again.

"Dear Dr. Price: Thank you for your response and the completed form of application. Your suggestion of Monday, February 27, as a suitable date for interview is quite convenient. I look forward to meeting you here in my office at 10 A.M. I am, sir, Yours etc." It was signed "A. K. Ballard."

Praetorius had pinned to it the typed letter he'd sent Ballard apologizing for Price's failure to appear. It was stilted, vague, and impersonal: "I shall travel to London, therefore, when my doctors advise me I am fit to do so, possibly at the end of April. Permit me to telephone you on my arrival."

An Englishman would never have written "permit me to telephone you." Nor would he have typed the letter. *Details*.

He bought a newspaper and found a bench on the Embankment where he could read it. A report from the House of Commons caught his eye. The provision of deep shelters "in the event of war" had been debated, and the establishment of a new Ministry of Supply to coordinate defense production was recorded in exhaustive and astonishingly candid detail. The secretary of state for war, speaking of Britain's lack of industrial preparedness, gave it as his opinion that "under our present system nothing can guarantee appreciable acceleration of output, nor can there be any enlargement of it in a given time."

Fact? Or propaganda devised to confuse the German government? It seemed inconceivable that a minister would admit his country's weakness so blatantly.

On the same page a whole column was given over to Adolf Hitler's fiftieth birthday celebration, and a large photograph taken from a rooftop overlooking the Unter den Linden showed part of the military parade. The report itself was as informative as the one which had no doubt appeared this morning in the *Lokal Anzeiger*; it listed the ambassadorial comings and goings at the Chancellery, the gifts showered on the Fuehrer by foreign governments and the thousands of telegrams received from heads of state, including one from King George VI.

Yet, on virtually every other page, the facts pointed inescapably to war. Italy and Yugoslavia were quarreling over the peace treaty with Hungary; Russia pledged its willingness to join France and Britain in "resisting aggression in Europe," while Benito Mussolini, in a speech in Rome, poured scorn on Roosevelt's appeal for a ten-year nonaggression guarantee and a world peace conference. Il Duce insisted that Italy was interested in work and peace, not war.

He dropped the paper into a wastebasket and began to walk, although with no clear idea of where he was going. He reached Trafalgar Square and stopped to watch a group of children feeding the pigeons; contemplated a brief sortie into the National Gallery, dismissed it as an indulgence, and drifted with the tide into Charing Cross Road. He pored for a couple of hours over old books piled on pavement trestles in front of a dozen secondhand bookshops, but his mind turned time and again to the letter in his pocket, and, finally, he could resist it no longer. *That* was the priority; he could stroll and browse and squander time to his heart's content in the pretense of getting his bearings, but in the end he would have to make that call.

His heart began to pound and he hurried away down a side street. Georg Sessler came to haunt him. Everything, everyone, is a threat. A telephone call made from a hotel is potentially traceable and might be overheard. Avoid the obvious. A public callbox is safer.

He found himself in a narrow alleyway, then another, and realized he was lost. A totally irrational panic welled up in him; he sprinted to the next corner and gasped with relief to see a busy street and, beyond, the gray stone facade of Charing Cross Station.

He was on the point of crossing the Strand to the station when Sessler's voice whispered again, "Watch your rear at all times and if you can't see anyone, find somewhere to roost before going on."

He backed nervously through the white and gold portal of a Lyons Corner House.

After five minutes he felt safe and rather foolish. People came and went but no one spared him a moment's idle curiosity. He sat for twenty minutes over a cup of undrinkable coffee, then paid his bill and left cautiously. By the station taxi rank he spun on his heel to surprise any plodding would-be pursuer, but the crowds were almost entirely composed of women and none of them reacted suspiciously.

He waited by the booths in the station concourse for several minutes before one fell vacant, then opened Ballard's letter to Tom Price, found the telephone number, selected a coin, and dialed.

"University College. Can I help you?"

"I want to talk to Professor Ballard, please."

"One moment."

His hands were shaking. This was ridiculous. There was nothing to fear. Nothing to fear.

A voice broke in on him, high-pitched and annoyed. "*Of course he isn't. Why should he be?* Hullo? Who is this?"

"Hullo? My name is Price, Thomas Price. I want to talk to Professor Ballard. I'm—"

"Price? Good Lord, yes. Hamburg."

"Er—is that Professor—?"

"Pepper. Philip Pepper. Bit of a mouthful. Just got in, have you?"

"I arrived yesterday. If I could talk to Professor—"

"Where are you?"

"I'm at Charing Cross Station. I thought—"

"Get an underground from there, can you? *Charles?*" The voice became indistinct. *"Get a tube from Charing Cross Station to Queen's Gate, can he? South Ken?"* The speaker returned to his audience. "South Kensington. You can take the underground from where you are. Remember the drill, do you? Down the stairs, Circle Line. *Circle Line is it, Charles? Yes, that'll do.* Make it by four o'clock, can you?"

"At—ah—" He opened out the letterhead again. "At Gower Street?"

The voice chirruped with impatience.

"No, Price. Queen's Gate, number 42a. Ground floor. Can't miss it."

"But can you tell me, please—?"

"Righto? Four P.M., 42a, Queen's Gate, South Ken. Got it? Jolly good. *So—where were we? Oh, yes. Why should the poor beggar—"* The line went dead.

He replaced the instrument, frowned at the letterhead, tapped it uneasily on the palm of his hand, folded it back into his wallet, and walked out of the station into Villiers Street. A sign over his head advised UNDERGROUND—STRAIGHT ON. The clock showed three fifteen.

Professor Philip Pepper was barely five feet tall, matchstick thin, and so generously layered in waistcoat, wool cardigan, and tweed jacket that he seemed weighed down by clothes. Tiny feet poked shyly from wide Oxford bags and his hands, potato chips of yellow skin drawn tight on the bone, clutched resolutely at one another as if in perpetual prayer. He was dwarfed by the drawing room-cum-library of his flat. The molded ceiling soared some twelve feet above his white head, bookshelves rose on three walls, and a giant log fire crackled in its grate under a mantelpiece he might possibly have grasped at arm's length if he raised himself on tiptoe. He had the face of a dyspeptic goblin, pointed chin and nose and ears, and eyes so large and banana-yellow bright they lent the whole of his face a pale primrose hue.

He brushed aside Price's apologies—"Ill, weren't you? Not serious, I trust." He waved him into a deep green velveteen-covered armchair commanding a view of six hideous oil paintings of the mid-Victorian "Love Lies Bleeding" school above the fireplace.

"Tea, do you?"

He indicated a teapot molded and painted in the form of a country cottage with roses round the door and garish petunias hanging from its window boxes.

"Thank you."

"So—you're Price." The little man pulled a half-dozen books from the seat of an armchair, decanted them onto the floor, and lowered himself into the velvet depths. "Where are you staying?"

"The Mendip."

"Mendip? Don't think I know it. Still, your business where you hang your hat."

Price submitted, with as much equanimity as he could muster, to the frail academic's cool appraisal. Pepper's yellow eyes seemed to cling to his clothes like burrs, snatching away every few seconds to move on to some other point of interest.

"I was hoping to arrange an interview with Professor Ballard."

The little man did not react at once; he seemed hypnotized by a button hanging on a long thread from his guest's jacket cuff.

"Not married, are you? Your curriculum vitae didn't say married."

"No, sir."

"No objection to that, of course." Pepper sipped his tea, burned his mouth, and ran a small pink tongue wildly over the scald. "Well, then. Ballard. Wrote you that letter, correct?"

"He said—"

"Interview. Absolutely. Very impressed. Could have had it for the asking at the time, no doubt about it."

"I don't think I—"

"Eh? Ah! Didn't write back to you—that what you're saying?" He clicked his tongue. "Got your second letter last month. Too late then, of course. Still, he should've told you not to come. Remiss. Not like Ballard; busy man and so forth, but a stickler for proprieties." He ventured another sip at the tea. "Couldn't wait, you see. Loved to have had you, but there were other candidates, you see. Gave the job to a fellow from Manchester. Edinburgh degree. You're Oxford, aren't you?"

He could not speak. At no stage in all the elaborate game playing at Hamburg-Wohldorf had anyone suggested for a moment that the job, the trigger for the entire operation, would not be his.

"Oh, dear." Pepper set his cup and saucer aside. "Taken the wind out of your sails, has it? Yes, I can see it has. Well. I really don't know what to say."

He assumed a look that so poignantly mirrored the misery of the man opposite him that Price felt compelled to say something.

"It's perfectly all right. I should have realized . . ."

"Set on coming back for good, are you?"

"Well, yes. I couldn't stay on there—not now."

"Adolf and Co. Get mixed up with them, did you? The Nazis?"

"Slightly. The local gauleiter set up a working party in 1933 to reexamine teachers in the city schools. I could see what they were after and I was damned if I was going to hand them my head on a plate. I let them think I was . . . sympathetic."

"Funny position to be in, though. Went there voluntarily in the first place, did you? I mean, bit of a desert for a pre-Renaissance man, Hamburg?"

The point of no return.

"I didn't really go there intending to work. It was a . . . well, a personal matter."

"Affair of the heart. Girl, yes?"

Price lowered his gaze but felt the yellow eyes drilling the top of his head.

"We met in . . . It doesn't matter. She was German. Wouldn't have me. Like a fool I thought she might if I followed her home to Hamburg. After a month my money ran out and I had to find a job. All I knew was teaching, you see. We got engaged in '32; unofficially. Her parents were . . . National Socialist people. Diehards. Then in '33, late summer, her father was offered a job in Munich and she . . ." He let his voice trail away.

Pepper leaned forward impulsively and patted his hand.

"I'm sorry. Painful for you, see that. Woman was ever thus. Decided to stick it out, did you? Your German must have been pretty fluent."

"Yes, it was. And there didn't seem much point in coming back here. After the first few months under the Nazis I thought about it, but . . . Oh, no excuses. I was set in my ways, I suppose."

"Join the Party, did you?"

"Oh, no."

"You must've felt very vulnerable."

"I can't deny that. The Gestapo, the SS, the SD—they're around every corner. A teacher has to watch himself, particularly a foreigner. Put a foot wrong and . . ."

"Absolutely. God knows why the people put up with them. Moral blindness; like Rome under Caligula. But . . ." He hesitated. "No business of mine, of course, but one can't help being curious. You didn't *have* to stay. A man needs a pretty strong stomach surely to put up with living under those conditions. Set in your ways—yes, I can see that, certainly; but after '36 . . . ?"

"I didn't . . ." He paused. "I'm afraid this may sound rather pretentious. After '36 I could see where it was all leading. Hitler never bothered to hide his real intentions in Germany. Quite the reverse. It was all quite open there. Aboveboard. I felt . . . I thought by staying on I might learn enough to be useful back here when . . . well, when war came."

"Inevitable, you think?"

"I do."

The pointed face slumped between the cavernous shoulders of the tweed jacket. "Mr. Chamberlain doesn't seem to agree with you."

"With respect, sir. Mr. Chamberlain doesn't live there."

"And you know better than he does what Hitler's about, eh?"

Price mustered a look of impatience.

"I don't think anyone here grasps what he's about, to be frank. The English judge Hitler by their own standards. Chamberlain has no more in common with the Fuehrer than I have with the man in the moon. I wish I could make you understand. At my realgymnasium, and at every school in Germany, history teachers study Clausewitz and hammer his first principle into every child's head from the age of six: War is the extension of politics by other means. That's the lesson. War. Against the Jews, against racial impurity, against anyone who gets in the way.''

He stopped, shrugged apologetically. He was surprised at the bitterness of his speech.

Pepper sat motionless for a long time, the acute angle of his chin buried in a cone of interlaced fingers.

Price pulled himself forward to the edge of the chair.

''I really think I ought to go, sir. I'm afraid I've wasted your time.''

Pepper came out of his trance and fluttered his yellow fingers. ''Go? What for, go? Sit where you are, my boy. Nothing pressing.'' He glanced up at the framed Victorian ladies above the mantel. ''Look here, Price. I've told you there's nothing we can do about that job now. Over and done with and nothing else on the cards at present. But—damnit, I'm going to take a chance on you. Listen to me—I've got a little enterprise in hand at the moment—cataloging the department's residual library. Now, it's not what you expected, God knows, but if you'd be prepared to take it on—few months, perhaps, no more—there's a possibility I might be able to fit you in somewhere.'' He rolled his lips into his teeth. ''You won't lose by it. Salary would be commensurate with the value I place on your potential, but you'd have to leave that with me. What d'you say?''

He said yes; his relief was so overwhelming he almost forgot that he was expected to show disappointment.

Pepper leapt out of his chair and Price rose to meet him. A small clawlike hand grabbed his and pumped it energetically. ''That's the spirit. First class. Excellent. You won't regret it, Price. My word on it. I'm not saying you'll enjoy it, but it's a beginning. I might even wangle you into the Grade Two lecturer scale; five or six hundred a year. You'll be your own man, of course. Couple of assistants. Not too bad. Just a few months.''

When Philip Pepper said good-by at the street door, Price asked if he could go to the library next morning to look around.

Pepper shook his head firmly. ''On a Saturday, my boy? Nonsense. Won't find even the caretaker there on Saturday. Monday's soon enough. About nine-thirtyish. Relax while you can. Take in a show this weekend. Afford that, can you?''

He said he might just have enough money.

Dinner was an obnoxious meal. A square of solidified Yorkshire pudding, potatoes, nearly liquid cabbage, and badly carved chunks of mutton. The dessert, rice pudding, had languished for some time on its plate in a hot oven before being brought to the table. There was no wine, no beer, and no carafe of water. When he finished, a desiccated crone in a white apron and a silly little tiara of starched white lace set the inescapable cup of tea in front of him and turned away before he could refuse it. He left the tea and went back to his room.

He examined his suitcase, still not unpacked but for a clean shirt and underclothes and his shaving materials. It had not been touched. It was tempting to believe luck was on his side so far—"The agent's most important accessory," Ritter had observed on the train to Amsterdam—but nothing in his life to date had given him reason to believe in luck. He would have to find a base quickly—but not too quickly. There were important factors to consider.

He went to the window and looked out; this was not a good place. A paved courtyard ran down to a wooden fence and an alley and, beyond that, the backs of other hotels, houses, and shops rose like cliffs. Always establish an escape route— Georg Sessler, 1939.

He took out the Morse key unit and sat at the marble-topped washstand to practice his handwriting, but his ineptitude depressed him and he soon put it away. He turned to the street guide he had bought that day and looked for Upper Phillimore Gardens, the address Pepper had given him of the library where he was to start work on Monday morning. West Kensington meant nothing to him. He studied the central London map and began to memorize the area bounded by Westminster, Oxford Street, Covent Garden, and Hyde Park, but it was a tiresome exercise and he could not concentrate. He pulled on his coat and went out.

Moving through a city at night was an art, Sessler had said. If you were being followed it was a nightmare; if you were doing the following it was a gift. Every shop window acted as a reflecting mirror and the lighted ones were better than searchlights. Street lamps were like furlong markers on a race course, perfect for judging pace and interval, and they threw good sharp giveaway shadows.

The golden rule: never hesitate and never run. A tail is there to watch you, not to catch you. Give him something to report next day and you'll make him a happy man. Walk a lot, keep him busy. A happy tail is a vulnerable one.

Easy enough for Sessler, but had he ever walked in Victoria Street at eight thirty on an April evening, shouldering through the crowds, avoiding stares, fighting down the urge to look back over his shoulder, flinching at the loud *parp* of a taxi horn, quelling his dread at the approach of a uniformed policeman?

He stopped in front of a small cinema and peered inside. The young woman in the ticket booth looked at him hopefully. He paid his one-and-ninepence and found a back-row seat in the scented stalls.

The film had started but it didn't matter. His ankle was throbbing painfully and he took off his shoe and massaged it as Sessler had done. He began to feel better and leaned back in his seat.

A man in white tie and tails was dancing agitatedly with a blonde in a diaphanous gown. He watched to the end and thoroughly enjoyed himself.

APRIL 23, 1939

Paul Curzon sat in the gloom beyond the outer reaches of Stuart Menzies' desk lamp and waited to be recognized. It was a few minutes short of midnight and he had been in bed when the call came. He had slept too much this weekend; there had been nothing else to do.

When he presented himself at the Buildings at four thirty on Friday, as ordered, Menzies had been "in conference." He returned to his flat. Saturday passed without further summons, and Sunday. He had turned in at eleven, satisfied that at that hour even the DCSS would be unlikely to open another file. He should have known better.

Menzies looked up at last from the papers on his desk and tweaked the bridge of his nose between finger and thumb. "Thanks for coming."

Curzon ducked his head politely.

"We've established a few facts about Price."

Curzon leaned forward expectantly.

"He left his hotel on Friday evening. Went for a walk and wound up at a cinema in Victoria Street." Menzies looked down at the report. "*Flying Down to Rio*. Fred Astaire and Ginger Rogers." His mouth puckered with amusement. "Two men shadowed him in series while Ritchie went through his things at the Mendip. Rather neat little Wehrmacht wireless set in a gramophone; £985 in new fivers, bottle of invisible ink and mapping pen, the usual cyanide pellet. Nothing unusual except for his codebook. The Golf, Cheese and Chess Society were quite impressed with that." The trade sobriquet for the Government Code and Cipher School dated from the twenties. "It's a checkbook. German-Dresdner. The day keys are overprinted as color tone on the stubs. Really very ingenious—for Hamburg."

Curzon puffed out his lips and fell back in his chair. "Well—I wondered why you hadn't called me. When did you have him arrested?"

"I haven't."

"But surely with all that stuff . . ."

"You said you'd look him up when you dropped him off at the hotel on Thursday."

"Yes. Nothing definite, though."

"You haven't called him?"

"No, sir."

Menzies' chair creaked as he forced it back on its sprung pedestal. He gazed steadily at Curzon's face as if searching for inspiration. "Dr. Price starts work at London University tomorrow morning." Curzon's eyes widened. Menzies was enjoying the shock effect. "He's been engaged to catalog a library for the history department of University College."

"I'm sorry, sir, I don't . . ."

"You said you thought he'd taken a shine to you. Enough of a shine to want to see you again?"

"I don't know." Curzon ran a hand through his hair. "Depends what you want out of it. And for how long. If he's good, I doubt I'll get within a mile of him."

Menzies nodded vacantly. "We don't know enough about him yet to gauge how good he is. He may have talked to you on the ferry because he's a professional who saw you as useful cover. But he could just as easily be a nervous amateur who needed someone to lean on." He referred again to the report under his hand. "No clues in his movements this weekend. He went to the Tate and the National Gallery on Saturday, but he made no contacts, didn't talk to anyone. Today, he went to the Natural History Museum, the Science Museum, and spent an hour looking over the Wallace Collection."

"Doesn't sound like a professional."

Menzies shook his head. "We can't take that for granted. They could all be future contact points, drops, transfer locations. Perhaps he was reconnoitering the ground. On the other hand, you could be right. He called the university on Friday and went to see the deputy professor of history. I'll let you have the report tomorrow, but that visit tells us a lot. Whoever he is, he's equipped to teach history. Even Hamburg wouldn't slip up on something that obvious. And historians, in my experience, aren't exactly Hamburg's strong suit."

"So he really is who he says he is."

"Maybe." Menzies stared sightlessly into the long distance. "Price grew up in Carlisle. He was at the local grammar school. Went to Oxford in 1920. Bennett's in Carlisle now, checking background, friends, schooling, home. Roythorne's covering Oxford."

"Parents?"

"Both dead."

"But we're bound to turn up people who knew him at Oxford."

"I know. On the surface, that suggests he's the real Price."

"You don't seem too sure."

Menzies shifted in his chair. "I know Hamburg, Curzon, and I know Canaris. The Abwehr is an opportunist's paradise. They're perfectly capable of pitching some poor fool into an impossible situation simply because a controller at the Knockenhauerstrasse thinks it'll improve his staff rating."

"They couldn't be *that* stupid. If he's *not* Price . . ."

"He's walking into a lion's den, yes. There are three Oxford men lecturing in history at University College and God knows how many in other subjects. He'd have to face up to them some time. A German wouldn't survive two minutes in one of those 'do you remember old so-and-so' conversations over the port.''

"With respect—" Curzon began diplomatically.

"I'm destroying my own thesis? Yes, I know." He gnawed on a knuckle. "You said his English was 'too perfect'—those were your words.''

"And I also said I could be wrong."

"Hmmmm." Menzies looked down again at the papers in front of him. "I don't think you are. There's something else about Price that doesn't fit and I've a pretty shrewd idea that the Hamburg people weren't aware of it when they sent this man in.''

Curzon came forward again on his chair. "What's that?"

"You'll know in due course. But for the moment I'd prefer you keep your mind open. I want you to meet Price. Get to know him—but don't press him too hard. I want a proper assessment of him: personality, weaknesses, strengths.''

"It won't be easy, sir. If he's already got a job . . ."

"He applied for that teaching post in February. It's been filled. The library option is something I had laid on for him. It'll keep him out of trouble and give us a chance to watch him.''

"D'you mind if I ask a blunt question, sir?"

"As long as you don't expect a blunt reply."

"Are you teeing him up to run as a double against Hamburg?''

Menzies rose stiffly and stretched his back with a grunt of pain. "One step at a time, Curzon. Go and see him tomorrow evening, when he's finished work. About six thirty or seven.''

Curzon rose. "And just talk to him?"

"No. Just listen. Let him do the talking."

APRIL 24, 1939

He tried on all three of Tom Price's suits and all six shirts
in front of the full-length mirror, but they all made him look
and feel like a refugee. He settled finally on a suit of dark
gray serge with a wide chalk stripe, but its flyaway lapels and
square-set shoulders were a travesty of English conservatism,
and when he joined the office-bound workers on the underground, his professional irritation turned to private shame.

The weekend had done nothing to relieve his skepticism
about the mission. In a half-dozen casual, largely self-indulgent
sorties around London on Saturday and Sunday, it had struck
him with growing horror that he was as well equipped for
active service as a tethered goat at a tiger hunt. Sessler's
orientation lectures on London geography and institutions
proved to be at least two years out of date; the ramblings of
Scholz and Praetorius lost all credibility in an inescapably real
world, and Ritter, in perspective, seemed even more of an
obscene joke. The training at Wohldorf, he now saw, had
been an exercise in fantasy. He had never felt more alone.

He stepped out into the warm sunshine at Kensington High
Street, crossed the road, and began the long climb uphill.
Phillimore Gardens was a sheltered artery of aristocratic houses
and apartment blocks punctuated at intervals by impressive
villas set back behind sturdy walls. From the top of the hill
came a steady trickle of cliché Englishmen in City black,
every one of them bowler-hatted and umbrellaed to perfection.
They were too polite to stare at him as the bourgeoisie on the
underground had stared, but by the time he turned into Upper
Phillimore Gardens his face was burning.

The house was a shock. He checked the paper Pepper had
given him and even walked on a little to look for a more
prepossessing address with the figure 9 in it, but there was no
mistake. It stood in a wilderness of uncut couch grass, holly
trees and rampant ground creeper; three floors, a chipped
green door under a peeling white portico, dirty uncurtained
windows. He walked down the broken stone path and rang

74

the bell. No response. His watch showed eight forty-five. Pepper had told him to appear at nine-thirty but he'd interpreted that as a first-day concession. In Germany the working day began at eight. He rang again, then knocked several times very loudly. Still no answer. Your first lesson, he thought idly: the English aren't always guilty of understatement, and they start work in the middle of the day.

He made his way along the side of the house and through an ornamental gate flaking with rust; a few yards from the back door, a paved fish pond was putrefying in its own slime. The garden was a jungle; overgrown lawns, choking fruit trees, broken glass forcing-frames, ruined paths. A pile of paper and cartons several feet high lay against a rotting wood fence. He was beginning to feel extremely apprehensive.

"Dr. Price? Is that you, Dr. Price?"

The voice seemed to come at him out of the ground. He turned full circle, feeling an utter clown. "Where?"

"Here. Down here." A girl's face smiled up at him over the rim of the basement area; just the face. "I'm awfully sorry," it said cheerfully. "Isn't it *ghastly*!"

He walked to the top of the basement steps. They ran down steeply to an area knee-deep in forgotten debris and the sad remnants of a potted garden, long dead from lack of sunlight and air. Two grimy windows gazed out blankly from behind a screen of solid iron bars. From the open door the girl said gaily, "Mind your step, doctor."

She stood with her arms clutched around her in what he took at first to be unallayed hysteria; when he stepped inside, however, he realized with a shudder that it was no more than a reaction to the chill. The place was as cold as a tomb.

"I said it was ghastly." Her smile warmed him. A rose, he thought, obliquely. An English rose. Who had no place in a weedbed like this. She was in her mid-twenties, he judged; dark brown hair teased into a cascade of curls that fell to her shoulders, fine innocent hazel eyes, the tip-tilted nose of the child, a small, inexperienced mouth. She wore her severe black skirt and crisp white blouse like Girl Guide efficiency badges.

She laughed—a joyous sound—and buffed the circulation back into her bare arms. "It really is the absolute giddy end, isn't it? I mean, do they actually imagine anyone can *work* down here?"

"Is there any electricity? We'll need light."

"No, but the gas is on, thank goodness, and I've found a kettle so we can make some tea. I brought a teapot and cups and saucers from home. Just a tick; I'll pop the kettle on."

It had probably been a servants' hall, he decided. Below stairs; a little hell of old England. Whoever had gutted it to create this one huge chamber had shown scant regard for cosmetic effect. Speed had been the priority. Deep channels of exposed plaster marked the lines of demolished walls and the decor ranged from white to green to blue to cream to brown in stretches of varying length corresponding to the size of the original rooms. On one side was a large porcelain sink; alongside it a vast black ironclad cooking range covered ten feet of wallspace. A small gas stove was tucked into a handy corner niche. Naked pillars of red brick, all that remained of the supporting walls, propped up the central area and around them lay piles of neatly stacked leatherbound books, some of them reaching above head height. He went over to the nearest stack and touched the heavily tooled blue leather of the topmost book. No dust. He sniffed. The air was sour with disuse.

He heard the gurgle of water being poured into a teapot.

"Is there a list of the books here?"

"I don't think so," she called from the cooking range. "I have an idea we're supposed to start from scratch. No one told me anything really. They just said 'would I take it on' and I said 'yes' and that was it. They seemed in an awful rush to start."

Awful rush. "When did they offer you the job?"

"Not till late Friday. I was just about to go home. When were you?"

Never yield to casual questioning—Georg Sessler. "What's your name?"

"Sally Logan."

"Are you with University College?"

She came around one end of the book mountain with a cup and saucer balanced expertly in each hand. "I was at the library in Russell Square." She offered him a cup. He took it and perched on the edge of a green baize-covered card table, the only visible working surface in the room.

"Professor Pepper mentioned two assistants."

She brightened. "Mrs. Petrie. Alice. You'll like her, she's

awfully sweet." *Awfully*. The bizarre contortions of middle-class English. He must remember that. *Awfully sweet*.

"Is she a librarian, too?"

"She's from registration. In Russell Square, like me. Oh—do you take sugar? I'm afraid I forgot to bring any."

"No, thank you."

A filthy cellar, obviously still being renovated. A hurried job, speed the priority. Several thousand books but no dust on them. The house unused for months, perhaps even years. Yet Pepper had talked of his "library" as if it were a going concern. *Residual* library? He shuddered and the girl said anxiously, "I can light a fire if you like. In the range. It won't take a minute."

"Please don't bother." No one had searched his luggage. Or his room. He was sure. And he hadn't been followed this weekend. Anyway, what possible interest could the history department of University College have in his belongings or his movements? But he *was* being used. By Pepper? Ballard?

He caught the girl inspecting his clothes. She blushed. "Tell me about Professor Pepper."

She gulped a mouthful of tea, coughed, performed a little dance to avoid slopping tea on her skirt and covered her mouth with her hand. "Oh, I'm terribly sorry. I didn't—"

"Why do you laugh?"

Something in his face pushed her close to hysteria. He watched in blank incomprehension as she fought to control herself. "It's—he's very sweet. Everybody likes him. Honestly."

"But you find him amusing?"

She blushed so deep a scarlet he thought she was about to choke. "Not amusing exactly. He's. . . . No, really, I mustn't."

"In confidence. Please. I don't know him, you see. I've only met him once. Does he teach at Gower Street?"

"Oh he doesn't teach anymore. He retired once, but Ballard brought him back to run administration. He sort of—hovers." The word, for some reason, triggered another paroxysm.

"You mean he's a little—odd." More middle-class convolution.

"Well—it's the way he goes about clucking over everyone. They call him Mother Hen. He can't help it, can he? I mean, it's the way some people are. You know, old maidish, a bit precious." It occurred to her she might have gone too far.

"He lives alone," she said as if that was the worst that could be said for him.

"I don't quite understand—" he began.

"And neither do I," echoed a competent voice from the door. "What *do* they call *this*."

"Alice!"

Alice Petrie was not a large woman and by no means a beauty, but as she crossed the threshold she seemed to consume every inch of space in the room. Her perfume robbed the air of its mustiness, her bright green summer dress subdued the slapdash colors on the walls and neutralized the brick-red columns; one flick of her finger, Price felt uncomfortably, and it wouldn't surprise him in the least if the whole house disappeared in a puff of smoke.

"Ah—Mrs. Petrie." He made the effort; put down his cup and took a pace toward her with his hand out.

She didn't appear to see or hear him. She gave ten seconds to a visual tour of the basement and its contents, another five to Sally—a small moue of recognition, a slight widening of the eyes—then, as if he'd emerged from a hole in the floor, she settled on Price. "Ah—doctor." She let him take her hand.

Her hair, piled high on her head like coiled black rope, was a device to give her added height; she was a woman who believed in height; he recognized that about her intuitively. Her dress flowed dramatically over large breasts and Venusian hips and there was a decided Mediterranean cast to her features; dark eyes, suddenly amused as they traveled his face, a wide sensual mouth, impeccably painted.

"I look forward to—ah—working with you, Mrs. Petrie."

She didn't answer at once; she appeared to be memorizing the precise geometry of his face, and her hand resisted his impulse to release it.

"Perhaps you'd like a cup of tea," he stammered.

"No, thank you." Alice Petrie's polished lips moulded the politeness and kissed it into open space. He extricated his hand.

"Well, then—" He gestured aimlessly around him. "I'm afraid it's going to take us a few days to—"

Mrs. Petrie handed her folded coat to Sally Logan and rolled up her sleeves. "Not *you*, Dr. Price. Sally and I. I'm not having you sweeping and cleaning like a charwoman. The department should be ashamed of itself. A mess like this on your first day.''

"I really don't mind lending a hand, Mrs. Petrie.''

"And I say it's woman's work." She turned, hands on hips, the question closed. "Sally, there's supposed to be a caretaker in at nine o'clock. Upstairs front, ground floor. Be a pet and see if he's got cleaning things—brooms, buckets, scrubbing brushes, soap, dusters. And tell him I want heat and light down here before the day's out or I'll be down on him like a ton of bricks.''

Sally pattered away obediently up the area steps. Price sipped at his cold tea for want of something to do with his hands and Mrs. Petrie, sensing his discomfort, ran her competent black eyes over him as if he were an errant adolescent sent to try her patience. She took the cup from his fingers as a practical first step, then slipped a hand through his arm and urged him toward the door.

"Now off you go, doctor.''

"Really, Mrs. Petrie—''

But she was adamant, immovable. "You take yourself for a nice walk; it's lovely out there just now. An hour or two should do us. Come back at twelve. That'll give the dust time to settle.'' She suddenly released his arm and stepped back a pace, her head on one side, lips pursed.

"Oh dear,'' she murmured and shook her head. "Wherever did you get that suit, doctor?''

"I—It's German. I've been working in Hamburg for several years.''

She shook her head again, very firmly. "We'll have to take you in hand, poor man, I can see that. You won't want to look like that now you're back with us, will you?''

Alice Petrie, he thought as he stumbled red-faced into the welcoming sunshine, would have to go.

When he returned a little after midday, the windows were wide open, dust floated like gunsmoke on the fetid air, and the newly scrubbed floor stank of carbolic soap. Alice Petrie immediately called a halt to the morning's work and announced that she and Sally had decided to take him to lunch. He protested in vain. They walked down to Kensington High Street—arm in arm, to his acute embarrassment—and Alice chose a neat white-tiled eating house called the Bluebird

Grill. She also chose the table, read the menu and ordered for him—a plate of steak and kidney pudding, roast potatoes and greens. "For energy," she explained in her competent way.

While they ate she cross-examined him on his life in Germany, his standing at the University, his *family*—she quite plainly meant *wife*—and "dear-deared" when he admitted he was a bachelor, advising him to "be careful" of Pepper. She did not expand on this warning, but Sally had another fit of the giggles.

Her curiosity finally assuaged, Alice reciprocated. Sally, she said, was a qualified librarian, a student of French, a lapsed vegetarian and a music-lover. She had a small flat in Edgware Road but went down to Buckinghamshire at weekends to be with her parents, who farmed there. She had a young man—blood rushed to Sally's cheeks at this—and they were working up the courage, as she put it, "to exchange parents." Alice herself was a widow—"five years, eight months, eleven days"; she had two children, Alan who was fifteen, and Dinah, twelve, and lived in Richmond in the house left her by her late husband, a civil engineer. "I really took a job just to get away from it," she confided. "Seventeen years of marriage and I was tied to the place day and night. Poor Leonard, he never understood why I hated it."

On the way out, Sally waved to someone at a corner table. The caretaker, she said. An old grouch.

Price began a cursory examination of the books after lunch but was interrupted at three when Pepper appeared without notice and insisted on a tour of inspection. He scurried around, pausing here and there to flick through the stiff pages of some faded volume, emitting little grunts that could have been recognition or surprise or simple bewilderment. Incredulity would have been more in keeping, thought Price. Of the hundred or so he had managed to page through, less than half a dozen merited shelf space in a university library. Even a *residual* library, whatever that meant. When he tried to pin Pepper down on the precise criteria for cataloguing, the little man wriggled away to talk to Sally about requisitions for office furniture and stationery. And when Alice began to lecture him sternly on the disgusting state of the basement, he made a decisive beeline for the door.

"Going then, Price." He closed his eyes tightly. "Something, though. What was it? Tip of the tongue. Oh, yes. Lodgings. Found anything, have you?''

''Not yet. I'll need a few days to settle in first.''

''Mustn't rot in that hotel for weeks, my boy. Not good for you. Must get you somewhere.'' And, having set in train a proposal he clearly had no intention of pursuing, he left, crabbing up the stairs in his black greatcoat like a crippled beetle.

The afternoon terminated abruptly at five. Sally put on her coat and hat and left to find a bus to take her to Edgware Road. Alice Petrie hung back; Price was all too aware of it and began preparing to leave himself, dreading the thought that he might be inveigled into walking her to the station. She caught him as he tried to sneak out.

''I hope you won't mind, doctor.'' A hand on his arm, a warm rich Mediterranean smile. ''I couldn't help hearing what Professor Pepper said. About your lodgings.''

''Oh, I'll get round to it sometime.''

''Yes, well—I was just thinking. If you need a nice clean room—''

''I'm not sure yet what I need, Mrs. Petrie.''

''No, but some digs are dreadful, aren't they? Hard beds, outside lavatories, queuing up in the morning for the bath, no proper heat. You wouldn't like that.''

''No,'' he sighed and edged nearer the door.

She followed, tightening her grip. ''I thought—you know, just an idea—well, I've got this lovely little room at Richmond and—''

''That's really very kind. I'll think about it.''

''You could come over for supper one evening. Just to look. See what you think.''

The idea appalled him. ''You're very kind.''

''The children aren't a bit noisy. They're no trouble.''

''I'm sure they're not.'' He lurched through the bog of courtesy, committing himself more inextricably at every step, and when she finally let him go he had agreed—or actively failed to disagree—to take the train to Richmond one evening for supper. *Soon.*

He trudged back through Phillimore Gardens in a daze. Achievements? A job that was not a job in a library that was not a library under the nose of an Amazon who would be

82

running his career in a day or two, if he let her. Reactions? Uncertainty, unease, confusion, doubt, concern. Conclusions? None. It was illogical to allow the insecurities of Wilhelm Sommer to influence the feelings of Tom Price. Nothing to date suggested he was vulnerable. He was not *unsafe*.

The journey back to the Mendip exhausted him; he avoided the underground, took a bus, discovered too late it was going in the wrong direction, took two more and walked the last mile. The open doors of the hotel greeted him when he arrived with the hot stale breath of cooking, and he almost turned his back on it; but he was overwound, tired, dispirited, and the thought of bed, if nothing else, was too attractive to resist. He went to the desk and reached for his key.

"Price, there you are!"

He spun on his heel. Paul Curzon was uncoiling his great length from a couch across the hall. "Hello, old man. I was in your neck of the woods so I thought I'd take you up on that drink if you're game. Do with a pint myself. Hot as hell in here."

The youngster grabbed his hand and pumped it heartily.

He was too tired to say no.

Winston Churchill's flat in Pimlico had been described by Brendan Bracken as "snug" and by a visiting newspaper editor as "spartan." Neither fitted the truth, but then no two people ever shared the same opinion of Churchill or his lifestyle. The flat was certainly smaller than any home he'd made thus far in his expansive and privileged career. Six of his closest collaborators had been in session with him there since eight o'clock—Admiral Sir Hugh Sinclair, head of the Secret Intelligence Service, Blinker Hall, William Stephenson, Desmond Morton, Duff Cooper, and Brendan Bracken. They had been joined shortly after ten by three others: Professor Philip Pepper of London University, Dr. Lawrence Reid of Cambridge University, and a young man Sinclair chose not to introduce.

Churchill fidgeted in his tall Jacobean carver. "What do we have then, Sinclair? In summary."

Sir Hugh was a small, neat man of great energy, renowned for the hurricane force of his intellect and the volatility of his temper. It was apparent that he was not well and his determination to hide the fact accelerated both his sharpness of tongue and his mental agility.

He raised the thumb of his right hand. "One. He is *not* Dr. Thomas Price. Two—"

"You're convinced of that? Beyond a shadow of doubt?"

The knuckles of the raised hand went white. "I'm dealing in *fact,* not speculation. The *fact* is, he's not Thomas Price. Two." He raised the index finger. "He's either unaware of Price's true background, or Hamburg failed to brief him efficiently, or they just weren't aware of all the facts themselves. Three. He *is* a spy. Wehrmacht wireless set, aerial and so on, code book, cash reservoir of £900-odd, cyanide pellet, etcetera, etcetera. Four. He's vulnerable. We could confront him with any of Price's former colleagues—headmasters, tutors, a girl he was attached to in Carlisle, men he roomed with at Oxford— and they'd denounce him on the spot. Five. Blinker set up a reception with Pepper here, but Price is unsure and possibly suspicious." He went back to the thumb. "Six. Our source in Berlin confirms he's one of Ritter's people, which means one of Canaris's. In my judgment, that implies that if he doesn't operate at strategic level he might as well not operate at all. They didn't send him here to blow up the Houses of Parliament. Seven. He's not a dyed-in-the-wool professional. We all accept, I hope, that they wouldn't be so foolish as to think he could function here as a lecturer in history if he weren't qualified. So we're dealing with an educated, intelligent, possibly briefly trained amateur. Don't forget that. It's important. Eight. He's the first of a planned series of infiltrators; Canaris won't be happy with one spy when he can muster ten or twenty—and our Berlin source confirms that Hamburg's planning a nursery. Nine. He needs a base of operations, a job that gives him scope for high-level contact, and a stable, established lifestyle. He must know that won't be easy. Ten. If we decide to"—he glanced threateningly at his audience—"*persevere* with him, we're committed to giving him more rope than we'd normally consider reasonable."

"That can be arranged," Desmond Morton said quietly. "The object is to—"

Churchill interrupted imperiously. "Let's go back to your second point. Why do you say this fellow's unaware of the real Price's background?"

Sinclair swiveled his head toward the diminutive professor of history. "Your area, Pepper."

The little man coughed. "Ah—yes. Background. The fact is, sir"—he looked over his glasses to measure Churchill's reaction to the courtesy—"Dr. Price had a somewhat unfortunate record as a teacher in this country before he left for Germany in '31. The feeling is—"

"Feeling?" Churchill's brows descended truculently.

"The assumption is that he—ah—withdrew to Hamburg as a direct result of incidents that destroyed any hope he might have entertained of a career in England. He was a bright young man but a rather impulsive one; prone to—ah—punish his pupils rather than chide. He was dismissed from two schools for excessive use of—ah—corporal methods. His intention in applying as he did for a post at London is a little obscure. His original letter of application was quite exemplary. Remarkable qualifications; a double first at Oxford, junior house master at Downside, two years at Ampleforth; a first-class teacher, in fact, and an obvious candidate for advancement. Naturally, my colleague Professor Ballard accepted this in good faith. He sent Price the appropriate form of application to fill in, said it was really just a formality, and suggested the man come to London for interview. Price returned the form and nominated a date when he could get away."

Churchill shifted restlessly in his chair. "A first-class teacher but he was sacked from Downside *and* Ampleforth?"

Pepper's small mouth stretched to reveal small uneven teeth. "Not quite, sir. As I explained, Ballard accepted Price's claims in good faith. However, when the completed application arrived Ballard wrote, as a matter of course, to the people Price named as references: the headmasters of Downside and Ampleforth and the—ah—warden of All Soul's. They had no knowledge of him. None at all. Price was never a teacher at either school. Ballard investigated at once, of course. He discovered Price got a second in history at Oxford and taught at prep and private schools in the North of England. He proved somewhat emotionally—ah—erratic and disappeared in 1931."

"What did Ballard do about it?"

Pepper squirmed uncomfortably. "Well—nothing, sir. He decided it was a preposterous joke or a very clumsy attempt at misleading the university and set the matter aside."

"He didn't write to Price again?" Churchill persisted.

"No, sir, we just let it drop."

"So Price was in ignorance of the reception he was likely to get when he presented himself for interview?"

"Oh, I wouldn't say that. The *real* Price had every reason to be apprehensive. I can't believe he would have had the nerve to turn up."

"Then, confound it, man, why did he apply?"

Sinclair raised a commanding hand. "We've got to accept two things about the real Price. The first is he *was* unstable. No two ways about that. Nobody with any sense would seriously believe he could get away with pulling a stunt like that. He knew the university would check up on him. Secondly—"

"So it was a . . . *joke*?" Churchill's mouth set in a crooked fissure of disbelief.

"More complicated than that." Sinclair glared challengingly at his audience. "In my view, it was an act of desperation, an impulsive attempt at wish fulfillment. He didn't expect it to work, so it left the stage clear for any amount of romancing he cared to put into it. And that brings in the second point: He'd almost certainly had as much as he could take of Hamburg. Wanted to come home."

"This *is* speculation," Churchill said testily.

"Informed speculation," Sinclair corrected him. "Reid?"

Dr. Lawrence Reid removed his spectacles and examined them for invisible smears. "The pathology of behavior isn't my field, but this man isn't the Price who wrote that letter. I can claim that on physical characteristics alone."

"Explain."

"The real Price had poliomyelitis when he was six. Right foot and leg. That's in the public medical record. *This* Price has a natural limp, but it's in the *left* foot; the ankle. The locomotive characteristics are quite different. We've filmed him. And this chap isn't neurotic; he shows none of the physical signs of deep-seated stress. Certainly nothing that fits the theory of a man desperate to escape his past. I had an opportunity to record his talk with Pepper at Queen's Gate. We're just not dealing with the same man, sir. I'll stake my reputation on it."

"Then who *are* we dealing with?"

"A balanced, reasoning—I should say controlled man.

Intellectually controlled. Afraid, suspicious, perhaps, but not emotionally ill.''

Churchill leaned heavily on his forearms and aimed a finger at Sinclair. ''We're getting away from the salient point. How—if you know and I know—is it possible for Hamburg not to know Price's real background? You claim this to be a highly sophisticated attempt by the Abwehr to infiltrate a spy of quality. Yet on this evidence they've made infantile errors of judgment.''

Sinclair contemplated his accuser. ''I brought Reid here tonight because I felt you should have credible scientific witness to the fact that Price is not Price. The next step calls for a certain amount of faith in that opinion. Our contention—''

''*Contention?*''

''No documentary evidence. A contention. Ours is that Hamburg has either arrested or subverted the real Price and intercepted his correspondence with London. Price, who'd be scared out of his wits if we judge him correctly, went along with Hamburg's plan to allow this man to impersonate him. What else could he do? Nevertheless, it seems clear he let them believe that the curriculum vitae he sent the university was true—and to look at it squarely, there's no reason why Hamburg should doubt it. He presumably made the same claims when he applied for a teaching job there.''

''And how do you propose to support that theory?''

''Seven weeks before *this* chap turned up in London—and long after Price must have known his game was up—Professor Ballard received a letter, purportedly from Price, saying he'd come to London for interview after all. That letter was typed; the first one was in Price's handwriting, but the signature on the typed one is an exact replica of the first. No one signs his name identically. The chances against are several million to one.''

''So?''

''So, *Hamburg* typed and signed that second letter. And they did so in the belief that the real Price was what he claimed to be. If they'd known he'd lied in his original application they wouldn't have touched him with a ten-foot pole.''

William Stephenson straightened in his chair at the right of Churchill's desk. ''What you're saying is that Hamburg saw what looked like a golden goose and grabbed it too quickly.''

"Exactly!" Sinclair bounced with uncontrollable impatience. "Which means that *our* Price believes what Hamburg told him: double first, Downside, Ampleforth, all the rest of it."

"Meaning?" Churchill growled.

"That he has to be protected," Morton interjected, "from people living and working around him and not least from himself."

"Unless we decide to have him arrested, of course," Duff Cooper grunted.

Churchill closed a hand around the brandy balloon on his desk and swirled the contents around its bulbous walls. "And if we did?"

"We can't," Stephenson snapped. "We *have* to give him a trial run."

Churchill turned to Blinker Hall. "What do you think, Blinker?"

The admiral emitted a sound pitched midway between a groan and a sigh. "Bill's right, Winston. You know it; we all know it. Hamburg's made us a present. We know more about the real Price than the substitute Price does. We know more than Hamburg does. That knowledge gives us an edge. We've given this chap a sanctuary. In due course, we can give him another, one that will take advantage of his talents and training. We can give him confidence—we have to if he's to function properly. We can give him access to information. We can make sure he transmits that information to Hamburg."

"What kind of information?" Churchill rumbled.

"That's something we can decide later," Desmond Morton said quickly. "First, he has to be protected—especially from himself."

"With respect," Pepper ventured mildly, "aren't we doing that already? He's out of the way, in a place where he'll have no chance contact with people who might have known the real Price."

"That's all very well for the time being," Sinclair returned severely, "But he can't function in a vacuum if he's to do what Hamburg sent him here to do. He's been sent in as an infiltrator, not a fence sitter."

"Then I suggest we create a group for him to infiltrate." Churchill drained his glass and lowered it thoughtfully to the desktop.

"Exactly what we had in mind," Morton interjected. "If

he's to make contacts—and we all accept he's bound to try—then we'll have to provide some for him. He's cut off in Phillimore Gardens and he'll soon realize it. So—Pepper will invite him to the odd soirée in Queen's Gate. We'll give him a ready-made social circle, populate it with people we can trust—chaps from Focus and the XYZ Committee, say, who share a common academic background."

"Six will provide round-the-clock surveillance and supervision," Sinclair added. "For the time being it's a cat-and-mouse affair. The problems will arise when Price is instructed to begin operations."

"And we're required to help him transmit information," Brendan Bracken said sourly.

Churchill tucked away his watch. "I think we can reasonably postpone that discussion till later. Duff, Morton, Pepper—I suggest you prepare a list of people suitable for Price to meet. Blinker, you'd better row in on that, too. We'll need that fine Italian hand of yours. Sinclair, when are we likely to know who this man really is?"

"In a week, hopefully. It might take longer."

"Quick as you can." He made a motion with his hands, palms up, a conductor calling the members of his orchestra to take a bow. "Keep me informed, all of you."

Sinclair turned to shake his head warningly at the young man in the far corner who had automatically got to his feet. The other guests trooped out to the hall, but none of them offered their host a farewell and he accorded them none himself. Brendan Bracken was the last to leave; Churchill's jaw jutted some prearranged signal as he closed the door.

"I hope this won't take long." Churchill consulted his pocket watch a second time.

"It won't." Sinclair beckoned to the silent young man, and he came forward hesitantly, brushing a swath of reddish hair from his eyes.

"This is Paul Curzon." Sinclair's pale eyes twinkled. "He's been entertaining Dr. Price this evening."

MAY 8, 1939

Tom Price inspected himself in the full-length mirror. An improvement. No, a metamorphosis, a miracle. The suit was a dark gray worsted with a faint pinstripe, double-breasted, on the advice of the tailor, to widen his shoulderline and narrow his hips. He fluffed out the white handkerchief in his breast pocket and settled the dark gray curly-brimmed trilby on his head. A mircle! The new Tom Price.

He went downstairs, dropped his key at the desk, and went out into Victoria Street, swinging his rolled umbrella. The Mendip was still anathema to him, although it no longer induced in him the old fits of morbid depression, but he was now thoroughly at home in Victoria. He found it astonishing that he had settled so quickly into the pace and atmosphere of an environment in every respect alien to him, but settle he had and he was actually beginning to enjoy the experience. The old man who sold him his morning paper near Westminster Cathedral ritually saluted him now, as a mark of friendly respect; he knew at least two ticket sellers by sight at St. James's Park tube station, and the tobacconist close by the Mendip greeted him warmly when he dropped in to purchase tobacco. (He had given up cigarettes in favor of a pipe after daily confrontations with a billboard stressing the incomparable Englishness of Wills's Cut Golden Bar at one shilling per one-ounce airtight tin.)

Philip Pepper had proved to be a tolerant and generous patron and Alice—quick to observe these things—gave it as her opinion that he should "watch his back." This advice was accompanied by feigned innocence and an explosion of merriment from Sally Logan, but they refused to enlighten him further.

Pepper ranked as number two to Professor Amyas Ballard in the hierarchy of the history department, but, as Sally had told Price that first morning, it was common knowledge that he had retired when it became obvious he would not be allowed to succeed his superior. Tougher, hungrier young careerists had challenged Pepper's position from below and, in his amiable way, the old man had cheerfully made concessions to their ambitions. He had come out of retirement to assume Ballard's administrative functions. There had been no residual library project until Pepper created it in a fit of combustive sleight-of-hand, and every member of the department in Gower Street was convinced he knew why. Pepper had found a mystery man, "a golden boy"—and his intention was to keep him in protective custody and groom him to snatch the crown Pepper himself had been denied.

Price had probed Pepper about this and had been pleasantly surprised to find that the stories were not denied; not confirmed, but not dismissed out of hand. The clearest indication yet of the professor's interest in him, however, had emerged on the previous Friday afternoon. Pepper had dropped in for tea and rather self-consciously invited him to a soirée at his flat in Queen's Gate.

"It's not a department thing," he explained guardedly. "I reserve the right to choose my friends, d'you see. Mostly old fools like me, but you'll find a few chaps your own age. Be glad to have you come, if you'd care to. Wine and cheese, nothing much, but the talk's worth the effort."

If he had needed unequivocal confirmation of Pepper's good will, this invitation to join his inner circle provided it. The evening was warm, and the deep windows of Philip Pepper's stronghold were opened wide to catch the faintest stirring of dusty air. A dozen bottles of Bordeaux stood guard over plates of sandwiches and cheese cubes on a side table, the lighted chandelier tinkled pleasantly, and some twenty men, most of them in their sixties, stood in groups of two or three or lolled elegantly in Pepper's velvet chairs. There were no introductions; he was armed with a glass of wine—"Just plonk, I'm afraid"—handed a plate of cubed cheddar, and insinuated into a three-part discussion of the Diet of Worms. Pepper neatly trapped him into a defense of Lutheran dogma and within fifteen minutes the group had grown to include half the guests in the room. Pepper came to his rescue before the debate became a diatribe and diverted the conversation into other areas, but he had achieved the desired effect; the newcomer was accepted. The group broke up and Price began to circulate under his patron's watchful eye.

It was too much to expect that, with Price present, war

with Germany would not intrude on the conversations, but it proved to be much less of a challenge than he feared. Pepper's friends—dons, many of them, with a sprinkling of academics working in political institutions and the civil service—were obviously chosen for their intellectual compatibility, but Price was surprised at how widely their political opinions deviated from Pepper's liberal leanings. At least half of them favored Chamberlain's efforts to appease Hitler, none were openly sympathetic to Poland and Czechoslovakia, and six of them advanced the view that Britain's interests lay much closer to Germany's than to those of France and America.

It was at this point that Pepper introduced the American, a lawyer named William Donovan who appeared to travel extensively in Europe and was currently on his way home to Washington after a business trip to Germany and Holland.

"Price taught in Hamburg for eight years," Pepper volunteered. "This talk of nuzzling up to Hitler goes against his grain."

"The Jewish question, Dr. Price?" Donovan asked politely.

"It's only the tip of the iceberg. If you travel in Germany you know that already."

The American nodded slowly. "I can see what's coming, if that's what you mean."

"War," said Pepper unnecessarily.

Donovan sipped his wine. "I don't see any alternative. Hitler and Mussolini have both gone too far in terms of polemic to pull back now. The only question is how *far* they'll go."

"Poland," Price said simply.

Donovan's jaw jutted in what might have been a humoring smile. "And the rest. France is the natural enemy. Always has been. At least, that's what they tell me in Berlin. But they won't be safe in France unless they take the Low Countries, and the extension to that is they'll need Norway, Sweden and Denmark to protect their northern flanks."

"Then they'll have Stalin to contend with. Russia's ready to sign a pact against Germany here and now."

Donovan shook his head firmly. "Don't count on Russia for anything, Dr. Price. They don't have a muscle worth flexing. Berlin's got Stalin shaking in his boots. Remember what Hitler wrote in *Mein Kampf:* Russia must be overrun; it's critical to the space equation."

Price stared provocatively into the wide serious face of the American. "Then we shall have to rely on your countrymen, Mr. Donovan. We have no one else."

The lawyer shrugged self-consciously. "I don't think you have the right to count on America, either."

"But surely you see that if Europe goes under, *and* Russia, you have no choice in the matter."

"There is a choice, doctor. I'm no lover of Hitler, but the fact is, our choice right now lies between involvement and trade. We don't have any political ambitions in Europe. So if it comes to war or trade, we'll pick trade."

"I'm afraid I can't accept that." Price sought sympathy in Pepper's elfin face and found it in full measure. "National policy, surely, turns on logic and—"

Donovan caught the side of his mouth in his teeth to hide a grin of pure cynicism. "National policy, Dr. Price, turns on self-interest. Next year the president's running for reelection. He'll be up to here in self-interest; mostly from American mothers. The message'll be loud and clear: my son for my vote. Do you blame them?"

Price shook his head, but before he could take it further Pepper grasped the American's elbow and towed him away.

The first guests began drifting out shortly before ten o'clock, an hour Price judged to be unnaturally late for Pepper. He decided it would be judged poor taste to be the last to leave and sought out his host to wish him good night and thank him. The professor was still arguing heatedly with William Donovan and spared him no more than a testy "Yes, yes. Good of you to come, Price," before returning to the fray. Price retrieved his hat and umbrella and went out into Queen's Gate.

Pepper squinted shortsightedly up at his guest of honor. William Donovan, one of Roosevelt's most trusted confidants, had been a last-minute bonus.

"Well—what d'you make of him?"

The American pinched his lower lip between strong fingers. "Carries the ball well. Seems intelligent. You think you're going to be able to handle him?"

"We can but try." Pepper rubbed his palms together in agitation.

"Bill Stephenson tells me you aim to play him back.

You'll have your work cut out for you, if you want an unbiased opinion. He doesn't look to me like a born patsy."

"Oh, he's not." Pepper looked out of the window, but Price had disappeared. "He's not at all. Up to us to make him one."

MAY 11, 1939

Tom Price toiled up the hill from the congested heart of Richmond toward Ellerker Gardens. The sun had disappeared an hour ago behind angry black-purple clouds, but it was still warm, uncomfortably so. He paused to catch his breath under an overhanging tree, then forced himself to trudge on.

That afternoon—day four of his third week in Phillimore Gardens—he had unearthed two eighteenth-century first editions from the literary rubble in his basement kingdom and Alice Petrie had insisted he come to Richmond for supper. The incidents were not unconnected.

They had found the books together, he and she, sifting and weighing and checking the work in the plywood "office" Alice had had built for him at one end of the room. Sally now habitually sat at the far garden end, alternately brewing tea and slaving over his handwritten reports to Pepper. That physical distancing symbolized the new order. He and Alice had fallen into a perfect working relationship—because she actively engineered it, he had to admit—and although they both liked the girl, their mutual rapport soon led to her exclusion. There was nothing intentionally hurtful in it; it was simply a question of age and temperament. It was, in fact, the little things Sally said, or more often failed to say, that laid the groundwork for the first small intimacies between Price and Alice: the knowing winks, raised eyebrows, nudges, and swiftly muffled laughter of adults in the company of a child. The jokes led to unspoken understandings, the understandings to a kind of mental telepathy, the telepathy to a growing physical awareness.

The unearthing of the first editions had been a godsend to Alice, a confirmation that he was not wasting his time or the precious scholarship of which she increasingly saw herself as guardian. At the moment of revelation, she very nearly hugged him; he was aware, instinctively, of her overwhelming compulsion to touch him. In the uneasy aftermath, she declared her intention of cooking him a celebration supper at Richmond. No excuses would be accepted.

The late, and apparently unlamented, Leonard Petrie must have been a man of some substance. Ellerker Gardens was a short street and proclaimed its middle-class respectability with quiet confidence. The gate of the Petrie home bore a polished brass plaque with the legend "*Middlemass House*" in Gothic script, and the garden was neatly paved. Price looked up as he approached the door; three stories, a triangular dormer window at the top, two identical bow windows on the ground floor draped with flounces of white lace gathered and tied. Neat, orderly, practical. Whatever else one thought of Alice Petrie, it had to be admitted she was all of those things herself. Well, he'd come a long way since that first day. In his attitude to her, in accommodating her attitude to him. All the way to Richmond. He rang the bell.

She opened the door at once, and he noted the changes as he was meant to. Her black satin dress was relieved at throat and cuffs by flourishes of white organza, a subtle hint of purity that did not quite survive the suggestive tension at breasts and hips. Her hair flowed free at her shoulders, framing her face, disguising its matronly fullness. She gave him a secret smile but no greeting, and he realized the children were probably waiting inside. An act of intimacy. *We have something to hide*. She took his coat and led him into the large front room.

"Alan, Diny—I want you to shake hands with Dr. Price." Alice spoke his name with hushed reverence.

The boy caught Price's eye and held it for several seconds without moving from a half prone position in one of the chairs. He was much heavier around the shoulders than Willy, swarthy, and remarkably striking in a sullen, brooding way. He sat upright but did not rise, and held out his hand. "Hello."

"Dr. Price!" insisted Alice sharply.

"Hello . . . Dr. *Price*," Alan Petrie repeated. One corner of his mouth twisted up and his dark eyes narrowed; contempt sat easily on his wide, flat face.

"Diny."

The little girl wore a dress of green velvet with a matching bow in her russet ringlets. She came to him, offered her hand and, as he bent to acknowledge her, dropped a wobbling curtsy. Without thinking he clicked his heels and bowed stiffly. The boy made a sound in his throat and turned away to hide his amusement. Alice was entranced.

Supper was served in an even larger room at the back of the house. Alice was a superb cook and had gone out of her way to impress him, but the meal was not a success. Alan Petrie ate in sullen silence while his mother prattled on about his brightness at school and his athletic prowess. Dinah seemed unmoved by her brother's black mood but also held her tongue, and by the time they had finished eating and retired to the front room to drink tea, the atmosphere was electric. Only Alice seemed unaware of the tension. After a while, she said brightly, "Diny, why don't you show the gentleman—ah—Dr. Price—the room?"

The child seemed as relieved as Price at the opportunity to escape.

It was the dormer room at the top of the house, somewhat restricted by sloping ceilings but large and comfortably furnished with a panoramic view of both ends of Ellerker Gardens. There was a brass-knobbed double bed with a plump feather mattress, a table and two chairs in the window nook, a huge wardrobe, bookshelves, and a small bureau. He had no doubt Alice had refurnished the room to anticipate his needs. How could he possibly tell her it was unsuitable?

"The bathroom's on the floor below," said the child, pointing shyly through the floral carpet.

"That's—ah—really very nice." His nervousness annoyed him; he must make an effort. He smiled at her. "D'you think I ought to take it?"

"I don't know," she said seriously. "Do you like children?"

"Well, I—" He stopped on the very brink of telling her he had two sons of his own, and took sanctuary in ingenuousness. "Well, I like *you*."

"Really?" She had her mother's eyes but they sparkled in the wistful face of a gamine. "Mummy says we'd have to be a lot quieter if you came. She says you don't like noisy children."

He dropped onto the edge of the bed. "I shouldn't think you're very noisy, are you?"

"Alan is," said the child confidentially. "He's got a wireless and a gramophone in his room downstairs. And a pair of drumsticks. He bangs on a book in time to the music. Do you like Woody Herman?"

He groped in vain for the connection.

"Alan likes Woody Herman. He's got five of his records. They're very loud. Mummy won't let him play them when she's home."

"I like listening to music."

"Mummy says Woody Herman isn't music. It's just noise. Alan likes lots of jazz." She glanced over her shoulder at the open door. "He says it has to be played loud."

"Hmmm." He made a serious face. "You don't think I'd be happy here, then?"

The dark eyes widened in surprise. "Oh, *I'll* make sure he doesn't upset you, if you really want to stay." Her gaze lifted to the ceiling. "You'd have the loft as well."

"The loft?" He followed her eyes to the trapdoor in the ceiling over the bed.

"You have to bend down because it's very low, but it's lovely and private. We keep our toys up there. But there's lots of space."

A stair creaked from below and Alice cooed, "What are you two doing?"

The child went to the door. "You can come up if you like."

"No, Diny. You and Dr. Price come down. We're going to have some chocolate cake."

They returned to the front room and, as they consumed tea and aggressively sweet chocolate cake, Price made one last effort to win over the boy.

"I hear you like jazz," he said pleasantly.

"Did *she* say that?" Alan glared furiously at his sister.

"I said you liked Woody Herman," Dinah retorted unrepentantly.

"Oh, he just likes noise," said Alice.

"It's not *noise*." The boy's awakening manhood showed in a hardening of the jaw. Price noted that he was already shaving. "My father thought Woody Herman was terrific."

In the silence that followed even Alice seemed at a loss for a proper response.

Price said lightly, "I'm sure he was right."

"He *was*!" The youth's body trembled with impotent rage.

"Did you like jazz when you were fifteen?" Dinah asked innocently.

"Well, yes," he lied, and scoured his memory for scraps of supporting evidence. "Bix Beiderbecke was my favorite. And—ah—Jack Teagarden."

Alan's anger was transmuted instantly to scorn. "They're old-fashioned," he sneered.

"I'm afraid I *am* a bit old-fashioned."

The boy eyed him insolently across the coffee table. "Are you coming to live here?"

"Alan!" Alice jerked forward in her chair. "I will not have you being rude to a guest in my house."

"I only said is he—"

"I don't care what you said. You've been doing your best to be unpleasant all night and I won't have it. Are you listening to me? Dr. Price—"

"Please. Al—Mrs. Petrie." Price touched her arm diplomatically, but even the tension of the moment failed to neutralize a thrill of sensation as his fingers made contact with her satin flesh. "I'm sure Alan meant nothing. . . ."

Alice ignored him. "Now take your plate and things into the kitchen and go up to your room." The boy swung angrily to his feet, his broad shoulders rigid. "And I don't want to hear that gramophone blaring all over the house. Is that clear?"

Alan stalked from the room, clattered crockery into the sink, and stamped upstairs. His door slammed loudly.

"If his father were alive . . ." Alice mourned.

Dinah piled the remaining plates and cups and saucers on a tray and lifted it experimentally. "Don't worry about him, mummy. You know he can't help it." She smiled at Price. "I expect you'll want to talk about the rent. I'll go to bed."

Alice pecked her cheek. "Who's my lovely grown-up baby?"

"Good night, Dr. Price." The child continued to stare at him with a curious blend of friendliness and doubt. He considered giving her an avuncular kiss but thought better of it.

"Good night, Dinah. I hope we meet again."

She turned to the door. "On Monday, Mummy said. When you move in."

Alice packed her off in confusion.

At ten o'clock he said for the second time that he thought he should be going, and Alice rose in a flutter of protest and went into the kitchen to make something "to warm you on your way." She brought in two large mugs filled with a sweet, creamy liquid.

"I should've asked you if you like Horlicks," she said. The tone was unusually self-critical, a major concession. She sank down on the couch beside him. "Do you?"

"It's very good."

She sighed happily. "I ought to know what you like and don't like. If you decide to take the room, I mean." She ran her tongue very slowly across her lip. "You're very good with children."

"Dinah's very sweet. Alan—"

"He's like his father," she said with vigor. "He'll come round, you'll see."

The unspoken question trembled on her tongue, but she didn't voice it. She seemed remarkably ill at ease and he wondered fleetingly if the question of letting the room was more important to her than she was prepared to admit. They had never discussed money. She folded her legs and ran one hand along her calf as if to smooth a wrinkle, but there were no wrinkles in her sheer black stockings. His eye followed the movement, up and down, up and down, and with a start he realized she was watching him, gauging his reaction. The hem of the dress had ridden well above her knee.

"About the room," she said delicately.

"Oh, it's very nice. Very comfortable."

"You don't like it!" Alarm. More than alarm.

"No, it's exactly what I need." Height, said Richard Wein. On a hill, at the top of a house. High.

"Oh, Tom, I—" She lowered her eyes demurely and a veil of ravenswing hair swayed tantalizingly across her face. "Funny, I feel—well, I never called you by your name before. You don't mind, do you?"

"Of course not. Alice." He felt a delicious tremor along his back. The need to touch. She'd felt it, too, this afternoon in the library; an unbearable compulsion. Her foot moved slightly, no more than a quarter of an inch; it touched his and moved away again.

"I'm so glad—Tom. I'll make you comfortable, you needn't be afraid of that. I'm a good cook, too."

"Alice, I'm sure—" His voice sounded tinder dry.

She drew the veil of hair across her mouth and caught a wisp of it between her lips. "I want you to think of it as home, Tom. As your home."

MAY 18, 1939

"Labor o' love, mate," the cockney said cheerfully.

Paul Curzon put the car in gear and rolled it down the slight incline of Ellerker Gardens and round the corner into Onslow Road. Lachie Heston climbed out with his squat leather bag and the little cockney followed him.

Curzon inspected them. They both wore anonymous blue workmen's overalls and flat caps. The cockney carried a length of coiled rope over one shoulder and a wooden-handled straw bag that clanked with steel tools. Heston, a long-faced lanky Scot in his late forties, looked in no way out of character as a Gas Board functionary.

"Fast as you can."

"Don't you worry, old cock." The cockney gave his bag a rattle. "No sense in pissing about, is there?"

"I'll be back in ten minutes to pick you up. Okay—hop it." Curzon pulled the snub-nosed Morris away.

The two men walked briskly to Middlemass House, turned in at the gate, and rang the bell. Heston used his substantial bulk to shield the front door while the cockney tooled the lock with a pick, and, when it clicked open, said loudly, "Oh, good morning. Gas Board. We're looking for a . . ." They slipped inside and closed the door.

"Loft," Heston whispered and they took the stairs two at a time. They entered the bedroom, took in the evidence of Price's occupation, and swung the table onto the bed under the trapdoor. The cockney had the trap open and himself inside in a matter of seconds. Heston followed.

"What we lookin' for?" hissed the cockney, taking in a bric-a-brac of toys and old furniture with a professional's eyes.

Heston turned away. The HMV gramophone lay on a long trestle under the sloping roof, its lid wide, a record on the turntable. He felt around it, pulled out a screwdriver, and released a half-dozen screws around the main component. The top lifted out smoothly. "That's my girl," he growled to himself. He touched the wireless set gingerly, then looked over his shoulder at his companion. "Up on the roof, lad! See if he's rigged an outside aerial. If he has, it'll be out the back, probably on the chimney. Get on with it!"

The cockney slipped down through the trapdoor and disappeared. When he returned to Price's room a few minutes later, Heston had smoothed the counterpane and was putting the table back in the window nook. He twitched the curtain and looked down into the street.

"Makes you wonder what neighbors are for," he growled. "We could've cleared the bloody place out and nobody'd know the difference. Is he using a booster aerial?"

"Nah. There's a wire from the chimney to the living room but it's for an old Phillips. Not much use to 'em. Bloody thing's rotten."

"Let's get out of here, then."

Curzon was already at the corner with the Morris.

Heston climbed in. "He's all set up. Ready to go. How'd you know it was in the loft?"

"I used my commonsense. Where else d'you think he'd put it?"

He let in the clutch and they rolled sedately downhill through narrow lanes toward the High Street.

"You're sure it's okay? It'll work?" Curzon pressed.

"I'm a specialist in wireless telegraphy, no a bluidy crystal gazer," Heston barked. "If he can work it, it'll work."

"You'd better be right," Curzon retorted. "If we miss that transmission, Menzies'll kick your spine through your bonnet."

"Lumme," said the cockney happily. "Labor of bleeding love."

The meeting with Palmer of the Government Code and Cipher School had run on until ten o'clock and, when Curzon thought it was all over for the day, the ubiquitous Desmond

Morton had floated out of the wainscoting and they back-tracked again over the Price preparations for his benefit.

Morton was obviously an intelligence mandarin of high clout and subterranean profile; his ease of manner in Menzies' presence and the authority he displayed were very nearly monarchical, yet he seemed to have no official rank and Curzon had never heard his name. But then, he reminded himself, he was as well acquainted as anyone with the fact that Churchill himself was an outsider, that dear old Blinker Hall was a ghost from the long-dead past, that Duff Cooper had resigned as Chamberlain's First Lord of the Admiralty after Munich, and that Bracken was simply Churchill's companion-in-distress. Stephenson, another imperial archetype, figured nowhere in Curzon's lexicon; his name did not appear in Vacher's *Parliamentary Companion*, in *Who's Who*, the Service or the civil service lists. For Sinclair himself, and Menzies, to be involved with these outsiders was outright heresy; it took very little imagination and only a simpleton's grasp of politics to appreciate that the Churchill conspirators were scheming behind the government's back in direct opposition to official policy. Delivering Price into their hands amounted to an act of treason.

Curzon reached Ebury Street just before midnight, let himself in, and collected his mail from the hall table.

He fitted the key in the door of his flat and turned it. It would not budge. He twisted it again impatiently, but the lock refused to yield. A faint stirring of unease touched his spine before it reached his brain and he acted without thinking. He turned the handle, felt the door give, and let it swing wide.

Rob was asleep in an armchair by the empty grate, his tie loose, collar open, long legs bridging the hearth rug, feet braced on the facing chair. The green aura of a student lamp on the writing desk at his side drained his face of its agricultural tan and cut deep gullies around his mouth and nose, but it could not disguise his youth. It was a family joke that Robert Curzon had taken twenty-five years to amass the physical characteristics of a fifteen-year-old.

Curzon kicked the door shut behind him and his brother leapt from sleep with a start that sent his heels crashing to the floor.

He rubbed his eyes blearily. "What time do you call this?"

Curzon threw his coat on a couch and perched on the arm of the facing chair. "How'd you get in here?"

"The motherly soul in the basement let me in. Housekeeper, she said. Why? Should I have bought a ticket?"

"You could have let me know you were dropping in."

Rob reached up to the mantel and took a half-dozen unopened letters from behind the clock. He selected one and flicked it in onto Curzon's lap. "I did. Why don't you open your mail?"

"I've been away."

Rob stuffed the mail back behind the clock and stretched out again.

"That's mother's line. 'He's away.' Every time the Bart goes off at the deep end about why you won't come home."

Lieutenant General Sir Martin Curzon, Bart, M.C., D.S.O., GCVO, had served king and country for thirty-six years as soldier and military administrator in India and the Middle East, only to be cheated of his field marshal's baton in his fifty-sixth year by a heart attack that had five years ago forced him to retire to his wife's estate in North Norfolk. The slightest exertion exhausted him; undue excitement could lay him low for weeks at a time. At the family conference called to decide who should manage the estate and farms for him, Paul had failed even to put in an appearance. Rob had walked out on his last year at Cambridge to prove how dependable he was and, by all accounts, had turned out to be a damned good farmer.

"How is Mother?"

"No better for worrying herself sick about you."

Curzon stared into the empty grate.

"How long have you been back?" Rob cocked his head on one side.

"Not long. Day or two."

"Takes no more than a second or two to pick up a phone and call home."

"I've been busy."

"And I always thought the wine-and-spirit trade was such a doddle. Well, we live and learn. D'you know how long it's been since you were last home?"

"Is that why you dropped in?" Curzon avoided his brother's gaze.

"Eight and a half months. Mother's reckoning, not mine."

He jerked forward impulsively. "Look, Paul, it's none of my business what you do with your life, but she *is* my business. I live with her. We eat at the same table three times a day." He fell back in the depths of the chair. "I can't pretend she's not there. Just explain to me, will you, for future reference, why you can't phone or write occasionally."

The same question had been thrown at him fifty times a year in his mother's letters and fifty times a day by the Bart on his reluctant pilgrimages to Norfolk. That question and all the others: Where will you be next Thursday? Where did you go last trip? What are the people you work with like? Doesn't everyone get time off at Christmas? Why don't you find yourself a nice young girl and settle down? And the threats that went hand in hand with them.

He said tightly, "I live the only way I can. I have a job to do."

"Is that *it*?"

"Look, I'm tired, I can't argue with you."

"No one's arguing, but if you think I'm about to swallow *that* old chestnut"—Rob mimicked his brother to perfection—" 'I live the only way I can . . . ,' you're out of your mind. Please, Paul—come home. Just for a weekend. Talk to her."

"I can't—just yet."

"Look, the longer you stay away the harder it is to go back and face them. I . . ." He faltered and peered suspiciously into Curzon's face. "You haven't been up to something you're . . . well, ashamed of, have you?"

"Oh, don't be a bloody idiot!"

"Well, how am I supposed to know! You could be a white slaver for all we can tell. I wasn't exactly keen to come up here this evening, I'll tell you straight. I didn't know *what* to expect. Were you in hospital? Were you in jail? Would I open the door and find you stretched out blind drunk on the carpet?"

Curzon shot to his feet. "Then you should have stayed away, shouldn't you! I'm going to bed. I have to be up early tomorrow."

Rob bounced after him. "We *care*, Paul." His whole body was shaking. "Why can't you? You know how ill Mother's been this past year. You know she won't let on about it to the Bart. It was bad enough with only him to worry about, but both of them . . ." He caught Curzon's arms. "If you don't care what happens to her, for Christ's sake *pretend*."

Curzon wrenched free and swung a stinging open-handed blow at his brother's face. It caught him below the ear and sent him sprawling off-balance over the arm of a chair.

"Dammit, Rob . . ."

The young man pulled himself to his feet and touched his ear tenderly. He shook his head, blinking away tears of reflexive shock. "I'd best be getting along," he said mildly. He crossed the room, picked up a small suitcase, and unhooked his coat from the door. "I'm sorry, Paul, I had no right to . . ."

"You can't go out on the street at this time of night, you maniac!"

"I'll be all right. I'll find a hotel."

"Don't be an ass. Take the spare room."

Robert Curzon shook his head. He pulled open the door and backed into the corridor. "I just felt I ought to try to understand, that's all."

Curzon let him go. There was nothing else to say.

MAY 20, 1939

Tom Price woke on the dazzling morning of the day of his first scheduled wireless transmission to Hamburg with a nightmarish premonition of disaster. He lay in the engulfing feather mattress and traced the course of his downfall, counting the mistakes.

Principally—overwhelmingly—he had failed Richard Wein. "Practice your keying at all times. You must develop a signature we can recognize before your first transmission."

There was no signature. He had certainly practiced—two hours every night—but it had served only to reveal the nervous vacuum that existed between brain and hand. He was incapable of keying at a consistent, even speed, the single most important prerequisite of an identifiable send. And tonight, at eleven forty-five, he would come face to face with the consequences.

Far worse—he had no faith in Hamburg. He could not

recall one shred of advice or instruction given him during his training that inspired confidence.

Tonight's transmission would be brief: the short precoded date that confirmed he was in place; but what was he to do if they ordered him to begin regular communication at once? He had learned nothing of value, could barely find his way unaided around central London, Ritter would be enraged at the futility of the work he was doing at Phillimore Gardens, at his isolation from the mainstream of university life; and Pepper's soirée could not make up for a whole month of inactivity.

He got up and went downstairs to wash and shave in the bathroom, making as little noise as possible. Alice had warned him that she and the children slept late on Saturdays. The thought pitched him deeper into despondency. Yes, he could tell Hamburg a great deal about the Petries. Very informative. He could tell them he had found—in the space of one ghastly week—an enemy worthy of Himmler's highest regard, a brooding tormentor who had reduced him to a condition of half-murderous, half-suicidal frustration. Alan Petrie possessed every virtue Willy and Else aspired to—and more. He could tell them he was in a position to seduce the boy's mother as and when he chose; he had merely to signify his willingness. He could tell them he was entertaining bizarre notions of paternal attachment—love!—for his landlady's daughter. He could tell them—

The door swung wide and Alan Petrie, in pajamas and dressing gown, burst in without warning.

"Oh. Are you going to be long?"

"No, I've already finished." He nicked the angle of his jaw with the razor and smothered an oath. The boy watched stonily as he staunched the flow of blood. But he did not retreat.

"Were you up in the loft last night?" he asked suddenly.

Price's fingers tightened around the razor's stem. "Yes, Alan. I brought some work home. I usually do."

"My father used to work in the loft." It was an indictment.

"I know. Dinah told me."

The boy riveted on Prince's reflection in the mirror. "He only went up there because Mum wouldn't let him work in bed. You've got a table and chairs and that old bureau. I don't see why you have to work in the loft."

"I thought there'd be less chance of disturbing you all if I worked up there."

"*I* heard you."

"I'm sorry. I'll try to be quieter in future."

He rinsed the soap from his face and went back to his room, shaking with anger.

"Now you stand there while Diny and I just pop down to the greengrocer's. I won't be two minutes. If you get to the counter before I'm back, ask the man for a joint of beef, about three pounds. For roasting."

He stationed himself at the end of the queue in the butcher's shop and tried to ignore the tolerant amusement of the women ahead of him. This was too much. He *had* to make a stand.

Alice's sympathy and support were essential to him; he had appreciated that from the beginning. When the time came he would need a buffer against Pepper at the library to give him the freedom to come and go in London as he chose, and in Ellerker Gardens against Alan. But yielding gallantly to Alice's whims and fancies was an exercise an self-emasculation. Much of her possessive zeal was benevolent; she handwashed his clothes, sponged and pressed his suits, even polished his shoes, but the price she demanded was total submission. To that extent she differed from Else only in method.

It was typical of Hamburg that they had offered no guidance on the conduct of relationships in his new world. Scholz would take it for granted that an agent functioned without hindrance in some kind of germ-free void, protected by his patriotism and sense of duty from unwanted human contact. If Ritter considered the problem at all, he would have dismissed it as "natural fieldcraft." And Praetorius—"Live a normal life; Dr. Price's normal life"—could have had no conception of what normality entailed. Sessler knew. He had diagnosed but, like the others, he could not prescribe. Alice was an enemy none of them had anticipated.

The most pressing priority was to neutralize her and that called for a major sacrifice on his part. He had no illusions about what it meant.

Since his arrival at Middlemass House, thanks to Alan's psychopathic refusal to accept him and the sheer weight of domestic reorganization Alice had had to cope with, there had been no repetition of the physical temptations of his first evening there, but she plainly regarded his moving in as evidence of his attraction to her. She was responding with every gift at her command. Dinah now walked alone to school in the mornings so that Alice could accompany him to town on the train; Alan had twice been refused permission to bring home friends from school in the evening to avoid disturbing "the doctor's" work; payment of rent had been airily postponed for a month on the grounds that he could not possibly afford it.

At the library, Alice took care to ensure that Sally had enough work at all times to keep her busy—to avoid her interrupting their sacred labors in the small partitioned office—and in the matter of his work, she was his slave, a humble and dutiful acolyte with the additional roles of surrogate mother, guardian, and intimate.

The rewards potentially outweighed the disadvantages. But he couldn't go on like this.

It was one o'clock before they climbed back up the hill to Ellerker Gardens. They ate a Saturday lunch of grilled sausages, chips and fried eggs, and then, at last, Alice packed him off to his room while she "ran" over the house with a vacuum cleaner.

He settled down to his keying. By five o'clock he thought he detected an improvement: a smoother "hand," a shade more speed, better coordination. He replaced the handset and codebook in the loft—he had found a useful hiding place under the torn saddle of Dinah's old hollow-bodied rocking-horse—and unlocked the door of his room. The major hurdle now was to avoid amorous proximity with Alice after supper and to find a reasonable excuse for retiring early without exciting her suspicion.

In the event, it was made easy for him. Alice was tired and, when Alan returned in a fit of pique resulting from his school's shameful defeat at cricket, his display of temper brought on one of her nervous headaches. All three of them went to bed before ten o'clock.

His hands were sweating and he dried them several times on his handkerchief. *Concentrate.* At 11:45 exactly, he tapped out his call sign: Gimlet. He repeated it three times and sat back to wait, his heart fluttering.

The response was immediate. As it bleeped in his headphones, he catapulted forward in shock and his head collided with the naked light bulb suspended over the table. He grabbed it to halt its swinging. He had prepared the date code block that afternoon but, inexplicably, at the last moment, his confidence deserted him. He stabbed out the in-place code form with painful slowness.

Richard Wein replied briskly. "Hotbed to Gimlet. Congratulations. Stand by."

Stand by? His heart pounded. Why stand by? Trautmann's order had been explicit: call sign, "in place" code, confirmation, and out.

He pulled notebook and pencil toward him. The ridge of his palm made a moist ellipse on the blank page. He applied the handkerchief again, turned to a new page and waited, pencil poised. Two minutes passed; three. Perspiration began coursing freely from his scalp onto his face.

Wein came on at last; perfectly consistent, generously slow.

"Page 43. Repeat. Page 43."

He lunged at the codebook and turned to check number 1778343; pressed the fold heavily and weighted each side of the book. Wein began again and he took it cleanly. He transposed the cipher: R*A*N*T*Z*A*U* H*E*R*E* A*N*D* Q*U*E*S*T*I*O*N*I*N*G* F*O*L*L*O*W*S*.

His body went limp. Questioning?

The carrier wave began its insistent piping; it was a long send, at least three times as long as the absolute maximum Wein had allowed him at Wohldorf. It took an unconscionably long time to decipher:

"Delighted and proud your accomplishment. All here conscious of honor serving with you. Anxious hear immediate in-place situation domestic and professional, contacts made, area of influence established. Climate opinion among your colleagues."

He flopped back in his chair, astounded. He had already been at the set for eleven minutes. It was madness, but then he had no doubt Wein had already registered that objection and been overruled by "Rantzau"—one of the dozen or so aliases affected by the oaf Ritter.

He encoded a brief meassage. "Established university post and domestic HQ Richmond. All satisfactory. Contacts university and governmental area developing. Opinion strongly in favor Chamberlain initiative. Americans reluctant engage European war.''

He sent it very badly, stopping a third of the way through to start again when he thought he heard someone moving about on the floor below. Even as he tapped it out he regretted embarking on it; it was nonsensical, absurd. Climate of opinion!

Major Ritter—he could envisage him at Wein's shoulder, peering excitedly at the lieutenant's take pad as the letters streamed from his pencil—considered it anything but absurd.

"Expand US opinion source," Wein responded.

Price flung down his pencil in disgust and looked again at his watch: 12:22! What was he to tell them? That he had sipped cheap wine and chewed cheese with a lawyer who regurgitated what every newspaper and every radio station in Britain and America had been saying for months? What else? Ritter was clearly collecting ammunition for his next visit to the Tirpitzufer.

"Source direct Washington. Major industrial contacts US-Europe-Far East. Washington views involvement war politically unacceptable. Business lobby violently opposed and anxious maintain German trade links.''

Wein was decoding simultaneously.

"Excellent. Beyond hopes all concerned. Cultivate US sources all costs. Coordinating presently US intelligence network to infiltrate aircraft and shipping industries. Your source invaluable future plans.''

For a moment he thought it was over, then Wein began to send again.

"From this time observe three-day radio silence security. Then transmissions appointed times your discretion. Omit nothing. Domestic address please.''

He sent it. His watch now showed 12:36.

"Expediting list London strategic targets. Letter via Lisbon conduit. Respond earliest. Hotbed out.''

Price switched off. When he tried to stand his legs buckled at the knees and he was forced to sit down again. His clothes were wringing wet. Twelve forty-six! One hour and one minute: a fifty-eight-minute overrun on Hamburg-Wohldorf's most rigidly applied maximum. And for what?

He was too shaken to feel anger. Ritter had no right to expose him in this way but he, in turn, had no justification for misleading them. He considered reestablishing contact, setting the record straight, but vetoed the idea at once. What harm had he done?

He replaced the Wehrmacht set in the gramophone case, hid the handset and earphones in the rocking horse, doused the light, and lowered himself into the darkness below.

His feet had barely touched the table balanced on the bed when the door handle rattled urgently. The shock was so complete he nearly lost his grip. He lowered the trap, dropped silently to the floor, swung the table back to the window, and stripped off his shirt and trousers with a blind disregard for buttons and cuff links. He rammed the clothes into the bed, dragged back the sheet and blankets, pulled on his dressing gown, and ruffled his hair.

He unlocked the door and peered straight into the beam of a torch.

"Oh, Tom, I'm sorry. Did I wake you?" Alice was an indeterminate swath of silk in the gloom behind the torch.

"Is something wrong?"

She lowered the beam to her feet. Alan Petrie loomed behind her, a dressing gown over his pajamas. Price could not see his face but he could feel the challenge in it.

"Alan woke me. He said he heard someone prowling about in the house. I was so—" She gulped. "I couldn't wake you. I tried the door and it was locked and . . ."

"We thought a burglar'd got in," the youth said impassively. "I heard him on the roof. Over the loft."

Price stepped back and opened the door wide. "There's no one here. See?" He gestured around him. Alan stared past him coldly.

"I'll go down and check the doors and windows, if you like," Price volunteered hurriedly. He pulled the door to and took the torch. Mother and son waited on the landing while he went downstairs and pretended to look into every room. When he returned Alice was alone.

She clutched at him. "Are you sure it's all right . . . Tom?"

"Perfectly. There's no one down there."

She hesitated. "Well . . . I mean your room. I can't understand why you locked your door. Alan said . . ." She decided it would be more tactful not to repeat what Alan had said.

He took her elbow and drew her closer, his lips on her ear.

"I'm sorry, Alice. Really sorry. I always lock my door. I know it's foolish, but . . . it was necessary in Germany. At night . . . so many times . . . the Gestapo . . ."

"Oh, my *dear*." Her hands touched his cheek. "I'm *so* sorry. I just didn't think. . . ."

She stepped away from him nervously. Alan was watching them from the half-open door of his room.

A discordant female voice, cracked with age, was singing "When I grow too old to dream" to the accompaniment of a rhythmically sweeping broom in a distant corridor. In Stuart Menzies' office, the green curtains were drawn and the tight pool of light from the desk lamp held four faces like Halloween masks in its glow.

Menzies pushed the written transcript of the decoded Price-Ritter exchange to the center of his blotter. "Right. What does it tell us? Heston?"

"Technically? Price is strictly amateur, sir. No technique. Hits the key like a club-footed camel. Slow as hell. Difficult to say if it's just his keying or lousy encoding and decoding as well. The Hamburg-Wohldorf 'send' was beautiful; that man's a pro. Too much of a pro, I'd say, to send what he did off his own bat. Half of it was superfluous. And thirteen-letter words! Christ!"

"I think we can take it for granted Ritter was the source," Menzies said dryly. "D'you think Hamburg-Wohldorf have enough to go on to recognize his transmissions in future?"

"You mean his signature? Not a chance. No fluidity. Some people never make it. Mental block."

Menzies turned to the specialist from the Government Code and Cipher School. "Palmer?"

The visitor brought his hand from under the table and pushed a comma of crinkly hair off his face. "I'm not ruling out a code-within-a-code."

"Why?"

"Oh, there's nothing in the encipherment itself. We've been over that. It's just that . . ." He pulled off his heavy hornrims. "That bit about 'coordinating presently US intelligence network' and so on. Why would Hamburg drop an admission like that into a simple in-place confirmation? Either it's a code or a tease. Has to be one or the other."

"Curzon?"

"Why did they keep him on the air for an hour? Breaks all the rules."

"Meaning?"

"Incompetence. Hamburg's too damn sure of itself and too damn cocky. Or Ritter is. I don't think there are any inner codes and I don't think it was a teaser."

Palmer's brow furrowed obstinately. "I still don't like it. It's not Hamburg form."

"We won't ignore it," Menzies said quietly. "You have anything else, Curzon?"

"Yes, sir. I think Palmer's right in pointing up the question of content—but for the wrong reasons."

"Explain."

"I've met Prince now seven or eight times. I'm beginning to get the feel of him. I think his response to Ritter's questions were totally out of character."

"In what way?"

"Integrity." He grinned at Menzies' scowl of incomprehension. "He's as straight as a die; no sense of humor, no tricks. I'd have bet a year's pay he wouldn't lie to Hamburg. But we all know he has. Why?"

"Because he was asked irresponsible questions," Palmer broke in. "He made the best of a bad job."

"Exactly!" Curzon pounded his knee. "He fobbed them off. He was bluffing to get out of a tight corner without losing face."

"So?" Palmer took off his spectacles and polished them with a large handkerchief.

"So he's told us something about himself we didn't know and couldn't guess. In spite of his natural instincts, if his back's to the wall he'll take the easy way out. He'll transmit rubbish if he thinks he can get away with it—if he thinks they'll swallow it."

"Ritter didn't give him much choice."

"No, he didn't, did he?" Menzies looked at Curzon. "We'll have to make arrangements to intercept that Lisbon letter. Question now is when will Price decide to make contact again and what we do about it."

"We have at least three days, sir," Heston reminded him.

Menzies glowered up at the clock on the wall. It showed three thirty. "We have five and a half hours," he snapped. "I'll expect all three of you back here at nine o'clock sharp."

MAY 21, 1939

"The problem," Blinker Hall said, interrupting Palmer gracelessly, "isn't a question of how *much* but how little. It's not what we can do to pin him down but how far afield we can let him roam."

Curzon caught Lachie Heston's grimace, a frozen-faced smirk and a rolling of the eyes that said plainly, "Who are these idiots?" He looked away. He had not expected to find Hall enthroned like a doge in Menzies' inner sanctum, and the later appearance of Colin Gubbins had done nothing to ease his disquiet.

Menzies himself was in a foul temper and looked as if he had not slept at all. He said shortly, "I'm perfectly well aware of the options. We're here to agree on method."

Gubbins fingered his red carnation. "I'm not suggesting for a moment you bring Five into this, but—"

"This is *not* a security matter!" Menzies seemed to have difficulty catching his breath. His face was uncharacteristically pink-tinged. "Price is a Hamburg operative. Strictly Six's territory."

"I was about to say, old man, that we might benefit from their experience in wireless management, that's all."

"Blinker, Palmer, and Heston have more experience among them than the whole of Five's Y section put together."

"Menzies is right," Admiral Hall chimed in heavily. "Let Five in and you can't keep out the rest. We'd be doing nothing but arguing among ourselves."

"Then we'll have to be damned careful."

"We'll be *careful*!" Menzies snarled.

"Contradiction in terms, isn't it?" Gubbins said good-naturedly. "How careful can you be if the principle is to let him run free? As I see it, you're stuck with letting him communicate with Hamburg. Can't control what he sends, can you?"

"We'll be listening. Curzon?"

113

"We've found a top-floor flat in a house in Onslow Road, just round the corner from the Petrie place."

"Ah—a listening post." Gubbins contrived to make it sound like a rapist's admission of guilt. "He transmits state secrets and you listen."

Curzon saw Menzies' shoulders hunch truculently and said quickly, "He'll transmit what we feed him, sir. Nothing else."

"You can guarantee that, can you? Are you telling me the fellow's deaf and blind? That he's utterly incapable of learning things for himself?"

"I don't think we have to be reminded of the risks involved," Menzies said icily.

"Good." Gubbins took out a slim gold case and palmed a cigarette. "I'm delighted you take my point. Let's not jump on the bandwagon before we're sure it's got brakes. All right—method. You feed him product and when he transmits, you monitor him. What happens when he sends information valuable to the enemy?"

"You're anticipating a situation that won't arise," Menzies said flatly.

"I repeat—what do you do if he *does*?"

Blinker Hall flapped away the smoke cloud issuing from his pipe with magisterial impatience. "Don't be so bloody negative, Colin."

"The devil's advocate has a right to be negative."

"Very well." Hall settled his diminutive bulk aggressively. "In our view, this man was selected by Hamburg solely because he has the physical and mental equipment to impersonate Price."

"It's a fact, not an opinion," Menzies broke in. "I've had confirmation from Berlin. His real name is Wilhelm Sommer, thirty-eight years old, married, two children. Taught history at a Berlin gymnasium. Good degree at Friedrich Wilhelm. Stood a pretty fair chance of getting a lectureship there. His wife's a Party official—Berlin Advisory Committee. He was recruited by Hamburg-Wohldorf in early March. Six or seven weeks' training no more."

He sat back to enjoy the effect of his revelation and Curzon thought: he's been saving it up. They waited for him to go on but he closed his eyes and propped his head comfortably on the chairback.

Blinker Hall's round face danced impishly. "Good. Fact, then. Just confirms what we suspected. An amateur with little or no training. Imagine what must be going on in his head. Snatched from his home, probably; his job, his wife and children. Six weeks of Ritter and dear Dr. Praetorius and suddenly—bang! he's in London, wearing another man's skin. Can you imagine the relief when Pepper saved his neck with that invitation? Good, God, Colin, I'd be sweating bullets in his place and so would you." The admiral stuffed his pipe bowl into a leather tobacco pouch and began to fill it. "Temperamentally—we have Curzon's word for it, *and* Pepper's—he's not a confident man. Not a professional. Suspicious and unsure—that's the reading."

"After exactly one month in place," Gubbins retorted. "Come *on*, Blinker. Six months from now he'll be a different proposition. You'll build up his confidence, all right—enough to make him bloody dangerous."

"Not if we build him the right way," Menzies said. "He showed us in his transmission last night that he's ready to clutch at straws. A trained agent, a committed professional, would have told Ritter there was nothing to report. Price took the easy option. That means he's not only insecure but scared Hamburg might realize it."

Gubbins looked at each one of them in turn and sighed. "All right, Menzies. I give up. Where do we go from here?"

"Heston will act as Price's case officer. Blinker's recruited a full-time w/t operator to man the listening post. If worse comes to worst, we'll use him to transmit in Price's name."

Gubbins stared at him in silence for several seconds. "But if that's what you've got in mind, why the devil use Price at all?"

Blinker Hall sucked noisily at his pipe. "Have to, Colin. We don't know enough about him yet. He might have special procedures arranged with Hamburg. We don't even know his transmission sequences—times, days of the week. It could take six months to build up a complete picture."

"Hmmm. Well—your show, old man. I hope he turns out to be worth the trouble."

Menzies caught Curzon's eye. "Oh, he will be. Take my word for it."

SEPTEMBER 1, 1939

It was twenty minutes to nine and night had brought with it the first damp tendrils of autumn chill. The trees bowing over the little cemetery in Vineyard Passage on the way from the tube station dripped raindrops left behind from an earlier shower, but the stars shone magnificently in a clear sky.

Price had rarely been so late leaving the basement in Upper Phillimore Gardens, but it had been rather a special day. It was done. Five thousand eight hundred and fifty-six volumes; catalogued, described, evaluated. He had signed his terminal report to Pepper and posted it to Queen's Gate on the way to the station.

It should have cheered him, but he was left with a feeling of anticlimax. The target date had been his, but the problem of what was to be done now with Dr. Thomas Arthur Leslie Price was wholly Pepper's. He didn't care; the work had been acting on him like a drug, narrowing his outlook and his vision, filling his days with profitless detail and his nights with frustration. His mission—he smiled sourly to himself at the gross pretentiousness of the word—has suffered incalculably.

His *mission*. An anachronism. Since the night of May 20, he had communicated with Hamburg-Wohldorf on no fewer than eighteen occasions. The legwork necessary to fulfill the demands of the Lisbon letter—wearisome miles of cycling through London's dockland areas—had taken up most evenings and every weekend in June and early July, but that necessary gap in his transmissions had in no way irritated or worried Hamburg-Wohldorf. In fact Ritter subsequently applauded him for taking his time, for proceeding with caution and subjecting every strategic site on the list to the closest scrutiny. What they appeared to overlook was that he had, in effect, merely rubber-stamped their own findings. He had established no method on these cycling tours of assessing the work going on inside the installations or the degree to which they were actually "strategic." He had chatted with workers in local pubs, watched lorries emerging from dock

116

and factory gates, noted the timing of day and night shifts; but in essence he'd learned nothing of value.

Still, Hamburg never failed to react enthusiastically. He was at a loss at first to explain why, but the truth of it dawned on him midway through August. His response to the Lisbon letter had, in a way, been a masterpiece of superfluous irrelevancy, a mass of detail confirming a known conclusion. His independent transmissions had been equally detailed and equally insubstantial; indeed, much of their content was derived from conversations at Pepper's soirées neatly dovetailed into reports from newspapers and radio broadcasts. He had developed a fine eye for interlocking information—a speech in the House of Commons and the report of a shipyard strike; the appointment of a specialist civil servant and a government grant to industry. Such things, strung out like washing on a line, looked impressive. None of it was exactly misleading, but Hamburg's interpretation of it, and of how he had come by it, was less than objective. They had taught him his first invaluable lesson: quantity is quality in the absence of any other source.

His technique at the handset had improved out of all recognition, and he was now able to "read" Wein's signature. Price had recently asked for progress reports on Else and on Willy and Kurt, and Wein—following "personal" inquiries by Ritter—had responded. Else was well, although working under great pressure, and conveyed "her thoughts." Willy was at the General Ludendorff Jugendheim at Demmin-in-Mecklenburg, and Kurt had returned from his first Jungvolk summer camp. The details were sparse but they assuaged some part of the guilt he was nursing for having blotted them from his mind. This guilt had mysteriously deepened as his "taming" of Alice progressed.

Since early July she had made a point of leaving the library at four thirty in order to have his tea prepared when he arrived home on the five-thirty train. She would let him do nothing for himself, even refused now to let him make his bed or clean his room. It would have been counterproductive to tell her that he regarded this as an invasion of privacy and, instead, he periodically bought her flowers or perfume, and on one occasion a gold cross on a slim gold chain. But gifts were only halfway houses to the commitment he knew she expected and, recently, he had offered to meet half the household expenses. She protested, of course, but her acceptance was a foregone conclusion. She interpreted the gesture as he knew she would; as an indication that he was preparing her for a closer, more binding relationship. Looking at it quite dispassionately, he could not hold out much longer.

The plain fact was that he wanted her. There was no denying it. Crude, inextinguishable lust, nothing more nor less. More importantly, she needed *him;* a fact he could not afford to overlook. He'd done nothing to encourage her; quite the reverse, in fact. Apart from his congenital shyness and total lack of experience—both of which conspired to keep her at a distance—he knew the time was not right. Alice, on the other hand, had launched an all-out campaign of enticement utterly devoid of subtlety. Silly things, like changing her cosmetics to add a dramatic Spanish intensity to her face and buying clothes specifically designed to excite him. (And they *did* excite him.) Then there were the little intimacies, sitting alone for an hour in front of the fire at night to talk over *their* day, a harmless preoccupation at first but one she had begun to use for blatant attempts at seduction. Before they sat down to their nightcaps, now, Alice would change into filmy night-gowns and lacy negligées; perhaps recline at his feet, her figure swelling dizzily under his eyes. She couldn't have been more explicit.

But he was determined not to commit the tactical blunder of yielding to her on her terms. Alice, whatever her needs, was still a woman of powerful moods and intractable will; in many ways the same Amazon he'd decided, on his first day at the library, "had to go." Well, he'd established his priorities and she must be made to adapt to them. If her sexual needs were great enough, she'd concede.

Her greatest value to him lay in two areas: as a protector at the library who could be relied on to cover his tracks should the necessity arise later; and as a buffer against her son. The second was infinitely more compelling. Alan Petrie was a threat to his peace of mind and, potentially, to his security. His hatred was open and intolerable. Throughout the summer Price had fought to keep his temper, but Alan would have broken the endurance of Job. As a grandmaster in the art of provocation he made Else seem pliable—and Alan was laying his ground with the cunning of a Heydrich!

Having failed to corrupt Dinah, the boy had turned to the

neighbors in Ellerker Gardens, Frank White, a genial, rather sickly old man who owned a chemist's shop in the town, and Fred Wilby, a customs officer at Northolt. They were both friendly, easygoing men and had had the decency to warn him that Alan was exercising a rare talent for "telling tales out of school." Nothing outrageous, of course; more suggestive than specific.

"Says you lock yourself up in the loft for hours, Dr. Price," old White told him apologetically over the garden fence one evening in July. "Said there were noises and scrapings—like a burglar trying to get in. He had my wife worried sick there for a minute or two. Made you sound sort of—well, criminal, you know."

He knew well enough. Fred Wilby confided a week later that Alan had spent an hour telling his wife how worried he was about what Price was "doing" to his mother.

"You mean—hurting her?" Mrs. Wilby had pressed him.

"I don't know. But she's changed. He makes her do everything for him; everything. He won't even let her take Dinah to school anymore. She's worried, I can see that much, but she daren't do anything about it."

As it turned out, Alan's whispering campaign backfired. The sympathies of White and Wilby, both of whom had grown sons, lay with Price. The boy, they said guardedly, needed a father. Both men were dedicated gardeners, and he quickly saw the advantage of joining their circle. Their conversations over the garden fence were now a feature of his evenings and weekends.

All in all, he was approaching a position of strength. In Alice, Dinah, Sally Logan, White, and Wilby, he had allies; in Philip Pepper, a professional confidant; in Paul Curzon a trusting, wholly undemanding friend. In practical terms, none of them were operationally useful; on the other hand he had learned enough about the chemistry of what Praetorius termed "solitary survival" to know that he could not exist without human companionship. He lunched with Paul at least twice a week, and for the past four Sundays Curzon had come to Richmond for a morning stroll in the park, a pint, and lunch with the family.

He turned in at the gate of Middlemass House and let himself in. Alice sang out from the living room, "Is that you, Tom?" and he heard a clatter of plates and tureens. As he entered the sitting room he heard the Greenwich time signal on the radio: "Here is the nine o'clock news." Dinah blew him a kiss. He winked at her and sat down.

"At six o'clock this morning," the newsreader began, "divisions of the German army crossed the border into Poland. The invasion forces struck deeply in a four-pronged attack . . ."

"Did you finish?" Alice asked excitedly.

He didn't hear her. He turned his head to catch the newsreader's next words, his heart in his mouth, but Alice kept right on.

"I said to the children, 'We'll wait tea and supper tonight and have it all in one as a celebration.'"

". . . at its heaviest in the southwestern sector of the front near the district of Częstochowa and at Chojnice and Mlawa, near the East Prussian border, according to a communiqué from the . . ."

". . . so I bought this lovely roast instead and we're having it with potatoes and cauliflower."

". . . the German High Command, announced this evening that German troops gained immediate footholds on all fronts and . . ."

It struck her at last that he was not listening. She clapped a hand to her mouth. "Oh my God, Tom! What is it?"

Dinah said with a long-suffering sigh, "The Germans are having a war, Mummy. You know Tom-Tom likes the news."

Alice reached out to him across the table, but she caught Alan's look and dropped her hand at once.

"Oh, Tom—I didn't know. . . ."

His elation was immense; it flooded him, suffocated him, stunned him. He grasped the seat of his chair and mastered the muscles of his face. They were staring at him: Alice open-mouthed, Dinah puzzled, Alan glowering. He couldn't stay there.

"Forgive me . . . Terribly sorry but . . . I think I'll have to go to . . ." He strode out of the room and bounded upstairs.

He locked the door and sat down on the bed, but he couldn't stay still. He got up again and paced the room, arms swinging across his body, punching the air.

Our plans for the invasion of southern England are fully realized. A year. One year.

A year. April 1940. Seven months! He vaulted onto the

bed; the mattress subsided under his weight and he only just suppressed a shout of joy. Seven *months*.

War was inevitable. The English wouldn't dare to renege on their pledge to go to the assistance of Poland in the event of a German invasion. They couldn't. He raised his legs high in the air and plonked them down, feet splayed, on the brass bedstead.

He had been unfair to Ritter, Praetorius, everyone at Hamburg-Wohldorf. He had allowed craven pessimism to blind him to the reality of German strength and honor; but he had no apprehensions now, no doubts. Their promises had matured. He caught himself. What of *his* promises? *His* obligations? He pushed himself up and set his feet on the floor.

There could be no excuses now; the game was on in earnest. Intelligence would be vital to the High Command in the months ahead. No more inspired guesswork; no more paste-and-scissors ferreting in newspapers. If England went to war—*when* it went to war—he must go with it, working from the heart. He would initiate the first of his orders on the day Chamberlain declared war by offering himself for service in the British Armed Forces. He would be rejected, of course, as Hamburg forecast; the asthma and the ankle deformity would see to that. But the gesture was important. It would be seen as a measure of his patriotism, his willingness to fight in spite of physical disabilities.

But gestures were not enough. He must find a way in: government, civil service, munitions, ship or aircraft building, docks—somewhere. A modest post at first, perhaps; then slow, painstaking progress to a position of trust. Dr. Tom Price had ample qualifications: a double first, teaching experience at two of the best public schools in England, a post at London University.

He must talk with Pepper. Pepper would advise him, introduce him to the right people. He already knew a few of them himself. Yes, he could call Pepper at Queen's Gate tomorrow. The one essential—

There was a faint tapping at the door, so hesitant at first that he had failed to hear it. It grew in volume and urgency.

"Tom? Tom, dear? Are you all right?"

He smiled wryly. War changed even the domestic perspective. He would have nothing to fear from Alan in seven months. And it was quite immaterial now what kind of relationship he had with Alice. He could take her or leave her. When the Wehrmacht marched into London next spring, Thomas Arthur Leslie Price would simply disappear.

He turned the key and opened the door.

She looked genuinely concerned.

"Oh, Tom!"

Then he saw she had changed the working skirt and blouse she had worn earlier for one of her newest dresses, a tight-fitting scarlet silk sheath with a deep V neck. She had also let down her hair and painted her face.

He took her hand without a word, drew her over the threshold, and pushed the door shut. She looked surprised but he gave her no time for second thoughts.

"I'm afraid I made a fool of myself," he said gruffly.

"You mustn't worry about that, love." Love! She had also found time to touch pefume to her wrists and throat. "I sent the children next door to Mrs. White. I didn't know. . . ."

"I'd been expecting it for months, but to hear it like that. . . ."

"My dear, you should have said." She came closer. Her skin radiated a heady musk of sandalwood. "I feel so useless, wanting to do something, not knowing what to say. You're so . . ." She stared at him adoringly. "You're so sensitive and intelligent and I'm so stupid. I never know what's going on in that head of yours. But if you'd let me . . ."

She closed the last inch of space between them and her breasts yielded as they met his chest.

"I didn't want you to worry . . . my dear." His cheek touched the fall of her hair and a new fragrance rose to tantalize him.

"Oh, darling, darling."

Her arms slipped around his neck and he clutched at the silken waist, binding her to him. Her mouth came to meet his and he brought his lips together, as he had done with Else, but her tongue plumbed hungrily between them. The shock of it freed him of all restraint, all reason; he clawed at her, his fingers gouging and kneading flesh, swooping from hips to shoulders, cupping the trembling breasts. She made small sounds in his mouth—cries, gasps, moans, entreaties. He caught her lip in his teeth and she reared back, her pelvis straining into his.

He tore his mouth away and buried it in her throat, in the straining scarlet of her dress.

"Please, darling. Oh, please! Oh, *please*, my darling love."

He lost his balance as she pulled him to her, but she held him upright, stronger than he, part of her still practical, planning the way. He felt her hands on his clothes, unbuttoning his shirt and trousers, slipping them off, but he couldn't help her, even hindered her, smothering her face and neck with his kisses, fumbling in that tantalizing V of scarlet for the imprisoned breasts.

She pressed him away, gently but with great firmness, and he stood naked, panting, obedient. She made a dexterous lunge for the fastenings at her back, freed the dress, and sent it plummeting to her feet. She took his hand by the wrist then and plunged it into the white satin at her waist. He gasped at the heat of her. She moved again, drawing his hand down. The cups slipped from her breasts and she pulled his face into them. Mouth and hand; liquid heat.

Then he was on the bed, straddling her, devouring her, and she was crooning in his ear, wetting his skin with her tongue, rousing him, plaguing him, taking him higher, higher, higher. . . .

And at the peak of it, the dizzying hallucinatory peak, he heard Dr. Praetorius's voice, so calm, so approving.

"A normal life, Dr. Price, a normal life."

SEPTEMBER 2, 1939

Ginger Haddon massaged his slim fingers, an impulsive reflex, half nervous, half indulgent. He was a stringy man in his late forties—long-nosed, blue-jowled, round-shouldered; prematurely aged by the veteran wireless telegraphist's preoccupation with unresolved sound. He had long lost the titian thatch that originally gave him his nickname and the thin horseshoe ruff around his ears and neck had faded to pepper-and-salt gray. He was anxious to be away, to get back to his equipment in the upstairs room on Onslow Road.

Appropriations and General Services had given the flat a

lick of paint and provided a few sticks of furniture, including a double bed, but Haddon rarely moved out of reach of his equipment and existed almost exclusively in the front room. He had set up a cot there that morning when he read about the invasion of Poland. He inched to the edge of his chair.

"He might break the sequence," he said gloomily. He was a Yorkshireman and his disposition was at best phlegmatic. "Better not hang about."

Paul Curzon grinned. "He hasn't broken sequence once yet."

"Always a first time. There'll be a war,. right?"

"There'll be a war," Curzon said equably. "That's why he'll stick to Hamburg's rules. But I'll drop round before ten tonight in case he sends."

"He'll send." The operator nursed his precious hands. "He'll want orders, sure as you're born. He's in it now. Up to his neck."

Curzon closed the folder on Haddon's weekly report. It recorded only one transmission—on Wednesday night. Haddon's reports were stark affairs, less concerned with the content of the messages he had intercepted—although they were duly enshrined in his cramped schoolgirl handwriting— than with the technicalities of signal strengths, speed of transmission, and Hamburg's "signature of the day"—in this case H-W 2, Sergeant Baruth.

The send had been another of Price's newspaper-oriented evaluations: the status of Air Raid Precaution arrangements in the home counties, with particular emphasis on the row between government and local authorities over the need to build public air raid shelters in urban areas. Curzon's opinion was that Price was doing them a favor by dressing up such publicly available material as covertly acquired "income."

Haddon was on his feet. He shrugged into his disreputable gray herringbone coat. "See you around quarter to ten, then?"

Curzon eyed him curiously. Haddon had not once questioned his role since the day Blinker Hall produced him. He had moaned briefly about the inevitable dislocation of his career as a senior radio officer with Cunard, then settled without complaint into the tedium of life at Onslow Road— the Isolation Ward, as Heston had christened it. He was a brilliant w/t man. He had not only reproduced Price's developing signature with an artistry that took Heston's breath away but, in the long breaks between transmissions, had perfected Wein's, Baruth's and Koehn's "for practice." Menzies' man in Berlin had provided the names of Wohldorf's wireless team and, with his help, Haddon had coupled names to signatures and identified the key men.

"Everything shipshape and Bristol fashion?" Curzon lay back indolently in his chair.

"Good enough," Haddon said shortly.

"All right, Ginger. Quarter to ten."

The midafternoon sun slanted down through tall windows, suspended dust particles glinting in its shafts. Paul Curzon closed his eyes against the prickling reflections from Sir Hugh Sinclair's brass inkstand. He felt stiff, hot, deprived of air, and bored.

Major Desmond Morton said gently, "We take the view" —the "we" embraced Winston Churchill, although his name had not been mention—"that Dr. Price is no longer simply a Trojan horse. The Polish ultimatum changes all that. He's the key to the whole principle of manipulating the Abwehr."

Sinclair nodded. "We agree, broadly, about Price. Matter of degree. Just get it clear in your minds—all of you—I have no intention of handing him the key to the door without proper safeguards."

Menzies squinted into the sunlight. "The problem's basically an executive one, isn't it? If the prime minister responds to the Polish ultimatum as we hope he will . . ."

Morton's gaze flickered briefly over Curzon's face and came to rest on Sinclair. "Very well. This is for your ears only. The P.M.'s invited Winston to join a War Cabinet of six ministers. Naturally, it's not a de facto appointment yet, and won't be till the crisis resolves itself, but I think we're all pretty sure, aren't we, what he'll be offered?"

"First Lord?" Sinclair murmured into space.

"It's just my personal opinion, of course, but I'd say he'll move into the Admiralty on Monday. If the debate in the House tonight permits, he might even look in first thing tomorrow. His . . . influence in this area won't be small."

Menzies' mouth puckered. "That does change things somewhat."

"So you see," Morton went on smoothly, "we're not talking academically, here. Price, properly handled, represents a major asset. We can't afford to waste him. I concede your point about safeguards, but we really do think you've been a little overcautious with him." He smiled tolerantly.

"We can't afford to waste manpower or money either," Menzies said slowly. "Price has a permanent watchdog team of seven, *plus* the Pepper network. The whole service is undermanned, undercapitalized, and—"

"Underrated," rapped Sinclair.

"Of course. Winston recognizes that more than anyone." Morton got to his feet and lifted coat and bowler from the coatrack. "He'll prosecute this war with every weapon we have—and some we haven't even dreamed of yet." He caught Sinclair's eye. "He's convinced Intelligence is the vital arm."

"Are you suggesting he'll have the *power* to prosecute the war?"

"I'm merely advocating optimism."

He closed the door behind him.

Sinclair released a hiss of pent-up irritation. "I wish to God we weren't so dependent on Winston's myrmidons." He became aware of Curzon's presence in the chair opposite him. "All right, Curzon. Get on with it," he said testily.

They watched him lope from the room. Sinclair sniffed, "You're putting a lot on that man's shoulders."

"They're broad enough."

"I wonder." Sinclair sifted through a sheaf of papers in the drawer at his left hand and placed a sheet of onionskin in front of him. "For the moment we won't burden him with this." He drummed his fingers on the quarto sheet. "We have some more from A-54 on Price. It's interesting."

Menzies controlled an urge to stare at the paper. A-54 was the code name of Hauptmann Paul Thümmel, a German Abwehr officer who had been feeding the Czech Secret Service since February 1936. After the German occupation of Prague, he had been jointly run by the expatriate Czechs and MI6. His product was wide-ranging and accurate, not only in terms of information on Wehrmacht and Luftwaffe technical resources and innovations, but in speedy forecasting of political decisions. He had warned of Hitler's drive into the Sudetenland as early as the summer of 1937, predicted the Czech assault in spring 1938, and since April had persistently underlined the imminence of a Polish invasion. He was the only

Abwehr officer wholly under SIS control, but his information had made little impact at government level.

"What does he say?"

Sinclair breathed deeply through his nose. "Our friend Wilhelm Sommer can thank his wife for falling into this little mess. She recommended him, apparently—without his knowledge. Sommer was Praetorius's pigeon originally, but Ritter and Canaris took him over when they saw the possibilities in him." He looked up at Menzies. "Pity is, Heydrich knows about him too. Still." He went back to the paper. "Sommer's out of the Fuehrer-prinzip stable. Wandervögel recruit as a boy; put his sons through the Pimpf and so on. Good Nazi. Ah—English mother. I'm having that checked now. Gave him his accent but not much else as far as I can see. She died in 1913."

"What about the real Price?"

"Price is dead—emphysema. It's a standing order that the deaths of aliens be referred to the Knockenhauerstrasse. Praetorius acquired the corpse. He sent out a round robin to Party officials to find a teacher fitting Price's description. Dear Frau Sommer was one of them."

"So she volunteered her Wilhelm."

"Doesn't sound like a love match, does it? Anyway, Hamburg-Wohldorf scooped him up and gave him six weeks' training. Couldn't be more, of course, because Price had applied for the job here in London and they needed Sommer at the interview."

"The application. Does Hamburg know Price trotted out a pack of lies?"

"As far as Hamburg and the Tirpitzufer was concerned, Price is one hundred percent genuine. A-54's seen the file. Price's application form and his first letter are both in it. Nothing to suggest they have any doubts about his background."

"Well—so our Price is a good Nazi, is he? I wonder if Morton would feel we'd been overcautious now?"

"Exactly."

Menzies contemplated the cat's cradle he had made of his fingers. "Do you intend to pass this to Winston?"

"No. It doesn't fit his view of the situation. He'd choose to ignore it."

"But we can't, of course." Menzies studied the ceiling,

eyes half closed. "Wandervögel, Party member; sons in the Hitler Youth movement, wife a Party official." He lowered his gaze to Sinclair. "And we defined him as nervous, inexperienced, probably reluctant. Doesn't fit, does it? Curzon was wrong."

"And Pepper."

"Pepper doesn't matter so much, but we can't use him as anything more than a baby-sitter from now on. I don't trust his judgment."

Sinclair exhaled noisily through his nose. "You'll have to learn to. Blinker Hall had a few words with him this morning. Winston's idea. He thinks it's time Pepper told Price why he *really* gave him that job at the library."

SEPTEMBER 4, 1939

At three o'clock in the morning there was a persistent muffled tapping at his door. Alice, wide awake, lavishly made up and fully dressed. For a moment he was completely disoriented, then she whispered, "I love the way you undress me first," and slipped into his arms. He stood gaping, clinging to her for support, still half asleep. The first hours of the first day of war, and she'd dressed and painted herself for the pleasure of being undressed?

He slept for an hour when she left his bed at six. At breakfast, he could barely keep his eyes open. On the way to the station, he told her he intended to join up. He told it badly. The stricken look on her face said plainly enough that she thought he was mad.

"But they need *young* men. You're too old for fighting."

"I have to volunteer, Alice. It's no good asking me why. You wouldn't understand."

"But what about your work? The library?"

"It's finished. You know that as well as I do. There's nothing left to do. Pepper won't need me now."

"But . . ." She switched the angle of attack. "I can't understand you. How can you think of leaving now? Leaving . . . me?"

"I don't *want* to. I *have* to."

But she couldn't accept it, and when she left the train at Kensington High Street she turned away tight-lipped and refused to say good-by. He got out at South Kensington and walked all the way to Victoria Street to steady his nerves. He had planned to get it over and done with in a couple of hours, and for that reason had selected Victoria, where all three services maintained recruiting offices within a few hundred yards of each other; but in the event it took up more than half the day.

His first call was on the Royal Air Force, the arm most likely to reject him without fuss. The small shopfront office was packed and a queue had formed on the pavement outside. The first volunteers were, in a majority, his own age and either office workers or executives, solid middle-class conservatives catching their patriotism at the flood before it ebbed in the cold light of reason. The processing was slow and it was ten forty-five before he was called into the bare room behind the office.

A uniformed clerk in spectacles took his "personals," filling in cramped answer blocks on a long buff form with a scratching pen, while a doctor in a white coat tapped his stethoscope impatiently.

They came to "medical history."

"Illnesses?" droned the clerk.

"Poliomyelitis, asthma, measles . . ."

The doctor came off his chair with a bounce of annoyance.

"Damnit, man, why didn't you say so at the start." He snatched the form from under the clerk's nose, tore it across and handed the halves to Price. "Wasting your time, man, and wasting mine, too. Here." He bent over his desk and scribbled his signature on a pink slip. "That's your medical release. You'll need it when you're required to register."

He acquired a blue slip to accompany the pink one in record time. The Royal Navy recruitment center was no less full, but the petty officer in charge picked him out of a dozen or so waiting aspirants on the visible evidence of his age. He was shown to the examination room and felt the petty officer gesturing to the doctor behind his back. The naval surgeon-commander received the message loud and clear; his first act was to make Price walk around him three times while he watched him closely from the center of the floor. He clicked his tongue.

"Oh, no, doctor. Won't do, will it? That's a bad limp you've got there."

"It's not serious."

"Polio?"

"Just in the ankle."

"Just in the ankle, eh?" The doctor flourished his signature on a blue rejection slip, tore it off the pad, and held it out with a sympathetic smile.

The Army had no time for sympathy or gentility. A starched sergeant major isolated him with a dozen other "previous serious illnesses and conditions" and treated him to a searching cross-examination about his medical shortcomings. Price received a green slip without ever penetrating to the back room.

It was half past one when he emerged for the third time in Victoria Street; he found a telephone booth near Westminster Cathedral and rang Phillimore Gardens. Alice answered and at the sound of his voice, gulped back her tears.

"Oh, Tom, I'm sorry. Forgive me. I was so upset, I . . ."

"There's nothing to forgive. I'm coming back. I'll be there in half an hour or so."

"*No!*" It was a squeak. "Professor Pepper's looking for you. He wants to see you urgently at Queen's Gate. He was in a terrible state when I said you'd gone to join up."

"What does he want?"

"He just said the minute you came back to tell you to go to Queen's Gate. Very very urgent, he said. Oh, Tom . . ."

"*Alice!*" He softened. "It's all right. They wouldn't have me."

"Oh thank God! Oh, darling, I want you to promise me you'll never—" The penny ran out and he clicked down the receiver.

Pepper pounced on him the moment he opened the street door. "Did they take you?"

"No, I'm afraid not."

Small hands clawed at his arm and dragged him inside. "Thank heaven for small mercies. Can't think what made you do it." He fussed Price into his flat and they sat down, face to face across the crackling log fire. "Nearly had a fit when Mrs. Petrie told me."

"You know how I feel about the Nazis. I thought it was my—"

Pepper tsk-tsked impatiently. "Please! If you're about to tell me it was your duty—"

"It was. *Is*."

The little man's banana-yellow eyes widened in irritation. "Duty has nothing to do with chucking your talents away on a uniform and a damned gun you'll never learn to shoot the right way round. Your duty, as an intelligent man, is to *think:* Where can I serve best? Who needs me most?"

"Well, they agree with you, if it's any consolation."

"Indeed! Now, look here, Tom, I . . ." He buffed his hands nervously. "Something to drink? I've only got milk at the moment."

"Nothing, thanks."

"Yes. Well." He came out with it in a rush. "We're friends, aren't we?"

"I hope so."

"Hope so? *Know* so. Why do you think I took you on here in the first place?"

"I often wondered. A first-year student could have catalogued those books—and for a tenth the money you paid me."

"Well—there you have it. Working under false pretenses, wasn't I? Hmph." He studied Price intently. "There *was* no library. I had those books trundled in over the weekend and a damn filthy business it was, too. Kept me up all night. Simple fact was, I didn't want to lose you. Had plans, you see."

"For a place in Gower Street?"

"Gower Street be damned! Thinking ahead. To a day like today. Remember what you said that afternoon you first came? You said, 'I stayed on in Hamburg to learn enough to be useful back here when war came.' Correct?"

"Something like that. I said it sounded pretentious."

"Still think that way?"

"Of course."

Pepper chuckled wickedly. "Or you wouldn't have been standing in queues all morning trying to join up. Right, then. Will you join *me*?"

"*Join* you?"

"Go to war. *My* war. No guns, no uniforms. Your brain's what I want. Your eight years in Germany, your German, your French—your instincts. What d'you say?"

"What exactly—?"

"Too early for exactitudes. Next week, week after perhaps. Not now. I can tell you one thing, though—it'll be hush-hush, top secret, lips sealed; that sort of thing. Are you game?"

Price stared at his feet for a full minute, until Pepper could bear the suspense no longer.

"Come on, Tom. Are you with me?"

He sighed. "I hope I won't let you down."

He caught a bus at the Albert Hall for Kensington High Street and stood all the way. Traffic paralyzed the streets, shoppers congested the pavements and jostled in long undisciplined lines at the bus stops, but there was no irascibility, no atmosphere of despondency. In the bus, the mood verged on the euphoric. Extraordinary. Or perhaps it was his own elation that led him to interpret all this frenzy as gaiety. Surely they couldn't seriously believe England stood a chance of defeating Germany? They had only to look at their morning newspapers to judge the effectiveness of Hitler's blitzkrieg.

In fact, all the signs pointed to a total collapse of morale and resolve in Europe. No one had a taste for war. The French were promising a diplomatic initiative "if the aggressor regained his frontiers"; the British Labour Party was divided on the question of Chamberlain's declaration; and the Foreign Office had issued a long statement that must have had Albert Kesselring in stitches at Luftwaffe headquarters that morning. It applauded Roosevelt's appeal to the combatants to avoid bombing civilian targets from the air and promised that Britain would "preserve in every way possible those monuments of human achievement which are treasured in all civilized countries."

A gale of laughter swept the bus. The conductor clattered down from the top deck to join the fun and showed his teeth in a smile as Price stepped onto the platform.

"We'll give 'im what for, eh, lad?"

Price smiled too, choking back laughter. "Oh, yes—we'll show him all right."

SEPTEMBER 6, 1939

He made love to Alice in a nest of blankets on the floor of her room, an erotic notion originally conceived to avoid alerting Alan with squeaking bedsprings. Alice could not be sated in an hour but, as always on a transmission night, he'd convinced her he was too tired for an extended romp. Her passions, he'd learned, took second place only to her ambitions, and his new temporary commission at Phillimore Gardens ranked as a sacred trust in her view. In fact it was no more than a way of filling in time: a tedious cataloguing of German industrial production quotas since 1936. Pepper had devised it as an exercise that might profit them some day, but Alice saw it as "war work" and therefore of national importance. The very mention of it was sufficient to cool her ardor to absolute zero.

He crept back to his room, moved the table onto the bed, and swung up through the trapdoor into the loft. Eleven forty-three. He'd run it damned close. He set up the equipment hurriedly and switched on. He was shocked to hear the carrier bleeping furiously as he clamped on the headset.

Hamburg-Wohldorf had never jumped the gun before; it was his privilege to open communication, the field agent's unchallengeable right.

"Hotbed to Gimlet. Respond. Over."

He tapped out, "Gimlet responds. Proceed."

The Hamburg signature was Baruth's; very fast tonight, full operational speed. "Rantzau for Hotbed, Priority One to Gimlet. Effective now suspend all transmissions until otherwise informed. Do you understand and confirm? Over."

His bowels turned to ice. Suspend?

"Gimlet to Hotbed. Expand order."

"Repeat. Suspend transmissions until reactivated. Rantzau orders as follows. Maintain penetration maneuvers and consolidate position. Observe radio watch once weekly on normal transmit schedule beginning Monday 2245 hours, Tuesday

133

134

second week same time, Wednesday third week etcetera. Discount Saturdays/Sundays. Do you confirm? Over.''

"Gimlet to Hotbed. Is my position threatened?''

"No threat your position. Suspension essential in anticipation overall strategic developments. Anxious protect your cover all costs. Confirm?''

"Confirm. Any other instructions?''

"None. Close down now. Good luck. Out.''

He signed off and removed the headset. For a few minutes he sat reading the take, then he stowed the equipment, switched off the light, and lowered himself to the bed. He stood at his window, watching the shadowy comings and goings of neighbors in the unlit street, trying to make sense of the message. He gave up, took off his dressing gown, and pulled back the bedclothes. He was about to crawl in when the significance of it struck him. Suspension. He pulled on his robe again and opened the door.

The landing below was a black void. From Alan's room came the sibilants of light snoring. He crossed to Alice's door and let himself in. She was where he had left her, in the nest of blankets under the window. He knelt and covered her breast with his hand.

"Mmmm.''

She was less than half awake but his touch roused an instinct that never slept. He pulled off his pajamas and slipped in beside her; lay on his back and let her wake to him, inch by inch. Her lips, silken soft, sucked hungrily at his tongue, moved down to his throat, his chest, stomach, thighs. The liquid furnace of her mouth found him, took him in, rose and fell, and his body tensed, flared with heat, relaxed, submitted. He closed his eyes and gave himself up to her. Suspension.

Dr. Praetorius would have approved.

BOOK TWO
1940

APRIL 20, 1940

In the street below a half-dozen small boys were playing football with aggressive abandon and a minimum of skill. It was raining mistily but not enough to dampen the children's high spirits or halt the mechanical Saturday morning routine of Ellerker Gardens. Frank White's Austin Ten, polished that morning before he left to open his shop in the High Street, was slowly being disfigured by blobs and trails of rain. Fred Wilby sat astride his front garden wall bolting a new paling gate in place. At one end of the street a baker's roundsman was delivering bread; at the other a horse-drawn wagon selling paraffin had attracted a cluster of gossiping women. There was a nerve-stunning domesticity about the scene. It was a fitting epitaph to his plight.

Here lies Thomas Price, who dug this pit and leaped into it unaided.

He had held out till Christmas Day, occupying her bed by night and—as she put it—her heart by day. Her heart! Things had been going so well. In October, he and Pepper had joined forces, with official Whitehall blessing, to set up a government research unit and find it a home. November and December had been spent in agitated searches and conclaves—irritating and exhausting, much of it, but manna from heaven in view of what surely was to come. Phillimore Gardens had been formally closed just before the Christmas holiday and Alice, by then its sole employee, was told she could return to her job at the university building in Bloomsbury. *That* was the turning point, the prelude to disaster. She had decided, she announced that night in bed, to leave work altogether, to devote herself to his every whim and comfort. She *belonged* at home—as long as he was there. Still, the word "marriage" had not crossed her lips—until Christmas Day.

Alan and Dinah had gone next door to the Whites' for the ritual Christmas morning mince pies and an exchange of presents. For an hour, they had the house to themselves. "Two minutes!" Alice promised the moment the door closed

137

on the children, and hurried upstairs. When she called him to her room—he was on fire at the prospect—he found her draped across the bed wearing the squirrel stole he'd given her; nothing else.

With "Hark the herald angels sing" blaring from the radio downstairs, Alice was under him, whipping him to climax, and at the penultimate moment hissing in his ear, "Marry me, darling. Marry me."

January 20: a Saturday much like this one but bitterly, memorably cold: ice on the register office steps; Alice clutching him for support as she slipped, the photographer's shutter snapping on cue. The picture stood on the piano as a permanent reminder of her gift for inspired timing.

For a while he was curiously happy. He'd engineered a fixed base, a sensible marriage, complete respectability—the normal life Dr. Praetorius had urged on him. Alice built her world around his, and Dinah became his daughter in name as well as spirit. The only shadow on their lives was Alan, but with Frank White's sailor son Donald egging him on, the boy had applied for entry to the Royal Naval College at Dartmouth and passed his entrance examinations with distinction. The one element he'd never dared hope for in this insane charade—peace of mind—was virtually within his grasp.

Then he destroyed it all in one blind act of self-serving pride.

He had been a victim of his own sensuality from the beginning; he saw that clearly enough now. He had an adolescent's appetites, the subtlety of a rutting hog, and the combination suited Alice perfectly. The act itself—the fusion of bodies, an expression of love—was of no importance to her. Extravagant foreplay, erotic charades, interminable arousal, was everything. She was wanton, provocative, and insatiable; she radiated an excitement that was beyond any earthly experience he had ever believed possible, and he wallowed in her carnality. At first.

After their marriage, for reasons he still couldn't put his finger on, this ceaseless physical hunger of hers began to offend him. More than that. His days with Pepper were long and tiring; the winter brought on a hellish attack of the arthritis that had long plagued him since his student days, and he was permanently doped with pain-killing drugs and lack of sleep. Alice ignored the signs, or perhaps was too insensitive to see them. Their sexual rampaging was already a routine; nightly, twice and thrice nightly, it provided an obsessive, repetitive outlet for her self-indulgence.

On the night he put an end to it he had been on his feet for sixteen hours. He was an aching, shaking bag of nervous tension. He said no. He pushed her away when she refused to take him seriously. And again and again. The soprano shrieking of her wounded pride, her rage and paranoia, must have awakened the entire neighborhood. Alan and Dinah undoubtedly heard every word. He spent the rest of the night in his old room and, when he got home from work next day, Alice had dumped his clothes and books there.

Had he made his peace there and then the whole childish affair would have been forgotten. But he offered no peace terms. He refused to surrender himself to her as a permanently primed pump, and his pride rejected the humiliation of admitting blame. By the end of February, barely a month after the wedding, they were avoiding each other at mealtimes and weekends. Paul Curzon maintained his Sunday morning pilgrimages but finally asked to be excused from further visits to the house; they fell into the habit of meeting in Richmond Park and ate their lunches in pubs. Dinah was not allowed to walk with them.

Alice supplied the coup de grace. Nothing was said, no messages conveyed by third parties, no notes exchanged; she simply tore up the contract. Literally. Price came down to breakfast one Tuesday morning in mid-March to find the shreds of their marriage certificate piled neatly on his plate. She didn't come home that night. Next day, she told Dinah she had gone back to work, that it was war work too secret to talk about and would probably keep her away a lot. That Friday she left to catch the London train and didn't appear again for four days.

In the past four weeks she'd slept at home on fewer than ten occasions. Dinah appeared to have taken her at her word; Alan exuded raw hatred and spent all his free time with the Whites, especially when Donald was at home. And Tom Price held his breath, waiting for the final blow.

Last night, she'd come home for the first time since Monday and unusually early. Price and Dinah had been eating supper and Alice sat down with them. The signs were all there; she told Dinah her lies—her travels around England, the "high-ups" she worked with, the pressures—and silently challenged Price to denounce her. He'd put off going to bed till nearly midnight, but she wouldn't be drawn. This morning she'd taken Dinah shopping. Price had sat at the dormer window for two hours waiting for their return. It would be her last, he was sure of it. He had already made *his* decision. His clothes were packed, the radio set lay in the old HMV gramophone case on his bed, his books in a stout bag. He'd decided, for the time being anyway, to take a room at the Mendip.

He saw them turn the corner from Onslow Road and watched them as far as the gate before going downstairs. As he reached the hall, Dinah came running from the kitchen, but she didn't greet him. One frightened glance, a hint of tears, and she bolted out the front door. He went to the kitchen. Alice was unpacking bags and baskets. He stood in the doorway.

"What did you just say to Diny?"

"Nothing. Why?" She didn't look at him.

"She looked scared."

"Your imagination. You're not God, you know."

"What's that supposed to mean?"

"I'm not going to waste time arguing with *you*."

He moved toward her and, sensing it, she drew her arms across her breast like a shield. He smiled. "Don't worry, Alice. I won't touch you." He propped himself on the kitchen table. "Why did she run out like that?"

"I . . ." She turned and busied herself at the sink. "I sent her round to Mrs. White. I'm going out."

"Where?"

"It's none of your—" She squared her shoulders. "I'll be away for a while. Maybe a couple of months, I don't know for sure."

"And what am I supposed to say to that?"

She bent lower over the sink. "Alan goes to Dartmouth next month. And Diny—" Her voice broke but he knew from hard experience that she was only experimenting; she held her tears in check for real emergencies. "She's very good around the house. She can cook and sew and . . . I've told her about my job. She understands. It's not as if she's a child."

He felt suddenly dizzy—rage, scorn, disbelief. "You can't *leave* her."

She swung on him furiously. "Who said anything about leaving? She's my—" She bit her lip. "It's my house."

"I'll go right away."

No response.

"Did you hear me? I said I'll—"

"Do what you like. It won't change anything."

"You'd leave anyway?"

"I have to. It's my job." Her cheeks flushed crimson.

He was totally unprepared for that and his resolution collapsed. "Look, Alice, we could start again. We—"

"Start *what* again?"

The blood roared in his head. "Acting like intelligent human beings instead of—*animals!*" he roared.

She put the table between them but she was no longer afraid. "It's too late for talk. You had plenty of time to talk if you'd wanted to."

"Who is he?"

"Oh, don't give me that!"

"*Who?*"

"No one." Her face grew flushed again. "Got that fixed in your skull, have you? No one. No one. *No one.* I'm just sick and tired of *you*, that's all. I can't stand the sight of you. And"—back came the control, like a steel door sliding into place—"when I'm ready I'll make . . . arrangements. About Diny. And the house."

"And in the meantime?"

"I wouldn't want to deprive you of your bed," she said sweetly.

APRIL 21, 1940

Richmond Park was lit by mellow spring sunshine.

Price and Curzon lay with their backs to an old elm and watched Dinah and the spaniel leap and play along the shore of the lake. The spaniel had deserted its elderly owners for the child's youth and readiness to frolic when they entered the gates; it showed no inclination to leave.

"You should buy her a dog."

Price pulled a face. "We've got enough mouths to feed."

"Man can't live by bread alone."

"In wartime he's damn glad to."

Dinah's appearance on the ritual Sunday morning stroll must have alerted Curzon to the fact that something dramatic had happened at the house in Ellerker Gardens, but he was too polite to ask and Price was vaguely uneasy about volunteering explanations. The watered-down version of Alice's departure he had given Alan and Dinah last night was drama enough for one weekend. He steered the conversation on to safer ground.

"How's the job hunting going?"

"Oh, well—you know."

Paul had known for several months after war broke out that his job at the wine shippers' was done for. He was the most junior and, as he put it, "the obvious one for the chop." He'd been handed his cards in February and immediately volunteered for the Army. He was turned down flat. Flat feet. His father had had a fit, he said, and ever since had been trying to wangle him a respectable niche in Whitehall. Sir Martin's latest target was the Ministry of Supply, where he'd unearthed an old Army crony, but so far his influence hadn't borne fruit. In a ridiculous bid for independence, Paul had taken a nine-to-five job in a furniture depository in the City. He seemed mulishly reluctant to leave it.

"Why don't you let me talk to someone at the university?"

"Oh, come off it, Tom. We've been through that. University!"

"As a clerk. Maybe something better. You don't know till you try."

"I wouldn't fit in."

The English preoccupation with fitting in! What he meant was that he now regarded himself as unemployable. He had no faith in the system or in himself.

"You're hardly fitting in now, are you? I wouldn't describe a job nursing furniture as a vocation."

"I'll get by."

"It's crazy, Paul. A country at war ought to be able to find you something useful to do."

"A munitions factory? Down the mines? No, thank you."

"What about your degree?"

"Third-class arts with dishonor. Ten a penny."

"And a good brain."

"Tell that to the Marines—and the rest of them. They all turned me down."

"They turned *me* down, too."

"I'm not in your league up here." Curzon tapped his temple. "Anyway, nepotism always comes through in the end. The old man'll find me something." So leave me alone, said the look on his face.

Dinah saved him further cross-examination. She came bounding across to them, the spaniel making spring-heeled leaps at the stick she held just out of its reach. She was panting with the exertion; her cheeks glowed, her eyes sparkled. How quickly children forget. The thought threw up an image of Kurt in his mind's eye, earnest and proud at the breakfast table in the Dortmunderstrasse. Had Kurt forgotten too?

"I'll have to go now." Dinah knelt to embrace the panting dog. "You don't have to come, though."

"Of course we'll come." Curzon levered up against the elm, but Dinah disengaged the dog and thrust Paul back.

"No reason for you to waste a nice morning. I want to see how the mutton's doing, that's all. And I've got potatoes to peel. Go and have your pints and"—she wagged a maternal finger—"be home at one o'clock or I'll throw it away."

When she'd gone Curzon said casually, "Do you think she'll manage?" and Price knew he'd guessed.

"Lunch?" he asked evasively.

"All of it. Cooking, cleaning, shopping. *And* school."

"We'll manage."

"It's damned hard on her."

"She's got guts."

"She's also got you."

Price chuckled, relieved at the chance to change the topic. "And you."

"Me?"

"She's got a crush on you, man. Stands out a mile." He laughed at the young man's discomfort. "It must be your sports car."

Curzon wrapped his arms round his knees in unconscious defense of his innocence. "I wish there was something I could do."

"Marry the girl, my boy." Price slapped him heartily on

the shoulder and got to his feet, amused at his own joke. "But get yourself a decent job first or I'll turn you down."

As they started back toward the park gates and their conventional watering hole, the King and Clown, three minute specks drew fluffy white vapor trails across the blue sky. Price made a binocular of cupped hands to watch them.

"Ours," said Curzon.

And the word, a cliché from the lexicon of English war, struck a chord. The Shining Day. It was to have been yesterday. The hour of Ritter's triumph; the Wehrmacht goose-stepping through the streets of London; his own message piping across the Channel to the Fuehrer himself. He saw the funny side of it in spite of himself and began to laugh. Curzon stared at him sharply.

"What's so funny?"

Price threw an arm round his shoulder. "Oh, nothing. Just something I forgot to remember."

MAY 7, 1940

Desmond Morton made a lightning survey of the room as he hung up his hat and coat, on the lookout for changes, the new man's stamp on the late incumbent's monkish style. It was his first visit to the Buildings since Hugh Sinclair's death and Menzies' appointment as his successor. He was disappointed; only the desk furniture was different.

He sank into a chair. "Sorry I'm late. I stayed on at the House for the Norway debate."

Menzies grunted, pretending absorption in the spill of paperwork in front of him. He wanted no part of the Norway fiasco. The German invasion force that had taken Denmark in a day only a month ago was presently engaged in driving the British-French expeditionary force into the sea near Trondheim. The planners, if no one else, had already conceded defeat. When he was satisfied Morton had nothing more to say on the subject, he looked up. "What can I do for you?"

"Your review of the Price situation." Morton tapped his briefcase. "I've read it. Not exactly sparkling with optimism."

"We *all* accepted from the start, didn't we, that Price was useful to us only if he was working for Hamburg. They put him to bed. Short of cutting our losses and arresting him, there's nothing to be done till Hamburg reactivates him. Or do you disagree?"

Morton sidestepped the question. "And there's no sign of their teeing him up again?"

"None."

"He's made no attempt to transmit?"

"You've read the report."

The visitor nodded moodily. "I blame Sinclair, not to speak ill of the dead. Lived in a fool's paradise as far as Price was concerned. I shouldn't be surprised if we've thrown the whole damn game away."

"We've thrown nothing away. We never had that initiative."

"Point." Morton gazed at his image in the reflecting glass of a watercolor seascape behind the desk. "You make a big thing about Pepper's role in the report. May I ask why?"

"He's out of his depth." Menzies' nose wrinkled perceptibly. "And I can't stand queers."

"I wouldn't have thought his—predilections mattered a tuppenny-ha'penny damn."

"He's closer to Price than anyone." He foresaw defeat on that score and switched direction. "Pepper's taking his role a damned sight too seriously. He's there to make sure Price has access to the material we want him to see. That's all. His department was created for that sole reason. So what the hell does he think he's doing squirreling away on pet research projects of his own."

"Oh, come; they're quite harmless. And he has to put up some kind of show, surely. Until Price comes back into play, the unit's a nonstarter. Pepper's job is to convince the fellow he's involved in a going concern. Top secret, Cabinet blessing, all the rest. A research team is bound to research." He lit a fat Greys from a slim gold cigarette case.

Menzies plumped forward on his arms. "He's playing with fire. He's opening channels of communication all over Whitehall, calling in background papers—Air, Navy, Army, Supply." He set his mouth in an accusing line. "I'm told he's getting support for it, too, not a million miles from your desk."

"He's simply the handle on the jug, you know that."

"I'd prefer a stronger handle."

"Immaterial, surely, till we have Price functioning again? You've got him under surveillance."

"That's not the point."

Morton waived the issue with a languid hand. "Has he done anything to alarm you?"

"Not yet."

"No deviations from established habits?"

Menzies' lip curled. "What does that mean? Precisely."

"Is he settled? Confident? Happy?" He showed his teeth. "Happy in his work?"

"He keeps a low profile. I don't live in his head."

Morton considered the luminous tip of his cigarette at some length. "I hear he's having squaw trouble."

"So I gather."

"Not in your report." The cigarette came upright in his fingertips in mild admonishment.

"Irrelevant."

"Hmm. First the stepson, now the wife. You wouldn't be amused, I dare say, if he went to pieces over a woman."

"That's Curzon's pigeon."

"Ah yes, Curzon." Morton brightened. "Fact is, we were talking about him before the debate this evening."

Menzies' flat gray stare made it clear he had no intention of asking who "we" were.

"You rate him pretty highly, I understand?"

"Yes."

"Plans for him, have you?"

"He's got his hands full with the Price project. He's still officially overall controller."

"You think he could broaden his horizons give the opportunity?"

"Perhaps. What do you have in mind?"

Morton looked hurt. "Oh, just thinking out loud. Looking ahead, preparing for eventualities. If Chamberlain were to lose a vote of confidence over Norway—could happen, you know— the whole intelligence area would be due for a shake-up."

"Is there a time scale to this—scenario?"

"Oh, no. Not really. Depends."

"On Winston?"

Morton flashed a brilliant smile. "On the prime minister, I'd say, wouldn't you? Whoever he is on the day."

MAY 10, 1940

Curzon shaved and showered in an alcoholic daze and, to avoid the mental effort of making unnecessary decisions, pulled on the clothes he had kicked off the night before. He tied his tie, ran a brush through his hair, and caught the girl's reflection in the wardrobe mirror.

He went over to the bed and shook her. "Hey. *Hey!*" He'd forgotten her name—if she'd ever parted with it, which seemed unlikely. The party where he'd met her, at Harry Devlin's flat in Mount Street, was a twice-monthly phenomenon, specifically designed for Toms on London detachment.

The girl came to, gin-pained green eyes surfacing through a cobweb of honey-blond hair. "What?"

"Come on. Get up. I've got to leave. Now."

"Oh-God-I-feel-terrible." She sank back on the pillow. He grabbed her arm and hauled her into a sitting position. For a moment she sat still, in shock, then she lunged down and clamped her teeth on his hand.

"Damn you!" He sucked at the four scarlet indentations in his skin.

She yawned and looked around. "Where's this?"

"Ebury Street. Now move, ducky. You've got ten minutes."

She was very thin, very pale, and very sure of herself. County stock, he remembered her saying. Shropshire. Harry liked to keep it in the family as far as he could: Foreign Office secretaries, Colonial Office PAs; the right type, hot-blooded and game for anything but guaranteed honorable. Legs open, mouths shut: you tend my itch, I'll tend yours, and a quiet St. John's Wood abortion thrown in if the cup runneth over.

"What time is it?" She stretched and he swore.

"Seventy thirty."

"Oh God!" She came off the bed like a scalded cat, grabbed his robe, and fled to the bathroom. The taps roared and he went into the sitting room to pace the floor.

147

Half an hour, Hancock had ordered on the phone. Why? *It doesn't matter why. Move!*

Loud splashing from the bathroom, an eruption as she launched herself from the water and hurried back to the bedroom. He watched her dressing; nothing sensual in it, pure mechanics. Harry's girls all dressed with the unhurried nerveless efficiency, as though they'd done time at the same finishing school.

Mrs. Silver, the housekeeper, was on hands and knees at the street door, scrubbing the already immaculate front step. "Had a nice time, dear?" she sung out amiably. No smutty implications intended; Mrs. Silver had few inhibitions and no subtlety. It came of being married to a milkman for thirty-three years, she said.

The girl waved down a taxi at the end of Ebury Street and slammed the door in his face in case he had ideas about climbing in beside her. She poked her head out of the window. "I'm Extension 171 at the War Office," she said yawning again. "You can ring if you like."

The cab shot into a break in the traffic and he set off at a brisk pace toward Buckingham Palace Road. Extension 171. He'd had less to remember a girl by after one of Harry Devlin's parties.

It was more than a domestic service flap, that much was obvious when Curzon came into Buckingham Palace Road. A company of battle-packed Guardsmen in tin hats scrunched out of Birdcage Walk on line for the palace gates; the pavements streamed with uniformed policemen in night capes; and as he turned into Buckingham Gate three staff Humbers roared by, bulging with brass hats. The Buildings wore a ruff of ministry cars at its curb and the entrance lobby overflowed. He waved his card at Trubshawe, the head keeper, and won a scowl as the old Marine tried to fend off half a dozen urgent callers in bowlers and black Burberrys.

He poked his head around Nick Hancock's door. Central Registry resembled a Whitehall dentist's waiting room. "Staff room!" Hancock bowled when he saw him. "And *wait!*" The horns of his mustache were fringed with creamy coffee and his glasses were pushed into his hair. One of the three phones on his desk trilled and he snatched it up, listened, groaned, and knuckled his forehead.

Curzon withdrew while he had the chance. He saw Heston at the window on the far landing and strolled over to meet him.

"Hey, Lachie."

The Scot beckoned, finger to his lips, and they pushed into the staff room. It was packed. Every field man on home strength was there, most of them unshaven.

"What the hell's going on?"

Heston leaned back against the door. He had a gleam in his eyes only marginally brighter than his whiskey-flamed nose. "We're away, laddie, that's what the fuck's going on." He seemed more than a little drunk.

"Away where?"

"Bluidy war. Stuffed the lot of 'em, the wee bastard has." Curzon clutched at his hair despairingly. *"Who?"*

"Jerry. They're running all over Holland and Belgium."

"When?"

"Early hours."

"What's the drill?"

Heston shut his red-rimmed eyes and blew steamy impatience through his nose. "God alone knows. Hancock's calling in the troops, that's all. Sit down and shut up—order of the day."

By midmorning the panic had cooled sufficiently for Nick Hancock to dispatch the assembled Toms in twos and threes to their flats to "pull yourselves together and dress like gentlemen." Curzon called Ginger Haddon from Ebury Street but the w/t man had nothing to report. Not a peep out of Price. It was beyond Curzon how any man could survive six months of grueling inactivity, as Haddon had done, and still remain sane.

He bought an *Evening News* on the corner of Elizabeth Street and topped up Heston's communiqué with the latest from the front. Two German Panzer divisions had breached the Albert Canal and were spilling onto the Belgian plain; mobile columns of the British Expeditionary Force and the French army were racing to cut them off. Meanwhile, von Rundstedt was rolling through Luxembourg toward France.

He had a mental picture of his father wrapped in his shawl and his cotton gloves, seething like a roman candle in his chair by the fire as he listened to the news on the wireless. They'd have to tie him down if the Germans ever reached the Channel coast.

The hardheads played gin rummy, the sophisticates whist and piquet, all afternoon. At seven o'clock, Hancock leaned in at the door and told them to push off. "Check the duty roster before you go. We're doubling up tonight. Everyone here tomorrow at eight sharp for reassignment, night watch included."

Curzon was the first to get to his feet but Hancock waved him down. "Not you. Menzies wants you. Wait for the call."

It came at ten thirty.

Menzies looked as if he had slept in his clothes for a week. "Are you up to date?"

"I've seen the papers."

"Churchill's prime minister."

Curzon wondered how he was expected to respond—even how he felt about it. He said nothing.

"Chamberlain broadcast a statement at nine o'clock. There'll be some reorganization over the next few weeks."

"Price?"

"Hamburg can't let him sleep any longer, not now. I've told Hancock to leave you out of his reassignment schedule." He grasped his jaw and sawed away at the stubble. "What's Price's status?"

Curzon shrugged. "Professionally—if he thinks of it that way—pretty good. Personally—I don't know. He needs people: me, the child, Pepper in a way. His wife . . . I think he's more worried than grief-stricken about her leaving."

"A threat to his cover?"

"Perhaps. He isn't talking about her."

"Where is the woman?"

Curzon stared at his feet. "She moves around."

"Explain that in English, do you mind?"

"She's clean. That's definite. We stayed with her from the day Price moved into the house up to the end of March. She doesn't have a fixed address at the moment."

Menzies cocked his head on one side; his eyes twinkled. "You mean she's living with other men."

Curzon colored richly. "I don't think you can call it living. Staying's nearer the mark. Ten days was the longest. With one of the clerks she works with at the university. His landlady turfed her out. There've been three or four others."

"But she's still working at Russell Square?"

"Yes."

"And you're absolutely convinced she's clean?"

"We run a random check every other week."

Menzies performed an introductory drumroll with his fingers, then stood up briskly. "Forget her. We've got enough work to do without trailing around after tarts. If Price hasn't recruited her she's of no possible interest to us." He rasped away again at the stubble on his jaw. "Stick with him. And keep your surveillance tight. He's about to become a very important man."

MAY 12, 1940

Alan Petrie pushed his mother away. "Look, will you stop it, for God's sake!"

She brushed his hands aside, went down on her knees in front of him, and took a needle and thread to the hanging button of his school mackintosh. "If you think I'm letting you go away like a throwout from the poorhouse you've got another think coming. Now stand still." She began to sew, clumsily, tongue in teeth.

He felt foolish and glanced out the window to reassure himself Don wasn't watching from the Whites' garden next door. Mummy's boy having his button sewn on, the day he joined the Navy!

"Oh, come on. I've only got ten minutes."

She'd been at it since Friday evening, packing and repackng his small suitcase, washing and ironing his clothes, cutting his fingernails, checking his documents. She'd come home unannounced on Friday afternoon expecting open arms and a fond son's gratitude. No explanation, of course. Well, he'd given her gratitude, all right. Enough to last her the duration.

"There." She got up with a look on her face that said, See how much I care, and he glanced out the window again. This time he saw Don in the next garden leaning on a rake beside his old man, sharp as a knife in his chief petty officer's uniform.

Alan went to check his case and when he straightened she grabbed him, arms round his neck, tears in her eyes. Bitch, he thought; turning it on to make yourself feel good.

"I've got to go." He felt ashamed when the words came out with a catch in them. She clung to him even tighter.

"Have you . . . got everything you need, darling?"

He couldn't bring himself to put his arm around her—but, yes, he had everything; up to here. More than he could ever forgive her for.

When he sat the Naval Cadetship Special Entry exam in January it had all seemed so simple. His brain, his efforts, his physique—they were the yardsticks by which the Navy would judge his right to cross the threshold of the Royal Naval College, Dartmouth; no one mentioned anything else. He had walked the written exam, scored 378 points out of a possible 400 at the committee interview, passed his medical board, produced his swimming certificate. Ideal executive officer material, the captain of the interview committee told him. A credit to your parents. Then they cut the ground from under his feet.

Pay as a cadet was a shilling a day plus messing allowance; not enough by a mile to survive at Dartmouth.

"The parent or guardian is required to make on behalf of the cadet a private allowance which will provide for all necessities incidental to his training (e.g., purchase of books, etc.). The sum required for the purpose is usually about £12 a term. Clothing, traveling expenses, and expenses on leave are not covered by his private allowance; any expenses for these items incurred at the College will also be claimed from the parent or guardian at the end of each term."

He'd explained it all to her but she was then in the throes of being a wife again, and it was like talking to a wall. When, later, the fights began and she went back to work, the truth came out. She couldn't find the money. The £6,000 his father had left her had gone; she couldn't remember how and where—it just went—and her wages wouldn't run to £12 a term.

Don White, the best mate he'd ever had, offered to chip in six of the twelve quid, the best he could manage on his pay, but when Alan telephoned the Civil Service Commission they told him it didn't matter where the money came from, the bill would be sent to the parents anyway. That was when she left home. He'd kept it to himself for days—worried sick—then, like a fool, he'd told Diny. She skipped off to Price straight away and blabbed it out. Price agreed to foot the bill, of course. That was bad enough, but when they sat down to work out how much he'd need, the rest came out: his allowance as a midshipman, £40 or so toward the cost of a uniform when he made acting sublieutenant, wardroom expenses. In the end, it toted up to a small fortune and he'd had to accept Price's bloody charity and pretend to be grateful. Every night since, he'd promised himself he'd make the bastard suffer for it. Today was the day.

She let him go, sponging her eyes with the tail of her apron; fussed with his tie, the lie of his collar; fiddled with his hair. "I wish you'd wait till Tom and Diny get back." As if she hadn't deliberately got them out of the house so she could play her broken-hearted mummy role in private.

"Don's coming to Waterloo with me."

"He's been a good friend to you." She gulped back her tears and turned away.

You wouldn't bloody think so if you knew what *he* knew, he rejoiced silently. Christ, you wouldn't.

They had no secrets, he and Don. Mates, brothers; all for one, Don said. Don had actually heard the screaming fit she put on that night back in February. Through the walls! There didn't seem any point in keeping him in the dark after that. Mates, said Don, stuck together—so they'd stuck together by going through her handbag and her letters whenever she came home to try to find out where she'd been. And who with. There's always a *who*, Don said. The searches were a waste of time, but Don wasn't the type to give up easily. He'd started chatting her up, very friendly. But there was no luck there, either. Still, he thought he was getting through, he said. *Getting through*. When he found out what was going on, Alan would be the first to know.

She came back from the kitchen with a packet of sandwiches and a bag of apples for the train. She looked as if she might pounce again, so he rapped hard on the window to attract Don's attention and held up his case. Don raised a thumb. A minute later he rang the bell and Alan shot to the front door.

"Fit, skipper?"

Don was all smiles and neat as a pin in his navy blue and gold and scarlet and his brass buttons. He was shorter than Alan and slimmer, but the uniform gave him height and more profile than Errol Flynn. Alan slipped down the steps to avert any possibility of a final doorstep hug, but his mother didn't notice; she was primping and preening like a schoolkid, her eyes on Don and his brass buttons. She was so absorbed she forgot to wave good-by until they were out of the gate.

At Waterloo station they shook hands and Don slung a brotherly arm around his shoulders. "Next time I see you, mate, I'll have to salute. Officer and gentleman, you'll be."

"Will you be staying on in London?"

"For the duration, I hope. I'm on Admiralty posting. Snuggest berth in the Navy, skipper."

"Well, keep an eye out for Diny when you're in Richmond, will you? Drop me a line to let me know she's all right."

Don gave his shoulder a squeeze. "Leave it to me. I'll keep an eye on both of 'em if you like. Your mum, too."

"Thanks."

Don offered to buy him a drink but he said no, he wanted to get a good seat on the train and settle down with his seamanship manual. The hint was taken. He watched his friend all the way to the exit and, when he'd gone, made a beeline for the row of phone booths near the ticket office. Right, you bastard.

"Richmond Police. Desk sergeant."

He'd practiced the call in his room several times, in a croaky voice with a touch of West Country accent, the only one he could do. "Are you the one I talk to about crimes?"

"You talk to me about anything, son." *Son!*

He dropped his voice to a hoarse whisper. "If you go to Middlemass House in Ellerker Gardens—"

"Ease up, there, son. Let's have your name and address first."

He pressed closer into the booth and spoke quickly. "There's a man living there—Middlemass House, Ellerker Gardens—he's German. Well, he was in Germany for years. He's up to something. A criminal. Look up in the loft, over his bedroom and I bet you'll find—"

"I can't register a complaint without a name and address,

boy, so why don't you tell me who you are and what you think this *man*—''

Alan dropped the phone on its cradle, his heart pounding violently. He backed away, his eye on the instrument. A great sensation of relief flooded over him. He'd done it! He made for the barrier, swinging his case, chock full of beans. When he reached the platform he began to whistle. "Who's sorry now?"

MAY 14, 1940

Tom Price negotiated the corner of Aldwych and Kingsway and slotted into the work-bound flood of clerks and shopgirls, moving as they moved, with a minimum of conscious effort, impervious to sight and sound. After four months of continuous commuting, the daily pilgrimage from Richmond to Southampton Row—one hour twenty-six minutes door to door—had nothing to offer the senses. Not even the sense of awareness. He'd given up spying on his fellow travelers after the first week, around about the time he became convinced none of them were spying on him.

One hundred and ninety-seven paces from the corner of Theobald's Road the double half-glass doors of the Pepperpot crouched under a gray overhang of Portland stone. Inside, Sergeant Cross sat at his scrubbed table and scanned Price's gray ministry pass minutely, rejecting physical evidence of identity as he rejected anything else that was not enshrined in Standing Orders. Into the lift—the stairs were closed to all personnel in the interests of security—and up to the third floor with the clank and moan of old machinery long past its prime. Turn right, twelve paces, turn left. "Dr. Thomas Price/Mr. Evans-Wyke" in tooled white Roman on a black plaque.

Coat and umbrella to the coatrack, Edwardian-severe behind the door. Briefcase to the hinged flap beside his desk. Pipe out, tobacco tin; scrape, clean, and refill the bowl. Light it. Walk to the window and check the clock suspended over Verney's cycle shop across the street. Eight fifty-five. Mr.

Evans-Wyke would appear precisely on the stroke of nine. Pepper arrived in his office next door just as the tea lady appeared. The routine was numbing—although, in truth, he appeared to be the only one to notice it. The English working animal gave him—or her—self unstintingly to habit and method; what was unnerving was a departure from them.

He brooded at the window. Eight fifty-seven. Four days since Hitler's lightning strike into the Low Countries and still no awakening call from Hamburg. Why? Because they'd abandoned him? Absurd. Because they didn't trust him professionally? There was something in that. They had no means of knowing what he'd achieved since their terminal transmission last September—all of *this*, a penetration deeper than any of them would have thought possible. Luck, of course. And to be fair to himself, his air of quiet dependability, on which Pepper now relied so heavily.

But it was a miracle the Pepperpot had ever come into being. The sobriquet, in honor of Pepper's bustling efficiency, had been bestowed on the house in Southampton Row even before they moved in. They first explored the four-story building in late October and by January had arranged government requisitioning and turned out its commercial tenants. The next stage was to have been a brisk conversion of the badly planned layout, but at that point there was a virulent outbreak of internecine warfare among Whitehall ministries also desperately in need of office space. A three-day conference of interested parties was convened, lines were drawn, bargains struck, and a communiqué was issued apportioning the Pepperpot floor-by-floor to as many claimant departments as could be squeezed in. Pepper drew the third. Honor was satisfied.

First priority, said Pepper, was a title. He created it himself: Central Government Research and Audit Service (Cabinet Office). Where initials were concerned, he explained, a banquet was preferable to a light snack. His next objective was to decide its function. (At no stage, Price was astounded to learn, was any pressure exerted on him to adapt to the requirements of higher authority; Pepper was regarded as a "brain-smith" and, as a First World War fringe-Intelligence veteran, eminently qualified to "fit in." That phrase again!)

It was his element. Since he believed no area was sacred, he marked the bounds of his empire with scant regard for the proprietorial rights of others. If he was intrigued by the possibilities of a line of inquiry, he manufactured "study lines" to justify wide-ranging demands for information—from Naval, Army, Air Intelligence, a whole bag of tight-lipped ministries, he didn't care. He was never rejected; Whitehall seemed to be awash with former colleagues and old students and, in the event of token opposition, he could always be relied upon to find a well-placed politician ready to exert some favorable influence.

The first CGRAS(CO) study lines were already in government circulation. They had been remarkably well received; Churchill had sent Pepper a personal note of congratulation on one and suggested two or three other areas worthy of his interest. They now had a secretary, Mrs. Plum, and four typists; a head of records, Archie Bassingthwaite, a former reader at the British Museum, and Price's personal assistant—

"Ah-hrum." Mr. Evans-Wyke presented himself as Verney's clock shivered to nine o'clock. "Good—ah—morning, Dr. Price." He doffed his bowler.

"Good morning, Mr. Evans-Wyke." A feudal litany, man and master, very English. Price moved to his desk and sat down, leaving the window free.

Mr. Evans-Wyke deposited briefcase, hat, umbrella, and coat, tested his punctuality against the silver watch in his waistcoat pocket and took up station. He spent much of his day at the window, elbow in hand, pouched jowl in palm, looking out at London but seeing only his beloved Eastbourne.

He'd retired there three years ago after thirty-nine years as a clerk in the Aliens Office, squandering his life away, according to his protector, Mrs. Plum, in tatty bachelorhood and a garret among the chimney pots of Fetter Lane. Retirement and Eastbourne; he lived for them both. He'd bought the bungalow of his dreams on the cliffs at the Beachy Head end of the town, he would tell you, painting pictures with his large knotted hands; quite lonely really. Walks with Pippin, his black scottie, mornings and evenings; gardening when he felt like it, fretwork to pass the time, a little painting—watercolor, not oils—and twice-weekly bridge afternoons with three fellow pensioners bungalowed nearby. The call to arms had genuinely shocked him and, although he returned to London because it was his duty, he was quite ill for a day or two.

Together—in body if not in mind—the four of them were now processing dozens of case papers a day, abstracting and summarizing information, composing analyses, making recommendations. Building a reputation.

"Morning all!" Mrs. Hemmings, daughter of dockland, came to the relief of the garrison in a clanking of tea urns and a crackling of waxed-paper-wrapped buns. CGRAS (CO) was officially cognizant of a new day.

Pepper reclined in his desk chair, sipping lemon tea and gazing, as was his habit, at the patch of damp which had stained a corner of his ceiling the color of burnt toast.

"It's all in our favor, my boy. Strike while the iron's hot, that's the rule. A few months from now every service'll have its own research branch. Trained academics, sharp as pins. So now's the time to act. Grab what we can. Agreed?"

"What do you have in mind?"

"Strategic forecasting, *that's* the future. A hard road, though. It'll put us in Intelligence country, and they'll yell like the dickens. Digging up their wicket, pinching their precious turf. Hard road."

It was to be *that* easy? He could sit at his desk, bombarded with classified information, and abstract at his leisure anything he judged worth transmitting to Hamburg? (If and when Hamburg had the fundamental commonsense to recall him.) And—equally unlikely—did Pepper really believe he could get away with such daylight robbery under the very nose of Whitehall's vested interests?

"They might easily finish *us* off first," he said cautiously.

"Nonsense. Keep 'em guessing; keep the devils arguing among themselves. Our best weapon, that. Winston's with us and we'll keep him. You can make a start on his review of aircraft production this week. Then there's the food supply project—Atlantic convoys and dock handling methods under fire; coastal defense systems and—"

"Philip, we've only got one pair of hands each."

"*Correct!* Told Winston so. He said we'll get more. Act One, we get rid of those blasted Ports and Harbors people downstairs and Archie can take over the whole floor. Records and Audit Control. I like the sound of it. We'll start today. Now." In his excitement, he bounced from his chair and came around the desk to Price's side. His small slightly damp hands locked on Price's lapels and fondled the fabric. Price felt a wave of revulsion. Pepper's compulsion to touch horrified him; the little man seemed to have no control over it or, worse, regarded their friendship as sufficient license to maul him at will. He didn't want to think about what it implied, but whenever those yellow potato-chip fingers reached for him he remembered what Sally Logan had said about Pepper on that first morning at Phillimore Gardens. *He's like a mother hen . . . old maidish.*

He said stiffly, "We'll need specialists, then."

"On tap, my boy." Pepper, to his vast relief, jittered away to glare amiably at the calendar pinned over his desk; a redhead in body-hugging black satin lounged suggestively over the month of May. "I'll take Whittingham from University College, I think. And Taylor-Morris." He rubbed his hands at the prospect. "Let Ballard pick the bones out of that."

The calendar appeared to remind him of something, and it was not to his liking. His pointed face nose-dived into acute melancholy. He returned to his chair. "Tom, I don't want you to think I'm interfering . . . ," The blush started from his throat and engulfed his whole face. "Your—ah—Mrs. Price. I hear it's not entirely . . . wholly . . . ah—satisfactory. Hmm?"

"You've talked to her?"

"Good Lord, no!" He recoiled in horror. "I met young Sally Logan the other day at UC; ran into her, d'you see. She's desperately unhappy for you. Of course, I didn't know what she was talking about. Felt I had to ask. She said one of her chums—mutual friend of your—ah—Mrs. Price—told her." He dipped his beak in the lemon tea to save further blushes. "Shouldn't be tittle-tattling like this. No excuse. Worse than a woman. But . . . well, damn it, I'm concerned for you, of course I am. My closest colleague, after all. Rely on you. If there's anything a friend can do . . ."

"I'm afraid, Philip—"

Pepper raised both hands in alarm. "No explanations, dear boy. Not one word." He fiddled with some paperwork on his desk but his leonine eyes fell longingly on Price's lapel. "I—ah—believe there are children."

"Alan's just started a naval officer cadetship. Dinah . . ." What could he say about Dinah? "Dinah's a very practical child."

"Bring her for tea one afternoon. What do you say? A Sunday. Do much on Sundays, do you?"

"Not much, no. That's kind of you, Philip. She'd like that."

The temptation was too great to resist. Pepper hoisted himself from his chair and slipped around the desk again, his little claws drawn irresistibly to Price's jacket.

"Count on me, d'you hear that? A young fellow needs an older man to talk to now and again. Think a lot of you, d'you see." His version of an avuncular smile of encouragement sent icy shivers down Price's spine. He leaned close. "We are friends, aren't we, Tom? I've always thought of us as . . . friends."

MAY 16, 1940

The champagne was warm and flat but Churchill offered no apology and Menzies pretended to enjoy it. Desmond Morton had wisely declined. He was lunching later in the City. The atmosphere in the basement room was oppressive; talk was the natural analgesic but none of them were anxious to begin.

Churchill lay poleaxed in his chair, arms close to his body, champagne glass sprouting like a funerary lily from his cupped hands. "I've had the security dogs yapping at my heels this morning, Menzies. They want your blood. Vernon Kell came to see me himself."

Menzies' burgeoning sneer vanished abruptly. Sir Vernon Kell, founder and head of MI5, was the least public of a solitary breed and celebrated for his pathological mistrust of politicians at all levels. It was no secret that Churchill regarded him as too old to function efficiently on a wartime footing—"a generation out of his time," were his words— nor that he was taking soundings in pursuit of a successor, but Kell, the snooper-extraordinary, would be the last to hear of it. He shunned the watering holes of interservice society, despised Whitehall fraternizing, and refused to pander to the committee system. In the one area where counterespionage was most vital to a secret servant—his own professional welfare—Vernon Kell was wholly vulnerable.

"Are the complaints for general circulation?"

"For your ears, yes." The prime minister sat up stiffly. "The police station at Richmond received a call—public telephone—last Sunday afternoon. Anonymous young man; silly accent, probably assumed. He was offering information about a criminal, he said. A German living at Middlemass House in Ellerker Gardens."

Menzies' face was set hard, smothering emotion. Morton selected a cigarette from his case with great care.

"The desk sergeant called the CID superintendent. They decided the wisest course was to inform Special Branch. Before the afternoon was out, Five were involved. They put a wireless detection van in the street and began to question the neighbors."

"Dear God." Menzies' face drained of color.

"Cannily, Menzies. They're not fools. Next day, Kell personally sent what he calls a 'Peter man' to the house. The caller told the police to look in the loft so that's what he did. They discovered Price's wireless set and the rest of the nonsense. In the early hours of Tuesday morning, I'm afraid, they also located your listening post."

"Damn them! If Kell's—"

"Kell's done nothing. Touched nothing. That's why he came directly to me."

"Looking for blood," Menzies said heavily. Six's stamping ground began at Calais; Five owned Britain. The gray areas in between, the overlaps, had been bones of contention since Mansfield Cumming, the original "C," dragged the Secret Service into the world in 1909. They had referred to each other, Five and Six, Kell and Cumming, as the Competition. The term was not designed to convey comradeship and affection.

Churchill's chins made a four-tiered nest on his shirt collar. "Your man Haddon's under confinement. Five found your equipment, of course; Haddon's files, interoffice memoranda, his log, the whole damn shooting match. Kell's sitting on it."

"The devil he is!"

"Wait!" Churchill waved Menzies back into his chair. "He's within his rights. We both know that and so does he."

"You told him about your"—Menzies eased out the word carefully—"personal interest?"

"Of course not." Two tiny scarlet rosettes grew on the old man's cheeks. "I must preserve my neutrality. I don't have to explain why, do I?"

"No, sir."

Desmond Morton intervened diplomatically. "Kell's in a corner, Menzies, you can see that, can't you? He had to make a stand, nothing else for it. It's his territory."

Churchill silenced him. "Kell wants an unqualified guarantee, my personal guarantee, in writing, that the Price operation will be transferred to his responsibility at once."

Menzies leaned forward, scenting more. "And?"

"*Your* signed undertaking that Six relinquishes any claims, now and in the future, to all enemy infiltration activity in this country."

"I'll see him in hell first," Menzies said mildly.

"You won't!" Churchill poured more of the tepid champagne but didn't drink. "We can't oppose him on this. We'd look damn fools."

Morton gasped the nettle dutifully. "Kell's been playing back a German double since 1938 and running a wireless link since early last year. B1a section have three agents in play as of now. All Hamburg; all Ritter recruits."

"And he's never seen fit to pass that on to JIC?" Menzies scowled.

"He applied the same criteria you did."

"*We* did."

"As you wish."

"And you expect me to hand over Price—and presumably Haddon as well—without a whimper?" He was careful to address himself directly to Morton.

"In a nutshell—"

"No."

Morton went fishing for help in Churchill's direction but the bait lay untouched. "No choice, old chap. Kell says the Price play is a scandal; no proper control, no backup, no cutout, no safeguards—his words, Menzies, not mine. He claims it could blow his own operations sky high. He's got a point."

"Is this an order, Prime Minister?" Menzies switched his attack.

"It's a position I have to accept." Churchill's glare was intractable.

"Then I'll need some guarantees, myself."

"And they are?"

"One, Haddon is detached to Five but remains on my strength. Two, Five makes available to me personally all files on their double agents. Three, Six retains a full share in all product deriving from Price. Four, full discussion on all material played back to Hamburg."

"And Five actively run Price? No other strings attached?" Morton, eyebrows arched expectantly.

"When Hamburg reactivates him—not before."

"And that's all." Hopefully.

"No. That's not all. I want Curzon appointed to a supervisory role, giving him access to Five's handling of Price and their existing doubles. He'll be responsible directly to me."

There was a long silence. From upstairs came the faint clack of typewriters, the jangling of telephones. Churchill stirred, nodded his head reluctantly.

"Very well. That's agreed. Kell will have to accept those conditions." He fixed Menzies with a stony frown. "And you'll be *bound* by them."

MAY 18, 1940

The taxi reversed into a gap between two Black Marias and Curzon pressed the night bell. It was raining lightly, the misty drizzle honest men associate with prisons and dawn executions; he pulled up the collar of his jacket and cursed himself for forgetting his coat. Menzies had said nothing about one A.M. phone calls, tricked-out taxis, and flying visits to jail when he'd outlined Curzon's new role. He'd made it sound sybaritically high-powered, a gift; scented secretaries and a carpeted office, exhausting mornings reading reports and protracted lunches. The office turned out to be a fifth-floor cell in Holborn (no lift, no carpets, and a sixty-year-old stenographer). He had yet to taste the power.

He rang the bell again and a voice behind the wicket gate growled, "Gimme a bloody minute, will yer!"

The gate opened and he stepped through.

"In 'ere."

Curzon came into the light of the gatehouse lodge. Stone floor, walls, and ceiling, two bare pine trestles, a pair of folding wood chairs. Welcome to Wandsworth written all over it. The big man in the duffel coat pushed himself off the far table. "I'm Frank Loughran. You're Curzon?"

They shook hands, matching grips like playground gladiators. Loughran won easily. He had more muscle in his fist than Joe Louis.

"What's the flap?" Curzon turned down his collar and dabbed at the rain on his face.

"No flap. Happens all the time. You'll get used to it." Loughran reached past Curzon and pushed the door shut. "One or two things to get straight in your mind before we go up. Nothing you hear is for circulation, verbal or written. I write the report when I'm good and ready and your people get a copy. Next: you take a back seat. Sit in a corner and keep your mouth shut. You're here because you have to be, not because I think it's a good idea. Last thing: no interruptions, no matter how important you think they are. Got that?"

"Your hospitality is truly overwhelming."

Loughran stepped back a pace and measured Curzon from head to toe, the pro's insolent assessment. He nodded slowly. "Let's go."

He opened the door and led the way to a flight of steps. There was running water on the great stone blocks of the walls. Hell on earth, Curzon thought fleetingly.

The duty officer pushed Arthur Owens into the room and closed the door at his back.

"Take a seat, Owens. There, where I can see you."

The man behind the desk was no stranger to Owens, who hobbled to the chair quickly, angling himself forward on the seat to ease his misshapen back. He had a peculiar deformity of the spine that not only rounded his shoulders but also forced one below the level of the other. He would have been small even if he could have stood upright like a normal man, but his head was grossly out of proportion to the rest of him, long as an African war mask, unbalanced, unfinished.

"Cigarette?" Black-and-white held out a leather case and Owens took two of the fat cigarettes greedily. One behind his ear, one in his mouth, hands shaking.

Black-and-white leaned across the desk with a match and Owens sucked smoke deep into his chest to calm himself. They'd given him another sedative last night and when the guard came to shake him awake he'd gone berserk, still in the nightmare. Black-and-white was no nightmare though and— His eye caught the second man in the dark by the window. Big. Red hair. New. Trouble. He sucked again at the fag and watched Black-and-white put the leather case back in his inner pocket. The bastard saw him and grinned like a death's head, but Owens didn't fall for it. Black-and-white; black suit, white shirt, black tie, white face, white hair. Black bloody heart.

"Sorry I had to get you up. You've had a caller."

Caller? A sensation like a quart of Andrews Liver Salts going off in his belly. "What caller?"

Black-and-white showed his teeth. "Your friend from Hamburg-Wohldorf. Major Ritter."

"Ah." He inhaled a great gush of smoke and it exploded in his head. For a moment he couldn't see for tears. Bastard. *Bastard*!

"Can't disappoint him, can we?"

"How'd you mean?" God, not Ritter! Not again.

"You remember what 'qrv' means?"

"Stand by. Yes, stand by."

"That's what he sent an hour and forty minutes ago. He's expecting you to respond at two A.M. I think you should, don't you?"

"Look . . ." He didn't know how to go on. "You said last time'd be the—what d'you call—last. You said—"

"There aren't any *last* times, Owens. Just next time; always next time. Remember what I told you. If you cooperate, you live. If you don't, I wash my hands of you."

"You said—"

"And if I wash my hands of you, they'll hang you. By the neck." He made a twisting motion with his hands and darted a glance at the man in the darkness by the window. Owens stared at the newcomer, eyes wide. Weeping Jesus! Him?

"So what do you say?"

Canada. God Almighty, he should have stayed in Canada.

"I can't—what d'you call—operate that wireless anymore. Look!" He held up his shaking hands. The cigarette sent a smoky squirl wriggling to the ceiling. "I haven't got the touch. I'm—"

"Enough." Black-and-white pressed a key on the squawk box and a connecting door opened from the anteroom: two men in shirt sleeves, the Wehrmacht set on the secretary's desk, a spare set of headphones. "Now then—" Black-and-white sprang from his chair with bullish briskness. "They'll make your call sign. What is it again?"

"Johnny," he said. Ritter, the bastard! "I shall call you Johnny," he'd said, that first time in Rotterdam.

"Right. You'll respond. 'Johnny to Hotbed, proceed.' One of my men will be listening on a Y-link—know what that is? Good. He'll take Hamburg's send and so will you. The other chap will decode for you. Then I'll tell you how to respond. Got it?"

"Suppose he asks me where I—what-d'you-call—where I am?"

Black-and-white came round the desk and grabbed a handful of Owens's gray tunic in his cruel hand, lifting him off the chair. "He knows where you are, you clown. At home. In Hampstead. Where you ought to be."

They went into the anteroom and Black-and-white shoved him into a chair in front of the key. The young one with the red hair came to stand at the door, staring in, enjoying it; you could see it in his face. Bastard! Then they waited, headphones on. When it came over he nearly fell off his chair.

"Johnny from Hotbed. Johnny from Hotbed. Respond."

The swine on the Y-link took like a demon, the other one decoding over his shoulder. He made his acknowledgment and, when he finished, Black-and-white struck his hand from the key and whipped the cigarette from his fingers.

"Rantzau here and greetings," beeped Hamburg.

"What do I—?" Owens began.

"Ritter," said Black-and-white and they all nodded at each other. "Make 'Greetings and await instructions,' " said Black-and-white.

He obeyed, but not very well. The man on the Y-link gave him a black look, but there was no time for recriminations; the Hamburg operator was going like a train. "Urgent you travel Lisbon earliest. Signify agreement."

"Bloody Christ!" He couldn't help himself. He stared up at Black-and-white and got that death's head smirk right back.

"Make 'Severe restrictions civilian travel here. Need cash.' "

"Cash available now. Consult Wahlstrep Swedish Embassy London all arrangements," flashed the Hamburg operator.

"Make 'Will consult Wahlstrep immediately. When Lisbon?' "

Owens couldn't believe his ears. "I can't go to bloody—"

Hamburg came back at once. "One week today latest. Contact Wahlstrep immediate and confirm flight plans. Hotbed usual schedule soonest."

Black-and-white grabbed a fistful of his shoulder flesh. "What does he mean usual schedule?"

"First available odd date. Eleven thirty at night. But—"

"Right. Confirm and sign off."

When they returned to the other room Owens collapsed, weak at the knees, head spinning sick as a dog. He gazed up at Black-and-white pleadingly. "That was just play acting, that there what-d'you-call, hey? Having him on."

"*That there* was an official invitation."

"Bloody Lisbon!"

"Bloody Lisbon. You'll love it."

"I won't go." Stuff 'em. What could they do—send him by post?

Black-and-white wove fingers into a cat's cradle, turned them inside out and cracked the knuckles. "Wrong attitude, Owens. If I say you go, you go."

"The bastards'll kill me!"

"Oh, I shouldn't think so."

"I don't! I can't! I'm not a—what-d'you-call—well man. I'll go to pieces if he—God Almighty, I'm past it; I told you all along."

Black-and-white fingered another cigarette from his case and flipped it into Owens's lap. "What you've done all along is lie your filthy Welsh head off. To me *and* Hamburg. Right? So what you're going to do is carry on lying—to him. In Lisbon, if necessary. Get the drift, chummy?"

Owens cupped his hands to his face and felt the tears hot on his palms. Bastards! No way out. Knew the minute he came through the door. No way out—unless . . . He let his hands fall.

"Suppose I don't come back?"

Black-and-white shook his head slowly. "Then I'd have to let Hamburg know what you've been up to since last summer, wouldn't I? I'd have to be honest. What you've done for us. How well you've cooperated." His big torturer's hands took the cigarette from his mouth and he blew a stream of smoke that bridged the desk and engulfed Owen's head. "I think Ritter'd kill you more slowly than I would. Don't you?"

Loughran had insisted on walking Owens back to his cell with the guard and Curzon tagged along. The Welshman was kept in solitary at the end of a basement tunnel echoing with captive snores. The stench of sweating bodies and urine lingered there, trapped like the inmates' dreams in the fabric of the stone. It was hard not to feel sorry for the poor devil.

Curzon opened the taxi window as they set off through the rain toward Westminster. Loughran was lighting another cigarette with steady fingers. He displayed no feelings, no tiredness. Curzon gulped gratefully at the air. "Now, what was all that about?"

"That was Snow."

"Who?"

"Real name, Arthur Owens. German work name, Johnny. Our code name, Snow."

"A double?"

"He came our way in 1936. He'd emigrated to Canada as a youngster, came back to England and got a job with a company on Admiralty contract work. It took him to Germany now and again. At that stage he was on the up-and-up. But people like Owens love playing games. It's a drug; worse than smoking. He began picking up odd bits and pieces of information, technical stuff, German naval developments. Nothing much, but he passed them on to Admiralty. Gave him a thrill. In '37, DNI gave us the tip-off he was active and we started intercepting his mail to Hamburg. Little swine was selling low-grade product to the Abwehr. Our practice in Five"—he sniffed, implying that Six had a lot to learn—"is to hold back on a Peeping Tom initially. See what he's made of. It paid off in Owen's case. He came to us one day and poured his lying little heart out. On his last trip to Rotterdam, he'd been recruited by the Abwehr, he said. Now he'd got cold feet and, please, could he drop out?"

"You said no."

"We told him it was his funeral," Loughran said casually.
"We didn't push him. Just let him float, kept him under
surveillance. Early in '39, Hamburg sent him a transmitter,
courtesy of his controller, Major Nikolaus Ritter."

"You mean he'd gone back to working for them?"

"Sure he had. Couldn't stay out of it. Anyway, that August
he hopped off to Hamburg. When he got back in
September, he called Special Branch for a meeting, thinking
he was still baby blue eyes and worth his weight in gold. It
didn't occur to him that the fact war had been declared made
a difference. We arrested him under Defense Regulation 18B
and filed him in Wandsworth—with his transmitter, of course.
We even had to teach him how to use it. Ritter assumed he'd
know. After that, they began regular communications. Usual
in-place stuff, weather reports; nothing big. Then Ritter called
him to Rotterdam for a face-to-face and we flew him out."

"He didn't run?"

"The trick is to make them too bloody scared to run. He
came back under his own steam with an order from Ritter to
establish lines to the Welsh Nationalist Army. Ritter had an
idea the Welsh would make ideal saboteurs."

"And you let him do it?"

"With help. We found a retired police inspector in
Swansea—George Williams. George made contact through
Owens's drop and offered his services as a link man."

"Owens didn't believe that?"

"In Wandsworth, you believe what you're told to believe.
More important, Ritter believed. He told Owens to bring
Williams out to Rotterdam so he could look him over. Loved
George on sight, old Nik. He gave Owens a London-based
German agent to contact when he got home and the name of
his paymaster, a woman living in Bournemouth. A month
later, the two of them saw Ritter again, in Antwerp this time.
George got a little training in fire bombing, and a cover
address in Brussels. After that, we fed Owens back in again
several times—once with an agent we recruited for him here.
We started with Owens and ended up with four doubles in
hand, all playing back to Ritter."

"Nice going."

The taxi swung onto Westminster Bridge and Big Ben

chimed the quarter hour: four fifteen. Loughran stuck his long legs up on the drop seat.

"No bad feelings? About Price, I mean."

"Ruffled feathers, that's all. You're the experts."

Loughran's granite inscrutability softened a little in the gray half-light. "We're ready to set up a briefing session for you—any time you want. You'll need it. How we run the links, cross-pollination between agents, control techniques, playback material, security clearance."

"What about Ginger Haddon?"

Loughran chuckled. "We're breaking him in. Absolute bloody genius as a w/t man, but a pain in the ass till we told him what was what." He tapped on the intercommunicating window as the cab pulled into Birdcage Walk and the driver stopped at the narrow entrance to Queen Anne's Gate. Loughran got out, stood at the door. "Let me know when you want to get started."

"Wait a sec." Curzon held back the door. "What happens to Owens?"

The big square white face went blank. Noncommittal shrug. "When I know who Wahlstrep is and we've walked round him a couple of times . . ." He paused; a glint of teeth. "Who knows?"

He slammed the door and winked at the driver. "Don't overtip him," he said softly.

JULY 7, 1940

"Darling, if you want to sit down, sit down. If you want to walk, go outside where it'll do you some good."

Eleanora Curzon looked over her spectacles at her son and, from his vantage point behind the Bart's chair, Paul gestured helplessly at his father who sat hunched over *The Times*. Please—don't get him going again, his expression said.

She smiled and went back to her sewing, Curzon studied her face anxiously and, as always, found in it a deeper reflection of his own. The eyes were greener, the hair more fiery—Irish red, his father had called it in the days when he was still conscious of her as a woman—but the lines bit deep, and pain, the old enemy, had gouged hollows in her temples and cheeks, discolored the skin around her mouth. Age was doing the rest—age and the Bart and his own damned selfishness.

"Go on, darling. Take the dogs. You'll find—"

Sir Martin dropped his paper in a fit of combustive pique. "For God's sake, Ellie, will you stop fussing over him. If he wants to go out—"

"I'm waiting for Rob," Curzon said defensively.

He turned his back on them, and Sir Martin thrashed his paper into shape and went on with his reading. Curzon crossed to one of the long Georgian windows and looked out across the paddock. A line of elms, old as the Conquest, stood like crooked sentries on the far side, and through their lower branches rose the square flint Norman tower of Great Westring Church. On all sides, actually farther than the eye could see except from the upper branches of the tallest elm, Great Westring Hall's quartered, stripped, and triangulated fields spread like a patchwork quilt around the old house: wheat and barley, stubbly-green potatoes, mangolds and rutabaga, velvety pasture and parkland; and, to the northeast of Holt, acres of breck and scrub and woodland. Rob's country now; passive and malleable and rich, impervious to war.

Still no sign of Rob. He'd gone to Norwich market yesterday, long before Curzon left London, and stayed overnight at the Maid's Head to have dinner with some Ministry of Agriculture pundit. Curzon had left a message with the hotel receptionist but Rob hadn't called back. He was a fool to have come. He caught a reflection of the fire in the windowpane and the Bart's profile bent over his paper. Thank God the weekend was nearly over.

The old man, sensing vibrations, stopped reading and peered at him. "Why d'you want to see Rob?"

"I haven't seen him since—"

"I know when you last saw him—*and* what happened. What makes you think he'd want to see *you*? He can do without your help, and he'll survive without your apologies. So will I."

Lady Curzon's stare warned: Don't excite him, humor him.

"I'd like to see him, anyway," he said lamely.

"Tell him how brave you are, is that it? Your fine new job.
That why you want to see him?"

"No."

"No? Any *other* reason for coming home after a whole
year without so much as a letter?"

"Martin!" Eleanora Curzon spoke sharply but without
menace.

"Martin *what*?"

"Ring for tea." She went back to her knitting.

"Damn tea!"

Curzon touched the bell over the mantel. She'd saved
him—both of them—from disaster a dozen times since he
stepped over the threshold yesterday, placating the father,
protecting the son. Twice Curzon had demanded to know
what was wrong with her; why the pains, the shortness of
breath, the fainting spells that had brought old Dr. Donohue
racing out from town and, on two occasions, a consultant
from Norwich; and twice she'd insisted it was no more than
could be expected of old age, thin blood, and a lifetime of
camp following. But he knew her too well. She had the true
Irishwoman's philosophy: when the truth hurts the people you
love, it's no longer truth, so hide it. Rob would know, which
was why Curzon wanted to see him.

"Milady?"

Cooper had opened the door and worked himself into the
room without a sound, butler by virtue of his tailcoat and
black tie but in every other respect, the batman who had
survived twenty-two years of the Bart's whips and scorns.

"Tea, please, Cooper."

"Milady." He paused, swiveling without apparent movement to face Curzon. "There's a telephone call for you, Mr.
Paul. In the 'all, sir."

"Hah!" The Bart exploded like a mortar bomb. "Tipped
somone in advance to get you off the hook, did you? Might
have known it. Who is it, Cooper?"

"The gent didn't say, sir. London, he said."

Sir Martin wrenched round in his chair and stabbed a
white-gloved finger at his wife. "What did I tell you! Got it
all sewn up now, you see. Telephones, everything! War
work, he tells us; *war work*. Sitting behind a bloody desk in a
bucketshop full of pansies."

"Darling, you know he tried to join up. You know—"

"So he *says*. We've only got his word for it, haven't we?
Spends a whole year selling liquor to profiteers—young men
dying all over Europe—and when the real fighting starts he
gets some monkey of a quack to tell him he's got flat feet.
I've never heard such shameful preposterous gutlessness in
my life. Did he come to me? No, of course he bloody well
didn't. Might have got him into uniform, mightn't I? Last
thing he wanted. Ministry of Gutless Supply! That's his kind of
war. Excused boots, excused parades, excused *guts*. God help
the country if the whole damned generation's like him, that's
all I can say. Big new job. *Important war work*. A *clerk* at
the Ministry of Supply." He flung himself back into the
depths of his chair and glared at Cooper. "What the hell are
you standing there for, you fool?"

"The phone, sir. For Mr. Paul," Cooper droned impassively.

Sir Martin buried himself in his paper. "Let him take it, if
he needs to keep up the pretense. And you can get out."

Lady Curzon motioned her son to the door.

"Not breaking anything up, am I?" Frank Loughran drawled
from the other end.

"No, it's all right. What's up?"

"I had no idea how important you were nowadays. I'd
have started without you but they wouldn't let me. Wait for
Curzon, they said. If it's really inconvenient, maybe they'll
let me come up to the Hall. Big is it, the Hall?"

"Vast. But you wouldn't pass the blood test at the gate.
Come on, what is it?"

"Our chum's back from his holiday. Brimming over with
it."

Arthur Owens. Well, that would save a few faces.

The Lisbon gambit had been cleared after a great deal of
soul searching and Owens had duly made contact with
Wahlstrep, a count of dubious German-Scandinavian origin
who appeared on the Swedish Embassy list as a third secretary.
Four weeks later, Wahlstrep produced money, tickets, and a
Swedish diplomatic passport. Owens flew out on June 17
under SIS cover. As of Friday, he had still been sitting in a
grubby pensione waiting for Ritter to materialize. No one,
including Menzies, thought he would.

"He's back in London?"

"Safe and sound. Brown as a berry. He's brought back presents for everyone. You'll be tickled to death with yours."

He couldn't ask. "I'm on my way. Where will you be?"

"Oh, the same place. The Big Hall."

Curzon put down the phone and squared his shoulders. The Bart wouldn't let him leave without a final round.

JULY 8, 1940

They had been over it twice, but Menzies was like a whippet with a cornered hare. He moved restlessly around the room and finally came to a halt at the window which gave him his favorite view onto the pavements fronting the underground station.

"Ritter actually ordered him to meet Price face to face?"

"Yes, sir."

"And Owens is to set up the meeting by hand-delivered letter."

"Yes."

Menzies shook his head. "I don't believe it."

"Owens is in no position to lie. He says he tried to persuade Ritter to keep him out of it and I'm sure he did. He was sweating blood waiting for Ritter to make contact. He thought he was being staked out for a kill."

"Then Ritter appears, talks to him *once*—for two hours—gives him £10,000 support cash and *written* instructions on sabotage targets for his Welsh Nationalist group."

"On microdot, yes."

"And at the end, in the last five minutes—almost casually—he says . . . what were the words again?"

Curzon sighed. " 'You are not alone in London. There is a man. Dr. Thomas Price . . .' "

"He said the name: Dr. Thomas Price?"

"Yes. He gave the Richmond address and told Owens to hand deliver a message telling Price to meet him at Brompton Oratory, St. Joseph's Chapel, a three forty-five on the afternoon of July 12."

"This Friday?"

"Yes."

"And Price is expected to think it's genuine because . . ." Menzies snapped his fingers impatiently.

"The bait line is 'Remember Father's farewell: Where I am, Germany is.' "

"What does it mean?"

"We don't know."

Menzies sank down on the window seat. "And then?"

"Owens's orders are to await key calls from Hamburg on the agreed schedule—that's eleven thirty P.M. on odd dates—beginning August 15."

"And Price . . ."

"Begins his regular transmission again the night before, August 14."

"And the rider to that was . . . ?"

"The Shining Day."

"Just that?"

"Just the Shining Day. GC and CS say it's arbitrary codelining, probably an invasion tag or a prearranged reference to Price's specific role in it."

Menzies shook his head. "Their invasion's code-named Operation Sea Lion. We know that. What does Five propose?"

"The consensus is wait and see. But if Ritter feeds him specific strategic questions on August 14, they want him pulled out of circulation. They won't play him under your present system."

"Kill him off as a source, in other words?"

"That would be the effect. I suppose in their opinion, it's too late to turn him."

Menzies got to his feet and paced off again around the room. He stopped directly behind Curzon's chair.

"Listen to me. Price is still the pivotal factor in Hamburg's plan. I know it. I believe Ritter intends using him in the next few months in preparation for Sea Lion. I'm convinced that's why they sent him here—to develop high-grade source material from the inside. People"—he waved his hand derisively, as if Vernon Kell were standing at his shoulder—"tend to forget that. He's not a tame playback pawn like the rest. A child of three could appreciate why Hamburg put him to bed last autumn. He'd done everything they expected—dug himself in, built his cover, put out feelers, made contacts. The last thing they wanted was to put him in jeopardy before they really needed him.''

Curzon remained silent.

"I intend talking to the prime minister personally about this. My point will be that Price is the best asset we've got—no matter who runs him. Does that strike you as reasonable?''

Curzon nodded and Menzies rewarded him with a rare smile. "Good." He came back to his desk and seated himself comfortably. "Snap decisions are always the hardest to make, Paul. I think you're developing a taste for them."

JULY 9, 1940

A group of fifteen toddlers, all girls, all dressed in long white cotton gowns trimmed with scarlet braid, formed a self-conscious arc on the platform and gazed up wide-eyed at the baton raised over the music teacher's marcelled head. And one, and two, mouthed the teacher.

"Little boy kneels at the foot of his bed . . ."

Word perfect, proclaimed the well-fed smile on the headmistress's face. And tone deaf, winced Tom Price. The program threatened a further twelve assorted songs, recitations, and dances; the only consolation was that the performers were ranked in ascending order of age.

He sneaked another look to his right, across the sun-dappled sea of hats, but there was no sign of Alice. He sank back into anonymous retreat, narrowing his shoulders to avoid contact with the mountainous curves of two enormous mothers on either side of him. As far as he could see there were only five other men seated in the audience, and two of those were patently dutiful grandfathers who had nothing better to do with their time. Mr. Evans-Wyke was the sixth, but he'd stationed himself by the door at the back on the grounds that he was an interloper and had no claim to a chair. He'd begged to be allowed to come. A treat, he'd said, meeting Dinah. Paul had promised to make an appearance if he could get away, but he'd warned Dinah not to bank on it;

his new job at the Ministry of Supply was lowly and tenuous and, with only a month's service under his belt, his request for an afternoon off was unlikely to be viewed with any great enthusiasm.

Of course, Price had had no choice in the matter himself. Dinah was the last performer and, by implication, the acknowledged star of the afternoon.

In a disturbed society where tens of thousands of children had been dispatched to the countryside as refugees, Dinah and her schoolmates were uniquely privileged; and this school in particular, where the plump bourgeoisie paid handsomely to have their daughters impaled on the proprieties of English niceness, good manners, Greek dancing, and flower arranging, was the archetype of its kind. The war was but a whisper here, a rumor, politely shunned. Unlike the very upper or the very lower classes, the "middles" saw no immediate cause for alarm. The absent husbands of these flower-printed matrons had not been among those who rushed to enlist in the first months of war.

When Dinah eventually climbed onto the platform Price sat up expectantly. The music mistress retired and the pianist closed the lid on her keyboard. The coughing subsided.

> "I will give my love an apple without e'er a core,
> I will give my love a house without e'er a door,
> I will give my love a palace wherein he may be
> And he may unlock it without any key."

Her unaccompanied voice was light, tantalizingly soft, perfectly pitched; a revelation.

> "My head is the apple without e'er a core,
> My mind is a house without e'er a door,
> My heart is a palace wherein he may be
> And he may unlock it without any key."

There was a pause, uncertain and plangent, then there came from the door at the back of the hall the clopping sound of Mr. Evans-Wyke's long hands and the audience erupted. The serried hats ducked and weaved and a few young women at the front squealed their delight, but Price sat motionless, isolated. All he could focus on were the words she'd whispered to him before the concert began: "It's for you, Tom-Tom. Promise you won't laugh."

Confronted for the first time by the recipient of his applause, the apple of his rheumy eye, Mr. Evans-Wyke blushed scarlet and hung his head like a teenage suitor. "Really very *very* nice," he managed and handed her the sweets he'd bought, wrapped and ribboned. Then he retreated in confusion to the marquee erected on the lawn to fetch cups of tea.

Paul Curzon—"late, but not too late"—dropped to his knees and hugged her and she spilled tears on his sport jacket because her crush on him had become intolerable and she was a martyr to it. Price was waiting to press his own undemonstrative kiss on her cheek when he sensed, rather than saw, a white-gloved hand waving at him from a knot of women at one side of the marquee.

He didn't recognize her at first. She wore a white turban, fixed with a bold green brooch, a white cotton suit, a white silk blouse, and white shoes: She looked like a bloated fairy queen. He backed away from Dinah and Paul, sidestepped into the crowd to avoid the cup-bearing Mr. Evans-Wyke, and slipped behind the marquee. He beckoned to her and she approached him, a frown of annoyance on her immaculately painted face.

"I didn't see you inside," he said accusingly.

"I wasn't there."

"Why didn't you come over and talk to her, then?"

"Why didn't you ask me?"

"Touché.

He stared at her clothes—expensive, new—and she folded her arms protectively across her body. It was two months since she'd been at the house to see Alan off to Dartmouth and the change in her was frightening. Her face was a mask, all the life painted out of it; the clothes cheapened her. He had a horror that someone might see them together—the headmistress, one of the governors.

He said, "Why are you here, if you had no intention of—"

"I knew you'd come. I wanted to . . . tell you to your face." She seemed to shrink, then her courage returned and she let her arms fall at her sides. A pouched white handbag swung from her shoulder, its mouth agape. He could see her identity card and ration book inside.

"Tell me what?"

"I said I'd—when I was ready I'd make arrangements about Diny. And the house."

"I see. And?"

"I've decided you can stay. With her."

"You're coming back?" For a moment he really believed it.

"No!" It was almost a squeak.

"What are you saying, then?" He couldn't quite believe what he was hearing. "Are you telling me you don't want to see her again?"

"I'm thinking of *her*."

"Her! Good God, she loves you, woman. She needs you."

"No, she doesn't! She couldn't care less about me—you made sure of that. You and Diny, all the time—no one else mattered, did they? You didn't want *me*. You pushed my Alan out because he wouldn't kowtow to you. Well . . ." She began to cry but it was more defensive than real. He offered her a handkerchief. She ignored it. "Well, you've got your way, that's all. You've got Diny and you've got the house and I hope you're satisfied. I tried my best. I—"

"Pull yourself together and stop acting like a child!"

"I knew you'd say that. I always tried to be a good . . ."

He glanced around nervously. "Look, Alice, there's no need for this. I'll leave. Tonight."

"No!" It was the last thing in life she wanted. "It's best if I go and you stay."

"Because you have someone to go to," he said viciously.

"I—" She bit it off. "You can phone me at the university when you like. Tell me how Diny's getting on; if you hear from Alan."

"And if I need to reach you when you're—not working?" She took a step backward. "I don't see why. . . ."

"Suppose Diny's ill? Suppose I have to go away? How could I . . . ?"

"Three Godwin Terrace." She wouldn't meet his eye. "It's behind Theobald's Road. You walk past it every day. You won't come spying on me, though?"

The absurdity triggered a convulsive smile. "I won't come spying."

"See you don't. Not that there's anything to spy on. I'll be living"—she was a pathetic liar, the kind who anticipates a bending of the truth with gulping hesitation—"with a friend of mine at work. She lost her husband in North Africa. In the war." She half-turned, putting distance between them. He could see the questions piling up behind her eyes: Is it finally over? Will he leave me alone? Does he accept it? But not, Will he look after Dinah?

He should have fought her, for the child's sake as much as his own, but he had no heart for it. He felt drained.

"I'll say it for the last time. You don't have to go."

"I've got a taxi waiting." She raised one hand in a ludicrous gesture of farewell.

"What about your clothes?" He moved toward her.

"I'm all right. Just . . . whatever you want to do with them."

She walked quietly into the crowd, keeping the marquee between herself and Dinah, Paul, and Mr. Evans-Wyke. The last he saw of her was a flash of the white turban through the trees as she hurried along the drive to the road.

The afternoon mail was on the hall mat when they got home but he didn't open it at once. All he ever got were University College notices, ARP warnings to householders, income tax, newspaper, gas, and electricity bills.

He turned to it, reluctantly, before he put out the lights to go to bed but got no further than the handwritten white envelope with no stamp and no postal mark. Alice . . . ?

The writing was flowery, the text ungrammatical and unpunctuated. "Dear Tom. Glad I caught up with you again after so long & thought we could get together Friday July 12 convenient to both Brompton Oratory 3:45 pm St. Joseph's Chapel when I take confession F. Dilke. Had to laugh remembering what Father said where you are G is Best regards Johnny."

For several minutes he stood with the scrap of blue-lined paper hanging limply in his hand. Then he burned it in the grate and went upstairs. For the first time in months he checked the wireless set in the loft before going to bed.

JULY 12, 1940

"You *should* get out, Dr. Price," Mr. Evans-Wyke agreed. "You look really run down. I was saying the same thing to Mrs. Plum only the other day. He ought to get out more, I said. Go on—I'll take care of things here."

Price took the underground to Marble Arch, walked across Hyde Park, and burrowed into the Friday shopping crowds in Harrods before making his way to the Oratory by the round-about route of Walton Street, Fulham Road, and Thurloe Square. Time-wasting nonsense, he thought; he observed Sessler's strictures nowadays more out of sentiment than fear. He was convinced that some primordial instinct would warn him were he ever followed and there was nothing professional, as such, in *that*. He felt remakably alert and not in the least concerned.

Points to remember: three forty-five did not mean three forty-five. More of Sessler's tortuous tradecraft. *Never approach a rendezvous at the stated time. Always add twenty-six minutes*. Eleven minutes past four. "St. Joseph's Chapel when I take confession F. Dilke." Father Dilke? Unclear. But that was deliberate; Johnny, whoever he was, had every right to protect his cover and his neck.

He paused at the foot of the wide steps, damping down an involuntary surge of excitement, checking his rear, playing Sessler's absurd games. *Decide your role, then play it to the hilt. Never act a part—be it*. He was a supplicant, a stranger in a large city approaching his God in an unfamiliar house. In need of comfort.

He went inside. For a moment he reacted as Wilhelm Sommer would have done: with a student's regard for sculpted mass. The vast nave, umbrellaed by soaring domes, six in all, was a pastiche of eighteenth-century Florentine church architecture—almost grotesque, a sweeping condemnation of the Victorian English taste for achitectural grand larceny. He advanced along the left-hand aisle, head bent in token genuflection to the high altar, eyes covertly flickering left and

181

right. He passed a large chapel on his left but there were no confessionals there. The next chapel had four imposing boxes, one at each corner, and before the altar, under a hanging brass halo lamp studded with leaflike bulb hoods, a marble image of a magisterial Joseph. He sat down on one of the small school chairs and bent his head to his palm.

He twisted round, inch by inch, playing out an agony of prayer, and scanned the nave. Two old ladies, shoulder to shoulder on their knees in a central pew, crossed themselves and climbed painfully to their feet. Beneath the great dome of the high altar, a young priest in an apron stepped back from a glowing brass ornament, folded his polishing cloth neatly, and disappeared through a door in the Lady Chapel.

The old women made their way down the aisle. He felt their gaze on him and bowed his head still more. He heard the muted boom of the door as they stepped outside.

The silence was complete. He sat up, looked around him hopefully, checked his watch. Four ten. The finely carved half doors of the four confessionals were closed. He examined the box to his right; on the triangular coping over the door, a name was inscribed in gold: F. Napier. He swung sharply to his left. The box in the far corner also bore a name: F. Dilke: Oh, Johnny! Clever boy!

He got to his feet, threaded through the lines of tiny chairs, and knelt on the hassock at one side of the box, elbows on the supporting ledges, hands folded, face to the latticed grille.

"You wish to make confession, my son?" No Catholic seminary had cultivated that flat, unpromising singsong.

"Yes, Father."

"You remember your father's advice?"

"Where I am, Germany is." He flashed another look into the nave, although he had only whispered the phrase, but they were alone. He tried to make out the shape of the features behind the grille but could see only the white folds of a soutane, the outline of hands bound tightly round a breviary.

Johnny's voice lost some of its tautness. "You're Gimlet. You call me Johnny, right? I'll keep it short. You listening?"

"Yes."

"I've seen Ritter. This is what he wants you to—"

"Where did you see him?"

"No questions! First: you start your transmissions again on August 14. Got that? August 14, usual timing. Ritter says,

'Tell Gimlet I'll give him instructions after he makes contact.' Meanwhile, you're to concentrate on preparing collected information for transmission.' '' Pause. "You hear that?"

Collected information? They had expected him to continue collating product even after he'd been shut down? "Yes. I've got that."

"Ritter says, they're very pleased the way you've—what-do-you-call—operated up to now. He says congratulations. And I'm to tell you personal from him: The Shining Day."

The Shining Day, the Fuehrer's birthday. April 20. Surely to God they didn't mean to wait another *year* before the invasion!

"Did he say anything else? About the Shining Day?"

"No. Just that. He said you'd understand."

"Why did he send you?"

"Didn't want to take any chances, did he? Not with you, he said."

"Meeting in public is taking insane chances."

"Ritter says it'll be only months now. Then the Shining Day. Know what he means?"

"Yes. Is that all?"

"No. He says he doesn't want you worried with—what-do-you-call—details. Day-to-day problems. There'll be plenty of them later on—after August 14. So I'm your backup, all right? Sometimes he'll transmit to you direct, sometimes he'll come through me and I'll pass it on. That's the way he wants it."

"He wants you to contact me again?"

"When he says. Only if he gives the word."

"Why?" Ritter had promised there would be no contact with other agents. Promised!

Johnny had no stomach for the broader questions. "He *says*, that's all."

"I won't have you or your runners on my doorstep again, understand? No more notes through the letterbox."

"Had to, this once. But I got something worked out now. Listen. There's an alleyway near your place in Richmond, between the station and Onslow Road."

"Vineyard Passage."

"That's it. Old cemetery on your left. Top left-hand corner, there's a grave, big grave, tombstone thing with a—what-do-you-call—angel on it, one arm busted."

184

"I know it."

"Back of the angel, between the wings, there's a split in the stone. Any day or night you walk past it and there's a handful of grass stuffed in that crack, just a few bits twisted up and pushed in, you'll know you have to meet me here next day, eleven past four in the afternoon, like now. Any questions?"

"How can I contact you?"

"You can't. That's for your protection, not just mine. The less contact the better."

Price swept the area beyond the chapel again. A door slammed somewhere, muted by distance. He said, "Are you really a priest?"

"Leave off!" Johnny's hands, small nervous hands, set aside the breviary. "Right, that's enough, chum. Off you go."

Price made the sign of the cross, stood back for a moment, then went to the wrought-iron frame and lit a candle for the look of it. As he walked back down the aisle there was still no sign of mortal life in the nave.

He pulled open the inner door and swung on his coat, then abruptly flattened his back to the wall. He peered through the glass panes. Still no movement inside. He waited another minute, two, three, then gave up. *Always plan your escape route first:* Georg Sessler. Perhaps Sessler had taught Johnny too. Still, he had to come out sometime.

By the back door!

The rain outside was torrential. He ran down the steps and made for a small iron gate in a high wall on his right. THE ORATORY HOUSE read the sign. He took a couple of paces and stopped. A three-story building of gray stone abutted on the church, forming a wide U-shape enclosing a great lawn. No way to the rear. He ran back through the gate, across the South Face of the church, and came into a lane paralleling the Oratory. The rain had already soaked his coat and the raised collar channeled small rivulets down his back, but his rampant curiosity, emotional not rational, wouldn't permit him to stop. He skidded to a halt at the end of the lane, perplexed. Ahead of him, blocking his way, was another church; high square tower, arched porches, separated from the Oratory by an alleyway and a high brick wall. He followed the wall, equally high. He paused for breath. No rear exits, either from the Oratory or the house adjoining it.

Thunder rolled aggressively from the north and, as he limped back into the lane, lightning slashed through the rainclouds. He ducked back under the cover of the portico and at that moment a red post office van swept round the Oratory House driveway, squeaked to a temporary halt between the double gates, and shot out into Brompton Road. It flashed past the Oratory railings and disappeared at speed into the fading light toward Knightsbridge. He ducked in an effort to see who was driving, but it was going too fast.

Why not? A post office van. It would have to be genuine, of course, but there was no reason why Johnny shouldn't be a post office worker. On the other hand, if he were he'd been taking suicidal risks; parking openly, walking into the church through the house—he couldn't have done it any other way—dressing as a priest in a place where he could at any moment have run into real priests, coming out again through the house. Madness. Or professionalism. A display of cold nerve that was light-years ahead of his own blundering inexperience.

He wiped some of the rain off his face with a handkerchief, buttoned the collar of his coat, and hurried down the steps. Brompton Road was a groaning mass of cars and taxis, trucks and doubledecker buses crawling nose to tail.

He stood at the curb waiting for a gap in the traffic; judged his moment and sprinted headlong for a traffic island in the middle of the road, stopping just in time to avoid plunging off-balance into another stream of cars. From behind him came a tortured shriek of brakes and the sickening hiss of skidding tires. A woman screamed and he swung on his heel. A bus thumped to a halt, its rear wheels angled crazily across the traffic lane. The bus driver swung down from his cab and ran to a group of passersby huddled at the curb.

Don't go back.

The lights changed again and he sprinted across to the bus. The driver was on his knees. Over his shoulder, Price caught a glimpse of an outstretched leg straddling the curbstone, a large laced ankle boot, a thick gray wool sock and a flash of emaciated shin, whiter than snow. The bus driver rocked back on his heels.

"Right under me bloody wheels. You saw him. Never had a chance."

"Is he . . . ?" someone began doubtfully.

The bus driver took off his cap and pillowed it under the bald skull.

The long wistful Eastbourne face of Mr. Evans-Wyke gaped lifelessly at the tormenting rain.

When the sickness stopped Price slumped forward on the lavatory seat with his face in his hands. The retching had brought tears to his eyes and now they rolled in great viscous clusters between his fingers. He stuffed a handkerchief in his mouth as the weeping enveloped him, gave himself up to it and buried his face in his coat.

There was a sudden clack of footsteps in the corridor outside, cleated heels on bare boards, and the outer wash-room door opened. He held his breath, almost suffocating in the folds of the sodden coat. A hand rattled the lavatory door. A hiss of annoyance. The outer door opened and shut again and the footsteps receded. He almost fainted with relief.

Johnny in a post office van. Mr. Evans-Wyke in the gutter. Alice in virgin white, a green brooch glinting from her turban. Curzon on his knees hugging Dinah; late but not too late. Else, distantly on the telephone: "We have our duty, you have yours." Praetorius: "A year. One year." Sessler and Wein. Ritter: "The Shining Day."

Like a silken chain, growing link by link, invisible . . .

He shouldn't have come back to the Pepperpot. Why had he? He couldn't remember; had no idea how he'd got back. His head began to throb mercilessly. Ignore it. Think. *Reason*.

Everything is a lie. I'm a lie and they're a lie. But they created the lie and I inhabit it.

Everyone? Even Alice?

From the moment Ritter left him at the Hook of Holland; perhaps even before, he had taken no step that could now be seen as his own.

Make plans, *any* plans. But not to run. There was no escape from the Lie. As they had unrolled a carpet at his feet when he came—drawing him first this way then that, luring him round the hidden snares, protecting him from himself, preserving his belief in his own pathetic deception—so they would unroll another carpet if he tried to run. Another Curzon, poised at another bar; another Pepper; another Mr. Evans-Wyke.

No; there was no point in running. Stay with the Lie, cocooned and safe, for the rest of the war if necessary. They wouldn't look for trouble there. Stay in the Pepperpot and let *them* show themselves. Which of them dogged his heels? Who watched him in Richmond, followed him home, walked in his wake in the park, read his mail, took his pulse? How could he have failed to *know*—feel, see?

What else? They'd known from the beginning about the wireless set, of course. Every transmission he'd made. Yet they'd allowed him his freedom. Protected him. Why?

A rhetorical question. The Lie was perfect but it was not yet perfect enough. They'd prepared him—Curzon, Pepper, the wine-swilling mandarins of the Queen's Gate soirées, an army of clandestine manipulators he would never see or hear or know—but the preparation was incomplete. Hamburg—the oaf Ritter—had unwittingly sabotaged all that by ordering him to lie low.

Johnny! The realization struck him with staggering force. Johnny was also part of the Lie. A double agent? Then Ritter was also known, penetrated, wired for sound, equipped with his own personal British spy. The implications were numbing. If Ritter had been tagged—and God only knew how long ago, how effectively—then Hamburg-Wohldorf itself was a farce, a theater of the absurd in which British Intelligence formed the audience. Nothing there was secure, no one was safe. How far back did the Lie reach? Praetorius? Canaris?

Then the realization came. *He* had not failed Hamburg. *They* had failed him. He was not to blame, had exposed nobody. They were already known.

Probabilities. Johnny *had* seen Ritter and Ritter had passed on instructions for Dr. Thomas Price. A reasonable interpretation. If there had been no meeting, Price's transmission at 11:45 P.M. on August 14 would alert Hamburg to the fact that their agent was blown. No, the British wouldn't risk that. The Lie was too secure to destroy for no good reason. So Johnny *had* met Ritter. Those *were* Ritter's orders.

So what to do about it? Answer (inevitable): exactly as instructed. *Prepare collected information for transmission.* There was no collected information. Then find some. Back to the newspapers, the propaganda talks on the wireless or . . . His brain seemed to somersault in his skull.

There was no need for that now. The Lie had given him a desk in the Central Government Research and Audit Service (Cabinet Office), knowing him to be a spy. *Because* he was a spy. The Lie had given him power and position; files and memoranda, access to information "of value to the enemy." Ergo, the Lie intended him to make use of it. The information, of course, would be inaccurate, designed to mislead, but there was nothing he could do about that for the moment and, in any event, the passage of information to Hamburg-Wohldorf was an exercise in futility from the start if London controlled both ends of the conduit. Much more important at this stage was the fact that London was, as yet, unaware that he had broken *their* cover. Unless someone else had been covering Mr. Evans-Wyke. A chance he would have to take. There was no choice but to go on playing their game, convince them he was still their pawn.

It was at that moment he realized he was no longer afraid. He went out to the washstand and began to clean himself up. What was the British Tommy's all-weather phrase? Carry on regardless. Why not? Regardless of Pepper, Curzon, Alice; regardless of Hamburg, Ritter, Canaris. The one supreme virtue was that the Lie which controlled him was also his shield and his guardian angel.

The outer door swung back violently and caught him a glancing blow on the shoulder. Archie Bassingthwaite, middle-aged and top-heavy with tangled hair and soup-strainer mustache, glared at him waspishly.

"Was that you in there? For the past half hour?"

"Me?" Price centered the knot of his tie. "No, not me, old man. I just came in to wash my hands."

"Well, I must say . . ."

Price hooked his head at the lavatory. "Be my guest, Archie. Carry on regardless."

AUGUST 13, 1940

It was a balmy, promising dawn. Dew lay heavily on the grassy sweeps of northern France and the Low Countries, bathing the land in shivering ground mist.

On the airfields lining the Atlantic Wall, the same dew was swept from the distended bellies of German gun turrets; cannons were armed, loading trucks trundled their cargoes to gaping bomb bays; squadron briefing rooms filled with sleepy-eyed young men dressed for battle.

Der Adlertag, the Day of the Eagles. At Cap Gris Nez, Hermann Goering was poised at his forward command post to loose his birds of prey at the English sparrows—an overly melodramatic turn of phrase, but the Reichsmarschall's own. It was to be the most formidable assault force in the history of aerial warfare.

Goering, up since three A.M., was in loud good humor, buoyed by engulfing excitement and a comforting injection of the drug on which he relied so heavily. As his crews prepared, he tramped impatiently from the plotting room to the grassy knoll outside the bunker and back again, waiting for the final weather report, fretting over his promise to Hitler.

Only one element threatened the success of Operation Sea Lion: Admiral Raeder refused point-blank to consider shepherding an invasion fleet across the infernal bottleneck to Dover unless the Channel skies were first cleared of RAF Fighter Command. An invasion date had been submitted by the High Command: September 15. Hitler was prepared to confirm it if Goering would guarantee the total destruction of the British fighter screen. An open challenge: Goering had been quick to see it, but he had given his word. More: he had boasted he would achieve victory in four days.

By nine in the morning on the Day of the Eagles Goering was nervous. The meteorological report revealed heavy cloud cover over southern England. He dispatched hasty postponement orders to his field marshals, Kesselring and Sperrle, but at 1040, on one of his impatient walks to the knoll overlooking the Channel, he was thunderstruck to hear the groan of high-altitude engines and then, eyes shaded, to see a string of bombers heading west from the Pas de Calais. He stormed back to the dugout but the disaster was too far advanced to be averted. His postponement order had failed to reach a half-dozen squadrons in northern France.

Three-quarters of an hour later the formations were limping home, decimated and torn, cut to ribbons by marauding Hurricanes before they had reached the target area.

It was two o'clock before the cloud lifted sufficiently to permit the command signal for a mass attack and, momentarily, the sight of the first coordinated wave, wheeling and forming directly above him, lightened Goering's mood. Two hundred bombers streamed toward the distant white cliffs, breaking in mid-Channel to take their separate paths.

It was 2200 hours before Goering was in a position to make a general assessment of the day's work and the picture it presented was depressing. The Luftwaffe had flown 1,485 sorties, twice as many as the RAF, but the returns were minimal when set against the monstrous effort involved. Two factors became clear at once: one, Kesselring's dive-bombers were sitting ducks under RAF attack and, two, much of the bombing effort had been dissipated on aerodromes that formed no part of the all-important British fighter network.

His first call, from the privacy of his quarters, was to Kesselring, his second to Sperrle. He told each of them, with a passion he regretted later, that he would accept no excuses tomorrow for a repetition of today's debacle. Tomorrow would be a triumph of tactics and human endeavor unrivaled in the history of warfare—or they would answer in person to the Fuehrer. It was an empty threat and both men knew it. There would be only one victim if *Der Adlertag* failed to break the RAF.

At 2220, he called Admiral Wilhelm Canaris.

Goering came to the point at once. Canaris, he said, had boasted for a whole year of his legendary agent in London, the impregnable Gimlet. The moment had come for the man to display his celebrated virtuosity. Luftflotten 2 and 3 required, as a matter of urgency, immediate, highly detailed reports of damage sustained by Fighter Command in the Luftwaffe assault. The information must be of impeccable character; nothing short of total accuracy would suffice if Goering was to justify his claims to the High Command. The Abwehr, he said, would be judged on its ability to supply this intelligence, day by day. The success of Sea Lion depended on it.

Canaris reacted with unusual cordiality. "You'll have your intelligence," he promised. "You can count on it."

Five minutes later, his call roused Ritter from his bed at Hamburg-Wohldorf. The Gimlet Initiative, scheduled for resumption at 2245 hours tomorrow, he said, was now subject to an emergency priority. All previous plans were hereby canceled. Gimlet would direct all his energies to acquiring official British government intelligence evaluations of bomb damage to the RAF's southern airfields. He would be re-

191

quired to transmit his first bulletin at 2245 hours on Friday August 16, without fail, and daily thereafter.

Canaris returned to his study and entered both calls in his private log. Ritter called Trautmann and Wein to his quarters and repeated the instructions.

When the radio men retired to the communications room to compose code blocks for the following night's Gimlet transmission, Ritter went back to his bed.

Unlike Canaris, he did not sleep.

AUGUST 15, 1940

Churchill's basement sitting room at Number 10 was shadowy and drained of color, the air in it tainted with cigar smoke and furniture polish. As the old man's unpredictable day ebbed toward its three A.M. finale, exhaustion flowed from him like air from a ruptured balloon.

Menzies, Curzon, and a remarkably quiet Frank Loughran sat stiffly in a semicircle around the glowing hearth, waiting for a response. The old man seemed disinclined to offer one. There had been a chiefs of staff meeting in the Cabinet Room a half hour earlier, and Curzon found himself wondering if the continuous demands on Churchill's concentration weren't proving too much for him. He had not spoken once during Menzies' briefing on the Price transmission and the verbatim transcript of Hamburg-Wohldorf's questionnaire still lay untouched on the stool beside him.

At length, he removed his cigar and stared into the fire. "Do you recall what I said in June, Menzies?"

Frank Loughran shot a look of bewilderment at Curzon. Menzies contrived to appear wise without breaking his silence.

"I said, 'Upon this battle depends the survival of Christian civilization.' I said, 'The whole fury and might of the enemy must very soon be turned on us.' I said, 'If we stand up to him, all Europe may be free . . . and if we fail, the whole world, including the United States, will sink into the abyss of a new Dark Age.' " He glanced at Curzon as if he suspected him of inattentiveness. Curzon nodded gravely.

Menzies came to his rescue. "I'm not questioning your forecast, sir. JIC agrees with you. There'll be no Operation Sea Lion until Admiral Raeder is convinced the Channel is clear of British fighter cover. Nobody's in doubt about what yesterday's action means. It's Day One of your Battle of Britain. The question here is—"

Churchill cut him short with a dismissive flutter of the fingers. "Menzies, I've had a difficult day. At this moment, I'm no great admirer of generals, admirals, or air marshals, and my capacity for unquestioning acceptance of military wariness is at the point of exhaustion. You agree with my forecast of events? I'm deeply obliged to you. Your Joint Intelligence sub-Committee is pleased to confirm my layman's view? I bow to them. So oblige me further by grasping the essence of what I've just said. I will not timidly preside over the Devil's subjugation of humanity in the interests of protecting short-term security goals."

Menzies showed no emotion. "With respect, sir, it's not a question of short-term security. Hamburg's asking Price for highly specific classified intelligence. Facts they'll use to program perhaps weeks of aerial bombardment of airfields and strategic positions. To give Price virtual carte blanche . . ."

"Be damned with carte blanche!" Churchill thumped forward on his forearms. "I told you a year ago—more!—that Price was the key to our counteroffensive against the Abwehr." He glared at Curzon and Loughran, his head nodding emphatically as he measured the truth of the statement and found in its favor. "The Battle of Britain will be fought at closing speeds of 600 miles an hour, Menzies. *My* war moves faster. In the same hour, the same minute, convoys are sunk in the Atlantic, armies clash in North Africa, the whole defensive effort of this nation flows apace—and I . . ." He poked a finger into his waistcoat. "I am the sole accessory before, during, and after the fact." Curzon watched hypnotically as his face worked to convey the dynamic convergence of ideas.

"Consider the proposition, Menzies. Consider the dilemma. I must have one overriding concern in every action I take, every decision I hand down: the probability of failure. The loss of a flotilla, the destruction of an army group—the invasion of English soil. For a political leader, the conduct of war is a continuous gamble. I live with the certain knowledge that each day will bring a succession of small defeats—lives, equipment, morale, allies. I concede them unwillingly, Menzies—but concede them I must. We shall concede to Price what we must. We shall exercise care and a high degree of alertness, but we will not turn our faces to the wall and hope. Price—as you were at pains to point out yourself—will repay us a hundredfold. Ten hundredfold.''

Curzon felt sweat oiling the palms of his hands and, isolated from center stage in his seat at the farthest end of the line of chairs, Loughran's eyes were fixed on infinity.

''Very good, sir.''

''All right, then,'' Churchill said. ''What do you propose?''

''Curzon?'' Menzies deferred without enthusiasm.

''The Pepperpot . . .'' Curzon swallowed the trade jargon hastily. ''Professor Pepper's operation in Southampton Row is geared to handle a whole range of evaluation tasks, sir.''

''Yes, yes, I know that. I made a few recommendations myself.''

''Ah—yes, sir. We can have intelligence digest input flowing by, say, midday tomorrow—if the service ministries can come up with accurate assessments in that time. If—''

''If they can't, I'll want to know why.''

Curzon looked appealingly at Menzies, but he was staring at the glint of firelight on his toecaps. ''The main problem's likely to be that we shan't have a unified report, at least for a couple of days. They'll come in dribs and drabs—RAF, Observer Corps, Ministry of Home Security, War Office, Air Intelligence. . . .''

''How easy do we have to make it for him, pray?''

Loughran's knuckles showed white on the arms of his chair.

''First,'' Curzon continued, ''we need the facts, sir. Then an hour or two with the services or ministries concerned to work out what Price can and can't see and how it can best be presented. Then—''

''Explain *how* it should be presented.''

''Finding a balance, sir, in essence. We have to convince Price it's genuine product, so the paperwork's got to look right. Five have the facilities but they'll need specialist help. Second, any statistics will need to be as near as possible to what the Luftwaffe expect.''

''What does that mean?''

194

"Aircrew are the same on any side, sir. They're prone to . . ."

"Exaggeration?"

"Optimism, sir. A bombardier will always claim he hit the target; a fighter pilot will claim two aircraft shot down because he scored two hits, even though he didn't actually see them crash. It goes all the way to the top, sir. The Luftwaffe's intelligence count on yesterday's raids will be inflated. So will Fighter Command's. Our aim is to take advantage of the German aircrew score sheets. The figures we give Price will reflect their claims, as far as we can guess. Probably three or four times the actual kill rate."

"Mmm." Churchill seemed to be almost asleep now. He roused himself with an effort. "So Herr Goering's intelligence from London will tell him what he wants to hear?"

"In general, sir, yes."

Menzies got to his feet. "I think we've detained you long enough, Prime Minister."

Churchill flicked his cigar wearily into the fire. "Keep Morton informed. Personally informed. The Cabinet Intelligence Committee must have final sanction on the Price material. And talk to Kell, Menzies. I don't want him turning up on my doorstep complaining about dirty work behind his back."

AUGUST 31, 1940

Fred Wilby came to lean on the fence. Price stopped digging and lit his pipe.

"You came round then." Wilby nodded down at the rich black newly turned soil wriggling with disturbed earthworms.

"It was Dinah's idea. 'We can't eat grass,' she said." He perched on the handle of the spade. "She's been listening to you, Fred."

"Dig for Victory," muttered Wilby.

Price shrugged. "I suppose so." He looked down sadly at what had once been a perfectly smooth lawn. "It'll take years to get it back to what it was."

"Oh, we'll have him on the run soon, don't you worry."

Fred, shifting the blame, invoked the universal demon, Adolf Hitler. "Winston won't take this for long. Year from now it'll be all over bar the shouting."

Fred Wilby was the archetypal English patriot. Too old to join up, he had thrown himself willingly into the fight on the home front. His garden had been converted to a vegetable food store, his living-room window displayed a "Help Buy a Spitfire" poster, and he had joined the Special Constabulary to prove that, even at the age of forty-five, every ablebodied man had a part to play.

He bit comfortably on his pipe stem. "Your Dinah all right this morning, is she?"

"Thanks, Fred, she's fine."

Dinah had been an unforeseen obstacle when Hamburg imposed their new regime two weeks ago. Since Alice left, Price had made a habit of arriving home punctually at seven thirty to join her in the evening meal and listen to her chatter before she went to bed. Their weekends had been spent in unexciting suburban hibernation and, apart from Paul Curzon's regular Sunday visits, their outside contacts were limited to the Whites and the Wilbys. There had been crises, of course—a day when the child, becoming woman, recognized that war work alone was not keeping her mother away so long; the afternoon of old Mr. Evans-Wyke's funeral—but they had walked through those fires hand in hand and, if possible, the experience had brought them even closer together.

Breaking the pattern had unsettled her, and for a few days she had made silly excuses for not going to school. On the fourth evening, she had waited up for him and, arriving home at ten o'clock, he'd told her, because there was no point in further pretense, a little about what he did at Southampton Row and how the Battle of Britain had made his work there vitally important. To win her trust, and not least to protect himself, he cautioned her that the work was secret and she must under no circumstances tell her friends, the neighbors, even Paul. Before he left for London next day she outlined her plan. Each night he failed to arrive home by nine o'clock, she would sleep next door in the Wilbys' spare room. This would put his mind at rest and leave him free to concentrate on his work, she explained. And, incidentally, avoid a clash with the local welfare department, who were bound to create a fuss if they heard of a child being left alone in the house at night. They had both been very sensitive to the threat of welfare busybodies since Alice left.

"She's no bother to you, I hope, Fred."

"Diny? Never! Good as gold. The way she and my Mable sit nattering at night you'd think she was forty instead of fourteen. Bit hard on you, though, working all hours. The girl misses you."

Price knocked out his pipe on his heel and uprooted his spade. "There's a war on, Fred. We have to do what we can."

SEPTEMBER 3, 1940

Dinah brushed his hand aside and pulled the paper toward her excitedly. "I've got it! I've got it!" She bent over her pencil, tongue between her teeth. "Blanket suffocation," she breathed, reading the crossword clue again, and began to fill in the squares. "Twenty down. Blanket suffocation. *There*!" She pushed the paper under his nose. "Asphyxiate," she crowed happily. "That's a word, isn't it?"

"Yes, it's a word." He grinned and ticked off the letters she had written. A-F-I-X-I-A-T-E.

They did *The Times* crossword together on all his "early" evenings and Dinah habitually filled in most of the squares. The teacher in him often rebelled at giving free rein to her ignorance but her ingenuity intrigued him and he hadn't the heart to spoil her pleasure. Later, he would tell himself; when things get back to normal. But then he would remember Mr. Evans-Wyke and Curzon and Pepper and the Lie and the hopelessness of everything would threaten to consume him. Later! He smiled at her.

"One more, then bed."

"Two more."

"Two more quick ones, then."

They settled down to fourteen across: A plague on both your houses, and he let her chatter. Alice had written to her a week ago and by a stroke of luck he'd got to the letter first. It was a travesty; a seasoned mix of protested love and emotional blackmail so totally lacking in honesty he'd torn it to shreds. There had been no address so, of course, Alice had expected no reply, but he had mentally cautioned himself to check the post every morning from then on. There were other worries, too. If Alice came to the house while he was in London one day and tried to take the child away. . . .

Dinah suddenly raised her head, a finger to her lips, eyes wide. He heard it, too. A floorboard in the hallway groaned under an unaccustomed weight.

"Who's there?" He raised his voice sharply.

The board groaned again. They both sat stock still. The doorhandle turned slowly. The door swung wide.

"Do you know there's a strip of light a mile wide showing out your side window?"

The special constable was a large young man in his early twenties, florid-faced and running to fat. A night cape was draped over his uniformed shoulders and his peaked cap was braced high at the front in the manner of a Luftwaffe ace.

Price and Dinah let out their breath simultaneously. Price fought to regain his composure.

"I didn't hear you knock," he snapped.

"Door was open." The insolent young swine hooked a thumb at the offending curtain. "Jerry could see that from ten thousand feet. One bomb and the whole street's done for."

Dinah ran to it and drew it tight. She pulled up a chair, climbed on it, and rearranged the slide rings at the top.

"Does Mr. Wilby know what you're up to?"

The young man was Fred Wilby's beat partner—a burden to him, he admitted quite freely. The Keen One. Each duty night, Fred broke his six-hour tour by slipping home for a hot cup of cocoa, leaving the youngster to roam the street for ten minutes alone. Three times in the past fortnight he'd rung the bell at Middlemass House to complain about inadequate black-out measures and three times Fred had backed down when Price confronted him with the fact. "Just doing his job, Tom. You can't complain, can you?"

The Keen One straightened his back. "What's that got to do with it? Orders is—"

"Then knock next time or ring the bell!"

The patrolman sniffed. "You're lucky I don't report you," he rallied. "Watch it, in future." He stalked out.

Dinah came back to the table. "What cheek!" she said.

SEPTEMBER 7, 1940

The thunder of antiaircraft guns shook the windows in their frames but Menzies was deaf to it. The first German attack had come in midafternoon and the East End was ablaze, but not a single incendiary had fallen within five miles of the Buildings. The target was dockland, not Westminster.

He stood at the curtained window, staring at nothing. "Who and what are they?"

Curzon swallowed a yawn. He had been awake for better than thirty-six hours. "Goesta Caroli is a Swede. Wulf Schmidt's German. They were both recruited the same way— they answered ads in the Hamburg *Fremdenblatt*, were interviewed by Dr. Praetorius, met Ritter, and went into training. They shared a room at the Phoenix Hotel, as a matter of fact. Caroli said they were supposed to drop together. Ritter changed his mind at the last minute. He didn't say why."

"What's their brief?"

"Caroli was trained to check on coastal defenses in the south—presumably for Sea Lion—but Ritter changed his mind about that as well. Two days before Caroli was due to parachute in, he was given new orders. He's supposed to dynamite four mainline rail links between London and the north of England."

"And Schmidt?"

"He's not talking yet. Interrogation say he'll be a tough nut to crack. Scraggy little devil, but he won't make a peep. If they hadn't had Caroli for three days beforehand, they wouldn't even know his name."

"Caroli's cooperative, is he?"

Curzon stretched his aching legs out in front of him. "He's a mess. Went to pieces after the first interrogation. He hasn't said much we don't already know."

"What's Five planning for them?"

"If they can twist their arms without breaking them, the idea's to turn them both and make them play back to Hamburg as doubles. They both came in equipped with radio."

"You think it'll work?"

"We'll know in a week or so."

Menzies made a slow turn and trudged back to his desk. "Does either of them know about Price?"

"As far as we can tell so far, no."

"Were they given any contact names?"

"Only Johnny—Arthur Owens. They were supposed to send a postcard each to his accommodation address in Hampstead when they were settled in. When they needed cash they were to drop him another card."

Menzies balanced his paperknife across his palm, adjusting it for balance. "Ritter parachutes two agents into England—three days apart and in the same drop zone, the Oxford-Buckingham Road. He tells Owens to expect them but not Price. Conclusion?" He looked up sharply.

"Price is to be kept out of it. Too valuable."

"Or . . ." Menzies touched one end of the balanced knife to set it swinging. "Owens, Caroli, and Schmidt are short-term assets and Price is long-term. Subtle difference. If Sea Lion fails, Price is expected to carry on alone. Higher and higher." He let the knife topple to his blotter. "If Five persuade Caroli and Schmidt to double for them—either or both—I want you to keep on top of it."

"What about Price?"

"No change. Maintain surveillance, keep in touch with him yourself, and . . ." He looked at the clock; it was nearly midnight. "Cut along, Paul. You know what to do."

SEPTEMBER 8, 1940

Price removed the headphones and sat back, eyes closed. Forty-two minutes from call sign to sign-off; too long, far too long. He blinked, opened his eyes wide, felt the stirrings of idiot laughter.

The Lie! Forty-two minutes or forty-two hours; what difference did it make?

He flicked playfully at the naked light bulb and set it swinging; drunken shadows swayed to its rhythms from floor to ceiling. He cradled his neck on laced hands and considered the information he had just transmitted, an overflow, like last night's, of Friday afternoon's gigantic take. The Cabinet Intelligence Committee's monthly assessment of Fighter Command strength after three weeks of continuous battle; an Air Intelligence résumé of damage inflicted on Chain Home stations and aerodromes; a Ministry of Home Security report on morale; an exchange of memoranda between Churchill and Lord Beaverbrook on plans for stepping up aircraft production. Really, Pepper had gone too far. The documentation had virtually spilled on to his desk and overflowed. They were insulting his intelligence.

"Sorry to pile it on like this," Pepper had apologized. "You're the backstop, my boy. Push it out to Archie as soon as you can, but get that indexing right first."

Indexing, a complex cross-reference system to ensure a proper record-and-retrieval service. Pepper had no time for such minutiae; he had invested his complete trust, and the efficient functioning of the machine, in Tom Price. And so they fed him: facts and figures, forecasts, reports and evaluations. So much energy, so much industry and care. Could he be *so* valuable to them?

Continue to live the Lie. He'd been right. Everyone was happy. He stood between them, like a referee, showing favor to neither and both; taking and giving, enjoying trust from London and Hamburg.

Except, of course, it hadn't worked.

He set the bulb swinging again, compounding his unease.

Starting on Wednesday of last week Luftwaffe attacks on southern airfields had slowed down; even the distorted versions of the truth the Pepperpot had so busily shoveled his way had been forced to concede that. Then, yesterday, the answer—or what he personally had construed to be the answer. From four in the afternoon till five o'clock this morning Goering's raiders had tumbled through the skies over London, splashing the city with molten fire.

The bombers were back again now, grumbling from the east along the Thames valley, emptying their bomb bays on the open hearth of the East End, turning for home to load and refuel and come again. It was an admission of failure; evidence of Goering's shame and Hitler's livid rage at the Luftwaffe's defeat in the so-called Battle of Britain.

He heard a stirring from below, feet on carpeted stairs, and switched off the light. Dinah? No—she'd gone to the Wilbys' to leave him free to work at his papers. Alice then? Impossible. Fred, perhaps; or . . .

Not that insolent young pup of his again? The Keen One? If he'd walked into the house again . . .

Was the front door locked? The door to the bedroom? He couldn't remember. He'd lost all interest in personal security since that day in Brompton Road. He fell to his knees at the rim of the open hatch and tried to plumb the darkness of the room below. Nothing. He felt a stirring of righteous indignation, frustration, anger, then blind rage. Damn him! He felt along the wireless bench and his fingers touched a screwdriver. He closed on it, gripped it hard.

He heard the bedroom door open. A pale softening of the blackness; the sharp outline of the door in its frame and . . . He squatted there, an arching in his calves and thighs, unable to see. The sound of breathing, not hard but perceptible, made him stifle his own. Then movement, black on black, to the center of the bedroom. Something hard making contact with something harder; breath squeezing through tight lips, holding down the urge to cry out.

The shape, although it had no shape, disappeared; he had not seen it move but it was no longer there in the middle of the room. The bed creaked, springs singing under great weight, then a foot, two feet, scraped on the table and . . .

The hands—black-gloved, shiny hands—appeared like spiders at either side of the hatch and a black wedge of cap rose between them. The tension that had held him paralyzed snapped. Without thinking, he struck across and down with the screwdriver, into the place where the throat should be. The steel lanced deep and grated sickeningly on bone. The black void beneath the cap made a harsh swallowing sound. The body fell. The table bumped to the carpeted floor.

For a full minute he could neither move nor breathe. Then he touched the blade of the screwdriver, felt blood warm and tacky at his fingertips, and knew what he had done.

* * *

For ten minutes his body shook uncontrollably. He slumped back into a sitting position on the floor of the loft and leaned his head against the hard edge of the table. Again his fingers touched the bloodied point of the screwdriver and this time he let it fall through the hatch to the bed below. He gagged, plastered his hands across his mouth.

No good. Must go down.

He couldn't see—it. He didn't want to. He fell on hands and knees beside the bed and—eyes closed, teeth gritted—let his hand flutter briefly over the shape. The Keen One lay half on the bed, half on the carpet, head down. His cap, miraculously, was still in place. Uniform jacket, embossed buttons. Price turned away, got up, went to the bedroom door. He stumbled downstairs, his balance gone. The front door was ajar; he closed it, locked and barred it, fell back against it, a steadying hand on the coatrack, gulping air to slow the hammering of his heart.

Presently, he was able to move again; nerves, muscles, joints functioned seemingly without benefit of orders from the brain. He unlocked the back door and walked blindly in the tarry blackness along the garden path to the shed. He reached under the tool bench and wrestled out the old tarpaulin. A memento of Leonard Petrie. He rolled it with agonizing slowness into a manageable sausage shape and hoisted it on his back. When he came out into the air again, he knew what he was going to do.

His first impulse when he walked back into the bedroom was to switch on the light; a reflex. His fingers actually touched the switch before his brain screamed, "No!" No light! A light would attract attention. Fred Wilby, drinking his cocoa next door. Someone in the street. He unshouldered the tarpaulin. That wasn't the reason, though, was it? Not really. Turning on the light meant looking into the face of the man he'd killed; looking into a pair of keen young dead eyes. He stripped a blanket from the bed and covered the face, then opened out the tarpaulin, dragged the body across it and rolled it into a long tube. He made three attempts at lifting it, but the weight was beyond him. He dragged it out to the small landing, pushing it toward the stairs and angled it for the descent. With a hoarse zipping noise, it slid out of sight under its own weight. He tore after it. Care. *Care*!

On the next flight he took a grip halfway down and bumped it step by step to the bottom. Along the hall, into the kitchen, a quick reconnaissance outside, then onto the concrete apron, down the steps, across the lawn to the newly turned earth. No lights showing in Fred Wilby's house. Where would he be? Looking for his partner? God, if he came back— He fetched the shovel from the shed, sank it and turned the first divot. Rain had made the soil sticky and unyielding; the clumps of upturned grass weighed like rocks.

Deep. Very, very deep. The Keen One was six feet tall and he would have to lie six feet down, no less. He set to work, finding a rhythm, changing hands when the effort became too much, stopping at intervals to question the night, digging again, avoiding excessive sound. Every five minutes or so he stopped—not to rest but to assure himself that what he felt, or did not feel, was real. He had killed; not for advantage, not in anger, not even in self-defense. In panic. He had taken a life, gouged it from a young unsuspecting throat. Nausea overwhelmed him at last.

He went into the house and washed his face and mouth. Three forty-five. His hands were shaking violently, this time from the sheer agony of digging. "No more." He said it aloud. He went back to the pit—four feet deep, perhaps, not much more—and rolled the tube feet first over the edge. He jumped in and dragged the Keen One after him, laying him lengthwise on the sodden ground. For a moment he contemplated the shape of him, becoming clearer now in the faint light, then he climbed out and began to shovel the earth home. It rattled like hail on the canvas shroud at first, and he stopped work, appalled, to stare at the neighboring houses. When he finished the hole had become a slight mound. He fetched a rake and leveled it.

He put the tools away, cleaning them first with uprooted grass, then reeled back to the house. At the kitchen door he stopped to survey his handiwork. This wasn't war. He could not excuse himself by calling it war.

SEPTEMBER 9, 1940

There was no such thing as passion, he thought, fitting into the crowd, letting it take him. Only fear.

The air stank of smoke and toasted oil and rubber and tar and gas, of ancient brick and plaster split by flame, but it was not the stench of passionate hatred. It was the bouquet of wild terror, like the moist smell of earth raining down on a canvas shroud. Tom Price was no part of it, he told himself insistently. None of it. But the sumptuous boom of distant explosions set the lie to that thought and his eyes turned apprehensively to the damson sky. It would be a blessing if the blitz took him, crushed him as it was crushing London. The alert had sounded for the sixth or seventh time that day about ten minutes ago, but the homeward-bound commuters, scenting tea and firesides and newscasters on the wireless telling them what they had already experienced, were flooding the pavements, talking and laughing, only occasionally flinching at the bigger bangs.

A great knot of them stood at the corner of Southampton Row and Bloomsbury Way behind a policeman's outstretched arm as a fleet of ambulances and fire engines clanged by. When the vehicles had passed, the policeman waved the crowd forward, but Price held back, the idea stirring him again, tempting. The extension of Bloomsbury Way was Theobald's Road. "You walk past it every day," Alice had said, leaving without a word to Dinah.

He crossed to the far corner, still unsure if he meant to go through with it. He knew it was insane, an admission of towering inadequacy, but the urge was overwhelming. Go to Alice. See her, talk to her. All he wanted, if he could only bring himself to admit it, was the comfort of another human presence; an inadequate like himself, an evasive, hopeless weakling who would recognize his misery in her own.

Godwin Terrace. Number 3, she'd said. Needle in a haystack, he thought, but it didn't deter him. He turned into Old Gloucester Street and it led him into Queen Square. He caught the stench again of burnt plaster and wood, soured by escaping gas. He turned into another side street and found it. Godwin Terrace was a slit cut between parallel rows of tiny terraced dwellings; pocket-handkerchief gardens on either side of a narrow central passage; little cottages standing back, gray-faced and modest. Modest from number 15 to number 7; nonexistent from 5 to 1. A bomb had torn the street in half, leaving only a saber-toothed wall at the far end. Number 3 was indistinguishable from its neighbors. The last three dwellings had become one.

His first reaction was disbelief, a stunned refusal to accept what he saw. Then despair, fleeting and impermanent. Then a grotesque kind of self-mockery. His last possible source of comfort—a joke in itself because Alice wouldn't have crossed the street to comfort him voluntarily—had been snatched away. He was alone with himself again.

"Are you all right, dear?"

Number 13. A gray-haired granny in housedress and slippers stood at her door.

"Oh—yes. Ah—thank you." He walked toward her little wicket gate. "I was wondering . . ." He pointed back at the avalanche of masonry. "When did it happen?"

"Last night, dear. Half past one." She came to the gate and eyed him soulfully. "It was a freak they hit it, the ARP said, but you can't believe anyone, dear, can you? The docks it was meant for. I bet there's more'n one in their graves this minute who could say the same. Friends, were they?"

"Well . . . number three. I think a chap I used to work with lived there."

The granny's expression changed instantly from sympathy to curiosity. "Oh yes, dear. Mr. Randall, that'd be."

Price looked back at the crushed cottages. "He had a . . . wife, I think."

"Lily, you mean."

"I—ah . . ."

"Little woman, about my height. Blond hair. Lovely dresser, she was."

"I never met her." Alice had said nothing about a married couple. A widow she'd said, husband killed in North Africa. "Did they have a guest staying with them?"

"In a little four-by-two like that? No. Never saw anyone else. And the rescue men only found two bodies. Burned terrible they were, both of 'em. Mr. Randall and Lily they said it was. Put a notice up in the Town Hall: Mr. and Mrs. Randall.''

In Queen Square he let the laughter bubble out of him, the racketing clatter of lunacy. Oh, Alice. In character to the very last syllable. *Not that there'll be anything to spy on*. Of course not. Because there *was* no widow, and she'd had no house in Godwin Terrace to go to. Alice was as good as her word; as long as it was understood that every word was a lie.

SEPTEMBER 13, 1940

It was treacherously cold. Price bent into the chill north-easter and drew the wool scarf tighter about his throat. The pavements were empty, the shops and theaters and restaurants of Shaftesbury Avenue locked against the promise of another night of carnage. It hadn't taken long to silence the West End, to wipe the tinsel smile off its face.

He took a short cut into Leicester Square and the boom and rattle of the nightly spectacular reached out of the sky to him from the Thames. He stopped to watch it, shivering in the cold and the dark, marveling at the sheer beauty of it.

The firestorm—a poet's word—splashed the eastern heavens with flame and he knew, because he had watched it before from the royal circle of Waterloo Bridge, that the light, brighter than a hundred sunsets, was blazing on domes and warehouse roofs, in water, in the diamantine reflections of glass and steel, as far as the eye could see.

He moved on, careful not to look behind him or give an impression of nervousness. It was the Plumber tonight; he'd spotted him within twenty yards of leaving the Pepperpot. Ruddy-faced, graying, square as a bookend; brown porkpie hat, buff mackintosh, stubby-toed black boots. A slow man, dependable, punctual as the Greenwich time signal.

The Plumber had been his first success. Why he had noticed him this week and not last, or the week before that, was a mystery he couldn't fathom. Informed blindness? Self-delusion? Knowing they *should* be there but not having the wit to see. The real joke was that it was too late to care. The Plumber had been Monday's child, the shadow at his heels; Tuesday produced the Curate, pretending to examine winter bulbs in a Kingsway shop when Price stopped to buy an evening paper. He had a round-shouldered stoop and a habit of walking with his hands clasped at his back; a pronounced clerical timidity.

After the Curate, it became second nature to identify the others. No tail could behave like a normal man.

On Wednesday, the Baker was waiting at the corner of Bloomsbury Way, a tubby, pipe-smoking extrovert in a bowler hat and check coat who had the confidence to shadow from the front when he considered his cover was threatened.

The fourth man was the Undertaker, a tall, severe figure in mourning black who favored a rolled umbrella and carried what appeared to be a leatherbound book under his arm. He spoke to no one, never entered a shop or paused at a news-stand to kill time, never hurried unduly or lagged. He had the knack of shadowing his quarry at a regulation pace that never faltered.

On the first night, the Plumber's night, Price had kept to his appointed route. The hideous shock of discovery, however, quickly gave way to excitement: triumph at spotting them at last, a gamesman's pleasure. On the second night he varied his pattern to test them, and on the third he led the Baker on a leisurely walk through the West End. Another week or two and he'd have their measure.

When the moment was right, he would find a use for the keys. He slipped a hand into his coat pocket and let his fingers close on them, counting them, eight in all. It was an omen—to have acquired them in the very week he identified his four shadows. Three days ago, strolling through the corridor to Mrs. Plum's hen coop, he'd seen the keys dangling on a ring from Pepper's office door. He removed them gingerly—a reflex, quite unpremeditated. He almost put them back when the thought struck him that they had been left there for him to find. A plant, another trap? But he dismissed that fear. They wouldn't tempt him with something they couldn't control. He left early that evening, reached Richmond before five o'clock, and went straight to Frank White's chemist shop in the High Street. House keys, he explained, dangling them under White's nose. He needed a new set cut by morning as a matter of urgency. Frank was owed favors by more tradesmen than he could lay tongue to and the local ironmonger was no exception. The copies awaited Price next morning. He sneaked the original key ring into Archie Bassingthwaite's pending tray where it was duly found and returned. Pepper was not in the least put out. It was his spare set, he told Archie; he always carried two to avoid locking himself out. Terrible memory.

Price had no idea what he intended to do with them, but the logic of possession was inescapable: they must be used. One clearly opened Pepper's office, another his wall safe, a third Archie's general office, a fourth the classified records room. The others were not Pepperpot keys. The big mortice probably fitted the street door at Queen's Gate, a Chubb the door to his flat. The last two were smaller security keys.

He turned into Charing Cross Road and the wind hurled the two ends of his scarf ahead of him in the dark. Home, now. There was Wednesday's key points bomb damage report to transmit and it was a long one, a full hour at least. He lengthened his pace, finding comfort in a mental image of his tubby pursuer accelerating to keep up.

The Plumber was doing well tonight. He hadn't shown himself for at least fifteen minutes.

A half-dozen letters lay on the mat inside the door and he scooped them up on his way to the kitchen where he put on his slippers and lit the gas under the kettle.

He gave one incurious eye to the stack of letters as he spooned liquid coffee into a large breakfast mug. A neatly folded page from a blue-lined exercise book lay on top: Dinah's nightly missive. Scrawled in pencil on the front: "Tom-Tom." Inside, a message that had not varied since the blitz began: "Going down to sleep in Mrs. Wilby's shelter. See you breakfast time. Remember to lock up. Milk on pantry floor. Love Dinah."

The kettle screeched and he made the coffee.

It would have been the neighborly thing to do to look in on Fred Wilby—but he couldn't face that. Not yet. So far, there had been no word of the Keen One's disappearance; no door-to-door inquiries, not even a paragraph in the local paper. Five days. Was it possible for a young man to have so little human contact that his absence could go unremarked for five days? Unsettling. Fred, he was sure, had told him once that special constables were required for patrol duty six nights in fourteen, in which case a five-day lapse was mathematically impossible. Still, there was nothing he could do about it.

He sipped his coffee and spread out the sheaf of manila envelopes: On His Majesty's Service, all of them. A postmark caught his eye. Dartmouth? He opened it. The letterhead was discreet. Royal Naval College.

"Dear Mrs. Petrie,

I have no wish to concern you unduly but I am required by Naval regulations to inform you that your son, Cadet Alan Petrie, has been officially posted Absent Without Leave. Since he was issued with a 72-hour pass on which his shore leave address is entered as Middlemass House, Ellerker Gardens, Richmond, and a rail warrant Dartmouth-Richmond-Dartmouth, I must assume you are aware of your son's whereabouts. In the event of sickness, a doctor's certificate should be forwarded to the College at once, but in view of the untoward delay involved in this case I would suggest you telephone me at the number above as soon as you receive this.

"I should add that the high opinion of your son's potential noted by the Selection Board has been amply borne out by his end-of-term examination results. It would be invidious to allow his progress to be overshadowed by a technical misdemeanor."

It was signed "A. H. Blackett (Capt)."

He pushed the letter away wearily. He might have guessed. For all his "potential," the boy was an arrogant little ruffian, a spoiled brat with no sense of responsibility. One term of iron discipline and he'd had enough. His mother's son. He stared moodily at the letter. Alan hadn't come to Richmond, of course; if he had, he would have made contact with Dinah. So he was on the run. He'd lose himself in London or scuttle to some obscure country town and cool his heels till the hue and cry died down. Then his problems really would begin. Finding money for food and shelter. And no ration book, no points; an identity card he dare not use. If the Navy didn't track him down, the police would. A deserter—the word Captain Blackett had been so careful to avoid—would find no sympathy and no sanctuary.

He poured the rest of the coffee down the sink, switched off the lights, collected his briefcase, and went up the dormer room.

Tomorrow he would have to call Blackett and, like it or not, tell him the truth. There were bound to be repercussions: policemen, investigations, council snoopers, and, when they found him, perhaps a court of inquiry.

Damn the boy! Damn them all!

At the end of his transmission, Baruth, the duty operator, tapped out a qrv—stand by. Price sat back, preparing for the worst. Ritter. The man's gratuitous paternalism aggravated him. No, there was more to it than that. Ritter was a fool— blind, inept, preposterous. If he had a gram of insight in him he would have spotted the flaws in the Gimlet operation months ago. He, not Price, was the puppet.

"Hotbed to Gimlet. Rantzau here."

"Gimlet standing by." Mechanical, the way brain and hand now worked the key. No codebook required for standard responses. A measure of his new professionalism. Baruth would notice it and tell Richard Wein.

Hamburg again: "Block One. Target date Sea Lion postponed. Do you receive and understand?"

"Understood." And expected. The Battle of Britain had failed. The blitz had failed. Sea Lion had failed. Why in God's name couldn't they accept the fact that *he* had failed?

"Block Two. Your wife and sons send warmest greetings."

"Understood. Please reciprocate." Ritter would like that. The reluctance of cold heroism.

"Block Three. Warmest congratulations magnificent effort recent weeks. Product invaluable. Fuehrer personally communicated Hamburg-Wohldorf this day following message. Quote your actions worthy highest commendation myself and all German people. In recognition bravery and devotion to duty take pleasure awarding you Iron Cross Second Class. Anticipate privilege soon meeting again. Adolf Hitler. Unquote."

The message took several minutes to decipher and when he finished he stared at the pad, willing it to make sense.

"Hotbed to Gimlet. Respond."

He coded quickly. "Aware great honor but am unworthy." And as an afterthought: "Where I am, Germany is."

"Understood. Out," flashed Baruth.

SEPTEMBER 14, 1940

"Captain Blackett speaking."

"Good morning. My name's Price. I—ah—received your letter yesterday. About Alan Petrie."

A cautious pause. "Are you related to the boy, Mr. Price?"

"*Dr.* Price. I'm his stepfather. My wife's away on business. I opened the letter by mistake and—"

"Is young Petrie there now, Dr. Price?"

"No, he's not, I'm afraid. We haven't seen him since he left for the college in May. I thought I'd better let you know right away."

Another lengthy hesitation. The telephone booth was like an oven in the unexpectedly warm sunshine.

"This is extremely serious." Blackett had a smooth sullen tone made weak by a slight lisp. "Is there no way I can get in touch with the mother? Perhaps the boy went to her. . . ."

"I shouldn't think so. I really don't know where she is." He had decided not to become involved in tortuous domestic explanations. Innocence was the correct attitude; innocence and apparent willingness. He could do no more.

"You realize this could jeopardize Petrie's chances of a commission?"

"Captain Blackett, I think I should explain that Alan and I . . . are not close. He hasn't written home and I haven't the faintest idea why he's done whatever he's done. *When* was he supposed to have come home?"

"Last Saturday, Dr. Price. September 7."

September 7? It meant something, but he couldn't recall for the moment what. He said, "We had very heavy bombing here that day. At least in London. Would he have passed through London?"

"I understand he would. But there's no question of his being . . ." Blackett shied from the word 'killed.' "Injured. We've made exhaustive inquiries."

"Then I'm sure I can't help you."

"The penalty for desertion . . ." the officer began darkly. It sounded like an accusation of complicity.

"But you said in your letter he'd done remarkably well at Dartmouth."

"He has."

"A boy who acquits himself well, Captain Blackett, doesn't run away. I'm a teacher; I'm not inexperienced in—"

He remembered, with sudden heart-jolting clarity, why Saturday September 7 registered with him. He said faintly, "Did Alan actually leave Dartmouth on the Saturday? Was he expected to arrive home that day?"

"He left Dartmouth at 2140 hours. We have the station-master's word for that. I gather he had dinner first with some fellow cadets and took the late train to Southampton. He planned to catch the London train from there to arrive home on Sunday morning."

Sunday?

"What was he—what was he wearing?"

"Uniform, naturally. We don't encourage the use of civilian clothes. Cap, jacket. Probably not his raincoat; it was very warm here last weekend."

"Gloves? Black leather gloves?"

"I'm not sure. Why?"

"I'll . . ."

He dropped the telephone and pushed out into the warm air.

Fred Wilby was in his garden. He came over to lean on the fence. "Good day for it, Tom." He looked hopefully at the well-raked surface of Price's unsown vegetable patch. "I've got a few winter seedlings in the shed if you're thinking of planting out."

"Yes. Thanks." Don't *rush* him. "I'm not up to it just now, Fred. Had a late night. I meant to come over and say hello before I turned in, but I never got to it."

"Turned in early myself. Out to the wide by half past ten."

"You're too old to tramp the streets at night, that's your problem."

"Can't argue with that. I was clapped out after Thursday night, I can tell you."

Now. *Now.* "You should find yourself an older partner, Fred. The Keen One's too damned hard on you."

Wilby broke a twig from an overhanging apple tree and used it to scrape out the bowl of his pipe in agonizing slow motion. "Young Rankin, you mean? Been sticking his nose round your door again, has he? Well, he's not so bad. Keen is what they teach 'em nowadays. And I s'pose you can't blame him, not being able to join up. Lungs, he says. Wouldn't have him because of his lungs. TB you can bet. But if he's good enough for the Force he's good enough for the army. I said to him Thursday night—"

"Thursday night?"

"I said . . ."

She was worried about him. He'd eaten nothing at lunch and slept all afternoon in his room; when he came downstairs she tried to get him to the table but he wouldn't have it. He went out into the garden, although it was too dark to see anything, and he was still there, mooching around.

The truth was she was too young to help him. Mrs. Wilby, who talked a lot in the Anderson shelter at night because she couldn't sleep, knew exactly what was wrong. "What that man needs is a woman to look after him," she said. "No discredit to you, love. You're old enough to understand, aren't you?"

She was, but she hadn't considered it before. Mrs. Wilby meant sex, of course, not that she'd ever lay tongue to such a word. "A man has to be loved" was the closest she came to it.

Diny took another plate from the sink and began to dry it. She must *do* something. The pictures? There was still time to get there for the last performance. Without thinking, she reached up and lifted the blackout curtaining from the kitchen window.

A great arrowhead of light blazed across the concrete step, the lawn, and the back fence, the shadow of her own head huge at its center, and when she realized what she'd done she dropped the curtain as if it were alive. But in that split second she saw. The plate slipped from her hand and shattered on the floor, but she was already running to the back door.

The streaming, incriminating light vaulted ahead of her into the garden but she didn't care. "Tom-Tom! Tom-Tom!"

And she saw him again as she'd seen him in that awful flash of light. On his face, stretched out like a fallen star, with his hands finger-deep in the black earth.

SEPTEMBER 15, 1940

Paul Curzon's distress was too apparent to be feigned. "Look, you're sure there's nothing I can do? Call a doctor or something?"

"No, I'm perfectly all right. Thanks all the same."

"You should have let Dinah call me at once. I'd have come like a shot, you know that."

"She wanted to. I said no."

"Why?"

Price indicated the bedroom door and motioned Curzon to shut it. He did, and returned to his perch at the end of the bed.

"I won't have her worried, Paul. She's got more than enough to put up with."

Curzon looked mystified. "What do you mean, put up with?"

"Alice."

"Oh."

"Look, Paul—" He gazed earnestly into the young man's face. "Can I trust you to keep something to yourself—at least, till I can think of some way of sorting it out?"

"You know you can."

Oh yes, he knew.

"I told you Alice walked out. I didn't tell you where she went."

"None of my business."

"No. Well, she said she was staying with a friend—a widow—at a house in Godwin Terrace. It's just behind Theobald's Road, not far from my office."

Curzon looked uncomfortable.

"I walked down there last Monday night. I don't know

why. I suppose I wanted to make sure she was all right—you know, after the bombing. I . . . the house was a pile of rubble. It took a direct hit on Sunday night.''

''Oh *Christ!* Was she . . . ?''

''The rescue people pulled two bodies out of it.'

''Both women?''

''A man and a woman.''

''Tom, I'm terribly sorry.'' Curzon reached out involuntarily and clasped his arm.

''I haven't told Diny. I couldn't. And I haven't done anything about . . . well, approaching the authorities. A woman there told me a list of names was put up at the local town hall but I haven't been to check it or . . . I suppose I should have told someone. I'm damned if I know what to do now.''

''Don't do anything. Leave it to me. I'll drive over there and sort it out.''

Price closed his eyes gratefully. He'd never doubted it for a moment. The Lie was all-encompassing. He said weakly, ''I feel such a bloody fool.''

''Don't. It's no fault of yours.'' Paul stretched his mouth in a white-lipped grimace. ''Look, Tom, we've never talked about the Alice thing and I don't want to pry—''

Price raised a limp hand, cutting him off. ''It was a mistake from the beginning, Paul. I was a fool. I didn't understand her, or what she expected of me. I don't suppose I knew very much about myself, come to that. A month after we married we both realized—well, it wasn't going to work. She went back to the university and I suppose she . . . met someone else.''

''I don't have to know this,'' Curzon began hotly.

''You have every right. After a while she started coming home very late; three and four in the morning. God knows what she was doing. Then she'd stay away for a day or two, then three or four. She left for good the day you came to Diny's school concert.''

''Do you know who the . . . chap was?'' Curzon flushed. ''No.''

Curzon wouldn't look at him. ''Why'd she leave? Why not simply kick you out?''

''Oh, some nonsense about Dinah being more attached to me than to her. I don't know. I suppose the man, whoever he was, didn't want a child trailing round after him.''

"She'd leave Diny for *that*?" Curzon was shocked.

"Don't ask me to explain how her mind works."

Curzon nodded. "You're sure Alice was in the house when the bomb . . ."

"I don't know." Always avoid an outright lie. "The fact is . . . there's something else. Oh, God, Paul, it's a mess."

Curzon opened his mouth to speak but closed it without a word.

"Yesterday, just before . . . I blacked out, I talked to Alan's principal at Dartmouth. A chap called Blackett. Captain Blackett. He'd written to Alice. Alan's gone absent without leave."

"Oh, for God's sake!" Curzon raked a hand through his red hair.

"Blackett said he left Dartmouth late last Saturday on a seventy-two-hour pass to come home. He didn't turn up, of course. I had to admit that. Then . . . I thought, if Alice wrote to him at Dartmouth—she must have, mustn't she? —she'd tell him where she was living. And if he went to see her when she got to London last weekend . . ."

"He could have been at the house when the bomb . . ." Curzon grasped the solution too eagerly. He looked down at his hands. "Were the bodies identifiable?"

"I don't think so. According to the woman—"

Curzon was on his feet. He held up a warning finger. "Now you listen to me, all right? I want you to put this out of your mind here and now. Leave everything to me. Whatever happened, I'll handle it. I'll go down there and talk to someone."

"It's Sunday. . . ." Prince offered a last despairing defense of his own incapacity.

"The Jerries don't stop for Sunday. There'll be someone."

When he'd gone, Price lay back on the pillows and let the tension run out of him in a burst of trembling that shook him from head to toe. The idea had hatched itself yesterday afternoon, and he'd acted on it in a kind of mindless daze, not daring to question it too deeply, trusting to instinct. A fainting fit in the garden. Wilbys and Whites clucking over him with Samaritan zeal, putting him to bed, nursing and nourishing; Dinah running to the telephone box first thing in the morning to call Curzon, pouring out her shock and concern.

The sheer audacity of it had unnerved him when Curzon first arrived, but it was too late then to change his mind, no matter how illogical the notion appeared in the harsh light of day: to persuade them he genuinely believed Alice had died in the direct hit on Godwin Terrace; to link her ''death'' and Alan's disappearance. He knew he could never hope to convince them of it rationally; but if Curzon could be made to believe that the mere probability of it had made him ill, brought on a collapse . . .

The trembling subsided. Theoretically, the outcome had never been in doubt. The Lie demanded that Tom Price be protected from *all* outside interference; his problems were *their* problems, Curzon's. All that mattered was that he continue to function. Thus his reasoning as the idea came to fruition. And it had worked.

Curzon had only to have the bodies exhumed, of course, to prove that Alice and Alan were not dead, but proof of reality was not the point at issue. The Lie was concerned exclusively with maintaining Tom Price's ignorance and his peace of mind. How Curzon chose to achieve that was his own affair.

He smiled. A new irony: now Paul too would know it was a lie. Their first indestructible bond. Allies in the cause of the status quo.

Menzies' observance of Sunday as a day of rest and withdrawal was minimal, but he was not at the office. Central Registry told Curzon to sit tight and he did, for an hour and a half. When they got back to him he was instructed to present himself on the Chelsea Embankment across the road from Carlyle's House at one. Menzies was waiting, casually dressed in foulard, khaki shirt, Harris tweed jacket, and old flannels. He looked unusually debonair.

They began to walk toward the houseboats on Chelsea Reach and Curzon related his bedside chat with Tom Price. When he finished, Menzies chewed on it for several minutes without speaking. The rank odor of bare mud from the exposed banks of the Thames seemed to shake him out of his reverie.

''Have you asked Five to make inquiries?''

''Not yet. I wanted to talk to you first.''

''Why?''

Curzon flipped an expressive hand. ''If you agree, I think

it's better I handle it myself. Loughran can deal with any necessary paperwork later on. The less said officially . . ."

"You think Price is lying?"

Curzon shook his head firmly. "No, I don't. If we ever had any doubts about his amateur status, this clinches it. He just went to pieces. Couldn't cope. In a few days, he'll have Dartmouth down on his neck about the boy, whether he's dead or not. There's bound to be a court of inquiry. And if the woman's dead and he hasn't come forward . . ."

Menzies propped his elbows on the stone parapet and surveyed the unlovely vista of reeking mud. "Bloody fool." He gazed moodily at a gull bobbing on the water in midstream. "All right, Paul. Wrap it up. All of it. Nip Dartmouth in the bud first. The last thing we need is a naval investigation. Then get on to the rescue services and the local coroner about the woman. If she was in the house at the time, good enough."

"And if she wasn't?"

Menzies looked at him quizzically. "Use your judgment."

"My judgment is that Price thinks they're both dead. He'd obviously prefer it that way—as long as he doesn't get involved in detail."

"Then that's your answer, isn't it?"

"It might involve a little jiggery-pokery."

Menzies pushed himself off the wall and looked at his watch. "I leave the detail to you. Just keep your man happy, Paul. Providing you keep the ends tied neatly, I don't much care how you do it."

SEPTEMBER 27, 1940

The danger area was the street door—opening it to confront some busybody coming out, or being unable to open it at all—but the big mortice key did the trick, and the hallway inside was dark and empty. Music, a wireless or a gramophone, seeped indistinctly from an upper floor, but it was more comforting than alarming; it would have been unusual to find the house totally empty at eight o'clock in the evening. He had two hours. Pepper's dinner at Claridge's, he'd confided to Archie Bassingthwaite, was due to end at ten o'clock.

He applied the little Chubb key to the door of Pepper's flat. It turned smoothly: a barely audible click.

He stepped inside, closed the door, and checked the curtains. Pepper was a careful man; he'd had stout wooden shutters made to fit inside the window frames and heavy curtains to mask them. Price switched on his torch. Search bathroom, kitchen, and bedroom first as the least likely areas of concealment. He hadn't the faintest notion what, if anything, Pepper might have cause to conceal, or why, but that was irrelevant. One step at a time.

The bathroom was a shock. In the cabinet he found tubs of ladies' cleansing cream, a muddy-colored face mask, astringent, and a disagreeably pungent lotion for the hands. A manicure set in a fold-over case, eye drops, nose drops, corn plasters, breath-freshening pills, hair restorer, skin tonic. A woman? The hair rose on his neck. "He's so old-maidish."

Bedroom: a sleeping mask and cough mixture on the bedside table, another breath sweetener, brush and comb, stud boxes, little else. In the wardrobe: a half-dozen suits Price had never seen him wear, the more familiar baggy flannels and sports jackets, shirts, underwear, ties, fine silk pajamas. In the dressing table drawers: pullovers, socks, and handkerchiefs, impeccably arranged and folded.

Kitchen: just a kitchen. Pepper appeared to eat little and drink less. The pantry shelves were bare but for a box of cornflakes, jam, bread, a packet of Mazawattee tea, sugar in a stone jar, some pickled walnuts, and a half-used package of cracker biscuits.

The dining room, familiar from Pepper's soirées, held no cupboards, no chiffoniers, no wall safe.

He went through to the drawing room and stood for a moment with his back to the empty grate. Windows on his left, two deep chairs and a couch immediately in front of him, a long sideboard to his right, a bureau at right angles to it in the corner, piano on the wall beyond the couch, the suffering ladies behind and above him on the chimneypiece. Sideboard first.

The cupboard space was quite empty. The drawers gave up three photograph albums, neatly bound, five sheaves of household bills, all inscribed with dates of payment, a visitors' book in which Dr. Thomas Price's name appeared several times, and three bundles of letters bound with elastic bands.

The albums revealed Pepper as child, adolescent, student, teacher, lecturer, and holidaymaker, but although places and dates had been lovingly inscribed in white ink, the names of his grinning compatriots in the pictures were not. The last one, dated October 1936, showed Pepper and two young men standing arm in arm before the Great Pyramid at Gizeh. One of them was strikingly effeminate; the other was built like a rugby forward. Price backtracked through the last album and recognized the same two men in a dozen other snaps, sometimes singly, more often together. Interesting: Egypt 1936; Cape Town 1936. Two remarkably extensive—and expensive— journeys in the same year with the same friends. On Pepper's university salary? But the faces meant nothing to him. He replaced the albums in the drawer with the bills and the visitors' book.

He turned to the bundled letters. The top one in each stack bore a date. He opened the earliest.

"My dear, dear Pippy, Ghastly time was had by all. Expected your call but not a peep all weekend. Where were you, you little turncoat? Guy said (I'll sift the expletives to save your blushes) that Tony told him you'd struck gold and were too busy mining away to spare precious time for less-than-precious castoffs. I loathe him! He had that awful pill Dorian in tow and devoted the *entire* weekend to reducing him to a nervous wreck. I can't understand what you *see* in him, Pippy, really I can't.

"We talked politics all weekend and Guy tore into everyone on Saturday night over the Stalin-Hitler thing. He's *mad!!* Halfway through, this terribly distinguished, tall, George Arliss-type, sickeningly good-looking, one of the dons (I don't know what college)—said very quietly, 'Cut it out, Guy, there's a good chap,' and would you believe it, he did!!!! Guy just sat down and looked sulky but he shut up for the rest of the night. The masterful one is Julian something.

"Must go. Knew you'd want the doings and all. Lunch on Tuesday all right for you? Or is the *gold* so ravishing you can't wrench yourself away? (This is not intended as an accusation, Pippy. You know I take the long view). Love, Gerry."

A man?

He replaced the pale yellow bond in its envelope and opened another.

"Pillface, I don't know what that litigious queen told you and I don't care. Either you take me as I am or you take me not at all. I'm coming up to London on Friday to mooch and prowl. K threatens a mild thrash in Clarges Street. If you're not already too debauched—or disillusioned by my sweet Columbine Gerry—come and join us. If you are (debauched and disillusioned) go to hell. As ever, Guy."

In spite of his detachment, Price grew more and more uncomfortable as he read through the first batch of letters. Gerry, Guy, Tony, Julian, Pyotr, Toots, Bili (with a final *i*), Willie, Dorian, Timmy. Their passions ebbed and flowed from undying to unrequited love with dizzying, always destructive, abandon; their gossip rioted with character assassination and their occasional bursts of seriousness were floods of sensual subjectivity. But one thread linked their ramblings, their invective and self-gratification: a preoccupation with politics. They paraded under a puzzling array of banners, but all of them were socialist or Leninist in tone. Price found this confusing, even implausible. Gerry was clearly a merchant banker, Julian an aristocrat of vast private means, Dorian's father was chairman of an international oil company; the others were predominantly writers, artists, dons, embryo civil servants, or itinerant playboys. Their backgrounds were essentially respectable and privileged.

The last batch of correspondence, though no less coruscating in the field of personal relationships, was surprisingly matter-of-fact. The letters from mid-September onward, more than twenty of them, referred continuously to the CP (Communist Party) and the PC (People's Convention). Another organization, the People's Vigilance Committee, had sprung from the first two and this, apparently, had won their seal of approval. The PVC appeared to have been launched in July, on the fall of France, to force Churchill to seek friendship with Russia, to reestablish "democratic rights," to defend the standard of living of the British people, and to end profiteering. Its ultimate objective was a new government "truly representative of the people."

Julian—"the masterful one," the don—had become, by late summer of 1940, the notional leader of the group. "We need," he wrote, "a corporate leadership strong enough to force Churchill, when the time comes, to launch a second front; otherwise Stalin's finished before he's begun. We'll need the Labor Party extremists and the Unions—plus . . ." The Pepper Circle lived in a dream world.

Price copied down a few addresses from the last batch of letters, not immediately valuable in view of the absence of surnames in any of them, replaced the elastic bands, and put the packages back in the drawer. He looked at his watch: eight fifty-five. Plenty of time yet.

He crossed to the rolltop desk. Locked. He selected one of the small security keys and inserted it. It jammed. The other one turned easily.

A will, Pepper's own; bequests to University College, a boy's home in the Isle of Dogs, to his Cambridge college, to Mrs. Davina Walton "my housekeeper for many years and, in the event of her decease, to Robert Edward Walton, her son and his issue." Nothing greater than £500. And the lease of Queen's Gate to "Bobby Bemmelmann with much love and gratitude for youth restored and faith regained" (the cosmetics in the bathroom? Man? Woman?).

A checkbook, Martin's Bank; payments to tradesmen, the Red Cross, yearly subscription to the Garrick. More letters, nothing significant. A large desk diary. He went through it page by page. Meetings were indicated by initials, but what they represented was unclear until: October 12—a Saturday, he noted. "Travis Hall, Bow, 7:30 P.M. PVC" (People's Vigilance Committee?) "No—but call Ws and plead previous engagement. Note to G."

Price copied the date, time, and place and put the diary back in its drawer. He relocked the rolltop and stepped back into the center of the room.

The music from upstairs blared louder for the space of two or three seconds, then stopped altogether. A door slammed and feet stomped heavily on the stone steps.

The street door opened and shut. Silence.

He gave them five minutes, then stepped out to the hall, pulling the flat door firmly into place. Opened the street door, went out, and let it crunch back into its frame on the suction valve.

He turned up the collar of his coat and set off for South Kensington underground station.

*　　*　　*

Frank Loughran sent the file skidding across his desk. Curzon caught it and riffled through the dozen or so pages without fully opening the green covers.

"Give it to me in words," he growled. "I can't plow through this."

Loughran's death's-head grin conveyed his mood. "How can I put it? Let's say that when the war's over you're going to have a hell of a lot of explaining to do. Point One: the bodies belonged to Mr. Ron and Mrs. Lilian Randall—not to Petries, mother and son. Unfortunately for you, the pathologist had already got at the remains. Point Two: the death certificates were issued and registered. Mr. and Mrs. Randall. Point Three: If Alan Petrie isn't on the trot somewhere, he's evaporated. Didn't tell his friends, hasn't turned up anywhere, isn't in hospital, doesn't appear on the casualty lists. Point Four: Alice Petrie never lived at 3 Godwin Terrace—and in that neighborhood you couldn't walk down the street without being noticed, believe me. Point Five: she left her job at the university on July 19. None of her hen friends've seen her since. We checked out eleven relatives—hers and her late hubby's. They haven't seen her either and there haven't been any letters. Point Six: she's what the Americans describe as a hot number. Fast and loose. Half a dozen clerks at University College have had a nibble, one time or another. You want to hear any more?"

Curzon sighed. "So what have you done?"

"Exactly what you ordered." He laid emphasis on the last word. "Phony death certificates for Alice and Alan Petrie. Killed as a result of enemy action, Godwin Terrace. Special Branch went white but they cottoned on. Your babies are as good as dead. On paper anyway."

"Hmmm." Curzon opened the file, found the documents, and eyed them sourly.

Loughran swung his feet onto the desk. "Mind if I ask you a question?" His mouth twisted. "I'll sign the Secrets Act first, if you're worried."

"Well?"

"What do you lose by telling Price they're not dead? Why all this?" He waved at the paperwork.

Curzon got to his feet and tucked the file under his arm. "How many doubles are you running at the moment?"

"Six in London. Why?"

"How many identity cards, ration books, birth certificates, and God knows what have you forged for them?"

"That's different."

Curzon opened the door. "See what I mean? It's always different when it's somebody else's problem."

SEPTEMBER 28, 1940

He had no stomach nowadays for the unexpected and the sight of Paul's MG sitting by the curb outside Middlemass House when he turned the corner set his heart fluttering in riotous panic. Paul's mood didn't help. When Price seated him in the kitchen and put on a kettle for coffee, his nervousness filled the room.

No, not nervousness, Price reminded himself. Paul was a professional. The realization plunged him into despair. On the day Mr. Evans-Wyke died, the greatest shock in a procession of shocks was the knowledge that Paul had betrayed him, and no matter how he intellectualized the reasons for it, the fact itself remained. Yet, even now, with all he knew of the Pepperpot and its Machiavellian goings-on, he could not quite believe that Paul was untouched by some human feeling; understanding, at the very least. Surely *that*.

The first sip of coffee broke the ice.

"I went to the coroner's clerk again today," Paul said quietly.

"Oh?" Price wondered if he'd considered the absurdity of the proposition; that Curzon, a lowly clerk, would be allowed the freedom of the coroner's office in a case involving people to whom he was not related. He decided he hadn't.

"It *was* Alice and Alan." Paul gulped at the coffee as if it were unwatered Scotch whiskey.

Price bowed his face in his hands, not trusting himself to display the required emotion.

"I'm sorry, Tom. Really."

He is, Price thought vaguely; but for what? Stage managing the dead? The living? For acting out a charade? For lying to—a friend?

"Will you tell Dinah?"

Ah, *that* was it. For a lie that might hurt Dinah.

"No. Not yet, anyway."

Paul dug into an inner pocket. He slid two long slips of folded paper between Price's elbows. "The death certificates. I have to take them back, but I thought you'd want to see them."

Price angled down to look at them: Alice's name on the upper one, boldly handwritten. He shook his head. "I don't." Then quickly, "Thank you."

Paul put them back in his pocket. "I wish to God I didn't have to be the one to tell you," he said gently.

And Tom Price believed him. Gladly.

OCTOBER 12, 1940

Price sat at his desk until five thirty, a set of files spread in front of him as if he were deeply engrossed in an exercise of some complexity, but there were no interruptions. No one came, no one telephoned. There had been signs of activity on the ground and first floors when he arrived at three, but in accordance with house rules he spoke to no one but Burton, Sergeant Cross's Saturday relief guard in the lobby. Burton, predictably, was surprised and suspicious, and Price had no doubt he had called the emergency number at once to report an unscheduled arrival by a member of the Pepperpot staff. Action would have been taken at once.

He watched the minute hand touch the half hour, put on his hat and coat, locked up, and went down in the lift. Burton eyed him with hostility from his table and ignored his cheery "good night." Price stepped out into Southampton Row and turned left, as he always did.

The trick, he reminded himself again, was to mislead without seeming to. It called for an acting performance the tail could actually observe and interpret. When he made his break, if he made it, it was essential his pursuer define it as bad luck or bad judgment on his part, not deliberate evasion on Price's.

He reached the corner of Theobald's Road, gazed around him as if deciding whether to cross or not, looked down at his feet, and shook his head. He missed a break in the traffic and let his shoulders droop, his body go limp; an act of weary resignation. A little flap of the arms, self-evident impatience, and he set off along Theobald's Road, shoulders bowed, eyes on the pavement. Two young women, approaching and passing, stared at him openly and exchanged giggles. Encouraging. From behind, he would have the appearance of a man daydreaming, temporarily cut off from the world about him. He dawdled to the corner of Gray's Inn Road, leaped back to the curb in time to avoid being run over by a Lyon's Tea van, turned completely around as if trying to get his bearings, and caught the Curate in the act of sidestepping into a shop doorway.

As he penetrated deeper into the City, the crowds thinned dangerously and he slowed to a crawl, forcing the Curate to hang back. The whole plan crystallized—or collapsed—at the acute-angled street corner where Poultry joined Queen Victoria Street; there for the space of thirty seconds, no more, he would be hidden from view. But only luck would yield the critical factor—a bus emerging from Cornhill or Threadneedle Street into Queen Victoria Street at the precise moment he needed it. Heading west. A bus or a taxi, he didn't mind which, although a bus would fit his aimless-wanderer performance better. A bus triggered recognizable reflexes in a homeward-bound City worker. A taxi might smack of premeditation.

It happened. He saw the doubledecker pull round the corner from Cornhill, feigned surprise, awakening decision, slipped round the sharp elbow of the intersection, sprinted across the road and leaped on the platform just as the driver pulled away from the stop. It took less than half those precious thirty seconds. From the window at the top of the stairs, he saw the Curate run into Queen Victoria Street, stop, and drop his hands despairingly. Perfect. Off the bus in Fleet Street; take an underground train at Blackfriars to Liverpool Street.

He was beginning to enjoy it.

Travis Hall was a gray-brick monstrosity tucked away at the end of a cul-de-sac behind the Bethnal Green Road, joined on both sides by small workshops and garages and overshadowed, two streets away, by a railway yard and a synagogue. The rough pavement leading to it was littered with wind-stirred paper, packing straw, cardboard box lids and tangles of knotted string. The gutters in front of the garages were stained with oil.

He was late by ten minutes or so, and when he entered through a double barrier of blackout curtaining the hall was packed and the meeting under way. "This way, brother," whispered a doorkeeper in shiny serge and squeaking boots, and he was led to the back of the hall and lodged in a corner under the megaphone of a public address system.

A small, round, rather sad little man with a bush of frothy white hair and half-moon glasses commanded the microphone on the raised dais. Flanked by four men, one of them colored, he stood behind a table covered with a large Union Jack. There were, he announced mournfully, over a thousand delegates in the hall, an overwhelming response and a significant rebuff to the undemocratic forces in British politics currently making themselves deaf to the raised voice of the proletariat. The paper he was reading from ran out of words. "I give you, brothers," he gestured grandly at the man on his right, "our comrade Harry Pollitt."

Mr. Pollitt was thunderously received and responded with equal passion. He was followed by "Comrade Palme Dutt," who opened by appealing to the trades union leaders, shop stewards, and air raid shelter committeemen present to redouble their efforts to bring "the international class war for survival into the open." The delegates gave him a standing ovation. Like Harry Pollitt, Comrade Dutt spoke for at least half an hour before conceding the floor to the colored man, an Indian whose name Price didn't catch.

Wedged deeper into his corner by the arrival of other latecomers, Price became aware of a nudging motion at his elbow. He glanced nervously at the source, uncomfortable reminders of the Pepper letters rising to chill the skin at his neck. A young man—mid-twenties, he guessed—lifted his head in a series of quirky jerking movements and rolled his eyes. Price glared discouragingly, his worst fears materializing, but the young man grinned and hooked a patronizing thumb at the elderly Indian.

Price nodded coolly and gave the Indian his undivided attention—at which point, the subcontinental evangelist stopped speaking and sat down. Comrade Pollitt leaped into the breach at once and announced that regional and district organizers should come to the platform for news of "the great London convention in January"; the rest were to fold their chairs, place them against the walls, and avail themselves of the tea urns, bearing in mind that the twopence-a-cup fee would swell the People's Victory Chest.

"You a shop steward?"

"Observer," said Price shortly, looking around urgently for escape. There was nothing here for him.

"Ah." The idea seemed to impress the young man. "Here." He took Price's arm and dragged him into the clattering swell of chair folders. "I'll buy you a cuppa, how's that?"

Two long tables had been erected at either side of the hall and good-natured queues formed in front of them. Price's companion bought two giant mugs of dense beige liquid, threw fourpence into the upturned hat serving as a cash box and, with a wink, added another tuppence. "For the pot, brother," he said to the man behind the urn.

His new friend then led Price through the blackout curtaining into the grubby cul-de-sac and lowered himself to the curb, feet in the oil-scummed gutter; Price followed suit. It was too dark to inspect the cloth-capped idealists squatting around him and too cold to be sitting on uncovered stone, but conformity seemed appropriate. He was suddenly very tired: the hours of waiting, the strain of the walk through the city, the deflation of anticlimax. Depression. What was he doing here? What had he expected to find?

"Oh, hell." The young man spat a mouthful of tea into the gutter.

Price tasted his; it bore the unmistakable tang of metal polish.

"I should've known better." The youth spat again to clear his mouth. "They can't make tea. Never could." He poured the contents of his mug into the gutter, and Price did the same.

The young man produced a paper bag from his pocket and held it out. "Sweet?" Price declined. "My mother makes them. Sends them to me every fortnight. Big tin. What do you think then?"

Price was confused by the question. "I don't eat sweets," he said politely.

"No, I meant the meeting. What did you think—as an observer?"

"Very well attended. Good organization."

"Oh, they're good organizers, all right. But the platform stuff's a bit *derrière le temps*, don't you think? All this"—he waved magnanimously at the invisible but noisy tea drinkers—"for an hour and a half of the same old dialectic claptrap. As group leaders we're a bit above that sort of thing, I'd have thought.

"That's what's wrong, you see." The young man seemed not to mind that he might be overheard. "The whole movement's still the domain of the inky-fingered. In this country, your intellectuals stand on the fringe and bow and scrape because that's the form. Not like Europe. Mustn't muscle in on the masses—oh, dear me, no. Their game, after all. They invented it. People forget that Marx and Lenin and Trotsky were all middle-class thinkers."

"That's a little simplistic, isn't it?"

"The whole bloody thing's simplistic, old man. You take Highgate—that's my stamping ground. Our cell leader's a bloody caretaker—and at my school, too!"

"You're a teacher?"

"Yes. Just a primary, though. We organize the air raid shelter groups up there. At least, I organize and Alf—that's this caretaker—Alf stands around biting his nails waiting for the revolution. Revolution! Bloody *pathétique*, old man. Offer him another couple of quid a week in his pay envelope and he'd vote for Churchill till he was blue in the face."

He helped himself to another sweet and, cheeks bulging, extended his hand. "Boyd Corrie, my name."

Price introduced himself as Robert Jardine and enclosed the damp uncallused palm.

Boyd—"I hate surname relationships, don't you?"—embarked on a snappy analysis of Highgate's tactical weaknesses and, in the process, revealed that he was twenty-five years old, a conscientious objector, a graduate of a teachers' training college and potentially the Party's soundest bet for London regional organizer.

"I can distance myself, you see, old man. And at the same time I'm in it up to the hairline. Perspective, that's what this lot needs. Perspective and new blood in and the sophistication to perceive the need for change." He had been talking continuously for several minutes and sensed he might have gone too far.

"Not boring you, am I, old man? I mean—an *observer* . . ." His emphasis lent the word enormous significance.

Price played up to it. When in Rome . . .

"I'm never bored by enthusiasm."

"Well, that's jolly decent, old man. I mean, coming from you."

Price wondered vaguely if "observer" was indeed a Communist Party rank, like regional organizer or cell leader. He shrugged. "It's my job to keep an eye on leadership material. It's hard to find."

"Get away. *Incroyable!* Sort of talent scout, you mean?"

"In a manner of speaking."

"Ah." Boyd tapped the side of his nose.

"As you said yourself, the Party needs perspective. The long view. And . . . discretion."

"Absolutely." Boyd Corrie looked at his companion curiously. He seemed much preoccupied; Price could feel the wide brown eyes studying his profile in the dark. Boyd was impressed, but he didn't know why. When they took their mugs back into the hall he asked Price how he intended getting back to "civilization" and, when he said he would probably walk, offered pillion space on his motorcycle. It would have been illogical to refuse.

Boyd parked the machine outside Waterloo Station and insisted on walking Robert Jardine to the train. They had ten minutes to spare and bought tea in chipped cups from the buffet.

"I'd be awfully bucked if you'd come and look over my organization one evening," Boyd ventured when they were settled at a table. "If you could spare the time, of course."

"I might manage that. I'd need a few days' notice, though."

"Where could I get in touch?" The young man produced a notebook and pencil with disconcerting eagerness.

"You can't, I'm afraid. I . . . travel a lot."

"Oh. Well yes, I suppose you must. Anyway, I'm in the book. Fire watcher at the school, you see—have to be available."

They discussed possible dates and times but Boyd's was a

crowded schedule; he was every inch the activist. Shelter
Nights (tea and buns served by "the lads" while Boyd preached
Marxist-Leninist materialism to shelterers and persuaded them
to sign round robins lambasting the government) depended on
the frequency of air raids. The Planning Committee and the
Funds Committee each met once a week. Collecting Nights
(door-to-door begging for food, clothing and blankets for
evacuees) once a week. Firewatching twice a week. "I sometimes think I'm doing too much," he confided. "And yet, in
a way, not enough, if you take my point."

"I should have thought that was plenty."

"Oh, absolutely!" Boyd was, if nothing else, absolute.
"But the way I look at it, anyone could do it. I mean, horses
for courses, don't you think?"

"You think you have more to offer?"

"Well, I should think *so*!"

"In what way?"

Boyd faltered. "Oh, lots of ways. If I say so myself I'm
no fool. No one can quote chapter and verse better than me.
I'm a teacher after all. I'd make a damn good Party lecturer.
And—ah . . ." He pawed his chin. "I've got the bike and a
petrol allowance. That's a big plus nowadays. And then
there's my wireless."

"Wireless?"

"Well, you never know, do you? If there was an invasion,
Jerries running all over the country—could happen, you know—
the Party'd be bound to resist, wouldn't it? They'd need
wireless communications." He stared unhappily at his tea.
"That's what I mean about perspective, old man. Nobody's
planning. Wasting their time on conventions and bloody
charters."

"What do you know about wireless, Boyd?" Price kept his
voice flat, almost condescendingly offhand.

"Everything, in a word. Should do—I've been at it since I
was ten. Radio ham—you know. You should see my rooms:
three hundred quids' worth of equipment and all my own
work. Shortwave, of course. Built it myself."

"I thought it was against the law to operate transmitting
equipment. Didn't I read that somewhere?"

"Ah, well . . ." Boyd blushed all the way down to his
throat. "I don't actually use the *transmitter* these days. Just

listen in. Anyway''—he smiled gamely—''that's not the point. It's the knowledge that counts, isn't it? What I *know*.''

They went out to the concourse and stopped by the barrier. Doors were slamming on the Richmond train. They shook hands.

''You *will* keep in touch?''

''When I can.'' His aloofness of manner set Boyd fidgeting inconsolably.

''Absolutely anything you need, old man. Just say the word and Corrie's there. Really, anything at all.'' He was still clinging to Price's hand. ''You won't forget, will you?''

''I won't forget.''

''Because I spotted right away you were—well, a cut above the rest. Stands out a mile. No''—he shook his head violently—''I won't ask questions. You can't tell me anything, I can see that. But''—the brown eyes were imploring—''if you think I could be useful—properly, I mean—just call.''

''I'll remember that.''

''I'm in the book,'' he said again anxiously.

The guard's whistle shrilled and Price broke away. He pulled himself into the last coach and slammed the door. Boyd waved agitatedly from the barrier. Price waved back.

''Absolutely anything at all, old man.''

He closed his eyes and settled his head on the cushion.

NOVEMBER 29, 1940

The cafe was on the corner of Euston Road and Birkenhead Street, a nest of a dozen tables enclosed by discolored floral wallpaper, sealed from the outside world by yellowing net curtains. King's Cross Station was visible through a hole in the voile covering the door. Frying chips sizzled in a vat behind the counter and a tubby man in a striped apron poked at them with a blackened spatula.

Price stirred his tea and inspected the room casually. Boyd was in the chair immediately behind him, eating a jam tart with a fork. Three of the tables at the end were occupied by a group of men in overalls and black railway uniforms, porters and greasers from the station. Their talk was loud and punctuated with whoops of laughter.

Price half-turned in his chair. "Could you let me have a match?" he asked politely.

Boyd Corrie nearly parted company with his skin. "Oh, absolutely, old man. Here, got some somewhere." He produced a box of Swan Vestas, dropped them, picked them up from the floor, and handed them over. His hands were shaking.

"Thanks." Price lit his pipe. "I think we'll have snow again tonight."

"Oh, absolutely!" breathed Boyd. He swiveled round to avoid dislocating his neck and accepted the return of the matches, "Absolutely."

"There's no need to panic. We shan't be overheard." Price shifted to a more comfortable position in his chair. "I'm sorry I couldn't make it on Thursday."

"Oh, don't mention it. Better in the long run, really. I mean . . ." Boyd nudged his head closer. "You said it was pretty vital."

"It is. And you're right. I'll be honest with you, Boyd, I had no intention of meeting your group."

"Ah." A world of understanding.

"I have a confession to make. No!" He raised his hand. "Hear me out first. There was nothing accidental about our running into each other at Travis Hall."

Boyd could not resist a smirk. "You know, it's funny you should say that. I was thinking on my way home that night, after I dropped you at the station—"

"I've had you under observation for six months. I and . . . other people."

"Go on!"

"We talked that night at Travis Hall because I needed to confirm my impressions at first hand. It was important you have the chance to—well, make your position clear. Without pressure from me."

"And did you . . . ?"

"I was impressed."

Boyd let out a great whooshing sigh of relief. "*Anything*, old man. I mean to say . . ."

"You have no interest in who or . . . *what* I am?"

"Look, I know the form. There's a war on. No names, no pack drill, right?" His soft brown eyes coalesced in what he clearly hoped was a penetrating gaze. "I'm a pretty good judge of character, myself. I was watching *you* that night, too. You probably didn't notice. All I'm saying is, I know a good man when I see one."

Price sipped at his tea. "I'm afraid I don't find that altogether comforting, Boyd."

"What?"

"If you decide to . . . assist me, our work, I'll expect more from you than acceptance at face value."

"Well, what I actually *meant* . . ."

"What do you really believe, Boyd?"

"Ah . . ."

"Your beliefs. Not the labels, Boyd. The ethic, the core."

"My dear old chap . . ."

"I'm not talking about shelter committees and collection nights."

"Well, if you don't know me well enough by now, there's no point . . ."

"You'd rather I left it at that? I see. That's honest, at least."

"No!" Eyes left and right, grasping at straws. "What I'm saying is, I haven't *changed*. Perspective, planning, getting down to brass tacks. That kind of thing . . ." He tailed off, imagination deserting him.

"War?" Price let the word hang.

"War, yes."

"You'd volunteer to fight?"

Boyd's pouchy jowls sagged in defeat. "I *objected*. I told you that. It's the line. The Party says . . ."

"Would you fight . . ."—he drew out the sentence tantalizingly—"for Russia?"

"*Russia!*"

"Would you?"

"Well . . ." Boyd's confusion was total but his fear of exclusion from the charmed circle was even greater. "Yes, of course I would. Like a shot. Anyone would."

"Not quite anyone," Price said dryly.

"But how could I . . . ?"

"*Service*, Boyd. Think about it. To *serve*. Not preach. Not organize. *Serve*."

"You want me to do something?"

"Do you want to?"

"Yes."

Price put down his cup and slipped his hand between the chairs. Boyd took it reverently, then glanced down with a sharp gulp as he felt a square of folded paper press into his palm.

"Read it when you get home, Boyd. Not before."

"Is it . . . ?"

"Let's say it's a chance to show what you're made of." Price withdrew his hand. "Nothing to it—for an old wireless hand."

BOOK THREE
1941

APRIL 20, 1941

The sky was low enough to touch; marbled cloud, smoky gray on stony black, full of rain. An English Sunday. Price stood by the garden shed, mesmerized by the invisible six-foot by three-foot rectangle in the corner of the vegetable patch where Alan Petrie slept deep in his blanket and tarpaulin.

The first warm droplets of rain kissed the back of his hand and he reversed the bowl of his pipe to keep it dry, squinting up at the sky. He had promised himself for a week that he would let the day come and go without noting its significance, but that was a little like pretending Alan was not over there in the corner, fertilizing vegetables. Closing one's mind to an idea locked it in, not out. The Shining Day was a fact; there was no hiding from it. Umbrellas along the Unter den Linden; the Wehrmacht goose-stepping by in greatcoats and capes; Hitler taking his birthday salute in the driving rain with the Junker generals around him. Else, perhaps Kurt too, watching from one of the special stands reserved for the Party faithful. Willy on parade?

A carnival in the rain. Ritter cheek-by-jowl with the Tirpitzufer crowd; if he could manage it, with Canaris's private party in the enclosure immediately behind the Fuehrer's, bathing in the reflected glory of Panzer generals brought home for the occasion from France and the Low Countries, from Scandinavia and North Africa.

Not one of them would be concerned, as the heels crashed and the salutes swung and the tanks rolled by, that Wilhelm Sommer stood waiting in the rain in a garden in Richmond for the real Shining Day. Would Ritter pause for a moment, recalling his promise at the Hook of Holland two years before? Of course not. The grand design now lay as deeply buried as Alan Petrie. Sea Lion was yesterday, a pipe dream overtaken by reality. If there was ever to be a Shining Day, an invasion, a triumphal sweep through London, it would take its place in a sequence of events ordered by necessity. For the moment, it was as remote as Judgment Day.

239

He shook himself out of his reverie and inspected what was left of his flower garden. Too much rain, too early in the season. "Told you so," Fred Wilby had said darkly last weekend. "You should've turned it over to veg, the lot of it." As if a passion for flowers was un-British, a sin to be washed away by the weather gods.

When the blitz ended last month Wilby had taken over the church hall; plastered the walls with pictures of whirling Hurricanes and Spitfires to celebrate the victory of The Few, and army recruiting posters showing desert tanks in furious action to honor Wavell's tumultuous victories against the scabrous Italians in North Africa. Saturday, March 29—a red-letter day, Fred had thundered from the platform, as the children dug in to margarine sandwiches and indigestible homemade ice cream.

Two days later Erwin Rommel had smashed through the El Agheila bottleneck into Wavell's Cyrenaica with only fifty German tanks as a spearhead and two untried Italian divisions at his back. In ten days he'd pushed Wavell's depleted garrison back into Egypt.

Fred had not appeared in his garden for a week after that, and when he found the courage to face the world again, he'd taken heart from the decay of Price's tulips. "A setback now and then is no bad thing," he argued, turning reason on its ear. "Learn from our mistakes; that's always been the British way."

But even Fred Wilby had his limits. Price had seen him an hour ago peering from his living room window, a furtive face behind a twitch of curtain. Fred had also read his *Sunday Times*. The fifty thousand Tommies Churchill had plucked from Wavell's arms and sent to Greece as a buttressing force to deny Hitler entry to the Balkans were reeling under the advance of List's 12th Army. There was no hope for them, except in a Dunkirk-style withdrawal to Crete. Fred had withdrawn.

Price jammed his hoe into the wet earth and leaned on it, his eye drawn again to the invisible grave. Greece was more than just another blow to Fred Wilby's native pride. It was another battle honor for the celebrants of the Unter den Linden. Another reason for postponing the Shining Day.

It was a mistake to dwell on it. He had nearly said it aloud.

He desperately needed someone to talk to, but there was no one.

The rain fell with suddenly renewed vigor and he made a dash for the house. The Shining Day! The rain god was an Englishman.

MAY 19, 1941

Pepper put his head in the door. "You ready, my boy?"

Price shuffled papers into neat stacks, slipped them into file covers, and locked them in his desk. They went down in the lift together. Pepper's official car, a recent bequest from a grateful government, stood waiting. The ATS girl driver, a broad-framed young cockney, remained at the wheel and engaged gear as soon as they were settled. "Home, Edith, please," ordered Pepper sharply.

They sat through the journey to Queen's Gate without speaking, Pepper's pointed chin resting on his chest in profound meditation, Price engrossed in an evening paper. It was Pepper's belief that Edith was a gossip, a parasite, and a liability; his defense against her was silence and an icy reserve.

At the flat, Pepper made toast and tea and they settled down in the drawing room.

"Well, now." He eased tiny feet from tiny shoes and pulled on a pair of ornately embroidered Indian slippers. "What's this idea of yours, my boy?"

Price stirred his tea reflectively, avoiding the banana yellow eyes. "Can we consider this off the record, Philip? Between you and me?"

"Of course." Pepper bit deeply into a piece of toast, scattering crumbs onto his lap and over his slippered feet.

"I've been thinking about the work note on Stronghold. At home mostly. I haven't attempted a formal analysis yet."

"Stronghold?" Pepper wiped his mouth with a crooked finger. "The Scottish Command paper. That's Joint Chiefs, isn't it?" He spread his hands. "I haven't really had time."

"As far as I can judge, forty thousand troops have been moved to camps on the coast north of Aberdeen. Four Marine

242

Commando units are due to join them in a week's time. The Navy's stepping up mine-sweeping operations and I see today that Air Intelligence want a reconnaissance facility at Garroch.''

"So?"

"All signs point to a Norwegian second front."

Pepper licked margarine from his fingers. "We both know that's in the cards. Sometime. Is that your point?"

"No." He concentrated hard on maintaining an expression of supreme discomfort. "Do you believe the Russian-German pact can last?"

It was Pepper's turn to look uncomfortable. "Well . . ."

"You told me once Stalin would be lucky if it survived six months."

"For heaven's sake, Tom." Exasperation.

Price grimaced apologetically. "I've been chewing this over for days. There are lots of other pointers, but Stronghold clinches it. I believe Hitler plans to invade Russia. Days or weeks. And I think Churchill knows. The buildup in Scotland is a Norwegian invasion force. I think it'll be timed to strike the moment the Germans cross into Russia."

Pepper left his chair and went to the fireplace. He set a match to a wigwam of paper and kindling and knelt in front of the hearth, watching it catch. "That's highly speculative," he said at last.

"But feasible."

Price allowed Pepper the privacy of his thoughts; he had anticipated them. Thought One: there was no Operation Stronghold; no buildup of men and arms in Scotland. Stronghold was just another paper deception exercise designed exclusively for the delectation of Tom Price. Thought Two: Price would not go to these lengths—a request for a private chat, off the record, away from the office—without good reason; i.e., to achieve an advantage. Three: What was the advantage?

Pepper murmured into the flames, "I don't see . . ."

Now the difficult part—the threat Pepper had to grasp, act on. He cleared his throat. "The implications, Philip. You and I both know we're not equipped for a second front. We'll be forced into it to take the pressure off Russia."

"*If* Hitler invades."

Price ignored the interjection. "Once we're committed to fighting at Russia's back door we're committed to supplying Moscow with total support—guns, tanks, planes, food, all the

243

rest of it. That's your own forecast. Production line capacity in British factories geared full time to arming Russia, convoys to transport supplies, naval protection. We'll bleed to death. We can't afford that kind of aid." His voice had risen to a hoarse falsetto; he stopped abruptly and looked down foolishly.

Pepper grunted to his feet and turned his back on the fire. He had difficulty in quelling a small smile of understanding. "What do you expect me to do about it? If it's true—and I'm not saying it is for a moment—it's policy. Out of my hands."

Price leaned forward eagerly, slopping tea into his saucer in his eagerness. "You hold the initiative in perspective planning, Philip. The next stage is strategic forecasting. Well, you'll never have a better opportunity. We've got the Stronghold papers. You're running an analysis of industrial productivity. You have a perfect right to demand a briefing on the Russian situation. Put them together and prove to Downing Street that a second front would be disastrous—that trying to supply Russia is madness." He sat back in his chair, smiled nervously. "That's what you believe, after all."

The little man's eyes were wide but sightless. "Speculative." He sighed. "Highly speculative."

Price relaxed. He had said enough.

There was little to choose between Pepper and Boyd, he thought, as the train jolted away from the platform at Waterloo. Boyd's naiveté sprang from knowing too little, Pepper's from knowing too much. What bound them in irons was their blind commitment to an ideal. A peculiar form of blindness; Else had it, Karl, too, in his day. Reason and common sense were no match for it.

And Pepper *was* committed, he had no doubt of that now. That weird correspondence of his was more than the pursuit of physical appetite. His circle—Julian, Gerry, Guy et al. —had common cause, common *political* cause. And they *were* active.

He pulled out his pipe and settled it in his teeth without lighting it. Pepper would feel compelled to act on what he had just heard. He—none of them—could afford to ignore a blatant attempt by a known German agent to forestall cooperation between Britain and Russia in the event of an invasion. They *would* act. Initially, by meeting to discuss the probability of a German assault on Russia. Then, by planning for the eventuality: through political agitation—the Communist Party, the People's Vigilance Committee, perhaps with the help of Labour Party extremists and union militants. Factory meetings, more conventions, carefully planted newspaper articles. They were quite capable of all that and more. Pepper himself would be under pressure to take more direct action. Yes, even a Pepperpot work note, but one that *pleaded* the Russian cause, not one that militated against it.

Now that would really be an unparalleled achievement; a document designed to persuade Churchill to cut off his right arm to favor Stalin's cause. The concept was Olympian and he pushed it to the back of his mind. He had no right to hope for anything so monumentally far-reaching.

Of course, at this very moment Pepper might be telephoning British Intelligence with a blow-by-blow account of their conversation. But the odds were wildly against it. Commitment comes before country. Boyd and Pepper shared that belief, too.

And if it worked? If Pepper wrote his pro-Soviet work note, if Julian, Gerry, Guy and Co. orchestrated a public clamor to rush to the aid of Uncle Joe Stalin? Well, given the opportunity to unearth more information about them—through Boyd Corrie, for instance; now *there* was poetic irony!—it might well be within his power to destroy them. Expose them, when it suited him, as agents working against the interests of the British Government. At the moment, of course, guaranteed to create the greatest possible public outcry.

Hmm. Pipe dreams. He removed the pipe with a rueful grin and put it in his pocket. He was developing delusions of grandeur. A puppet had to free itself before it could learn to pull its own strings.

MAY 30, 1941

The answer to complexity was simplicity. It was a continuing source of amazement to him that he had not recognized it before.

The Price surveillance effort was a machine, well-oiled and continuously maintained, but a machine nonetheless. Automatic. The Pepperpot was its heart and brain, its soul, but it drove a mechanism composed of innumerable smaller parts. A few cogs—Pepper and Archie Bassingthwaite, Curzon, the shadows and their masters—knew the machine existed and why. But that secret was critical to the efficiency of the Lie. It was not open to such toilers in the vineyard as Mrs. Plum and her corps of clacking secretaries. For them, Tom Price was no more than he appeared to be. It couldn't be otherwise.

They knew nothing. Who else was excluded? Sergeant Cross, perhaps. A mere functionary. The three young acolytes Pepper had recruited from University College to increase the handling capacity of the research unit. Presumably, many if not all the lower- and middle-grade civil servants Price dealt with by telephone in Whitehall.

It was simple enough to prove who *did* know and what arrangements existed among them to nurse and coddle him, and he had set about the task assiduously. When he was in the company of Pepper or Curzon—working, eating out, at a concert, walking in Richmond Park—the Plumber-Baker-Curate-Undertaker ménage miraculously disappeared. When he was alone, they reappeared. When Pepper was out of the office, Archie Bassingthwaite was in situ. When Archie left early for one of his spellbinding evenings of poetry reading and chamber music, Pepper worked late. On Saturdays two of the surveillance quartet—one in the morning, the other from midafternoon to late evening—lurked at the window of a top-floor flat in Onslow Road. On Sunday Curzon presented himself with religious punctuality at ten o'clock and usually stayed for lunch and supper.

Before they left the building together, for lunch or an

evening concert, Pepper would make a call—unquestionably to release the surveillance man of the day from further bondage. Curzon presumably phoned from a callbox each time he left Middlemass House. The system, like the Lie itself, was perfectly interlocking. It cried out to be manipulated.

When it was necessary to meet Corrie—once, sometimes twice, a week since mid-January as his reshaping of Boyd's life accelerated—he would persuade Pepper to join him for an evening drink or a light meal or find some excuse for accompanying him to Queen's Gate in the car. Only once, on an atrociously bitter night in late January, had he been followed from Pepper's flat and, on that occasion, the Baker had deserted him at South Kensington station and left him to make the journey to Richmond on his own. The machine had run smoothly and faultlessly for two years. It was beginning to take him for granted.

He left Pepper's flat in Queen's Gate at nine thirty. The street was quiet but not empty, and he stood for a few minutes under the porch to adjust to the dark and the tempo of the night walkers. There were few strollers abroad at that hour and loiterers were instantly identifiable, but he went through the motions for simple peace of mind. He set off toward South Kensington at a brisk pace, stopped abruptly at the corner of Bremmer Road, tapped his pockets as if he'd forgotten something, whirled on his heel and marched back. No one behind him; no one hugging the wall on the opposite pavement. A man and a woman turned the corner behind him, giggling and chattering at the tops of their overbearing young voices, and he stooped to untie and retie his shoelaces, letting them pass. They crossed the road and pattered up the steps of a block of flats. He crossed into Kensington Gore and found an eastbound bus stop.

Railway station buffets and bars were no longer secure meeting places. Too many policemen, military patrols, and service transport officers, all of them suspicious and on the lookout for fly-by-nights on the run in civilian clothes. On the other hand, public houses buried away in back streets around mainline stations were ideal; the clientele was more often than not transitory, the regulars kept themselves to themselves, and the only uniformed invaders were Salvation Army zealots with collecting tins and copies of *The Warcry*. Price varied the locations from one meeting to the next, but he favored the area around Liverpool Street station. The Cross Keys was ideal—obscure, small, grubby.

Boyd was at the dartboard, the agreed signal that he had not been followed. Price went to the bar and bought a half of bitter, then sat at a table to watch the doors for ten minutes. When he was satisfied, he walked over to Boyd and asked if he'd care for a game of 301 up. Boyd won easily. When they were well into the second game, Price opened the conversation.

"Is the set ready?" He covered the question with the wide grin of a loser recognizing the inevitability of having to buy the next round.

"Perfect."

"And the power pack?"

"No problems. About the same weight, near enough. Can't get the set below twenty-two pounds, as I said."

"No matter. I've got another job for you, Boyd. A few telephone calls, nothing much. Will you have time, d'you think?"

Boyd winked, playing his victor's role with panache. He raised his tankard and drank. "Nothing but time now, have I? No more shelter work, no more firewatching, no more collection nights. Free as a bird, except for the lectures. What's the brief?" He had inherited the word from Price and used it liberally.

"We talked about your colleagues on the People's Vigilance Committee. The young ones. Your inner action group." Boyd loved labels.

"Ah. The lads."

"You said they'd cooperate in . . . certain ways."

Boyd threw a triple twenty, a double nineteen, and a six. He was within a double four of winning again. Price went off the board with all three arrows and conceded the game. He refilled their glasses and they started the third round.

"Absolutely," said Boyd as Price got off to an unnervingly good start with his first throw. "What line exactly?" Boyd threw a remarkable double twenty, then a triple and a triple nineteen. Price slapped him on the back and laughed good-naturedly. He said quietly, "The Germans are ready to invade Russia."

Boyd swallowed hard. "Blimey—"

Price cut him off, still grinning for the benefit of possible

248

onlookers. "It could be any day now. In the next week or so I'll need ten or twelve men I can trust; young, committed. Not cowards."

"Oh, absolutely."

"Can you bring them together?"

"You want to brief them?" That word again.

"No. I'll instruct them through you. You'll coordinate and handle their product."

"Ah—product?"

Price scored a bull's-eye with his last dart. "I want men working in shipping, railways, munitions, docks, the civil service. All over the country—Liverpool, Southampton, London, Birmingham. We'll want to know production figures on war assembly lines, troop and supply movements around the country, delivery dates and destinations, food cargoes landed from abroad. I'll give you the fine detail later. Are you sure you can lay your hands on such men?"

"Pretty sure. I can let you know in a day or two."

Price threw his last arrow aimlessly, knowing he had no hope of finishing on a double one. It was his blind side. The dart thunked home in the very center of the slot. He beamed. "Everyone wins sometime."

He took a cab to Waterloo. An extravagance, he reminded himself soberly. His original nest egg of £1,000—the Barclays Bank fivers, banded and new—had finally run out, a small miracle of conservation. The last £200 had gone to Boyd to purchase black market spares for the wireless set; the rest had simply evaporated on essential trifles—a bill he hadn't anticipated, a new school uniform for Dinah, traveling expenses, food. He was as vulnerable to inflation as anyone else.

But he was starting over now. There would be more groping in the dark, more pitfalls of his own making to avoid, more to hide, more to lose. Creating trouble for himself, to put it in perspective. And why? For the Fatherland? Hitler? Karl's Roman-Spartan idealism? The sanctity of hearth and home?

He grinned to himself in the dark. A line from the *Desiderata* came to him and he tasted it. "Go placidly among the noise and haste." Hamburg wanted precisely that and so did London. Go placidly. And alone.

A vassal with two masters owes loyalty to neither.

JUNE 21, 1941

Halfway through the evening someone discovered it was Pepper's birthday. There were shouts of "Encore! Encore!" and a crescendo of nasal braying noises of the kind grown Englishmen feel it necessary to indulge in when private details are revealed by accident in a crowded room. Pepper blushed and Price, trapped in one corner of the dining room by a large young American and two lofty dons, felt sorry for him. The dons, neither of whom could have been much younger than Pepper's confessed sixty-six, plowed off in his direction roaring a tuneless "For he's a jolly good fellow." It was a performance of great volume and as they approached the end of it a loud thumping broke out on the floor of the flat above. Gales of laughter greeted this, and the chorus died of mass hysteria.

The young American tried to appear worldly. "I guess they need to let off steam now and then."

Price shrugged. "Perhaps."

"Nice guy, the professor. Friend of yours?"

"We work together."

"Ouch!" The American brought hand to mouth. "That does it. Lips sealed, okay? You don't have to say a thing."

Price groaned inwardly. The last thing he'd expected tonight was to be drawn into one of Pepper soirées, but he'd been given little choice in the matter. Pepper's insistence had been draconian. "Short notice, I know, my dear fellow, but I need your support. You can't deny me." Which, translated, meant "you have something to learn tonight and it's urgent." Something Hamburg had to be apprised of and no time for the subtleties of inspired forgery.

He knew the American was to be the conduit; Pepper had thrown them together the moment he arrived. But the fiddler couldn't find the tune. This was their third confrontation in an hour and a quarter, and the fool was still circling for an opening.

Price said petulantly, "There's no need to be coy. No one comes here unless he's . . . cleared."

The American's acute embarrassment was not part of his cover. "Well, I guess so." He grinned sheepishly to relieve the strain. "Watch your big feet, they told me in Washington. Don't make a fool of yourself. Keep your mouth shut and your ears open."

"We welcome advice. We haven't won the war yet." Now there's an opening, you wilting clown; use it!

"You run it like you were winning it. In the—ah—unorthodox areas, shall we say."

"You're interested in the . . . unorthodox areas, are you?" Price gave the phrase precisely the tonal emphasis the American had.

"Pretty much. I don't get in as deep as you and the professor, naturally, but . . ." He made a ridiculous production of flapping a hand to his mouth in a manner that made Price cringe. "Sorry. Out of line again."

There would be no escape until it was over and done with. "What line are you in?"

"You could say kind of security."

This time Price could not contain his irritation. "Then why not say it? We're all in security one way or another."

"Look, I haven't offended you, have I, doc?"

Doc! "Not at all. I'm just trying to point out that when you're in this room you're among peers. It's a privilege and we all make use of it. A kind of club. You wouldn't be here if Pepper didn't think you were qualified."

"Wheeew." Half whistle, half sigh. "That takes a load off my mind. Okay, start again. I'm with the embassy. Dick Strachan. Aliens control. We—"

"Yes, I know what you do," Price interrupted impatiently, making it up as he went along. "We work with your people now and then. Background on German nationals, East European émigrés, trade delegations, that sort of thing." Surely somewhere in all of that the fool could find a peg to hang a confidence on?

"Right! Well, there you go. You probably know Gordon Royce."

"Yes, of course," Price said mechanically.

"My boss. He's—ah—back in the States for a couple weeks. I guess you knew."

"He told me." His last, his *very* last, offer. "The Nazi business, I suppose." What else could it be, after all?

"You mean you're in on the roundup?" At *last!* Strachan threw in a bit of business to add texture; eyes over his shoulder, hand to his mouth. "I thought it was—"

"We supplied the original input." Price was imperturbable.

"Well, I'll be goddamned! Keep your big mouth shut, Strachan. *Hell!*" He converted to a confidential croak. "You know the FBI are making the sweep day after tomorrow? The Krauts' entire American network."

"I knew it was coming up soon. Not our province, though, once the reins are in your hands." From the corner of his eye he saw Pepper watching them anxiously.

"Yeah, well, I hear Hoover's running the case himself. Thirty-three German agents in one swoop. That's gonna make somebody in Berlin feel pretty damn sick, wouldn't you say?"

"I'm sure it will," said Tom Price with relief.

Go placidly, he thought, and give Hamburg the placid truth.

It was past one in the morning when Curzon parked his MG outside the house in Ebury Street. There had been no good reason for driving out to Richmond. There was a permanent case officer sitting on Ginger Haddon's shoulder; he was fully briefed and perfectly capable of confirming the fact that Price had transmitted the information. Not that confirmation was necessary. Tom Price was as predictable as a bell; strike him and he rang. Menzies had sweated blood to persuade the Americans to let him pass Price the roundup plan forty-eight hours ahead of time; he'd sleep better for knowing that everything had gone smoothly. No sleep for Ritter, though. Nor Canaris. Price's revelation would put the fear of God into them. Reinhard Heydrich had been on Canaris's back since last autumn, chipping away at his reputation, investigating his claims of Abwehr successes in Britain, America, and Portugal, preparing to cut him down. There would be no hiding this scandal.

The only saving grace the Tirpitzufer would have to its name was the ineffable Gimlet. First with the news again, jumping an ocean to prove his omniscience. Even Heydrich couldn't help being impressed by a performance of that caliber. It would double Price's value as a source overnight.

There were no letters on the hall table and he tramped upstairs to his flat without turning on the light. On the last flight he sensed a presence at the top of the stairs, dropped to one knee—and Rob hissed, "That you, Paul?"

It was an uncomfortable first five minutes but they got through it without too much bruising. There was no light— another electricity failure—and that helped. Curzon poured them each a Scotch and they blundered in the dark till they found the fireside chairs.

"I'd be glad of a bed this time, if it's okay with you," Rob said awkwardly.

"You don't have to ask."

"I should've dropped you a line to say I was coming up."

"Doesn't matter. Liberty Hall. Drop in when you like, you know that." Curzon squinted into the darkness. There was something different about Rob: a leanness, a crispness of outline. Unlike him. He had always dressed like a scarecrow— floppy tweeds and cardigans, knitted ties, shapeless hats. Evening dress? He said, "Have you been up for a night on the town?"

No reply. Not at once. "I'm—ah—I'm on seventy-two hours' leave." In a rush. Glad to get it out.

"Leave?"

Rob's hand reached out and took his wrist, guided his fingers to his chest, along a Sam Browne to an epaulet. Service dress. One pip.

"Congratulations." Grudging. He sensed Rob's hangdog dejection and said quickly, "Well, good for you, Rob. Really, I mean it."

"You don't mind?"

"Mind? What's a war without a Curzon?"

"I mean about . . . leaving mother and the Bart to get by on their own."

"Well . . ." No, wrong moment. "They'll manage. I bet the Bart's tickled to death."

He was and he wasn't. Rob had sneaked off to Norwich and signed on as a private soldier after persuading the Ministry of Agriculture to drop his reserved-occupation status. He'd told no one until a week before he was due to report for training. At which point the Bart had exploded.

"He said I had no business trying to be what I wasn't. Curzons had been born to lead for three hundred years. The glorious tradition and all that. I said it wasn't the same Army anymore. Generals' sons were like everyone else."

"I can imagine the way he took that."

"He got over it."

"How will they manage?" The inevitable question. He wished he could see his brother's face.

"I brought Brian Wilbraham in as steward. Damned lucky to get him. He caught a packet at Dunkirk. Lost an arm."

"I hope he knows what he's let himself in for."

"Brian was a company sergeant major. They eat generals alive."

End of conversation, Curzon thought sadly. Minds at rest, the peace signed. Nothing more to say. But he tried. "What mob are you in?"

"Well, I joined the Norfolks and they put me up for a War Office Selection Board. I did sixteen weeks' officer cadet training at Eaton Hall and they sort of shoved me into the first square hole they could find." He was clearly embarrassed.

"So they stuck you in the Catering Corps."

"Well, the Commandos, actually."

"Glory, glory Hallelujah," Curzon sang softly.

Rob changed the subject quickly. "You still with the . . . Ministry of Supply, is it?"

Cautiously, "Yes."

Rob cleared his throat. The chair grunted as he shifted his weight. "I tried to call you here last September, the week I joined up. The woman downstairs said you were away."

"Yes, I was."

Curzon heard a series of soft clinking sounds—Rob's fingernails playing nervous arpeggios on the rim of his glass.

"I thought you were a clerk. You know, deskbound. The Bart said . . ."

"We have to travel sometimes."

Rob said nothing and went on saying nothing for so long Curzon braced himself for an attack. About to do the Bart's duty for him, he thought. *I'm* in uniform, why not *you.* He finished off his Scotch at a gulp. "We'd better turn in. I suppose you'll be off at crack of dawn tomorrow?"

"Yes. There's a good train at eight fifteen."

"Norwich?"

"Yes." Another long silence. Whatever he had to say couldn't be said sitting down. The lean shape of him came out of his chair and loomed over Curzon. "Paul—" False start. "Look, there's something I've got to say. Tell me to shut up if you like but I'd rather you heard me out."

Curzon closed his eyes. "Go ahead, Rob. I don't think I've got the strength to knock a Commando off his feet."

"It's about that firm you used to work for. The wine shippers . . ."

"What about it?"

"Whenever I telephoned you there you were always abroad, but they never had an address I could write to or even an overnight number where I could call you. I believed it at first. . . ." He couldn't say it standing up either. He dropped back into the chair. "I called them one day about two years ago, the summer of thirty-nine, I think. I was coming up to town and I thought we might get together for drinks. But they gave me the usual line: you were abroad, they couldn't be absolutely sure where, didn't know when you'd be home, would I like to leave a message."

"Nothing unusual in that."

"No. Anyway, I came up, spent the night at Browns and went to Liverpool Street for the early train next morning. I suppose I had a premonition or something because when I got to the station I telephoned you here at the flat. You were in bed."

"I probably just got back."

"That's not what you said."

"Oh?"

"You asked me why I hadn't looked you up. You said you'd been in town for a week." He paused unhappily. "I didn't mention I'd called your office."

The clock on the mantel tinged the half hour.

"What do you want me to say, Rob?"

"I don't want you to say anything. That's the point, don't you see? You never had to breathe a word. You didn't have to lie."

"What should I have done?"

"Simply made it clear to all of us, Mother more than anyone, that you couldn't talk about it. We'd have taken the rest on trust."

"And now?"

More fingertip arpeggios on the tumbler. "I think I know what you're in—and it's not the bloody Ministry of Supply, is it? The only thing I'm sure about is that you can't tell—"

"You're coming round to my way of thinking."

"Only because it's too late now. A damn sight later than you think. Mother's been in bed with pleurisy and God knows what other complications for six weeks. The Bart's skin and bone. Donohue has a full-time nurse there."

"I didn't know." Or care, or think of finding out.

"The important thing . . ." Rob set his empty glass by the hearth; something to do. "I respect you for what you're doing, Paul. I don't think I could have kept mum about it all these years. I suppose it *has* been years? Since Cambridge?"

"Yes." He daren't ask Rob what he thought *it* was.

"I thought so. I wouldn't have brought it up, honestly, but—oh, I suppose things have sort of piled up. The Army, Bart and Mother, handing over the estate. And—ah . . ." Another river to cross. They'd never been good at confiding in one another. "I've gone and got myself engaged."

"You what?" Curzon laughed; pure relief.

"Her name's Nicola. Nicola Stacey. She's a Wren, third officer. We met when I was doing an assault course at Fort William."

Curzon avoided the obvious comment.

"Does Mother know?"

"She will tomorrow. It happened a little too quickly for announcements in the *Times*."

"When's the big day?"

Rob got up and unhitched his belt, unbuttoned his tunic. "When it's over, I suppose. Don't make any false moves; isn't that what they say about wartime romances? Marry in haste, repent alone."

Curzon nodded in the darkness.

Rob peeled off his tunic and swung it over his shoulder. "I just wanted you to know . . . in case anything happens to either of us . . . that I understand."

"Nothing's going to happen, idiot."

"No, of course it isn't." He wanted to laugh it off but couldn't; young men need their fears as they need their passions, Curzon thought gloomily. "But just in case, all right? You for me, me for you. If I caught a packet I wouldn't want Nicky to hear it from—well, you know, some twerp who never knew me. Is there anyone you'd want me to . . . ?''

Curzon wondered whose bed Extension 171 was decorating tonight and tested his feelings on the subject. All clear. No feelings. ''No, there's no one,'' he said solemnly.

JUNE 30, 1941

There was a moon but it was soured by the mountainous black cloud. A perfect night for the bombers, Price thought, as he wedged himself into the telephone booth.

He laid out three piles of pennies, took off his gloves, and massaged his fingers. The arthritis began to throb as soon as the sun went down; the old enemy of his university days. The cold winter had brought it on again—arms, hands, legs, and feet—and the warmth of spring had done nothing to banish it. He held the luminous watch face close to his eyes: ten fifteen.

He checked the wide sweep of Victoria Embankment both ways, then dialed. Boyd's hand must have been poised over the instrument at the other end because it rang only once.

''Yes?'' The tremor in his voice was not excitement.

''Were you followed? Is there anyone close by?''

''No. There was a woman on the phone when I arrived, though. Thought she'd never come out.''

''Good. Keep your eyes on the street, Boyd. Now—first point: we shan't be meeting again.''

''Ever?''

''Have you made a list of the public telephone numbers I asked you for?''

''Yes. Fifteen. But I mean to say, old man—''

''Give them to me. Now.''

Boyd recited them in his bored schoolteacher's monotone. Price penciled them into his notebook, using the simplest code to hand: HAM 0316 became GZL N_2H_5, the first three letters of the dialing code taking the letter preceding it in the alphabet, the four digits taking the preceding number; the figure zero he transposed as the letter O, the figure 1 as the letter I. Boyd reached the end. ''Got that, old man?''

"Thank you. Now—from this moment, Boyd, you will avoid any attempt to make contact with me. Is that understood?"

"Well yes. But—"

"I shall always contact you. Every night at ten fifteen, go to one of the telephone booths on your list; number one on the first night, number two on the second and so on, in rotation. Punctually at ten fifteen. I shall telephone at that time if I need you. If I don't call in five minutes you'll go home. But the system's important. You must go *every* night. There'll be other times when I need to pass messages too long for a box-to-box call. I posted the first of these to your flat this morning. It's in a copy of the *Financial Times*. Open it and turn to the first leader. Do you know what that is?"

"Well of *course* I know!" Wounded pride was Boyd's strongest emotion.

"Always the leader columns, Boyd. You'll find sixteen coded letter-blocks pricked out there. Pinpricks *under* the letters concerned. Under some letters you'll find two pinpricks; that denotes the end of a sentence. Under others you'll find three pinpricks. That marks the end of a message block. You know what that means?"

Boyd seemed grateful for the chance to talk. "End of a sentence, a three-second delay in transmission—and *one* and *two* and *three*. End of a block, twelve seconds delay or—"

"In this case, twenty-five minutes delay. But *only* in this case. Let's go over the procedure again. Where do you start?"

He was more confident now. "When I leave the Evening Institute at Broxbourne at a quarter to nine, I ride south and take the left-hand turn at the traffic lights, the Waltham Abbey road. Eight miles exactly to Claban's farm. Push the bike up the lane to the woods. Nine twenty exactly, I make the first transmission."

Hamburg couldn't be warned in advance, so everything hung on the effectiveness of their shortwave sweep system. First block: "Gimlet to Hotbed via Sibling. Part One of three-part grouping. Second group twenty-five minutes hence five miles due north this point." Repeated three times. If they picked it up they would get a fix with their direction finders long before Boyd reached the second position. Wohldorf maintained six mobile signals units in a ten-mile arc around

Hamburg, all trained on England; they could be called into service in a matter of seconds. It would be child's play to take cross-bearings and pin Boyd to earth.

"Excellent, Boyd. What next?"

The phone fretted plaintively for a new injection of coins. He pushed them in quickly. "Boyd?"

"I ride five miles north to the crossroads by the pub, the King Charles. Left there and down to the river, a hundred yards from the bridge. Nine forty-five exactly, the second block."

Wohldorf should be quivering with suspicion at this point. Someone was bound to alert Major Trautmann or Richard Wein. Second block, again repeated three times: "Sibling to Hotbed for Gimlet. Moving five miles east of this point for next transmissions in twenty-five minutes. Prepare and fix. Tell Else to say hello to Hugo under the railway bridge."

An open invitation: to refix the final transmit position, to get Ritter from his bed, and to have Else roused by messenger in Berlin. Hugo under the railway bridge—one of the few genuinely private memories they shared: Hugo Schildburger's bookshop near Bellevue station where they had broused as children.

"And then?"

"Then five miles east and stop at the top end of the sandpit. At ten ten exactly I send the third block."

The real message, the one they *had* to accept. It had taken him hours to write. Short, unambiguous, sufficiently assertive to command respect but not so urgent as to alarm Ritter (who at this stage was likely to be in an advanced state of convulsive neurosis over the roundup of his American network). To suggest that Gimlet's cover was blown in Richmond would have been enough to persuade Ritter to close down on him instantly. The final block read: "Have recruited sub-agent Sibling in view overwhelming burden of product for transmission. Exhaustive inquiries his background full year. Will use him mobile sites this transmission area and wavelength 2130 to 2230 as necessary for product of highest and most urgent quality. Require your response via Sibling July 6. Essential you make no disclosure Sibling conduit in routine Richmond transmissions. Where I am, Germany is. Gimlet."

Corrie was sucking his teeth impatiently at the other end.

"That's perfect, Boyd. And if you run into . . . difficulties on the road?"

"I say I lost my way at Broxbourne and show my WEA lecturer's card."

"Are you happy about the wireless?"

"No problems. I guarantee it. The power pack balances it pretty well."

He'd begun designing it in December, built the frame in three days, and scoured the black market for valves and essential components with the £200 Price had given him. The set was portable, flat and wide, made to fit snugly into a steel motorcycle pannier. Shortwave, of course—medium wave would have required cumbersome aerials—operating in the 1.5 to 30 megacycle range on a power output of 15 watts. (Price had told him he would be signaling to a Red Army Intelligence pick-up located in a quarry near Gdynia in Poland.) Boyd had designed his own Morse key as an extra safeguard; a silent one, quite ingenious.

"Boyd, I'm proud of you."

"Oh, I say, old man. Gosh—"

"It's not been an easy seven months. I've been hard on you, I know. I hope you realize it was for the best."

"Oh, absolutely, old man."

"All right. You'll make your first transmission on July 2. Wednesday."

"Wheeew."

"That worries you?"

"I just didn't think it would be that soon."

"It must be that night. Do I have to explain why?"

"Oh, absolutely not. The invasion, you mean, right? My God—I mean, I know we *talked* about it before it happened and all that but—well, I'll be honest with you, old man, I thought you'd got it round your neck. Hitler invading *Russia*? Barmy! No other word for it. Where'd he get the troops from, that's what I'd like to know."

"More than a hundred divisions in the field, Boyd," Price said quietly. "That's probably two-thirds the tactical strength of the Rus—of our armies. We need every man we can find—over there and here, too. Your work is critical, Boyd. I mean that. You're more valuable than you can imagine. So be careful. When you're transmitting and, later, when you're receiving."

"When do I—"

"You'll go back to Claban's farm on the night of July 6. You'll make your call sign. Then they'll respond. On the following night you'll go to the next number on the public phone box list and wait for my call. Then you'll pass their message to me."

"I'm a bit worried about this telephoning business, old man. You don't mind my mentioning it, do you?"

"Nothing to worry about. There's no way our calls can be intercepted, and as long as we keep conversations to a minimum we're hardly likely to attract attention. You're sure the call boxes are well spaced out?"

"All over, old man. Camden, Highgate, Seven Sisters Road, Harringay—all over. Just as you said."

The pips broke in again and Price rammed home more coppers.

"We're over-running, Boyd, so listen carefully. Have you made contact with your friends?"

"I've had five replies so far. All saying yes."

"And you're sure you can trust them? Tell me if you've got any doubts in your mind. I don't want to find the security police turning up on your doorstep one day because someone's had too much to drink and started boasting to his friends."

Boyd's tone was reproving. "I hope you don't think I mix with *that* sort, old man. I really don't. I mean—"

"Yes, Boyd. I know what you mean. I trust your judgment. Has the chap in Peterhead replied yet?"

"Geordie? Yes; day before yesterday. He's all for it. I told you he would be."

"You're quite sure he's not due for call-up?"

"Fishing's a reserved occupation. He'd have registered as a conscientious objector if they'd tried to make him join up, but they didn't. It's a damned dangerous business, fishing. Especially up there. He was telling me once—"

"Right, Boyd. We'd better finish. Any further questions?"

"No, sir." Boyd being militarily correct. Price had told him he would probably be given the honorary rank of lieutenant if all went well.

"Well, then, good luck."

"Nothing to it, old man," said the honorary hero.

"Good night, Boyd."

*　　*　　*

He had selected the call box on Victoria Embankment at random by jumping on a moving bus at Piccadilly and getting off where the fancy took him. He came out of the box and walked westward to find a bus to take him to Waterloo. It was a bitterly cold night; the wind sheered gustily off the Thames and flayed the wide street, cutting him to the bone, and when he found a bus stop he backed into the shelter of an office building entranceway.

So far, so good. The main hazard now was to retain Boyd's loyalty and enthusiasm without ever meeting him again face to face. From here on *all* genuine product must be channeled through Boyd. His own transmissions would have to go on as usual to allay suspicion, but there might be a way of scaling them down in time, perhaps distorting them. He'd think of something. Far more pressing, though, was the need to generate genuine product. Boyd's couriers represented his only possible source in that direction; not a glittering prospect by any means but they could be trained, given the right conditions. Best of all, they constituted no threat to his personal security; Boyd would deal with them at every stage and, if the system broke down, there was no way of linking Boyd with Robert Jardine.

Besides, they were ripe for manipulation, these people; indoctrinated to the hilt with their own dialectic pap and bursting to show their mettle. He was merely redirecting a conditioned reflex. Like Boyd himself, they were Communist Party cell-leaders, teachers or perennial students registered as conscientious objectors who, at the outbreak of war had been pushed into munitions factories, railway goods offices, aircraft production plants, hospitals, docks, mines—anywhere at all where labor shortages were critical and their conschy attitudes could be harnessed without compromising the national interest. Geordie McNeil was rather different, an exceptionally interesting case. He was the son of a trawler operator who ran a fleet of inshore boats from Peterhead on the Scottish east coast. A small-town lad with big-city ambitions, according to Boyd; strong as an ox but a mite underpowered in the brain department. "The last thing he wanted was to be a fisherman. Joined the Party to see the world but didn't get far, if you see what I mean."

A bus droned from the upper reaches of Chelsea and he

stepped forward, automatically tugging his coat collar around his chin and his hat brim over his eyes. He waved; the bus slowed and stopped. What happened in the space of the next five seconds appeared at the time to be so obviously the product of his overwound imagination that although every detail etched itself in his mind's eye, he experienced no emotion whatsoever. A young man in naval greatcoat and cap leapt from the platform and a woman stepped down behind him. The sailor marched away, furiously, shoulders hunched against the wind and, as Price climbed into the bus, he heard the woman's anguished, "Donny! Donny!" He watched her run after him, clumsy in her high-heeled shoes, and his brain said, *Alice*.

The bus had traveled a good thirty yards before the message registered. Alice and Donald White! Without thinking, he leapt for the curb.

He thought he'd lost them. He ran, his weak ankle trailing in an agonizing skip-and-drag shuffle; then he heard her again. "You mustn't! Oh, Donny, please!" and from White, "Shut up! Shut your fucking trap!"

The voices faded; Alice's heel clicks died. Price reached a corner, located them again. A narrow street of tall terraced houses, black as pitch. He caught up with them but after fifty yards lost their voices again. He loped on, cursing his ankle, then froze in mid-step only yards from a darkened archway set in a high wall—windows above it; an apartment block of some kind. The two of them were arguing in barely controlled whispers. He was almost on them. He looked around for cover and ducked behind a parked car.

"I *can't*!" Alice, her voice straining and breaking. "I won't stay there alone. Not anymore. I go out of my mind sometimes, thinking someone's going to come knocking at the door."

"I'm going. First thing they'll do if I don't turn up is—"

"I'll tell them, if they do come."

She gasped suddenly, a hard asphyxiated sound; a throat closing under pressure. Donald White hissed viciously, "And I'll cut your bloody throat out, you bitch. Hear me? One word out of you and I'll shut you up for good."

Alice, gulping air: "I didn't mean it. Oh, Donny, I didn't

mean it. I'm so scared. Why'd you have to do it? He was just having a bit of fun.''

"Fun, was it? Well, he won't think it's very bloody funny now, will he?''

She was sobbing, muffled sounds, hands over her mouth. "They'll come. The police. Someone.''

"They will if you don't stop shouting all over the fucking street. Shut up!''

"Stay with me, then. Just tonight. You can say you were ill. I'll phone and say you're ill.''

"You'll do what you're sodding-well told.'' Silence for a moment. "Look, love.'' Gently. "There's nothing to worry about, okay? No one saw. It was pitch dark. And it's been six weeks. If the coppers had anything to go on, they'd have been round here. . . .''

"They'll remember you having that argument in the pub! Someone will.''

White's voice lashed out at her. "And whose bloody fault was *that*? Chatting him up like some tart on the game! What'd you expect me to do, stand and bloody watch?''

"You didn't have to *kill* him.''

Price froze.

"Nobody killed anybody! And don't you bloody forget it. He fell, that's all. Pissed as a newt and he fell over the edge. Couldn't see a thing, could he? That's why we haven't heard anything. Accident. Under the influence of drink.''

"Oh, I wish we'd never gone there. I didn't want to. You said—''

"You said you were sick and tired of being cooped up! That's why we went, you moaning bitch! You didn't think it was so bad when you were putting it on for him like a sow in heat, did you?'' Donald White tried again to get himself under control. "Look—no one knew me up there, love. Or you. I've never been there before in my life. And people forget faces. Specially in pubs. Anyway, we left before he did.''

"We should've come home when I said. You're mad when you get like that. You scare me, you really do.''

"Then shut up and go to bed.'' Silence. Then, "Christ, it's half past bloody eleven. I'll be shot if I'm late on watch. Go on, up you go. I'll be home at six.''

"Donny . . .''

"Up! Now push off. I'm not going to tell you again."

White's face appeared around the brick arch; he glanced up and down the quiet street, hunched his coat collar around his face, and set off briskly in the direction of Victoria.

Price was holding his breath. He let it out slowly. He was trying to remember something Frank White had told him, months ago. Boasting about his son. "In the thick of it, my Don. At the Admiralty. They only pick the best for the Operations Room."

He was startled back to the present by the hollow clopping of Alice's heels. Go or stay? His reflexes decided for him. A wide courtyard opened out beyond the arch. He caught a faint flash of reflecting glass in the far corner as a door opened and clunked shut. He made for it, paused, stepped in.

Stone stairs. She was climbing slowly, two or three flights above. He followed on his toes, clutching his coat to his body to smother its rustling. Third flight; fourth. She stopped. He moved up, hugging the wall, saw the shape of her against a pale painted door, grubbing in her handbag. Key in the lock; the door swung wide. She went inside and switched on a light, took off her coat and hat, put down her bag; returned to the door and pushed it shut, leaving the keys dangling in the lock. True to form.

He waited five minutes then moved to the door, number 434; he put his ear to it. He could hear her crying. He took off his hat, wiped his face and neck with a handkerchief, and adjusted his tie. So he'd decided to go in. Why? To achieve what? The answer came back: to know. He took the dangling keys in his gloved hand and anchored them. Last chance to pull back. He turned the key in the lock.

A short hallway ahead, then another door, half open. He closed the outer door and squeezed home the latch without a sound; took a breath, collected himself, and walked into the room.

She was curled in a fetal ball in one corner of the scruffy couch, her face buried in her folded arms, legs drawn up under her. She didn't hear him; ten seconds slipped by before some sixth sense made her look up. Then she opened her mouth to scream. He lunged across the room and slapped his palm across the lower half of her face; found her neck with his free hand and squeezed. She made no sound. Her eyes were round with shock, her body stiff.

"One sound, Alice. Just one sound." He put his mouth to her ear. "I don't want to hurt you. Agreed?" Her eyes rolled wildly. *Yes*. He released her and she gagged at once, hands to her mouth. He lowered himself to the coffee table in front of her and pulled it closer till his knees were touching the couch. Her only escape route was over the back and he seriously doubted she was up to that.

He gave her a few seconds to quell her leaping stomach and her nerves. She was a mess. Black tributaries of mascara fanned out from twin pools under her eyes and raked her cheeks. Her lipstick, a thick scarlet gloss, had smudged and shredded. She looked a hundred years old.

"Are you ready to talk now?"

She turned away.

He grabbed her chin in the cup of his hand and wrenched her face to his. Again, shock. She flinched away.

"We'll *talk* now, Alice. Say yes."

"Yes." A reflex. No defenses.

He studied her for a moment, feeling the vulnerable underbelly of her throat against his gloved fingers. Her eyes dropped, closed.

"Now tell me what happened. Exactly, every detail."

"What . . . ?"

"At the pub."

He had to grab her by the shoulders or she would have collapsed on him. Her eyes rolled upward. He slapped her face hard and she jerked in spasm. He pushed her into the corner of the couch. "The sooner you tell me, the sooner it'll be over. You were in a pub. What was it called?"

"The Hay Wain. In the City Road." Her voice was rasping, dry.

"You were talking to a man. What did Donald do then?"

"He was . . . he went out for a minute. To . . ." She hung her head.

"And when he came back you were talking to a man and Donald was angry. What happened?"

"I daren't! He'll . . ."

He hit her across the face again with the back of his glove. One slap, light, but the effect was instantaneous.

"He told the man to . . . go away. He wouldn't. He poured

beer on Donny's coat. Donny tried to stop him and the man pushed him about. Everyone laughed. He pulled Donny's coat and jacket off and threw them . . . outside. Then he pushed Donny in the street.''

"And you and Donald waited outside."

"Not me! Not *me*!" She wept anew. "I said, 'Come home,' but he wouldn't. He's like that when's he's got drink in him; *terrible*! Then this man came out, the one who did it. He was drunk. Rolling about. Donny followed him and . . ."

"Did you go?"

"I couldn't stay on my own!"

"No. Go on."

"He went along, this man . . ." A burst of sobbing set her shaking inconsolably. He waited. "He went down some streets, singing. Then there was an open place; water and barges and cranes . . ."

"A canal? A mooring basin?"

"Like that. The man went near the water, high up. He started to . . . go to the toilet, on the edge of this place. Donny ran very fast and pushed him in the back. Oh, God! I thought . . . I waited for a splash but there wasn't one. Then I went where Donny was and looked down. There was another sort of dock thing, made of stone, a long way down. He was lying there, all bent and . . ."

"Did you go down?"

She shook her head, knuckling her eyes, gulping on her terror as she relived it. "Donny went. When he came back he started to cry. He's so . . ." There were no words for it. "He said his neck was broken. He couldn't feel . . . anything. Any pulse."

"He was dead?"

He let her cry, got up and went into the kitchen. He found a glass and filled it with water and brought it back. He watched her drink. She clutched her stomach. "I want to be sick."

"No you don't. Now listen to me, Alice. Are you *listening*?"

Her head rose and fell mechanically.

"You know the penalty for murder?"

"Oh, *Donneeeee*!"

He grabbed both her hands. "Listen! There isn't a court in the country that won't convict him. The evidence of the people in the Hay Wain. He'll hang, Alice. And you'll go to prison. Perhaps for life.''

She collapsed on him. He put his arms around her to push her back, thought better of it and let her be. His mouth found her ear. ''Listen. *Listen!*'' Her head moved on his shoulder. ''I can help. *Perhaps.* But you'll have to do exactly as I tell you. Understand?''

She pushed herself up, rubbing her eyes, smudging the liquefied mascara.

''You know I work for Professor Pepper.'' He felt it growing, coming alive—a seedling idea, breathtaking. ''Alice?'' She nodded mutely, watching him. ''I work in—national security. You remember my telling you I couldn't discuss my work?'' Another nod. ''Well, I have some influence. Not much; I can't guarantee anything. But . . .'' He took her chin in his fingers. ''Donald works in Admiralty Operations, doesn't he?'' *Yes.* No sound. ''Then he can help me in my work. If he does, I'll help him—both of you.''

She formed a word but nothing came at first. She tried again. ''Will he go to prison? Will I . . .''

''I'll do what I can. Tell him that. But the most important thing you have to tell him is that he must come and see me. In Richmond. Tomorrow night, about half past seven. Tell him to go to his father's house. I'll be in the garden. Now do you understand all that? Will you remember?''

He made her repeat it, then got up and backed away. Leave now. Quickly. She followed him with her eyes, like a dog ordered to sit without knowing why.

''Tomorrow night. Half past seven. His father's house.''

Her eyes stayed wide, terrified. He went to the inner door and turned once more to look at her. She gulped at air.

''To-om!''

He waited.

''Is . . . Diny all right?''

JULY 1, 1941

Seven forty-five. The sun was low, but it was mild in the garden, balmy. He was clipping the patch of lawn with hedge shears and his back and forearms were beginning to ache. He straightened, leaning back on his heels, spikes of pain in his knees, and a voice said lightly from Frank White's garden, "Nice and easy, skipper."

He turned too quickly and canted over sideways.

"I said *easy*, skipper. Dad's looking out the window. Just walk over and shake hands."

Donald White had the setting sun in his face; it gave him a bronzed and sturdy look. He was neat and sharp and newly pressed and his brass buttons glinted bravely. Price shook his hand unwillingly.

"So—a copper are you, now?" His gray eyes were narrowed against the scarlet glare but they were bright with anticipation. No fear in them; not even embarrassment.

"No—not a *copper*."

"Oh dear oh lor'. Security, then. That's what you told her, right?"

Price eyed him coolly. Strip that uniform off him—as the man in the pub had done—and he was nothing. Weedy; 150 pounds, perhaps less. All mouth. And the Devil's cheek. A hero when he was roused, an assassin who pushed from the back. And then spilled tears.

"You killed a man."

"Oh yeah?" White's mouth curled into a grin of bravado but the rest of his face fell short of the mark.

"Six weeks ago. Alfred Edward Tillett, furnaceman. Married, three children. Lived in Micawber Street, just off the City Road. Death from internal hemorrhage caused by acute compression." He paused. White's expression gave no hint that the facts meant anything to him. "He broke his neck and his ribs. A bone punctured the lungs and heart."

The grin stayed intact. "Prove it."

"Have you killed Alice yet?"

White stiffened in shock. "Have I what?"

"If you haven't," Price went on matter-of-factly, "*she'll* prove it. She's an eyewitness. And there are the people at the Hay Wain, remember. They can prove motive, at least."

Donald White looked over his shoulder toward his parents' house. His mother waved from the kitchen window. He waved back. "So what's the game then?" One eyelid flickered down and almost closed. A nervous tic? A concession of defeat?

"Alice told you?"

"*You* tell me. I don't trust bloody women."

Quickly, forcefully, unequivocally; as he'd planned it. Don't question its credibility; consider Donald White's dilemma. "I'm a security officer. I'm engaged in an investigation of national importance. You can assist me. If you do, I'll cover your tracks. If you don't, I'll hand you over to the police."

"You and whose army?"

"If necessary, your father."

It rocked him on his heels. He clutched the fence for support. "Why should you help me?" Sullenly.

"No reason at all—but you can be useful to me. And compared with my work, your murdering a drunken ruffian is nothing. Do I make myself clear?"

White shrugged. "What, then?"

"Next Monday, you'll come to Richmond again to see your parents. You'll have an envelope. You'll climb over this fence, knock at my back door, and give it to me. Then you'll go back to London."

"What envelope?"

Price went on remorselessly, battening down his own fluttering misgivings, staring White into submission. "Between tonight and the night of July 6, the day before you come here again, you'll collect copies of any papers that pass through your hands in the Admiralty Operations Room. You'll—"

"You off your fucking rocker, mate?"

"Copies! You'll make sure you're not observed. When you get home each morning you'll hide them. At the end of each six-day period, you'll bring what you have to me."

Donald White kicked the fence heavily, less in anger than incredulity. "Bollocks to that! You think I'm barmy? Anyone cops me stuffing a flimsy up my bleeding shirt and—"

"No one will. I said you'll make sure you're not seen."

The sun dropped below the western rooftops and White's

face paled to the color of weathered cement. "What the fuck are you up to, Price? All I've gotta do is pass the word to Naval Intelligence and you're up the gunga without a paddle, mate." The grin returned, a little worn at the edges but secure. "And where do you think you'll be going, then, cock?"

"To your superior officer, I imagine. To explain *why* you're trying to blackmail a security official. What's the Navy's attitude to murder in wartime?"

Donald White stuck his hands in his pockets and looked at his feet. He was no longer grinning.

"Is this on the up-and-up? You're really in security?"

"That doesn't concern you. You'll do it. That's all."

"I'll think about it."

"No you won't. For the sake of your neck. For Alice. For whatever future you think you have."

"Don't tell me what I'm going to—"

Price dropped a hand on his shoulder very lightly. He closed his fingers on the flesh of the lower neck. Hard. "I've told you. I won't tell you again. You'll work for me and you'll work hard. And you won't ask questions. When I'm satisfied . . ." He relaxed the grip but kept his hand in place. "Perhaps we can arrange something for you." He jerked his head at the house. "Alice can't be too happy, cooped up in that grubby little bolthole of yours. She'd be better off here."

"She's not coming back to you, you bastard!"

"And I wouldn't dream of asking her."

White's brow furrowed uncomprehendingly.

"Perform well, Donald—efficiently—do what you're told, and perhaps later on you and Alice can have the house. It's hers, anyway."

White caught the flavor of the bargain and grinned. "You canny bugger, you. I suppose you expect me to tell *her* that."

Price let his hand fall. "You will, Donald. And she'll agree. Your life and a roof over your head. Now tell me you'll go to Naval Intelligence."

Donald White retreated a few steps, pivoted slowly on his heel and slouched away. For a moment he seemed about to stop, to make a last stand, but the impulse died and he walked on into his father's house.

JULY 7, 1941

Philip Pepper was being exceptionally attentive. He had started the day by drawing Price into his office to unveil his strategic forecast on the Russian situation. "Bearpit," he'd scrawled on the red file cover. It was a weedy document of fifteen foolscap pages penned in his own hand, a résumé of current British industrial chaos liberally spattered with graphs and figure tabulations. A three-page summation pointed out the awesome hazards that could be expected if any attempt was made to further burden the productive system by supplying the Russians or by launching an ill-considered second front.

"You'll note that—ah"—Pepper hovered at his shoulder, a small hand digging possessively into Price's jacket—"most of your ideas are embodied in the recommendations."

Price nodded. "You don't mention the tactical area, I see."

"Oh . . . ." Pepper dismissed the point with an airy wave. "Hardly our business, is it?"

"It's important in terms of timing, surely. The bad weather's bogged down the German advance, perhaps for weeks. The countryside around Minsk favors the Russians. And don't forget they're still active behind the German lines. There'd be a big temptation to rearm and supply Stalin now and take advantage of the situation."

"Well, you're right, of course." Pepper had swept the file away. "I'll make that point before I have it typed up."

The forecast, Price judged later, must have taken up at least a day of Pepper's time, and the fact gave him a small glow of satisfaction. It was encouraging to know that he was considered worth a day's work. More important, Pepper had reacted precisely as he'd anticipated, which meant that he'd also reported their conversation of six weeks ago to Julian, Gerry, Guy and Co., discussed its implications, and determined on a course of action. The forecast, Bearpit, was the

271

result. It was not the document that would reach Churchill's hands of course. He felt a giddying sense of achievement.

But Pepper had not finished with him. First, he bought him lunch, an extravagant spread at a small French restaurant in Soho. Then he treated him to a wide-ranging dissertation over afternoon tea, crystallizing his ambitions for the Pepperpot and Tom Price's singular part in them. Just before Price left for the day, the little man trailed into his office and entered into a vague conversation about work and play. He reminded Price that he had still not brought Dinah to Queen's Gate for Sunday tea; he fretted over the hours Price spent working both in the office and at home, demanded to know when he'd last been to a party or a decent concert.

"I'll have to take you in hand, my boy. No other way," he said at the end. "You need to get out and about more. Make friends. A party's what you need. Let your hair down."

Price walked to Waterloo Station on a carpet of air. They'd taken the bait. More, they were shaping something more positive. There was no other interpretation.

Donald White came to the kitchen door at exactly seven thirty and when Price opened it to him he drew in breath for the attack he had plainly been preparing since London. Price snatched the envelope from his hand before he could get out a word. "Make it the same time next week," he snapped and slammed the door in the boy's face.

The envelope was bulky and he was sorely tempted to open it right away, but he'd laid his plans and followed them rigidly. He slipped the envelope in a larger one, sealed it, and wrote on it, "The Director of Naval Operations, Admiralty, London." He left it lying on the kitchen table and went back to his supper tray in the living room. The first pass would be the most dangerous. If White had weakened and talked to Naval Intelligence they would be outside, waiting to catch him red-handed opening the envelope and checking its contents. No defense would be watertight, but he could at least confuse them. "I have no idea what's inside. Donald asked me to keep it for him, but when I saw the Admiralty seal on the back I began to worry. I thought it best to just put it in the post. Look, I've already addressed it."

The excuse was weak enough to appear genuine—for the first few hours. Then . . . He chewed nervously on a meat paste sandwich, conscious for the first time of what he was doing; or more practically, of what he'd set in train. He had stepped out of the protective aura of the Lie, sacrificed his cover, offered himself as a target. He, Wilhelm Sommer. Again—why? Not impulse; his actions were premeditated, the product of months of thought and planning. Self-justification, then? Not even that; he was not impelled by any allegiance to a cause. Momentum? He smiled at the absurdity of it. Perhaps that's all it was. Momentum. A certain anger—or was it shame?—had motivated him after Mr. Evans-Wyke's death; such a wasteful, pointless death. Then the accident of Pepper's keys; then Boyd. Momentum.

At nine thirty he took the envelope upstairs to the loft and opened it. Thirty sheets of flimsy: yellow, white, and blue.

The white sheets were made up entirely of attenuated letter blocks followed by number groupings. Coded, unintelligible. He'd expected that. Yellow: more letters and numerals, but this time in odd wave forms across the paper, each line numbered—1,2,3, and so on—running to a definite tail at the end like the poem in *Alice in Wonderland*. The blue papers were composed of much denser letter blocks ten or twelve lines long, three blocks to a page. At the top of all the pages was the same notation: DNI/Flag/Sigint.

Considerations: One, there was no question of his evaluating the material himself. Two, at a conservative estimate it would take three or four weeks of continuous nightly transmissions to pass it to Hamburg. Three, it could, however unlikely, be a plant, with Donald White playing hero in a scenario designed by Naval Intelligence. Only careful assessment of all the sheets at one time by an experienced team of naval cryptologists could establish that. Four, the value to Hamburg lay in what the sheets could reveal about British naval codes and convoy handling methods; but its greatest potential was in its immediacy.

Conclusions: It must be passed to Hamburg in its entirety. That ruled out Boyd and his wireless set. It must be passed quickly. Safely. By a method that permitted Hamburg a degree of control.

He put the sheets back in their envelope. There was only one course open to him. But then he'd known that for days.

*　　*　　*

He took a circuitous route to the telephone box near the gates of Richmond Park and stepped inside five minutes ahead of time to register his claim. At ten forty-five, he dialed the second number on Boyd's list of public call boxes and waited with his heart in his mouth.

"Yes?" Boyd.

Dizzying relief. He said without emotion, "How did it go, last night?"

"Like a dream, old man. Absolutely downhill all the way."

"They responded?"

"Clear as a bell. Could've been in the next field."

"Dictate it to me now, please."

Boyd recited the code blocks letter by letter in his classroom voice. It was short. Price said, "Keep talking, Boyd. I'll decode now." He opened the checkbook, switched on his pencil torch, and turned to the day's key stub.

"I was there a bit early," Boyd said eagerly. "Bit of a fog, so I started before I normally would. *Murder*—fog in those country lanes. And I admit I was a bit nervous, wondering if they'd come through. You know, after last week; no response to my send. Anyway . . ."

Price let him chatter. The groups dissolved into plain text. "Applaud recruitment Sibling. Concur your transmission sensitive product his hand. Will avoid all reference this conduit in future Gimlet transmissions. Await further messages. Hotbed."

The phone needed more coins. Price waited for the line to clear. "Boyd, this is excellent. I'll read the part that concerns you. 'Agent Sibling congratulated. Perfect signature. Your request granted his appointment rank of lieutenant.'"

"Well . . ." Boyd laughed to cover his embarrassment and whatever other fantasies he was indulging at the other end. "Really, old man, I don't know what to say."

"There's nothing to say. You deserve it. I have some more material for you. Usual form. *Financial Times*. I posted it this morning. A single message block this time and you transmit in one continuous send."

"Absolutely no problem at all, old man. Claban's Farm?"

"No. The King Charles. Down by the river. Vary the sites, Boyd. As long as you stay in that ten-mile sector."

"No sooner said." Boyd was walking on air.

"That's tomorrow night. Tomorrow morning, early, I want

you to make a telephone call for me. To your friend in Peterhead.''

"Geordie McNeil?"

"Is there a number you can call?"

"His old man's house. Geordie lives at home. But he may be at sea. It's on the cards.''

"Try him. Ask him . . .'' He thought quickly, juggling with words. "Ask him to come to London for a weekend. *This* weekend. I'll pay his fare—but don't tell him that. Say you've had a windfall; you've got a bunch of PVC members coming up for a party.''

"But—ah—I mean, I haven't, have I?"

"Then," Price forged on, "call a half dozen of the others. I've made a note of the ones we need. Simmons, Lock, Davis, Caunt, Adcock, Brill. Got that?''

"Look, I don't want to seem difficult, old man, but these chaps do have jobs, you know. Most of 'em are on shift work, weekends included. And they're not exactly millionaires.''

"I'll pay the fares. You can find beds for them, I'm sure. Get your people at Highgate to put them up.''

"It's not just the money; it takes days to get anywhere by train, and—''

He refused to listen. "I'll want to talk to Geordie McNeil myself. By phone. Call box number four on your list. You'll take him there at ten fifteen on Saturday night.''

"And if he can't come?"

"Make him come. Boyd. Use your rank.'' A joke. It fell flat. "Tomorrow morning I'll send you another two messages. They're not for Transmission. One will be the usual newspaper; the message will be pricked out in the leader column but not in code. Those will be your instructions for Simmons and Co. You'll also receive an envelope. A large one—bulky. Open it and you'll find another envelope inside. Hide that, Boyd, and don't open it under any circumstances. When I talk to Geordie McNeil on Saturday, I'll tell you what to do with it. Understood?''

Boyd dug a soldier's mettlesome "yessir!'' from his mental kitbag.

"So—tomorrow night you make the transmission from the King Charles site. On Wednesday night, I'll call you

276

at box number three for any messages received. Saturday, you have a party. Saturday night you bring McNeil to the telephone at box number four." He paused. "They're proud of you, Boyd. So am I. Don't let us down."

JULY 9, 1941

Curzon pulled his arm free and rolled gently over the edge of the bed to the floor. He looked down at her face, the outlines of it indistinct under trailing strands of honey-blond hair. He settled the sheet over her narrow shoulders. Extension 171 slept like the dead from the moment they fell apart. He tiptoed out to the living room and poured himself a Scotch, well watered.

The Bart had woken him—or thoughts of him, insistent pipings of memory. Guilt, perhaps. The Bart would have a fit if he knew about Extension 171. But then he'd have a fit about all of it: a career as a "sneak"—even as a soldier he'd detested the whole philosophy of spying; a son's refusal to confide in his father; the dirtier tactic of befriending an enemy as a preliminary to destroying him. It was not the Bart's idea of war.

"The good general's supreme gift is a clear conscience." Sir Martin, in a rare moment of confidence. "Battle, some people'll tell you, is a board game. Chess. Pieces repositioned, pieces in check, pieces removed. Hogwash! War is the deployment of flesh and blood against flesh and blood. No matter how dense the logistics, you can never erase the human element. If you can, you've got no right to command."

Curzon pulled back the curtain and looked down into Ebury Street. He had more of the Bart in him than he thought. Tom Price was no longer a chess piece to be played around the board without feeling. There was too much humanity in him to ignore. Yet he had to be played; that was the job—Curzon's duty. But the logistics were denser than any the Bart had ever envisaged. Five's BIa section were now running upward of twenty-five German doubles against their masters in Hamburg, Oslo, and Berlin. Every one of them was personally handled by Loughran's team of case officers and wireless men, and each was cross-indexed to complement the activities of the rest. It was a new industry and a stunningly successful weapon. Of the ten agents who had made it ashore to Britain in the past ten months, only three had refused to work voluntarily against their own kind. One had been too ill to be of use, one had lost his mind, and the third had been executed—as an example.

The Bart wouldn't be able to grasp that, either. Turning against one's country for any reason was cowardice; doing so to save one's neck was ungodly. But the terms of reference, like the art of the double cross itself, came from a new lexicon. Another language, another ethic, another England.

He dropped the curtain into place and gulped the last of the whiskey. He went back to the bedroom; Extension 171 hadn't moved. He rolled into bed, propped his head in his hand, and studied her face in close-up. In sleep she had all the innocence of an unmarked child. A clear conscience. Or no conscience at all?

He lay back on the pillow. Did Price have a conscience? Yes. Emphatically. He ran too deep to be able to isolate himself from a sense of honor. So how did he justify it? Where did he find the moral rage to go on?

Answer: Where Paul Curzon found his. In the end, no one did it for king and country or glory or the hell of it. They did it for themselves—in the name of vanity, guilt, or escape. The Bart was right. The good general had to have a conscience. Only the very good could be trusted to perform the very dirty.

Boyd was bubbling over with self-importance. His telephone manner, thought Price wryly, wore a pip on its shoulder.

"Your chap's an absolute wizard, old man. Keys like the wind."

"But you got it down?"

"Well, I'm pretty fast myself, you know."

Boyd read out the letter block. Just one. Price again let him chatter while he decoded: a silent Boyd was a nervous one. He held the pencil torch over his notebook.

The plaintext read: "Your request for pickup feasible but dangerous. Essential drop made minimum one mile outside repeat outside mined War Channel 22 miles east-northeast Peterhead bar. No earlier one A.M. GMT no later two A.M.

GMT. Method: Buoy equipped radio oscillator directional flash as you suggest. Confirm date. Good luck."

Price cut in on him. "It's good, Boyd. Have you spoken to McNeil?"

"Fortune favors the brave. Isn't that what they say, old man?" He'd held that in readiness, thought Price. "He's ashore till Tuesday, so he's coming down. Journey will probably take all day, he says. Tickled pink, actually. He hasn't been up to town since '39."

"Why Tuesday? Is there something wrong with his boat?"

"The Navy runs a group of minesweeping trawlers out of Aberdeen, he says. They're doing a big cleanup in the fishing grounds. No boats allowed out till they're finished."

Relief emptied his lungs of air, misting the mirror over the coin box. "And Simmons and Co?"

"They'll fiddle it, they say."

"Excellent. Have you received the—ah—material?"

"Big envelope and the paper. I worked out the F.T. stuff tonight after tea. I better not say too much but there's no problem, believe me. What you want from . . ." He paused. ". . . Simmons and Co., I think it'll be safer in the long run if I tell them to use verbal messages only. They can call me your way—callbox to callbox. I take the stuff down and pass it on to you. That's okay, is it?"

"That's perfect, Boyd. You'll receive another envelope tomorrow. Put it with the first one. Now, tomorrow night, I want you to make another transmission. The sandpit, this time. Can you manage that?"

"If it's the usual time. I'll be lecturing at Broxbourne Institute till a quarter to nine."

"You'll always transmit at the same time. Even dates. This one's very short so I'll give it to you now. Got a pencil and paper?" He checked the day code blocks, looked in his diary, and encoded, "Pickup date: Wednesday July 16. Time: One A.M. GMT." He read it over to Boyd.

"Do I get a response to this one?"

"Probably just a single word. Pass it to me when I call you on Saturday night."

"Till Saturday then, ten fifteen. Box number four," said Boyd with military crispness.

"Same time. Good luck, Boyd."

He rang off and dialed the operator; he gave her the fourth number on Boyd's list of public callboxes. "I've been calling it for ten minutes," he said, "but my friend isn't there. I wonder if you could tell me where it is exactly."

JULY 12, 1941

The box was on the corner of Shepherdess Walk and Micawber Street in a tangle of byways behind the City Road. He arrived fifteen minutes early and turned back to reconnoiter the area. He found an alley between two shops that gave him a clear view of the phone booth and slunk into it.

They came thundering down Micawber Street on Boyd's motorcycle and pulled up immediately in front of the box. No attempt at concealment, no thought for who might be following. The pillion passenger lit a cigarette and they sat on the parked machine, feet on the curb, talking in whispers. At ten past ten, Boyd entered the callbox and wedged himself half in, half out, as a safety precaution. At ten fifteen exactly, he beckoned Geordie McNeil and they both squeezed inside. Price let another minute go by, then stepped out on the blind side and wrenched open the door. Boyd let out a whoof of terror.

"Good evening, gentlemen," Price said witheringly. "Why don't you bring a brass band, next time?"

JULY 14, 1941

Donald White held the envelope at his back, out of reach. He regarded Price's outstretched hand sullenly. "I've got a question first," he said.

"No questions!" Price grabbed him by the shoulders and hauled him into the kitchen. He slammed the door at his back and rammed the boy hard against the wall. White offered no resistance, but he managed to keep the envelope wedged behind him.

"Remember what happened to the last bloke who thought he could kick me around, skipper." It wasn't much of a show but Price let him go.

"*You* remember it. Give me that."

"When I'm ready." White smoothed the creases from his jacket and straightened his tie. "I want to know how long this is going on."

"Until I'm satisfied. Until the case is proved."

"What case?"

"That's not your affair."

"It's my fucking *neck*! Look . . ." He tried a smile, an appeal from one sportsman to another. "I'm doing it, aren't I? What you want. Okay. But I'm not stupid. If they cop me one night, I'm buggered all ways. *They* get me for pinching classified information, then *you* step in and get me for murder. Now, you're a brainy type; see it from my point of view. I'm sweating bricks every time I go in there. You make mistakes when you're nervous. So I need something to hang on to, don't I? Like when it'll be over."

"That depends on factors outside my control."

"Have you told your boss about me—what I'm doing for you?"

"He knows, of course."

"What about . . . that bloke I . . . ?"

"No. Not that. You'd be under arrest if I had. He doesn't make allowances for murderers."

White brought up the envelope and handed it over reluctantly. "What about the house?"

"What about it?"

"You said you'd be moving out."

It was the moment to end it. Price snatched open the door and pushed him outside. "You've got a long way to go before you get the house. That's a bonus, Donald. Earn it."

JULY 15, 1941

Geordie McNeil had a Viking's hatchet jaw and sea-blue eyes and, in the faint glow of the binnacle light, a skin tone of peppermint green that undercut the youthful geometry of his face with fierce shadows. He brought the *Dolores* abreast of the inner pierhead and held her against the rip from the outer harbor. Bigger boats entering the refuge from the sea had to warp in through the gut, but the *Dolores* was small, just fifty feet, and quick as a dolphin. He gauged his moment and spun her on the screw through 45 degrees, boosted her on full power, then eased off and probed the darkness ahead for the lifeboat station slip. The second pierhead loomed to port and he calculated his distance from the half-submerged rock sitting there awash to one side of the slipway. Hard aport, 120 degrees; she came around unwillingly, heeling as she met the southeast swell scudding through the outer harbor piers. Force Four to Five, moderating, according to the Navy's Weather Ops Room at Aberdeen.

He pushed out the door of the tiny wheelhouse and shouted to Jock and Iain who were sheeting down the slung nets in the forepeak. They couldn't have heard what he said but they didn't need to; Iain waved and the two of them bucked and rolled down the open decks and flopped down in the lee of the engine housing.

He brought *Dolores* on line for the outer entrance, darted a measuring glance at the prison bulking on his starboard hand, and pushed the controls full forward. She got up on her ladylike arse and headed for the open sea.

Clear as a bell, thank God. Luck again, like getting the go-ahead from FOIC Aberdeen to go out tonight unsupervised. The permission came on the express understanding that he would be fishing well inshore of the mined War Channel and no man in his right senses—fisherman or Englishman—would expect him to take a run-down tub like *Dolores* farther than he had to. Geordie knew the dangers better than most, and the

281

least of them, tonight, were the Aberdeen coastal patrols and the converted trawlers sweeping the approaches. The sea, as ever, was enemy enough.

Boyd's ''Control''—a word new to Geordie but it fitted the man fine—had heard him out on Saturday with the professional's ear for nuance. When he finished his résumé of the hazards of the voyage, Control had recited it back word for word, as if he were reading from notes. War Channel buoys could be shifted off their marks by heavy tides, so the special container buoy with its precious cargo of message envelopes was bound to drift if left too long. The chance of a patrol boat spotting the pickup vessel was high, the likelihood of a low-flying Anson or Blenheim or a long-range Spitfire doing so even greater. The container's radio direction flasher could be picked up by shipboard w/t. Plotting a course along the edge of the War Channel mine field was like dicing with the devil—hit a half-knot tide change at the wrong time, miss a buoy or range too fine on one that had floated off station, and—*bang*. The gaps through the Channel into open sea were narrow and, in the dark, almost invisible till you were on top of them. A sudden squall, a Force Ten blowing up from nowhere, and *Dolores* was driftwood. And so on and so on. It said something for Control's gentle persuasiveness that Geordie, who knew it all, came away with the firm conviction that he couldn't back out, even though it meant talking Jock and Iain into putting their lives in his hands for no apparent good reason.

He glanced back at the great stone sea walls as they rose and fell astern. Sanctuary. It had always struck him as ironic that they'd been built by the inmates of Peterhead Jail, who must have thought that they were simply adding yet another wall to the one that already cut them off from life. He knew that feeling only too well himself. He'd been cut off by birth, by family ties, by necessity, from everything he'd grown up yearning for. George McNeil didn't belong in Peterhead. London was for him; London and men like Boyd Corrie and—Control. No name. Just Control. A man who talked of Moscow and Berlin and Paris and Rome as if they were village stops along the bus route to Aberdeen. A man who talked of armies and beachheads and lines of command and strategy as if he directed the military effort of a continent.

And like all great men, he recognized his debts. When they

turned the tide against Hitler—and he seemed to imply that he and Boyd and Geordie had the power to make that happen— there would be no stinting rewards. For Geordie, a place at university—Oxford or Cambridge; his choice—extra-mural courses at the Sorbonne in Paris, and in Moscow. Travel. A position of Party trust.

When the war was over . . .

Jock and Iain had lit their pipes below the coaming and were alone with their thoughts. He'd told them he was going "abroad," which meant off the inshore grounds, but they didn't know how far and he hadn't told them. With a six-knot cruising speed and an early start, they'd probably guess. But they wouldn't question it. "The skipper's bairn" had earned his right to command years ago.

He went up into the bows himself with a pair of night glasses and Jock took the wheel, responding to his hand signals. Iain was in the stern, rising and falling like a kid on a seesaw but firm as a rock and no handholds.

If Jock and Iain took fright when they saw the War Channel marker buoys they kept it to themselves; greasy black and small as corks they were at this distance, but dead in line. Pray God they hadn't shifted. Then the narrow break channel; thin as a cormorant's gizzard it looked across the wide brace-let of mined water, but that, he decided, was his imagination. He kept *Dolores* smack on the centerline and Jock wrestled with her as she yawed in the keening southeasterly. Moderating, now. Jock claimed afterwards that for a Channel that was only two-point-eight miles across, it seemed like twenty, but then he held the fisherman's irrational superstition that *Dolores* was a living thing, could feel, was crying out in her panic to come about and run for home.

Twenty-two miles dead east-nor'east; two miles exactly from the outer markers on a direct line with the break channel. Good enough. He went back to the wheelhouse and sent Jock and Iain into the bows to shoot the nets. Madman! they'd be telling each other. But he was the skipper's bairn and they knew their place. One hour GMT, said Control. That gave them two hours on the drift before the tide turned.

And heaven help him if the nets came up empty!

*   *   *

A plane flew over just before midnight; at least Jock said he heard it, but they listened and there was nothing. They hauled in and there was weight to the net. Geordie left the two of them in the bows, backs bent, eyes on the net and the flash of silver in it, and unshipped the container buoy from the lifejacket locker under the wheel. Three feet long, six inches across. He unscrewed the cap and set the interrupter, checked the thick brown envelope rolled in the float chamber, then slipped astern and unbattened the afterlocker. The disc was two feet across and maybe turned the scales at a hundredweight; light as a feather in a head sea but it would hold a wee bauble like this long enough—if the weather didn't make up. He bent the long warp under the ring, lowered the disc over the stern and let it run, praying the warp was long enough. He looked forward; Jock and Iain were well occupied. The warp ran out and he let the container buoy kiss the water. For a moment it disappeared—gulp; then it surfaced and rode fine, maybe halfway down its length. He breathed hard and went back to the bows to lend a hand.

JULY 18, 1941

The bare boards of the dining room creaked and squeaked under the rubber-shod heels of aging female bondslaves. The maître in wing collar and tails bowed and scraped at the door as yet another party of Whitehall warriors came in. Menzies, displacing cabbage and boiled mutton around his plate in a pretense of eating, looked up and fixed the newcomers with a defensive scowl. The room was uncomfortably full for a summer Friday, but so far they had kept their corner table free of intruders. Curzon had not eaten at the Travellers' since the outbreak of war and had already made a mental note not to come again until it was over.

The invaders seated elsewhere, Menzies returned to his uneaten main course. He kept his voice one decibel level below the din of the members' gossip.

"Price is in better form nowadays, is he?"

"Emotionally, you mean?"

A fatted slice of mutton went off on a tour of Menzies' plate. "I suppose I do."

"Much better. After the Petrie business he was on his feet in no time."

"The death certificates, all that."

"It's what he wanted to hear."

"Hmmm. No change in his operational pattern?"

"None. He takes what the Pepperpot gives him and pushes it over lock, stock, and barrel. No complaints in that area. Pepper himself—"

"Ah, yes—Pepper. Spreading his wings, that little queer. He's put up a proposition to Downing Street, I hear. He wants exclusive rights on strategic forecasting of the Russian situation. Anticipation of needs, coordination, forward planning of war industries, convoying, lines of supply. He sees himself as a kind of middleman between Stalin and Winston."

"They're letting him do it?"

"Full speed ahead."

Curzon swallowed the comment he was about to make. None of his business.

"Which, of course"—Menzies touched a napkin to his mouth—"puts Price behind what I believe the Americans call the eight ball. Pepper's been told to find other premises for his Russian nonsense and at the same time maintain a partial presence in Southampton Row. A foot in both camps. Sounds uncomfortable."

Curzon put down a forkful of boiled beef and carrots. "It sounds crazy to me. Can't we stop it?"

Menzies sidestepped the question. "Perhaps it'll work. I don't know. There're altogether too many damned academics cluttering up the field play, nowadays." He tested his glass of white wine, made a face and put it down. "I have an idea our friend Price's days are numbered, anyway."

Curzon's head spun so fast it ricked his neck. "There's nothing to suggest that. I told you—"

"You haven't heard, then? Ritter's been sacked."

"When?"

"Three weeks ago. Canaris under pressure from Hitler under pressure from Heydrich. He's been flown out to North Africa. Tripoli, I believe. A decent burial, professionally speaking. His deputy Julius Boeger's taken over."

"But that doesn't mean . . ."

"Oh, come, Paul. Don't be arch. A change at the top, new broom. A fallen idol leaves no assets, just a sour taste in the mouth. Price was Ritter's prodigy. How long do you think he'll last under the new regime?"

"If it hadn't been for Price, Hamburg wouldn't have known about the American roundup till it happened. In a way, Price lost Ritter his job."

Menzies pushed his plate aside. "Times are changing, Paul. Price isn't out there on his own anymore. Loughran tells me the doubles are playing back day and night. Immense output. And Wulf Schmidt's the cock of the walk. Hamburg are leaning on him now far more than they are on Price. He's making twenty to twenty-five transmissions a month—and it's all material Hamburg specifically asked him for." He sat back in his chair. "I'd say that puts Price in the shade, wouldn't you?"

Curzon carried on eating. It hadn't struck him before but Menzies' tone and manner were remarkably mild, almost flippant; yet no one in the Intelligence community had fought harder to establish Tom Price and maintain him in place, and few were more convinced of his value than Stuart Menzies. There was an essential element missing from this conversation. Anger.

"You've changed your mind about him, then," he said guardedly.

Menzies shoulders rose and fell. He looked around him plaintively. "Do you suppose there's anything else to eat?"

Curzon signaled a passing waitress and asked for the table to be cleared. They ordered jam roly-poly for dessert.

Curzon returned to the subject. "About Price . . ."

"The picture's getting too big for its frame, Paul. Price occupies just one small corner of it. And we're no longer functioning in isolation. Special Operations Executive have their own interests in Europe now and they're not exactly bending over backward to cooperate with anyone." He leaned forward, his voice dropping perceptibly. "Heydrich's to be named Reich Protector of Bohemia-Moravia next month. He'll be headquartered in Prague. In Berlin, they're saying Hitler's grooming him as his successor. As Protector he'll have carte blanche to put his pet theories into practice—total suppression of impure racial stock, all the rest of it."

"I fail to see how that affects—"

"Don't you? We've been processing a great deal of agent traffic on Heydrich in the past couple of months; all for SOE. Habits, appetites, movements. Personal stuff. I wouldn't be surprised if SOE were setting him up for assassination. A dramatic gesture—striking at the Nazi core; one step from Hitler. The—"

The jam roly-poly was brought to the table: two squares heavier than housebricks filled sparingly with gooseberry jam. Menzies attacked his fearlessly but one mouthful was enough to spike his enthusiasm.

"If Heydrich gets his comeuppance," he went on quietly, "the whole Abwehr machine's in jeopardy. Heydrich's been pouring poison about Canaris into Hitler's ear for eighteen months. If he's killed, that poison becomes his epitaph. Canaris might not survive it. Nor would Hamburg. Ergo, nor would Price."

"That's a pretty tenuous argument. If—"

"It's the best we have!" Menzies snapped it out with uncharacteristic heat. He regretted it at once. "We now have a new head of Five; good man, we see eye to eye. The double-cross system's working well. The Pepper complication is bound to force a change of tactics." He spread his hands. "New circumstances, new game. I've accepted a JIC proposition that Price be run down. Slowly, mind. He won't be aware of it."

Curzon bit back a rejoinder. He said, "What does that mean? In practice?"

"We restrict material passing through his hands, reduce the operation at the Pepperpot. In a week or so, if I'm satisfied he's taking it as I think he will, we'll scale down his surveillance." He cocked his head on one side. "Well? No comment?"

Curzon shrugged. "All other things aside, doesn't that make me redundant?"

"Mmm. It does." Menzies grinned widely. "I'm sending you to Washington next month. You'll need to pack a bag or two. I expect you'll be there through the winter at least."

"Washington!"

"We've been invited to set up a special liaison office with American Intelligence—or the ragbag they're pleased to call Intelligence. The president's planning to put all their foreign operations in the hands of William Donovan. He's been canny enough to ask our advice and cooperation. You'll represent me till we can set up a proper organization there."

"I see." It was hard to contain his pleasure. And something more poignant: a sense of release. He wiped the self-satisfied smile off his face. "I suppose Loughran'll handle the run-down on Price?"

"Initially." Menzies tapped the napkin to his lips and laid it over the ugly remains of his dessert. "But I don't want Price alarmed. No unscheduled shocks. Nearer the time, you'll have to tell him you're going away. Ministry of Supply posting to Washington to coordinate convoy handling; that should impress him. Tell him your father wangled it." Menzies' eyes twinkled.

"That might be difficult. Suppose he wants to keep in touch?"

"Oh, you'll write to him, of course. Why not?" He pushed back his chair and got up. "Splendid meal, Paul. We must do it again before you leave town." He shoved the chair neatly under the table. An idea occurred to him. "If I were a member here I'd drop a line to the Catering Committee. That mutton was all fat."

Frank Loughran planted his size tens on the rim of the wastepaper basket and lit a Woodbine. "I'm lead fiddle, not the conductor," he said flatly. "They say play, I play. Stop playing, I stop. Anyway, Price isn't more than half my business."

"He's under your surveillance," Curzon retorted.

"Five's surveillance. A hell of a lot's changed since Churchill fired Vernon Kell. The new man's a committee juggler. He and Menzies are thick as thieves. For the past few weeks the only part I've had in the Price operation is keeping Ginger Haddon happy—you know that. They control the street furniture, decide what material he's fed, and write the weekly reports."

"Why? Doesn't it strike you as a little strange?"

Loughran rolled his eyes. "*Everything* strikes me as bloody strange. That's how I stay sane. I convince myself everybody else is crazy."

"Would you roll him up if it was your decision?"

"Like a shot."

"Why?"

"Economics. At BIa we're starved of money, men, and

resources. We're running twenty-eight doubles. Every one of 'em's got a case officer, wireless officer, housekeeper, uncle, and driver. That's the minimum requirement necessary to run one German agent full time. Everything's controlled down to the last dot and comma and none of them moves an inch without an escort. Now look at Price. You, me, Ginger Haddon, the Pepperpot team, a whole unit dummying up material for him to pass, four tails in rotation—and he can still float any time he wants. He costs the taxpayer £25,000 a year to run and he's peddling low-grade ore most of the time. It's not worth the money—money I could use to better advantage on Double Cross.''

"His record's good, you'll admit that."

"Record! He's been coasting. Without our back up he'd have caved in like all the rest. You said it yourself—at rock bottom he's pure amateur." He flicked ash from his cigarette onto the floor. "Anyway, what are you complaining about? He's not your problem anymore."

Curzon nodded slowly. "I don't like waste. And I don't like the feel of it. Too many people jumping to too many conclusions."

Loughran pinched out his cigarette on the sole of his shoe. "Things are tough all over," he said in his best Bogart. "Be grateful you're getting out of it."

AUGUST 22, 1941

The plat du jour was corned beef fritters and mash and there was nothing to drink but tea. They ate slowly to delay the need for conversation, a mutual decision. In Paul's case it probably sprang from uncertainty; he had something to say and couldn't for the moment find the right words. Tom Price was simply the victim of his own self-induced trauma. Geordie McNeil was making another run out to the drop point tonight, his fourth in almost as many weeks. In his imagination, Price made that perilous trip over and over again, always with disastrous consequences. Paul's telephone call an hour earlier—

"quick bite at Hopper's. I've got something to tell you"—
had set his heart bounding into his throat.

Paul cleared his plate at last. "They're shunting me out of
town, Tom." He still seemed unsure of himself. "The
ministry."

"Oh?" Alarm signals.

"I'm being posted to Washington. On the convoy lark."

"Permanently?"

"Through the winter, anyway. I don't know for sure."

Price made a thin smile. "Well, congratulations. That's a
bit of a leg up, isn't it?"

"Oh, I don't know. I had a letter from my old man
yesterday. He wangled it."

"Nepotism always comes through in the end."

Curzon grinned weakly at the memory of his own joke. "I
wish he'd leave me to live my own life."

"Oh, come on, Paul. That's unfair. You haven't been
exactly happy here, have you? He's done you a good turn."

"I prefer London." Curzon looked down at his hands. "I
leave tomorrow. I'm afraid I shan't be able to say good-by to
Dinah."

"She'll miss you."

"I'll be back."

True? Or the first subtle move in a complex reprogramming
of Thomas Price? He could feel his pulse beating insistently
in his throat.

"Can we write to you somewhere? She'd like that."

Curzon shifted uncomfortably. "I'll drop you a line when I
find somewhere to live."

"Won't they do that for you?"

"When I get there."

"Well, don't forget."

The rest of the meal was a trial for both of them, and they
put a swift end to it. A handshake on the pavement in
Holborn, the ritual backslapping, and they went their separate
ways. When Price got back to the Pepperpot, he closed his
office door and stood at the window for a timeless hour,
staring at the clock over Verney's cycle shop.

If Curzon was being withdrawn, the implication was that
the tempo was either rising or falling. In terms of the material
he was currently milking here for passage to Hamburg, the
trend was downward. The volume of reports and statistical

data had fallen off markedly during the summer. The only possible interpretation was that London were either losing interest in him or they'd found better alternative channels.

Boyd! His pulse raced out of control momentarily. He reined it back. No. If they'd located Boyd's Essex transmission sites he'd be under arrest. The same went for Geordie McNeil. The rules that applied in the manipulation of Tom Price couldn't be applied to them.

Wait and see. The coward's philosophy again.

SEPTEMBER 9, 1941

Lunchtime offered the only opportunity of the day; a departure from the office that wouldn't excite curiosity—he always left at one o'clock—dense crowds, heavy traffic, bucketing rain to confound the trailing Curate if, indeed, he was trailing that day. He would simply have to hope Alice would be at home.

He made for Holborn tube station, bought a ticket for St. Paul's, and went in the opposite direction. He changed at Oxford Circus and buried himself in crowds that carried him to Leicester Square. Down to the tube again and up without stopping. A fast walk through the back streets to Lower Regent Street and on to a bus, any bus. He walked from Parliament Square, backtracking at regular intervals to cover his rear. It was nearly two o'clock when he finally climbed the stone stairs, and he was soaked to the skin. Five minutes, not a second longer. He must be back by three at the latest.

"He knocked at the door of number 434 and Alice called out fearfully, "Who's that?"

"It's me. Tom."

The door edged open; he could see the links of a security chain running from the lock to the lintel. An innovation. "Quickly, Alice. I can't stand out here."

He stepped past her and walked into the living room. She chained the door and came in after him, darting here and there around the room to pick up the detritus of what appeared to be days of accumulated chaos. There were two plates on the table under the window, stained with coagulated fried egg. Three or four cups and saucers; a man's clothes, civilian clothes, slung across the back of a chair; three or four newspapers piled in a corner of the couch; Alice's clothes.

"Where is he?" he said sharply.

"Donny?" She looked absurd; a hoyden in a long quilted robe, fluffy pink slippers on her feet.

"Of course *Donny*!" He looked behind him and strode to the bedroom door. The bed was unmade and showed all the signs of recent occupation.

"He's been *ill*!" She shouted after him. "You made him ill!"

He barged back into the room and took her by the elbows. "Do you have any idea how dangerous it is for me to come here? How dangerous for you?"

She jerked her head upward and away, expecting a blow, and that defused his temper at once. He couldn't strike her again. Foolish, but he couldn't.

"Where is he?"

"He went . . ." He read her thoughts; could almost hear White's parting threat. "He's . . . out."

"On duty?"

"No."

"Why not? Is he still on the night watch?"

"No. He's . . ." Her look was imploring, and he almost weakened. She'd aged ten years, or maybe that's how she'd always looked under the makeup. When had he last seen her face free of paint and powder?

"He hasn't been to Richmond for two weeks. Why?"

"I told you—he's ill. He's been off ill."

His heart tripped violently. "Has anyone been to see him? From the Admiralty?"

"A Navy doctor came. And before that two sailors. Navy police."

"What did he tell them?"

"Just he was ill. The doctor gave him tablets and some medicine. It's his liver. He's been in terrible pain."

"How often does the doctor come?"

"Twice a week. Tuesday and Friday."

"Today?"

"Tonight, about half past five usually."

The speed of his cross-examination was panicking her. He let her sit down on the couch.

"All right, Alice. Where is he? If he has to be back by five thirty he can't be far. Where?"

"Oh, *please*, Tom! You don't know what he's been like. He gets so he doesn't know what he's doing. Look!" She plled up a sleeve of her robe, then the other. The bruising was purple and yellow.

"He did that?"

"Only because he's . . . You've got him so he doesn't know where he is. You're *killing* him."

"And he seems to be killing you. Where, Alice?" He took a threatening step toward her.

"He's gone!" Her arms came up to shield her head.

"Where?"

"I don't know where. He just goes. To be safe, he says. To give him time to think. He only comes back for the doctor, then he goes away again. Honestly, I don't know where. He won't tell me anything. He says . . ." The sobbing burst out of her; tears welled, huge and pendulous. "He says it's all my fault. He says he *hates* me for what I did. And I didn't do . . . anything. It . . . was . . . all . . . you."

He sat in the underground train shivering in his sodden clothes. He could imagine precisely the scope and nature of Donald White's "illness" and what had triggered it, and there was no doubt what White had in mind for a cure. He'd bolt—and probably leave Alice flat. Another complication.

So—make the decision now before it makes itself. Cut Donald White loose. The Operations Room ploy had been a godsend, had worked without a flaw for nearly two months, longer than he had the right to expect. Besides, he'd pressed White's luck and his own beyond reasonable bounds. White could have broken at any time; God knows, he had only to be offered a way out, a vague promise of clemency, to spill everything. White would do him a favor by running. Give him time, a week or so; then back to the flat to confront him or, hopefully, to confirm he'd flown. Alice was a born follower. With luck she'd run, too.

Which left a temporarily unemployed Geordie McNeil. Bad policy. The boy was thriving on his nerve-racking games of blindman's buff. He'd reported, in fortnightly callbox-to-callbox conversations with Boyd, three close shaves with patrolling minesweepers—one on the inner edge of the War Channel—two confrontations with the fleet officer in charge at Aberdeen, and a near capsize when *Dolores* hurtled through Peterhead's outer wall on the back of an eight-foot swell.

He must be kept at it; and luckily there was plenty of material worth passing along the McNeil conduit, much of it so familiar to Price that he'd overlooked its potential. The Pepperpot War Establishment list—names, titles, and telephone numbers of Whitehall functionaries, none of them high grade but all active. Addresses of ministerial outhouses in suburban London and the provinces. Sample letterheads, forms, and report sheets from the service arms, the Cabinet Intelligence Committee, and the Ministry of Supply—the raw meat on which he was fed each day. And newspapers. Today's *Times*, for instance, claimed that Britain was winning the Atlantic war against Germany's U-boats; convoys were getting through in increasing numbers. A patent lie in view of the havoc Hamburg must have created with the help of Donald White's Admiralty material, but a lie the German High Command planners should be aware of. If nothing else it indicated how extensively propaganda was being employed to prop up British morale.

He got out at Holborn. Bright sunshine greeted him at street level, tungsten sharp where it slashed the storm clouds. A quarter to three. He walked slowly back to Southampton Row.

For the second time, a week or so ago, he had considered sending a coded letter to Hamburg via McNeil, urging them to discount all product transmitted from Richmond, but having written it he burned it. Firstly, because if the container had been intercepted by a British naval patrol vessel, the letter would have exposed all of them—himself, Boyd, Geordie, even Simmons and Co. Secondly, because he now had absolutely no faith in Hamburg's judgment. They barely acknowledged his nightly sends. Wein occasionally added a private addendum before he signed off, but Ritter no longer issued personal directives and to all intents and purposes appeared to have washed his hands of Gimlet. Either he'd been removed after the disastrous collapse of his American network or he was punishing Price for being the bearer of bad tidings.

He reached the gray stone portico and dug for his pass. Go *placidly among the noise and haste*. He grinned at the recollection. Good advice.

Pepper was on him like a terrier the moment he stepped from the lift. "Tom, my boy. Looking for you." He fingered Price's sodden coat. "Good God, man, you're drowning."

"I got caught on the way back from lunch. No umbrella."

"Get yourself dried out, then, before you catch your death. I'm taking a glass or two with a close—a few chums this evening. You're coming with me. Spot of relaxation."

"I'm afraid I can't tonight, Philip. I've got something on."

"Can't?" Pepper clapped both hands to his ears. "Rubbish, *can't*! All work and no play? Won't listen, my boy. Not a word. Seven thirty. We'll go down together in the car."

Price was in the washroom, stripping off his jacket and shirt in a mood of seething rebellion when the significance of it struck him. We'll go down together in the car. Not at Queen's Gate, then. And a *few chums*. The term was quite foreign to Pepper's lexicon; not his style at all. Unconscious verbal camouflage? *Chums*. The Pepper Circle! The thought took his breath away. He hung his shirt on the radiator to dry out, stared at his haggard reflection in the mirror.

Well, why not? Pepper's Russian bandwagon had been trundling merrily through the Whitehall bogs for weeks now, gathering speed and support on every hand. Hitler's invasion of Russia had seen to that. In the space of a few days, Stalin's dilemma had triggered a tidal wave of native British sympathy. Uncle Joe could do no wrong: the papers said so, the Labour Party, the Communists—inevitably—the man-in-the-street. Clementine Churchill was personally organizing a food-and-clothing aid program, Washington was urging London to despatch arms convoys to Archangel, the "Tanks for Russia" Week had been an immense success in British factories. Julian, Gerry, Guy and the rest had reason to congratulate themselves. And reason to meet a neutered enemy on safe ground?

He put it out of his mind. Like it or not, he would have to go.

*   *   *

296

"Back at eleven please, Edith." The dumpling face of
Pepper's ATS driver pouched in sullen recrimination. "This
way, my boy." Pepper led him to a half-porticoed door and
rang the bell. Price looked back down the quiet street and up
to the bulk of Broadcasting House rearing over the rooftops,
hard against the moonlit sky.

"Pippy?" A face appeared, then a body, jacketless. "You
old . . . Come on, you little devil. Who's that you've got
there?"

They entered. Light flooded down the stairs ahead of them
and a silhouette, indistinct, stood at the top. "That you,
Pippy?"

"Hello, Adrian. I've brought a . . . colleague. Working
late; thought he deserved some relaxation."

The dandy who had opened the door to them took their
coats and pitched them casually in a heap on the floor.
"Won't you introduce me, Pippy?" He winked conspiratori-
ally at Price.

"Ah—" Pepper waved from one to the other. "Gerry, this
is Tom." No surnames. A precautionary measure. Price took
the long slim hand. It gave under his like warm Plasticine.

"Hmmm, Pippy!" breathed Gerry theatrically, and led
them upstairs. Adrian had withdrawn to the room at the back
of the landing and, as they rose to it, a swell of animated
conversation and tinkling glassware greeted them. Gerry pushed
them inside, slammed the door loudly to gain silence and
bawled, "Mai lords, others, gentlemen—" and received a chorus of braying abuse in return.

"Pipehead!" A dark-haired, good-looking man came at
them with a wide indulgent smile and a glass in each hand.
Pepper performed the rites with something less than enthusiasm.

"Guy, this is—ah—Tom. Colleague of mine."

Guy shoved a glass into Price's hand, grabbed Pepper's
elfin chin and shook it affectionately. He evaded Pepper's
attempt to pluck the second glass from his hand, wrapped an
arm around Price's shoulders and drew him into a corner.
Pepper looked on nervously.

"So you're Pippy's protégé, are you?" At close quarters
Guy's rakish good looks deteriorated dramatically; his skin
was gray, heavily pouched at the jowls, his eyes dazed and
bloodshot. When he smiled it was with his mouth in a crooked

leer. "He picked you out, I heard. One in a million, he says."

Price shrugged uncomfortably. "I wouldn't say that."

"Just a poor old toiler in the vineyard, eh?" Guy offered his Gorgon's grin. "Modest type. *Invita Minerva?*"

"Without natural talent or inspiration?" He rendered the Latin tag automatically, oblivious to the trap. "That's hardly for me to say, is—?" He stopped, shocked; Guy's rubbery mouth was performing a manic parody of his own, shaping his words without sound. The dazed eyes watched him with deadly expectation, looking for trouble; the cigarette at the corner of his mouth jutted up and out like an accusing finger.

"I really wouldn't know."

Guy threw back his dark head and roared with derisive laugher. The talk stopped, every eye in the room turned on him. "Hear that, you fiends in human shape? He wouldn't know if the secret war's hellish or not." He jabbed a finger into Price's chest. "They *know*, you see. The whole bloody war's secret from top to bottom. You know *why*, don't you?"

Price shook his head.

"So no one will know who to blame when the whole bloody bloodstained disaster's over and lost. Hey? Hey?"

Price turned away abruptly. The man was either unbalanced or drunk, and probably both; he had no defense against this kind of aggressive lunacy. But Guy was not done; with a roar, he grabbed the back of a gilt chair and snatched it from under its middle-aged occupant. He leapt on it, wine slopping from his glass, the cigarette jumping convulsively in his mouth. He held his arms wide, commanding silence.

"*Never* . . ."—Churchill's free-verse delivery, plummy and emphatic—"in the field of human decency, have so many been incinerated for so few, *or*, to take arms against a sea of troubles and, by opposing, go forward to the pit of Hell. We shall fuck them on the beaches, on the untamed hills, in the hedgerows, behind the lavatories in Leicester Square, under the clock at Victoria *Station*. Man*kind*, looking back—or forward or up its arse, according to its taste—will say of this moment—"

"Get his trousers off!" bellowed a voice, and there was a wild charge for the chair. Guy hurled his glass into the fire with spectacular force and kicked out violently as the first rank of the scrum lunged at him. The chair toppled and he went down in a welter of bodies.

The wrestling match was violent but short-lived and Price was relieved to note that at least a dozen other men in the room were as thoroughly embarrassed at the spectacle as he. He recognized their pained frozen faces; he had met them at Queen's Gate, from time to time; dons, civil servants, diplomats. Not regulars here, he decided (nor, for that matter, were they ever likely to accept an invitation again). So what were they doing in this bear garden? The truth penetrated as Guy freed himself from the maul on the floor. *They were here for his benefit*. A smoke screen. He was meant to recognize them, identify with them, suppress any lingering suspicions; write the whole thing off as just another conventional gathering of placid academics. In which case, someone should have made allowances for Guy.

The villain of the piece was sitting on the floor, his attackers gathered round him in a semicircle. His shirt hung out at the back, half the fly buttons had been ripped from his trousers and his tie was smoldering gently on the fire. He didn't seem to care. Maniac, Price thought as Pepper edged him toward a matched pair of Cambridge dons he knew from Queen's Gate. They can't control him.

Slowly, the atmosphere returned to normal. Pepper engineered him craftily around the big room, steering him into the company of old hands, bedding him down. The talk was dull, sluggish, pedantic, and a few of the older men began to move to the door. Price became aware of a pair of eyes in a far corner, a man standing alone, avoiding talk, contact, waiting. He knew instinctively that Pepper was working toward him, but the game couldn't be hurried. It took another half hour of aimless talk before they reached him, and the reunion was a pantomime of rehearsed surprise.

"Julian!"

"Pip, my dear chap!"

The parts fitted Price's mental image—the hand behind the letters, the leader, "the forceful one"—but the whole was flawed. He was overpoweringly tall—six feet four or five— fine wavy brown hair flecked with gray at the temples, a high broad thinker's brow, a lantern jaw, square and curiously mobile. Poet's eyes, a penitent's secretive mouth. But the paradox, the flaw, lay in the poet's eyes; one gray, one blue; impenetrable depth. No depth at all.

"Tom, this is Julian."

"*Mountford*." The voice was melodically deep, soothing, but it delivered the surname with unmistakable emphasis. "Glad you could come, Price." The square jaw moved a fraction. "Forgive us this day our roistering." His fine head angled discreetly at the group on the floor. "You mustn't mind Guy. He's a bit wild."

"Julian and I were at Cambridge," said Pepper hurriedly. "The long dead past."

"Oh dear." Julian shook his head in mock despair.

"In government now, of course."

Julian Mountford unsheathed two rows of yellow tombstone teeth. "Defense," he said helpfully. "Your line of country."

Price pretended a sip at his wine. "A wide field."

"Isn't it? You're in—?"

"Tom was the chap who put up the Cabinet study line on Russia." Pepper clamped his little fingers on Price's wrist. "Julian was on the Steering committee. He wrote the minority report. Thought you were right, every step of the way. Said so, didn't you, Julian?"

Mountford raised his glass and studied the golden liquid minutely. "A minority of one, I'm afraid, Price. We were victims of circumstance."

Price shrugged. "Circumstances don't change basic realities. The reality is we can't supply Stalin and survive our own shortages."

"The proletariat doesn't seem to agree with us." The blue eye closed; the gray, isolated, burned like a beacon in the long pale face. "War is emotion. Emotion feeds on expediency." The yellow teeth appeared again, a wall of primrose tiles. "Don't you find?"

"I—"

But Guy, in mid-diatribe to his circle on the floor, had the ears of a lynx. "Come then," he roared suddenly, "in the foundries and forges of Britain, in the engine works and the assembly lines, to the task and duty of helping Russia repel the savage invaders who bring *torment* and *torture* to mankind."

Julian smiled indulgently. "Beaverbrook," he said, giving

the speech a languid footnote. "No one's pitching in stronger for Stalin than Beaverbrook. The national mood, you see."

"And Maisky." Gerry swiveled his thin body from a prone position in front of the fire. "Don't forget Maisky."

"The Russian Ambassador," sighed Julian and chewed an invisible lip fretfully. "Charming fellow, of course, but one draws the line at putting him up for the Athenaeum. Hardly one of us, is he?"

"Odds are all against, Tom." Pepper again, plucking at Price's sleeve like a hungry bird. "Dragging us into a second front by the scruff of our neck. Your point again."

"I blame the Americans." Julian rolled the word off his tongue disdainfully. "Roosevelt's chipping away at Winston day and night. Help Stalin, hit back at Rommel, go for a second front. Tedious little man. Knows he can't stay out much longer and be damned if he'll come in on the losing side. Sound Wall Street thinking, you see: never invest in failure." He raised a tobacco-stained index finger to his mouth and chivvied away with the nail at an obstruction in his teeth. "So you and I, my dear chap, wail unheeded in the wilderness and Pippy here—" a fatherly hand descended on Pepper's shoulder, "scampers around London drumming up collateral for a second front."

"Has to be Norway," Pepper snapped as if he were arguing a hopeless case. "Told them. No good. Norway—only way in."

"Norway?" Price was genuinely astounded. Surely to God they weren't in all seriousness playing back to him his own invention?

"Oh, spring at the latest," Julian said wearily. "Absolutely nothing to stop it now, I'm afraid. The gang's all here. Can't beat 'em, join 'em."

As they were on the way out, Pepper in the lead, Guy lay back on the floor and shouted after Price, *"Forsan et haec meminisse juvabit.* Hey?"

"What was that he said?" Pepper asked when they were settled in the car behind the shimmering Edith.

"Perhaps this, too, will be a pleasure to look back on one day," Price said slowly.

Price giggled. "Idiot! He's a bit of a handful at times, Guy, but pure gold underneath, you know. Solid gold."

"Yes, I'm sure he is."

On the train he considered the entire performance, act by act, word for word. He wracked his brain for nuances he might have missed, points he hadn't absorbed, and unearthed none. Why had they got him there? To look, touch, smell? Test, tempt, divert? Or simply to crow? The Norwegian second-front gambit, of course, was pure theater; they couldn't believe he was that gullible. So?

Perhaps he was making the mistake of looking too deep, too far. Motives could be simple. What would he have done in their position? Inspect the victim. Yes, that was reasonable. They had nothing to fear from him and nothing to lose. And the extension to that? Make use of him, perhaps; use Pepper to channel occasional tidbits of disinformation useful to the Russian war effort. But it would be British policy to do that in any event. It was happening already.

He closed his eyes and forced the storm of speculation away. No profit in speculation. Know thine enemy. How many weeks since he'd ordered Boyd to initiate inquiries into the membership of the Pepper Circle? Six? Seven? And no results. He had no one to blame for that but himself; he'd set it aside in the press of more urgent considerations, put it out of his mind.

There was no sanctuary in ignorance. Begin again. Know thine enemy: Julian, Gerry, Guy, Adrian. . . .

SEPTEMBER 11, 1941

"Well, I did tell them, old man. I mean, the order went out." Boyd's discomfort was acute.

"When did I ask you to begin making inquiries, Boyd?"

"Oh—ah—I should think . . ."

"In early July. Seven or eight weeks ago. That's unforgivable, Boyd. I expected better of you than that."

"I'll start ringing round. First thing in the morning. Don't you worry, old man—I'll give them a towsing they won't forget. *Control*—that's all I have to say. You wait."

"I've waited too long already. These men are dangerous,

Boyd, can I get you to grasp that? They're secret men, professional agents. They've worked their way into the Party and they've got a lot to lose. We must know who and what they are—and quickly.''

"I know. Surnames, details of wives and children, family backgrounds, jobs past and present, known friends and—"

"And *discreetly*, Boyd. One word in the wrong ear that your people are asking questions behind their backs . . ."

"We're not exactly without experience, old man."

"Nor are they. Some of them are very powerful in private life, Julian and Gerry particularly, I suspect. So I want hard facts. Their movements, where they live in London, if they have homes elsewhere. Do they have relationships outside their marriages."

"Ah." Boyd caught on. "Compromising stuff, you mean."

"Yes, Boyd. Compromising stuff."

SEPTEMBER 16, 1941

He made a long diversionary approach to Alice's flat, leaving the Pepperpot at four o'clock and doubling back and forth in Victoria to clear his tail. He'd left without a word to Pepper or Archie Bassingthwaite, but he'd chosen his day and his excuse well. Tomorrow was Mrs. Plum's birthday—intelligence direct from the hen coop. He'd bought her a handbag. Ruthlessly expensive.

As he expected there were far too many people about; home-going workers, women with shopping, children playing street games. He crossed the courtyard with a handkerchief to his face, blowing his nose mightily. Luckily the stairs were deserted and there was no one in the corridor outside the flat. He tapped at the door. No response. He tapped again, a little harder this time. Still no reply.

Cautiously, he leaned his weight into the door. The tongue moved in the lock with a plaintive groan. He checked the staircase and walked to both ends of the corridor to make sure he was alone. He took the handle firmly in both hands, bent his knees to bring his shoulder to a point level with the lock, found a purchase on the coconut matting for his feet, poised, and threw his weight upward and forward. The door jinked inward and he fell sprawling.

The curtains were drawn. He shut the living room door and switched on the light.

Nothing much had changed since his visit a week earlier. Clothes were still draped on chairs, strewn on the couch, on the floor. A newspaper spread on the carpet under the coffee table was stained brown (spilled tea, coffee?), and a cup and saucer had rolled under a chair. One greasy plate, a knife and fork, on the table. An aging loaf of bread, hard as rock where it had been sliced; butter dish, an open pot of jam. Dust everywhere. And a terrible, cloying odor.

He went into the kitchen. The sink was full of unwashed dishes. He moved on to the bedroom; it stank of stale cigarette smoke but not powerfully enough to overwhelm the other all-pervasive stench.

He stood in the middle of the living room, stepped on the newspaper under the coffee table, and bent to examine it. The *Daily Mirror* of September 12. Friday. Stiff and illegible under a coating of . . . coffee? He carried it to the light to see it better, began to pull off his gloves but thought again. It was not coffee.

He took it back to the low table and got down on his knees. The carpet was thick with blood. *Don't touch.* His eye caught a glint of steel under the couch; he poked it out into the open. A pair of scissors. The closed blades were stained a coppery red all the way to the pivot. Something else under the couch. He worked it forward and it rolled. A work basket; Alice's.

He became aware of that hideous musk again, got up and checked his watch. Ten minutes past five. He couldn't stay much longer. The doctor, if there *was* a doctor, would be arriving any moment.

Who had spilled blood? Whose blood? Get out, his brain said, but his curiosity was stronger. Nowhere else . . . The bathroom? He crossed to the door in four strides and turned the handle. Locked, and the key removed. He tested the mechanism by pressing his shoulder to the woodwork. No stronger than the one outside. He collected himself and shoulder-charged the upper panel. It gave with a screech of splintering wood and old steel and he catapulted into the dark. His knees cannoned into the bath and he flung out his hands to break his fall.

As he pushed himself upright, something struck his head. He ducked in panic and the object struck him again. He reached out tentatively, his pulse hammering in his throat, and something brushed his fingers; once, twice, a third time. He grabbed at it. It was a shoe.

There was a foot inside it.

He had to leave for a few minutes because he couldn't breathe; then, with a handkerchief tight around the lower half of his face, he returned and switched on the light.

She'd been dead for some time; days, at least, he thought. Decomposition had set in, releasing the odor of . . . He touched the pipes running along the walls. They were hot; the room was a hot house. Little wonder.

He fought down his nausea and went back to the living room. No sickness! Not here. Something wrong—fundamentally wrong. What was it? *Think.* The blood on the floor. It wasn't hers. There was no trace of blood on her clothes—the pathetic robe, her nightgown—and no wound. What else? Something else. He screwed up his courage and went back yet again; looked up at her.

The face and neck were one vast purple-brown bruise. Eyes closed. *That* was it. Closed! At the point of death by hanging? Wouldn't they be wide open, bulging with the terror of anticipation, frozen that way in the instant the neck snapped?

And how had she got up there? There was a tiny window, eight inches square, in a recess just below the ceiling, but a woman of Alice's weight couldn't possibly have climbed up herself. And her feet swung at least a yard above the rim of the bath. The rope had been slung from a solid U-bolt in the ceiling, the sort used to suspend a drying rack. The knot at her neck was precisely placed, expertly tied.

And that finally showed him the truth. He turned away, switched off the light, and pulled the door shut. He felt dizzy; the odor seemed part of him, in his mouth, his nose, his stomach. He stumbled over the coffee table, went down the hall to the outer door, listened. He pulled it wide, stepped out, and shut it behind him.

A voice on the landing above shouted, ''I'll give you what

for if I catch you, you little bugger!'' and a child's derisive laughter echoed after it. He started down the stairs.

Halfway across the courtyard he remembered her face and the tears came so quickly they temporarily blinded him. He'd killed her as surely as if he'd tied the knot himself. A second's rational consideration of her dilemma rather than his own would have saved her. But no—he'd turned his back on her as he had on Donald White. Wait and see! And the pressure of waiting, not knowing, had been too much for both of them. An argument; a fight; Alice swinging hysterically with the first thing that came to hand—a pair of scissors. White, bleeding, losing control, striking her, knocking her senseless. Then cold-bloodedly finding the rope, tying the knot. . . .

OCTOBER 5, 1941

The lead violin reached for the final ecstatic note of Scheherezade's triumph and Charles Hambourg brought the London Philharmonic to a breathless finale. Applause rolled round the great dome and Price found himself on his feet with the rest of the audience. It was in keeping with the times that Rimski-Korsakov's symphonic suite should have been chosen to end the program; 1941 had become the year of the Russians. Stalin the monster was now Stalin the father figure, the unbending champion of freedom. The British, worshipers of underdogs, would cheer the devil if he presented himself as a plucky loser.

Hambourg came and went four times, acknowledging the ovation, and finally withdrew. The audience swayed toward the exits and Price stood patiently in the middle of a row, sobered by the experience but at peace with himself. It had been so long since he'd sat alone, embraced by pure melodic sound, and, ironically, he had a great deal in common with the legendary Scheherezade. They'd both saved themselves from death for a thousand and one nights by telling tales.

He sidestepped slowly to the aisle and descended toward the exit, flanked on all sides by talk and laughter, feeling in a strange way almost part of it. In front of him a woman was frantically pulling on a light coat, an umbrella and handbag wedged under her arm, and he pressed to one side to avoid her, but the umbrella caught in his jacket and plopped onto the stairs, followed at once by the handbag. He bent to pick them up, rose unsteadily, and held them out to her. "I beg your—"

He stared at her open-mouthed. "Sally!"

"Oh." Dismay. She took the bag and umbrella in confusion. "Dr. Price."

Her embarrassment was disconcerting—an accusation in itself—as if he'd deliberately waylaid her to cause her pain. As they joined the cascade on the stairs, she drew ahead of him; and, because he understood, he allowed her to. What in heaven's name had happened to her? To the bright innocence, the flushed cheeks, the quick smile and the child's gaiety? *Was* it Sally? He caught up with her in Albert Court.

"Sally?"

She was almost running. He touched her elbow, and she flinched away as if she thought he were about to strike her.

"Do you have to rush off?"

"It's late. There's a bus. . . ." She waved vaguely, head down, still walking hard.

"Can I walk with you?" He took her arm before she could object. She seemed uncertain where to turn, and it occurred to him someone might be meeting her. A friend? Her husband? "If you'd rather I didn't . . ." he said politely.

She looked up briefly. It *was* Sally. But only just. "I think I'd rather go alone, if you don't mind."

He dropped her arm at once. "Well, some other time then."

She walked on as if she hadn't heard and he stood foolishly in the middle of the pavement, watching her go. Why? Because of Alice? Some impulse goaded him on; he hurried after her. "Sally!" She stopped. "Look, I can see I've caught you at a bad time. I won't hold you up. I'm just . . . well, glad to see you, that's all. It's been so long."

She turned, and he was astounded to see that her eyes were brimming with tears. She clapped both hands to her mouth, helpless to stem the flood, and swung away.

He took a step back. "Look—if I've done anything to . . ."

"I'm . . . I've not been too well." She found a handkerchief and blew her nose. "I was a bit surprised."

"So was I."

"I didn't mean to be rude."

"Of course not."

She looked longingly down the street, seeking escape. "I really have to catch that bus. . . ."

He knew he should let her go but he heard himself say, "I'm going to South Kensington. For the train. I'm still at Richmond." She said nothing but he plowed on. "If it's on your way . . ."

"Yes." She wiped her eyes. "There's a bus stop in Cromwell Road."

It was hardly an invitation but he took her arm again and they began to walk; very quickly, she dictating the pace.

She seemed so *old*. He said lightly, "Are you still at University College? Pepper mentioned running into you there once."

"I left. A . . ." Her voice broke. "A year ago."

"Yes, I suppose it must have been at least a year." He tightened his grip on her arm, reassuring her. Now that she was on his arm he could think of nothing to say but the idiot banalities of accidental reunion. "Do you work now?" She nodded and he felt her arm go tight, as if she were making a fist. "Where?"

She didn't want any of this. "An office. A chartered surveyor."

They turned the corner into Exhibition Road. "I suppose you're married now. When I last saw you you'd just 'exchanged parents.' I remember you said . . ."

She stumbled, fell against him, tried to pull away, swayed unsteadily, and collapsed on his chest. She made no sound but her body shook uncontrollably against his. He touched her face and she clung to him. He let his arm encircle her. The husband?

"Sally?"

"I'm all right. I'm really . . ." She pushed him away, found her handkerchief again and covered her face. "I really shouldn't have come out . . ."

"I'm not going to leave you like this," he said firmly. He closed his hand on hers and when she tried to free it, began to walk, drawing her with him. "We'll get a cup of tea

308

somewhere. There's a place near the station. If you miss your bus, we'll take a taxi."

We.

"When he came back after Dunkirk we eloped." She was under control now, steadied by the light of the cafe and the people around them. There were dark circles under her eyes and the deep clefts running down to her mouth were crusted with mingled tears and face powder. "We sent telegrams from Sheringham. His people were terribly angry—they were against it from the start. They had plans for him. A local girl. Anyway, after a while . . ." She stared unseeing at the spoon in her fingers.

"Last summer?" he said gently, for something to say.

She nodded. "We had two months. They gave us married quarters at Aldershot. He was teaching officer cadets. We thought . . ." She ran the spoon over the surface of her tea. "He said it was bound to be only temporary but I thought, 'If I want it to be permanent, it will be.' You get like that. Make-believe. Then he came home early one afternoon. They'd posted him to Egypt and he had to go right away. Thirty-six hours. His mother and father came down on his last day. There was a row about . . . oh, everything. . . . John couldn't cope."

He was unequal to it. The moment she'd begun talking about her husband he'd guessed the end.

"He said he'd write to me at my parents'. We agreed I'd live there, but I couldn't stand it after the first week. I got my old job back at UC and took a bed-sitter. For some reason I felt I had to be on my own; I didn't know why at the time. Then I realized I was going to have a baby." She let the spoon drop into the cup, splashing brown teardrop stains on the check tablecloth. "I wanted so much to tell him." She looked up at Price, half surprised, as if she couldn't expect him to understand. "I'm no good on my own. I learned that quickly enough. I was working up the courage to go home again but I was scared stiff. I hadn't told my parents or his about the baby. Then my mother called. She always phoned on Friday mornings in case there was a letter. She said they'd just had a telegram. For me. My father opened it."

He reached out impulsively and covered her hand. "You don't have to. . . ."

"I never had much in my head. John used to say I married him to have a grown-up doll's house to play with. He only meant it as a joke but he was right. I never talked to him once about the war—what Dunkirk was like, if he was frightened. Things like that. All I thought about was the house we'd buy when it was over, and his job, and holidays, and schools for the children. I took it for granted he'd always come back. He was a *possession*. . . ." She traced the letter P on the table-cloth in front of her. "He belonged to me. . . . My mother read out the telegram but I didn't believe it. I just put the phone down and went home to the flat and started washing things. I didn't think about it. I just did it. Clothes, crockery, glasses, the sheets on the bed, tablecloths, anything I could find. Then I remembered some paint I'd bought for the kitchen ceiling and I got everything ready and—"

"Sally, don't. . . ."

She ignored him. "I'd been meaning to do it for weeks. It wasn't a very high ceiling, but I got the stepladder and stood right on the top. I was bent over, under the ceiling, looking down. I couldn't stand upright. It was like sleep walking. Suddenly you're somewhere you didn't mean to be and you get a terrible feeling of . . . I don't know. I didn't fall, I jumped. Just let go."

She freed her hand from his, took up the cup, and nursed it tightly. "I held the paint pot on . . . where the baby was. As I was falling. To make sure."

Some perverse memory cupboard opened in the dark reaches of Price's mind and showed him a picture of Else lying on a nest of towels in the Dortmunderstrasse, knees raised high to contain his seed.

"When I came out of hospital, I couldn't go back to UC and I couldn't face my mother. I found another flat and got this job in Wigmore Street. I haven't talked to anyone. I haven't been out like this since . . . then. When I saw you . . . ."

"I really am so very, very . . ." He stopped, frustrated by his inadequacy. "I'm not much use, am I? I can't think of anything to say."

She set the cup precisely in its saucer and buried her hands in her lap, out of sight. "I'm glad I met you." She couldn't look at him. Her face puckered, reaching for a smile, not finding it. "You have to tell someone in the end, don't you? You and Alice . . . I suppose you're . . ."

"Alice is dead," he said, too quickly, too harshly. He didn't want any mistake about that; no misunderstandings. "She was living with—*in*"—he changed the word quickly—"a house behind Theobald's Road. A direct hit."

"But she had children." As if that bequeathed incontrovertible rights.

"Her son, Alan, was with her. He was killed too. Dinah's all right. She . . ." He groped for a way out of it. "She's leaving school this summer. We're thinking of moving into town. It's a long way to trek home every night."

She sat motionless for a long time, hands in her lap, eyes downcast. Then she touched her hair, lifting it from the back with splayed fingers; an unconscious vanity. "Are you still with Professor Pepper?"

"Yes. As a matter of fact he gave me his ticket for the concert tonight. He had to go to a meeting at the last minute." Another chapter opened and closed. He looked at his watch. "It's ten to eleven. What time's your last bus?"

"A long time ago. But it's not far."

He checked the bill and dropped a shilling on it. "We'll take a taxi if we can find one. There's a rank across the street."

She didn't argue.

NOVEMBER 26, 1941

They'd had a letter from Paul Curzon that morning; he'd been shamed into it, he confessed, by the one-way flood of lettercards and essays that had streamed from Dinah's scratchy pen at the rate of two and three a week. He painted a Wellsian picture of Washington. Something called air conditioning in summer, piped heat in winter, dream kitchens, an ice-water machine in his office, a motor car so big he could fit his little MG in its boot (sorry, trunk!). But he missed London and he missed Dinah. She loved every word of it.

She read it aloud from beginning to end for Sally's benefit when they dropped around to pick her up at her flat in Earl's Court Square. That was Dinah's idea, too. A man shouldn't be allowed to go house hunting without a sensible woman to spot the pitfalls, she said, and Sally was perfect. He couldn't disagree with that.

Sally was perfect.

He couldn't remember why he'd told her on their first meeting that he had decided to leave Richmond but, in the weeks that followed, his determination to do so grew. Dinah was delighted. She'd fought a hard campaign for the right to leave school when she was fifteen and then announced her intention of finding a job in London as soon as she could. Moving solved both their problems, she argued. He would have to spend less time traveling to and from work and she could take a job *and* keep house.

They strolled along Fulham Road and turned into the narrow terraced artery of Elm Place. From the outside, the house looked minute. Inside, Sally and Dinah agreed at once, it was simply perfect. Not cramped; *cozy*. The front garden was a stone-laid handkerchief; the rear courtyard was paved and enclosed by a high brick wall. No garden. Price entered a black mark against it. He went upstairs.

Sally was measuring the front bedroom window with a long folding ruler as if his acceptance of the tenancy were a foregone conclusion. He concluded, wryly, that it was and sat on an upturned box to watch her. He'd been relegated to the status of spectator from the moment they crossed the threshold.

He caught her eye and waved around him. "Green, I think, don't you? Strip off this wallpaper and paint it green."

"Oh no!" She frowned at him. "White, I think. A nice white paper. And white net here." She made flounce shapes with her hands. Her smile was infectious, glorious. The sparkle was back in those hazel eyes again, life in her face. He'd put it there; he and Dinah.

"Well, a red carpet, then."

"Green would be softer," she said without looking around. "Apple green. And apple green and white for the door and window frames."

"I was thinking of tartan for the—" But he couldn't hold it in. She looked at him blankly as he spluttered with laughter, then, seeing the joke, smiled again. The old Sally—young Sally—eager and open and wide with innocence. Her brows knitted a mock rebuke. He wanted to go to her but something, as always, held him back; and at that moment Dinah came clacketing up the wooden stairs.

"It's *perfect*!" She flung her arms round his neck, rocking him on his unsteady perch. "We *must* take it. There's a lovely little kitchen and a shed in the yard and *hundreds* of cupboards and——"

"And it feels like two telephone booths knocked into one," he said to tease her.

"Oh, it's not!" Sally, coming to her rescue.

"It's *perfect*!" Dinah pleaded. "Admit it."

"For two pounds a week? I expect Buckingham Palace for two pounds a week."

"I'll help with the rent as soon as I get a job." Dinah started out the door to continue her survey.

"You'll be lucky to earn five bob a week," he called after her. "How much do you think that'll pay for?"

"Well . . ." Dinah paused, her face set, taking him seriously. She chewed her lip. Then, "I know!"

They both looked at her gravely, trying not to laugh.

"We can have Sally as a lodger."

BOOK FOUR
1942

APRIL 20, 1942

For the tenth time he raised a hand from the sheet and reached in the darkness for her shoulder; and for the tenth time he let it fall again without touching her. She was still sobbing; small tremors shook the sprung mattress, entering him at the nerve ends, compounding his misery. She lay curled on the farthest edge of the bed, abandoning him.

He should have gone home when they finished supper. He'd planned to. It had been no different at that point from any of the other evenings they had spent together. But she hadn't wanted him to go. They had washed up in the small kitchenette, not talking, and that had made him uneasy because they always talked. Their friendship was built on disclosure. He put it down at first to an attack of guilt; her husband's ghost rarely left them in peace, particularly when she was happy. But that wasn't it. Not tonight. Without warning, his brain had begun telegraphing urgent messages to his body; what they whispered shocked him, and he'd looked at her in bewilderment when he realized the messages were flowing from her. He had no clear recollection of what happened after that; if it happened there in the kitchen or later, if they exchanged words or signals or touched or looked, if she moved toward him or he to her; but one moment he was drying a plate and the next she was in his arms. He hadn't led her to the bedroom, he was sure of that, so she must have led him. Incomprehensible, but she *had*. No memory, either, of entering her, feeling her move under him; only that split second of electrifying stillness when his mind returned to earth and he raised his face to look at her, and she stared back in horror and began to cry.

That look. He draped a forearm across his eyes to blot it out. Reaction. What else could he expect? She'd submitted to impulse, not to him, and when it was over she'd looked up and the face she'd seen was not John's.

She stopped crying, and the silence sent a shiver through him. He contemplated getting up, dressing, slipping out.

315

Never coming back? Her body straightened very slowly and she rolled over. They'd forgotten to draw the curtains; the moon, very bright now, played shadowy games on the wall above their heads.

He kept his eyes riveted on the ceiling. "I think I'd better go," he whispered.

She said nothing, but an instant later her hand touched his arm; not the whole hand, just a trailing of fingertips. He made no move to respond.

"I don't know why I did that." She spoke so softly he barely heard. Self-examination, he thought; she doesn't care if I hear or not. "It was like"—the fingertips touched him again, very briefly, preparing him for the truth—". . . like waking up in the middle of the night. Not knowing who you are."

He swallowed hard. "I had no right to . . ."

"Don't talk about it. Please."

He closed his eyes tightly and, with a start, touched a hand to his face. Tears?

"I'm sorry, Tom, I didn't mean it that way." This time her fingers curled round his arm and stayed there. He could feel a pressure point at the base of his bicep beating into her palm. His tears rolled out of control down his cheeks into his mouth, into his ears. A great constriction rose in his throat and he felt an overwhelming urge to give in to it. That's how it must have been for her. So easy to give in.

She was speaking again, a new note in her voice—persuasive, pleading. ". . . always talked things out. But never about us. Now I know why."

He nodded up and down on the pillow. He couldn't trust himself to speak, and for several minutes neither could she. Was he free to touch her now? He kept his arms rigidly at his sides, his fists clenched.

"Do you believe a person can . . . love someone without being honest? About—what they are?"

"I don't know." He felt her eyes on him, but he didn't dare to look at her.

"Did you love Alice?"

He laughed; a snort, a sneeze of contempt.

"But you married her."

"Yes."

"You weren't honest with her."

He felt a stirring of righteous anger but there were no words to express it. Alice with her purple-brown face hanging over the bath, lifeless in a dirty dressing gown.

Sally turned to him, closing the gap. "I loved John," she said flatly, as if he'd challenged her. "I never loved anyone else."

"No." He felt her move again; her hand tightened possessively on his arm.

"When . . . A long time after the telegram, they sent his things home. My picture, his watch, his wallet. I suppose they think wives need . . . objects. And they sent his letters; the ones he'd kept. Afterwards, someone told me they're always so careful when they go through a dead man's belongings. In case they upset his . . . family." He screwed his head round to face her, his heart thumping. "They weren't *my* letters."

"Sally . . ."

"I think it was the girl his parents wanted him to marry. They wouldn't if they'd seen what she wrote."

He dragged her to him, felt her face hot and wet on his chest, but she couldn't stop now.

"I don't think he really loved her. It was something he— whatever men need. She wrote about being in bed with him . . . physical things. I couldn't have given him that even if he'd asked me. I wasn't angry. The only thing I felt was . . ." She pressed her face into his throat. "I killed the baby for the wrong reason."

His own tears started again and flooded his eyes, racked his body. She stiffened in shock as she felt it, then her lips reached up and found his eyes, his cheeks, his jaw, his mouth, very quickly, weightless butterfly movements of pity and tenderness. "Please don't. Please. I love you." She pulled his head to hers, crooning and crying, dabbing his eyes with the sheet, and he let her do it, unresisting. After a while the storm passed and he lay still.

"I won't care . . ." Her voice was muffled, framing words into his hair as she cradled his head; but firm, gathering strength. "I won't care if there are things that happened before me. After Alice died. But there mustn't be anything . . . anyone else. There isn't, is there? Anyone?"

It was a kind of insanity, he thought with half his mind; the walls of the brain collapse and the chambers empty one into the other, intellect into emotion, fantasy into reason, balance into imagination, fear into fortitude.

He fought the words as they rose to his lips but he had no power over them. "In Germany. There was a woman." Why was he saying it? "We had . . . two children. Boys." He heard her catch her breath, but all he could think of was that the truth had to be a lie, that confession was deceit. Price had been in Hamburg for eight years. Kurt would be . . . his mind reeled . . . four then, and Willy seven? No, Kurt three and Willy . . . It wouldn't come right, but the madness drew him on, inventing lies for him. "She left me." He gasped with relief at the inspiration. "I had no money and she wanted what her family could give her. For the boys, too. I never saw the youngest. She left before he was . . ."

It was a long time before she stopped crying, and when she released him he felt her exhaustion seeping into him as his seeped into her. He fell back on his pillow and groped through misty layers of encroaching sleep for something real on which to concentrate. The time. What was the time? He must go home. Now.

"Do you . . . want to love me?"

His brain grappled with the notion, the construction of the question. Not "Do you love me?" but "Do you want to?" He lay too long thinking about it and when he realized she was waiting blurted out, "Ever since that day in Elm Place. When you were measuring the curtains." He didn't mean it but he knew only too well what she wanted to hear.

"I want to love you."

"There isn't anyone else."

Her hand seemed almost too heavy for her to move but it found his and curled inside it like an embryo. "I don't *care* about anything else," she whispered passionately. He tried to open his eyes but they seemed shut; locked and bolted. What did she mean "anything else"? Of course, Else and the boys. She meant Else and the boys.

"There isn't anything else," he said emptily.

Her breathing became deep and steady; she was on the edge of sleep. Then she roused herself with an effort and her arm fell across his chest. "Don't leave me. I couldn't bear to lose anyone else."

JUNE 3, 1942

It was one of those mornings that make war seem an absurdity. The birds sang in Kensington Gardens, exotic trees bathed in bright spring sunshine along the ornamental walks, mothers with prams paraded in lighthearted convoys around the lake, and pretty girls in short-sleeved summer frocks dallied in the grass with confident young men in well-cut uniforms.

Curzon drank in the sights and sounds greedily. It was a perfect day to come home. His companion, Stuart Menzies, was less impressed. He was glaring disapprovingly at a couple locked in unheeding embrace under a tree. The man was an American Army Air Force lieutenant, very dapper and, in his ardent attention to the girl, totally uninhibited.

He averted his eye with an ill-concealed shudder. "What the devil does he think he's doing? In uniform!"

Curzon grinned. "Well, at least they're here."

It was almost true. The American 34th Division, the 1st Armored Corps and detachments of the US air forces had recently arrived in Northern Ireland. Much of their equipment had yet to follow them, a condition described by the War Office mandarins as "ragged arse chaos." America's belated entry into the war was still regarded in the more hidebound Whitehall circles as a mixed blessing, and the imminent transfer of US troops to English soil as a major social catastrophe.

Menzies stabbed the turf with his umbrella. "I gather you approve?"

"Not approve. Understand. They do things differently over there."

"Hmph. That applies to their intelligence operations, too, does it?"

"I guess so."

Menzies spared him a withering sidelong look. "Guess? Oh, of course. Different language, too. Perhaps it's as well I brought you back when I did. You'll be able to translate."

319

Curzon kept his peace. Menzies had met him off the plane at dawn, had bought him breakfast at a hotel on the Great West Road and brought him into town without once revealing why. They had touched lightly on Curzon's Washington sojourn, discussed the weather and the North African campaign, and mourned the passing of the traditional English breakfast; there was more to come.

They strolled for five minutes in silence. Then, "How often has Price written to you?"

"Maybe a half-dozen times. His daughter—the Petrie girl—sometimes two or three times a week."

"And you? You replied, of course."

"When I could. I've never been much of a letter writer."

"How did he come across in his letters?"

Curzon tapped his jacket pocket. "I've got them all here. They're not worth your time."

"You know he left Richmond, obviously."

"Yes. I called Frank Loughran the moment I heard—one of the girl's letters. Loughran said Price didn't tell Hamburg he was on the move; just started sending from the new address one night. Hamburg spotted the change in signal strength and ran a fix on him. There was quite a panic at the time."

"Did Loughran advance an opinion on why Prince didn't report his change of transmission site?"

Curzon stole a glance at him. Why ask when he already knew? He let it go. "He didn't have to. Hamburg ordered Owens to contact Price and find out. Price said he'd used Richmond for far too long. It wasn't secure."

"But he's still transmitting," Menzies said softly.

"Is he?"

"Oh, yes. What your friend Loughran describes as low-grade ore. Not very discriminating, Price. He takes what he's given and sends it religiously. Twice a week now, Tuesday and Thursday nights."

"So you were right."

"Right? Oh, about running him down? Yes, we ran him down. Took off his surveillance, scaled down the Pepperpot operation."

"But you kept him in circulation. I don't see the point of that."

"No, you wouldn't." Menzies was lost again in thoughts of his own. "Did he write to you about the girl?"

Curzon made a face. "Sally Logan. Is she one of yours?"

"Not at all!" Menzies looked shocked. "For heaven's sake, Paul!" He removed his bowler and wiped the inner band with a large vermilion handkerchief. "They met at Phillimore Gardens when he first came to London in '39. Planning to marry, I hear."

"But you'll scuttle that."

"Scuttle it? It's hardly my affair, now is it?"

"Then we have to warn her."

"Of what exactly?"

"Of . . ." Curzon pulled back from the edge. "We're obliged to legally, if nothing else. Alice Petrie's alive somewhere." He shot a hard look into Menzies' face. "Isn't she?"

"You arranged the death certificate, old chap. Not I. You'll have to ask Loughran." He upended his umbrella and swung a chip shot at a twig with the curved handle. "In fact, if you're not too wrung out, I suggest you go see him today."

"Why?"

"You'll be coming back into circulation again, yourself. Loughran can brief you. Better to get it over with, don't you think?"

They came to the foot of the Albert Memorial. Menzies' car was tucked into a no parking area beside the Royal Albert Hall.

"You'd better call on Price, too. Today."

"I'd rather not, if it's all the same to you. I don't see the point."

"No, you wouldn't," Menzies said again, and shaded his eyes to gaze up at the memorial. "But do it. Be rather silly if you bumped into him in the street and you hadn't told him you're back. I'd like your opinion of him. He'll be glad to see you."

"And then what?"

Menzies twirled his umbrella reflectively. "He's an old and valued client, Paul. We have obligations." He settled his bowler squarely on his head. "Find your own way to Loughran's office, can you? I have an appointment."

He strode down the steps to his car without looking back.

*　　*　　*

Loughran slammed the door of Donald White's flat in the janitor's face and latched it to sabotage any idea the old fool might have of eavesdropping. Curzon went immediately to the bathroom and glanced up at the U-bolt in the ceiling. It looked innocent enough now; a drying rack hung from it, festooned with two pairs of pink bloomers and three collarless shirts. He backed out, peering briefly into the kitchen and bedroom.

"How long have the new tenants been in?"

"A week after it happened. Empty flats don't go begging for long."

Curzon dropped into a chair. "All right. Let me get this straight. Alice Price hangs herself."

"So they say. September 15."

"And two weeks ago, for the first time, you hear about it."

"Million to one chance. Dick Pierce, one of my blokes, was running a trace on classified personnel with Admiralty access and he—"

"He finds Donald White's status card—"

"Showing that White was transferred to the Far East Fleet on September 1. And a covering note from DNI: Alice Price found dead in his flat two weeks after he left."

"And their conclusion?"

"Suicide while the balance of the mind was disturbed." Loughran rolled his eyes. "Broken heart."

"But the death certificate was issued by an Admiralty pathologist, not a civilian coroner."

"DNI got bloody snotty when I asked why. White was on their Red List, they said, and Alice Price was his popsy, so there were possible breaches of security involved. Blah-blah."

"But you pointed out, I hope, that Alice Price also happened to be—"

"Course I bloody-well did. I went knocking on the chief's door with a stack of bloody files under my arm a foot thick. Sat and listened for half an hour then told me to shove it up the old back passage. Forget Price—he wasn't my business anymore. Nor Alice. Nor Donald White. Terminate the files and hand them over to chief of staff, Five. End of conversation."

"Which you did."

"What else was I supposed to do—argue?"

"But you discovered enough to find your way here."

"Put it down to an old hack's pride."

"What happened to Alice's body?"

"They didn't confide in me."

Curzon nodded vaguely. He looked up. "What else did you do?"

Loughran grinned sheepishly. "I took a shot at Donald White's old man."

"You didn't tell him about Alice!"

"Don't be daft. I got talking with him in a pub. Said I was in the Navy; just back from the Med. He said his boy was in the Far East. Got himself posted there last September." His grin widened. "Proud as punch, he was. Important lad, his Donald. Only had five minutes to talk to him on the phone before they whipped him off to fight the Jap."

"White *phoned* him?"

"September 9, about half-past eight at night. No doubt about the day. It was the Whites' wedding anniversary."

Curzon opened his mouth, shut it again, got to his feet and sauntered back to the bathroom. "Donald actually said he was going out East, did he? To fight the Jap?"

"No." Loughran stretched his hard mouth in a self-satisfied smirk.

"Well, then—?"

"Donny boy didn't say he was going anywhere. Secret work, he said. They wouldn't be hearing from him for a while. The old lady got worried, though. Just before Christmas, White called up Admiralty Operations and asked where he could send Donald's Christmas present, lah-di-dah. They rang him back and gave him a FARELF address. I checked it out. It's a Combined Ops London letterbox, unofficial. Run by your lot. I reckon it goes straight to Menzies. Bet on it."

"So they buried Alice and got White out of the way. Why?"

"Perhaps they thought it wasn't suicide. You tell me."

"You think *Price* killed her?" Curzon's jaw dropped.

"Who's Price?" asked Loughran softly and washed his strangler's hands in invisible soap and water. "I never heard of him. Official."

The obvious approach would have been to go to Elm Place and simply ring the bell, but the idea lost its charm the more he thought about it. Alice, White; suicide and foreign postings;

dead letterboxes. Oh, no. He'd lost too much ground in the past seven months to step blindly into a face-to-face lie. Let Price surprise *him*.

Curzon wound himself up for the effort all day and even then very nearly called it off at the last moment. He posted himself at the corner of Holborn and Southampton Row a little before five thirty, lurking in the doorway of a bank from which he could keep watch on the Pepperpot front door. When he saw Tom Price limping toward him he came close to aborting the whole thing. They collided in a ruck of jostling commuters.

"Paul!"

Price beat a passage through the crowd, grabbed his arm in an excited hammerlock and swung him around.

"Tom! I was just about to try and catch you before you left."

"Well, I'll be— Look at you! You've grown a foot. And you've got a paunch!" He slow-punched Curzon's waistline. "When did you get back, for goodness' sake?"

"Four hours ago. Just got off the plane. You're looking pretty fit yourself."

"Fit? Me? You make me look like an invalid." They fell into step and were caught up in the crowd. "Are you free tonight?"

"I only called in at the office to let them know I'm back. I haven't been home yet."

"Good." Price steered him firmly across Holborn. "First, I'm going to buy you a pint. Then you're coming home for dinner. No—no arguments. Diny'd kill me if I let you get away now."

They walked through to Fleet Street and joined the first of the evening drinkers at the long bar of the Cock Tavern. Price maintained a continuous flow of gossip so obviously innocent of deceit that Curzon found himself drawn into it irresistibly. If Price was *not* genuinely happy to see him he'd perfected an acting talent to rival Olivier's.

Without the slightest hesitation, Price told him how he'd met Sally Logan. It was a long story, studded with nuance and insights into his own feelings at the time, and he was completely caught up in it. Curzon, watching his face intently for clues to this man who might have been capable of strangling Alice Petrie and swinging her from a rope, felt a flooding sense of relief. There was no murder in Tom Price's make-up. He hadn't changed.

But he had *been* changed. Softened. Redeemed. "After Alice . . ." He spoke her name without emotion. "Well, I was worried sick I might be making the same mistake again. The coincidence apart from anything else—you know, having met both of them on the same day. Then there was Sally's first marriage. It wasn't . . . all it should have been. None of them are, I suppose, but in her case she didn't find out till after her husband died and the shock . . . well it's worked out. I'm not much of a catch for her but . . ." He stared unseeing across the bar for a long time, then snapped out of it and grinned infectiously. "We're getting married on the twentieth of June. It's her idea; the last day of spring. You're hereby appointed a witness." He slapped a restraining hand on Curzon's shoulder. "And I won't take no for an answer."

They reached the house just after seven o'clock and Curzon thanked his lucky stars he had discarded his original idea of turning up there unannounced. He wouldn't have survived it. Dinah hurled herself into his arms the moment he crossed the threshold and they clung to each other while she poured her tears on his neck. Sally was there for one of her ritual midweek suppers and she embraced him as if he'd been an integral part of her life and Tom's for years. The meal was a riotous affair; Dinah never stopped talking, Price squabbled with her good-naturedly for the right to make himself heard, and Sally Logan presided over them both with touching pride. When he got up to leave, Curzon had consented to be a witness at their marriage in June, had promised to come to lunch on Sunday as the first step to rekindling the Richmond habit, and had agreed to take Dinah to see *Gone With the Wind*.

Tom Price saw Paul Curzon to the South Kensington station and strolled back to Elm Place through the unlit streets. He was curiously proud of himself but for two quite separate, even diametrically opposed, reasons. That first sighting in Southampton Row had shocked him into a state of near paralysis, yet he had recovered with remarkable speed and presence of mind. He had discovered in himself a new professionalism, a by-product no doubt of his work with Boyd; a new resilience, a reserve of animal cunning. That

326

was one source of this feeling of well-being. The second had shocked him in another way. Paul *was* his friend. Whatever bound them together—the impermanent, artificial obscenities of war, perhaps—there existed beneath the surface a genuine human regard for one another.

Midway through supper, the solution to all his problems had come to him—so simple, so perfect, so patently heaven-sent it momentarily robbed him of his senses. Now, on cooler reflection, he knew it would work. All that mattered was the timing. It had to be after the wedding, of course. When Sally had settled in at Elm Place. When Dinah had found a job to occupy her. When Boyd and Geordie McNeil and Simmons and Co. were safely out of the picture.

But before Paul Curzon was forced to set in motion whatever deception he had been brought back for.

JUNE 4, 1942

The familiarity of the Buildings was oppressive, a reminder of days left behind, of parts of himself cast aside. Menzies' office was no longer an undisturbed tomb but a forcing house for deceit and retribution. It closed in on him.

Curzon felt his anger growing and, because he couldn't isolate a reason for it that might seem rational in this room, to this man, he found himself retreating into sullen resentment. It wasn't lost on the chief.

He tried again. "With respect . . ." Weakness; backing down. "I don't see why you couldn't have told me all this yesterday."

"I wanted you to learn firsthand, Paul. You have."

"At the expense of my credibility."

Menzies bridled. "You're a career officer, not an emotionally arrested adolescent. We're dealing with a threat to the security of the country, not your ego."

Curzon rolled on his chair in exasperation. "I take it I have the right to ask questions."

"Go ahead."

"Did Alice Petrie commit suicide?"

"Alice *Price*." Menzies was turning his paper-knife pacifier in his fingers. "The judgment was suicide."

"An Admiralty judgment. It wasn't publicly disclosed. Why?"

"Any other questions?"

Curzon checked the impulse to shout. "Was Donald White really posted to the Far East two weeks before she died?"

"It says so in his record."

"Is it true?"

"I have no reason to challenge an official document."

A sudden gust of wind hurled a broadside of rain at the windows, turning years of accumulated dust to muddy tears.

Curzon got himself under control. "I met Price last night—as you ordered. I met Sally Logan. I'm elected to be a witness at their wedding in June."

"Congratulations," Menzies said dryly.

"But I'm damned if I'll do it if he's got the Petrie woman's blood on his hands. This girl's a fine, decent—"

"Yes. She is, isn't she?"

"We can't let her go through with it. The moment you decide to finish Price, she'll—"

Menzies' desk chair sprang upright with a creak of released tension. "You have a great deal in your favor, Paul—intelligence, persistence, craft, energy, dedication. But you have the perceptive faculties of a jackass. I pushed you at Loughran and Price yesterday with all the subtlety of a bulldozer. Even you can see it was intentional, surely? I wanted you to learn, digest, and assimilate. When the time comes, not long now, I'll explain why. All I'm prepared to say at the moment is that I have reasons for wanting you to reestablish yourself with Price."

"But . . ."

He fished his watch from his vest pocket and grimaced at it. "I don't have time now. Just remember this. The tempo's changing. Eisenhower will be in London shortly, and I've a shrewd idea what his priorities will be. This department—you and I—will be invited to sit in on his councils of war. We'll be expected to concoct miracles, and I have no intention of disappointing him. In essence—" He sat back sharply, withdrawing from his own indiscretion. "Just stay close to Price, Paul. He's an odd bird. He needs—" He corrected himself with a quick frown. "He'll need someone to lean on."

JUNE 8, 1942

In late February 1942, British families clustering around their wireless sets for the customary evening devotional of the nine o'clock news were treated to a bizarre, even comical, "appeal to the nation." The nation was, in one way or another, constantly being appealed to——to grow more food, to "make do and mend," to save, to work harder, to avoid gossip——but the smooth voice that emerged from the wireless that night was in search of something more.

It invited all British families who had made holiday trips to the Continent before the war to look up their snap albums at once for pictures of German, Dutch, and French beaches, cliffs, harbors, and rivers. The photographs should be carefully labeled, giving dates and precise locations, and sent to the Admiralty in London. They could, the broadcaster said, be of inestimable value in the conduct of the war and might even play their part in an Allied invasion.

Public reaction was immediate.

Thousands of photographic prints, albums, and picture postcards arrived at Admiralty House and were dispatched at once to the headquarters of Special Operations Executive in Baker Street where they were sorted and labeled. Some offerings were considered more important than others, and these were passed to squads of young women of the First Aid Nursing Yeomanry based in strategic areas of the country. The FANYs, on the surface just another branch of the women's army, were in fact an energetic sister service of SOE. In this case, their job was to follow up the more interesting snaps and letters received.

Which is why FANY Joy Macklin set off from London on this bright June Monday morning to visit Mrs. Katherine Logan at Billdyke House Farm near Gerrard's Cross in Buckinghamshire. It was a wasted journey. Mrs. Logan's letter about her family's prewar visits to France implied that there were hundreds of snaps in her collection. But when Joy arrived, Mrs. Logan confessed that the bulk of them were in the possession of her daughter Sally and eventually admitted *that she had no idea where Sally was.* Since the girl's husband died . . . Joy took the last-known address and returned to London.

She had other people to see but this case seemed worth pursuing, so she began a long, frustrating search through civilian records for Mrs. Logan's unhappy daughter.

Because Special Operations Executive had a passion for working alone and without fuss, an instruction was issued that all contact with other security agencies or the police should be avoided. The undertaking, as the man on the wireless had told the nation, was to be conducted in the strictest confidence. But since the search was part of a vastly complex exercise in public relations, there was no time to be wasted on niceties. Joy Macklin cut corners by calling the Ministry of Food's ration book documentation center; they produced Sally's address in a few hours.

The case of Sally Logan was no different from ten thousand others. She was just an unhappy widow who didn't want her mother to know where she lived. It was a confidence Joy Macklin was prepared to honor.

JUNE 9, 1942

Tom Price climbed briskly into the evening light of Earl's Court Road on a rising tide of home-going tube travelers. He hated this daily subterranean crush, and on a hot day experienced a profound German distaste for the English and their one-bath-a-week mentality. War had encouraged the national disinclination to expose bodies to soap and precious water, in a way had almost made it an act of patriotism.

Air! He lengthened his stride for Earl's Court Square. Another two weeks and there would be only one destination at the end of his day. Since April he had held rigidly to the ritual: Sally's first for tea, then Elm Place for supper with Dinah. Sentimental nonsense, but they both encouraged it. His whole week, in fact, was programmed down to the last available hour. On three mornings a week, Sally picked him up at the house and rode part of the way with him to Southampton Row; on two evenings, she came to supper; on the weekends, they spent the days and evenings together. But not the nights. The covenant she had made with herself ruled out their sleeping in the same bed again "until the day."

He entered the square and felt the magnetic effect of her tugging at him. His irritation and weariness evaporated at once; he walked faster, straighter, arms swinging. He loved the anticipation of those last few yards.

She had the kettle on the hob and fussed as always with his coat and hat, brushing them before she hung them up. He went into the living room. The dining table was spread with photographs and, on a chair, a small leather handcase stood open with several dozen more inside. "Hello. What's this?"

"My grisly past." She chuckled, warming the teapot from the kettle.

He sat down and began to sift through the photographs. He recognized John immediately. A thin young man with a small mustache; not handsome in the conventional way, but striking. Good bones. The wedding group at a country church. Derbyshire, wasn't it? The honeymoon at Shevingham. Not one snap showing them together. Then a very young Sally, in her late teens, with an elderly man and woman on a beach, at a cafe table (yes, France; there was the inevitable Pernod Pontarlier poster behind them). Sally by the rail of a ship; on a headland looking out to sea; walking alone against a sprawl of sky and winding beach and splashing surf. A hundred pictures, at least.

He smiled at her over his shoulder. "Is this significant?"

"Wouldn't you just like to know."

He got up and went to stand behind her. Touched his lips to her hair, very gently. "I would, to be honest. You're not getting worried about . . . ?"

She turned her head quickly, startled at his seriousness, then pecked his cheek comfortingly and returned to the job at hand. "It's the woman who's supposed to get last-minute nerves, not the man. Go and sit down. Would you like a biscuit?"

He obeyed and looked at more of the pictures. She came to the table with the tray and pushed a whole section of snaps to one side; the John snaps. "In case you were about to ask,

I've had a marvelous day," she said, arranging cups, saucers, and spoons.

"With these?" He nodded down at the mementos of another life.

"I was just going out this morning when a girl came to the door. I thought she was one of those door-to-door salesgirls at first; you know—a big attaché case, a list on a clipboard. But she wasn't. She was doing a sort of survey."

He bit into a biscuit; her own, homemade. "Oh?"

"I made her some tea and . . . well, I don't think she left till three. We got on like a house afire."

A cold hand touched the base of his spine. "What did she want?"

"Just pictures. And what I could remember about them." She ran a hand lightly over the snaps. "Joy—that was her name—she said they were terribly important. There was a talk on the wireless—oh, months ago—asking for photographs of France for the war effort, and Mother wrote in to say we'd got hundreds. We used to go every year. Joy went to see Mother yesterday." She pulled a face. "She said it was awful—gossiping about me mostly. I had all the snaps, you see. So Joy traced me under my married name. I made her promise not to tell Mother where I'm living."

He braced his hands one in the other, holding down his anxiety. "She went to a lot of trouble, didn't she? There must be thousands of people who went to France before the war."

"Oh, there are. They've had *thousands* of replies. She's been working on it for months. But we used to go to the area Joy's specially interested in: Boulogne and Dieppe, around there. She said my pictures were perfect."

He picked up a few of the beach scenes. "These?"

"No, she took the best ones."

"How do you mean, the best? These look pretty good to me."

She pointed. "Well, take that one. Lovely picture of me and Mother, but you can't see the dunes, can you? There was a better one showing the shingle running up from the sea, then the dunes, and the cliffs in the background."

His pulse quickened. "Where was it taken?"

"That one was Dieppe."

"I see. It looks very pretty."

"Yes, she thought the Dieppe ones were best. She took a

few of Boulogne—we went there in 1937—but we went to Dieppe a lot, the last time in August 1939.''

He raised his cup casually. ''You seem to have had a fine old time.''

''Oh, she was *lovely*.'' Sally colored and burst out laughing. ''Well, let's say she's a good listener. I haven't talked so much to a girl my own age in years. And she was *interested*.''

''I suppose she wanted to know how you spent your time there, did she?''

''Everything. How we traveled, where we stayed, what we spent, what we thought of the hotel. But then it was mostly gossip. What the beach was like—''

''At Dieppe?'' he put in quickly. ''Or all the beaches you went to?''

''Well, Dieppe mostly, because those were the best pictures, but Pourville, Varengeville, and Puys as well.''

''A little difficult to describe a beach, isn't it? I mean, a beach is sand or pebbles with sea at the edges.'' He chuckled to put her at ease.

''My mother was the world expert on beaches. They were either too hot or too windy or too close to the sea or too far away or there were too many people or . . .''

''And Joy thought that was interesting?''

''Everything's interesting, she said. She made lot of notes. Things like: Did the beach slope very steeply? Could you swim out very far before you got out of your depth? Was it sand or shingle? Were there any rocks? More tea?''

''Hmmm? Oh, yes, please.''

''It's to help the war effort. At least, that's what they said on the wireless when they asked, according to Joy. I don't suppose it is really. I mean, they wouldn't announce it on the wireless, would they?''

He stared at her, his cheeks bulging with biscuit. ''She told you—she said the pictures were needed for an invasion?''

''No, she didn't say that. The war effort. I think she did, anyway.''

Would they go to these lengths to pass him an invasion scare? Work through Sally to make him accept it more readily? Nonsense. First of all, he'd never once failed to transmit a Pepperpot plant. His record was unblemished. They had no justification for using outside sources. And why go to the mother first? It made no sense, unless—

Unless it were true. Unless it had nothing at all to do with the Pepperpot, no connection with Tom Price's Lie machine. Unless there *had* been a broadcast appeal, Sally's mother *had* written and the girl—Joy—*had* paid an innocent visit in the line of duty. Well, the BBC story could be confirmed simply by calling them, pretending he had pictures to offer. He might even persuade Sally to call her mother. What then?

He said, with a carefully defensive grin, "Did you talk about anything else? John for instance?"

"*No*, for instance." She leaned across the table and kissed him. "And we didn't talk about you, either, if that's what's bothering you. She wasn't like that. She just wanted pictures of France, that's all."

Only the pictures. Beach gradients, inshore sea depths, coastal rock formations, photographs of the shoreline, the dunes, cliffs, inlets, and presumably harbor installations. Essential information for military planners mounting a landing from the sea. Dieppe, Varengeville, Pourville, and Puys. When?

He smiled at her and touched her cheek. "Well, you have had a day, haven't you? Tell me what else she said."

June 20, 1942

In the best traditions of wedding-day womanhood, Dinah cried fulsomely through the ceremony at Chelsea Register Office and finally flung herself into Curzon's arms to be comforted. Philip Pepper, Curzon's fellow witness, footed the bill for lunch at the Hyde Park Hotel and astounded them all later on when they returned to Elm Place by presenting Sally with an antique Georgian silver tea service that had belonged to his mother. Archie Bassingthwaite looked in long enough to take a cup of tea and produce a finely bound first edition of Shelley; and Sally's mother, belatedly informed of the event, had three boxes of china and glassware delivered from Harrods depository, where they had languished since 1932.

Pepper withdrew after supper and, at Sally's insistence,

Price took Curzon across the road to the Queen's Elm for a pint of beer.

"More like a family party than a wedding," Curzon told him jokingly at the bar and Price took it as a compliment. He and Sally had decided against a honeymoon on the grounds that it would be too short to satisfy either of them; besides, they didn't want to face up to the necessity of leaving Dinah alone. Family party was accurate on all counts.

Before he followed Sally to their bedroom—in as nervous a state of mind as he could ever remember—Price went out to the shed in the small paved rear courtyard and, for no good reason, pulled out Hamburg's transmitter. He sat looking at it for half an hour, challenging the bond that made him its slave. Timing. He would go to Curzon—in time—and hand him this thing, himself, his services, his special talents. And he would be free of it; at least, the fear of it. He would have guarantees of his own safety, Sally's, Dinah's. He would have a future.

He locked the transmitter back in its case and replaced it under the workbench.

Timing.

After the wedding, he'd decided. After Dinah had found a job and Boyd and the others had been taken care of. But those decisions had been made before Joy Macklin walked into Sally's life and asked for photographs of Dieppe, Varengeville, Pourville, and Puys.

Why should that make a difference?

He went outside and stood for a while staring up at the stars.

It shouldn't make any difference.

But it did. God help him, it did.

JULY 7, 1942

This was more than mere nervousness, more than fear, doubt, anxiety. He could feel his pulse in his throat, a constriction in the muscles of the legs, a tightening of the nerve delta at the base of the skull. Sickness, dizziness, distress.

Dieppe, Varengeville, Pourville, Puys. A landing force from the sea. It was nearly a month now since that day at Sally's flat, yet he'd done nothing. Well, he'd checked the sources; the BBC, Sally's mother. He'd even called the Admiralty department concerned with a manufactured offer of pictures he had just that moment found. It all held together. He was convinced.

But he'd waited a month. Correction: he'd ordered in his mind every single justification for doing nothing and then, in the space of an hour last night, had changed his mind, called Boyd, arranged a rendezvous, and prepared a line of inquiry.

For what reason?

He'd been over *that* ground endlessly, too. Not compulsion. Not his father's bloodstained concept of patriotism. Not love of Germany. Not a hatred of the enemy; Sally and Dinah were "the enemy." So was Paul. The truth, as ever, was that he felt powerless to stop. It was the philosophy of the psychopathic killer.

He walked through the arcade above South Kensington underground station, turned right, and circled the block through Thurloe Square, entering the arcade again the way he had come. No one on his heels. He ran down the stairs and bought a ticket for Notting Hill Gate. He got out there, changed to a Central Line train, and came up into the night at Holland Park station. He'd chosen Holland Park because the only exit from the platform to the street was by way of a clanking double-gated lift; anyone following him would have to enter the lift with him or waste valuable minutes kicking his heels below. Three women and an elderly railwayman joined him in the ascent.

At ground level, he slipped into a side street off Holland Park Avenue and devoted fifteen minutes to doubling and redoubling back and forward, north to south, but he surprised no one except for a startled young couple embracing in a doorway. He was careful to retain his sense of direction and began to move northeastward toward the church in Westbourne Park Road.

Again the old indecision returned and, with it, a jumping at shadows, a cringing at unexpected night sounds. A cat curled on a wall under a privet hedge spat at his passing and he leaped with fright, his heart in his mouth. No good; he must get a grip on himself. None of it was *real* fear; not for himself, anyway. Sally was the cause, directly and indirectly. Fear for her. All kinds of fears. After this, no more. One final initiative, then Boyd, Geordie, and Simmons and Co must be run down. They would understand. The country was awash with pro-Russian sentiment. Open public agitation to arm and supply "Uncle Joe Stalin" was an accomplished fact, supported by the press, the Americans, and the Labour party. The raison d'être for undercover activity, he could argue, no longer existed. Boyd would accept that—however unhappily. An end to "active service" would consign him once more to the gray anonymity from which Robert Jardine had rescued him—all of them—a year ago; but he was infinitely malleable. The important thing was to be done with it. He couldn't run the risk of Sally's being sucked into—

"Evening, sir. See your identity card, can I?" The policeman stepped out from behind a telephone booth without warning, and Price uttered a low "aaaah!" of shock. "Sorry, sir. Didn't mean to make you jump."

"All right. Quite all right, officer." He dug for his wallet; identity card, Ministry pass.

The officer shone his hand torch on the gray card, shading the beam to release only a strip of light through his fingers. "Oh, government." He was impressed. "Live around here, do you, sir?"

"No. I'm going to a meeting in St. Stephen's Gardens."

"Mind telling me what for?" The torch clicked off.

Price retrieved his papers and put them away. "I'm afraid I can't. But if you'd like me to walk with you to the station, we can make the necessary telephone call. I don't want to divert you from your duty." A nice balance of contempt and tolerance; the effortless bonhomie of the ruling class.

The policeman retreated before it. "Oh, I don't think I'll bother you, thanks all the same, sir. Have to keep an eye out, you know. Sorry I held you up."

"You haven't. It's comforting to know the police are on their toes. Good night to you."

"Good night, sir."

When he was sure the dark had swallowed him up, he let out his breath. Luck! One life gone.

St. Stephen's Church was empty, but he scouted every nook and chapel to reassure himself. He looked in at the vestry door; rolled blankets and pillows were piled in one corner. At the height of the blitz, many people sought the sanctuary of churches and more particularly their crypts rather than huddle on tube platforms or in street shelters, but the days of sheltering were over.

He heard the main door scrape open and ducked down behind a buttress of the flying pulpit. The altar candles burned under small steel hoods to conform with air raid precautions and their light was minimal, but light was unnecessary to recognize the voice of Boyd Corrie. "I say, old man?" he hissed nervously from the pitch black of the nave. They found a bench in a small chapel across from the door.

"It's damn good to see you again, old man," Boyd whispered warmly.

Another rule broken, meeting Boyd again. Sheer folly.

"Have you talked to Geordie?"

Boyd nodded eagerly. "A couple of days ago. He's winkling away, he says. Doing his best, but the FOIC office in Aberdeen's his only bet and he says if there's something really big on they won't know till the last minute."

Price snapped disagreeably, "If there's a cross-Channel invasion planned no one will know till the last minute. But there'll be clues. A suspension of fishing, perhaps, or diversionary exercises off the Scottish coast. Tell him . . ." He pondered. "You said his sister's fiancé tows boats down to the English coast?"

"Dumb barges, I think they're called. He picks them up in the Firth of Forth and brings them south. To Brightlingsea, one time, and to a place called Queensborough in the Thames Estuary. He didn't tell Geordie why. I don't think he's doing it anymore."

"This man, the fiancé; he's in command of a minesweeper?"

"Yes, a converted trawler."

"Then tell Geordie to concentrate on the fiancé. He'll probably be ordered to standby a few days before; all shore leave canceled, a change of duty, something out of the ordinary. Do these trawlers go out at night?"

"Not this chap's. He did when he was stationed on the Tyne, but it's different at Aberdeen. They sweep during the day and put in at night."

"That's useful. It's possible he'll be ordered to sea that night; on patrol or standing off the War Channel. We've *got* to know that date."

Boyd pulled on his gauntlets nervously. "We can only try, old man."

Price grabbed him by the shoulders with both hands. "Don't ever say that to my face again. Do you understand? *Never!*"

Boyd's eyes bulged with shock. "I only meant . . ."

"We have to be *right*, Boyd. Nothing less. *Exact*."

JULY 28, 1942

"What do they give pips for these days?" Curzon joked. "Good looks or spit-and-polish?"

Rob pushed away his plate and blew out his cheeks with artificial pleasure. "Both—and it also pays to have a general in the family." He wore three black pips on his shoulders now, and the burden of them seemed to have matured him. He was tanned, alert, sharp in his movements; he'd put on weight around the neck and shoulders. "Anyway—a year and a half's pretty good going for our bunch. Stay alive that long and you're bound to get promotion." It was intended as a joke.

Curzon said anxiously, "You're not sticking your neck out, are you?"

Rob looked idly round the Travellers' dining room. "Oh, you know." He shrugged uncomfortably.

"Don't play the modest hero with me, numbskull. I said are you sticking your—?"

"I'm not in it for the money, am I?" Rob took a pull at his water glass; he had refused the wine. "What do you expect me to do—pick and choose?"

"Who are you with now?"

"Four Commando."

"Hairy?"

"Sometimes. We've done a couple of raids on the French coast. That's all." He couldn't resist that.

"That's *all*!"

Rob stared at him coolly. "I shouldn't think *your* job's exactly a bed of roses, is it?"

Curzon brushed the comment aside. "Have you told Mother what you're up to?"

"Of course I haven't. Nor the Bart."

"Your fiancée?"

"Nicky wouldn't expect me to. She's up to here in secrets. She knows the drill."

Curzon finished off the last of his Spam and potatoes. The thought of two young people in love diplomatically avoiding the one topic of conversation on which their entire future rested struck him as inhuman. He wondered how well they really knew each other. "What's she like?"

"See for yourself." Rob grinned broadly at his brother's surprise. "She gets in at Euston at five o'clock. She wangled a few days off so we could . . . well, you know."

"You're not thinking of getting married on the sly, are you?"

"And miss all the trimmings? She'd rather be a spinster for life. No, I've got five days and—ah—" He looked away again. "Never know when you'll get the chance again, do you?"

Nicola Stacey was tall and slim, honey-blond and green-eyed, but Curzon registered the components only when the total shock effect of her began to wear off. And by then he was lost. There were clichés to describe what he felt—all inadequate. From the moment he caught sight of her—thirty yards or so away, indistinct, a blur obscured by impatient crowds—he knew what he was about to feel and nothing could change it. She seemed to come at him in a cloud of electrostatic energy and he was caught up in it.

Rob performed the introductions, proud as Punch. "Go on, give her a kiss," he said. But Curzon only shook her hand as if it were a bomb about to explode.

In the car, she talked about the journey down. Her voice was silken, hypnotic. Rob had booked her a room at the Connaught, and they dropped off there before going on to the In and Out where he was staying. They agreed to meet at Curzon's flat in an hour, and he tore back there to give the place a lick and a promise before she arrived. God, it was a muck heap. How could anyone live like this? He pushed clothes and coats and old newspapers and stray junk out of sight in the handiest cupboards and ran a duster over the more exposed surfaces.

She arrived as he was running a bath. Mrs. Silver brought her up and gave him a wide-eyed gleam of approval behind the girl's back. He circled around her cloddishly, like a flat-footed wrestler, until she pointed out, with a slow smile, that water was running somewhere and hadn't he better do something about it. He let the water out and came back, plastering his hair down, then realized what he was doing and what it might imply to her and grasped at the safest straw.

"Can I get you something?"

"Not now, Paul. I'd rather just sit and talk."

He poured himself a stiff four fingers of whiskey and sat down across from her, conscious for the first time in his life that he had more leg than he could decently cope with in a sitting position. He slouched in the chair with his knees under his chin.

"You're not what I expected," she said, smiling.

"Oh?" It had always been accepted that he was the mis-shapen half of the progeny. The Bart said they'd improved the mold before they got to Rob.

She caught his look of discomfort. "Funny, but I imagined you were much older. Rob never described you. Any of you, really. I pictured your mother as dark and rather tall and your father . . . well, Mount Everest with a military mustache."

"You haven't met them, then?"

Her face fell. "Not yet. We planned to several times but Rob always had last-minute duty. I thought we'd have time this week, but he says he'd rather stay in London."

Friction? He seized on it. "He wants to keep you to himself. I don't blame him."

Her face lit up. He'd never known such torment in his life. Why can't she look somewhere else? And where the hell are you, brother? Get your big fat uniformed ass over here and take her out of my sight. And smell. She smelled of flowers.

"You know we're engaged?" She touched a sapphire stud in a silver ring.

Yes, he nodded. I know you're engaged.

"I wanted to get married right away. Rob said no. I can't do much about it if that's what he wants, but I think he's wrong, don't you? Putting it off?"

"I—ah—" I—ah—what? "Yes," he snapped sharply. And

then, because his anger combusted with his disgust at himself and what he was feeling, "I think it's bloody stupid, shortsighted, and selfish. If he had a spark of guts in him he'd grab you before you got away." He took a long snort of neat whiskey. It added a comforting heat to the red mist in his head, but he knew he'd gone too far.

"Nicky—" He stopped short. He had no right to use her nickname. "I didn't mean that. Well, I mean I did, but not in that way. If you see what I mean."

She watched him dispassionately as he gulped again from the glass. She said quietly, "Why are you angry?"

"Angry? Good God above, child . . ." Insult. She was no child. Nor was she in any way, shape, or form designed to be the reflecting half of an ambling adolescent like Rob. Captain's pips don't make him the man you have to marry, he stormed silently.

"I'm not a child, Paul." She said it without rancor, but precisely, like a teacher conjugating Latin verbs.

"I didn't mean that, either." Lie to her, lie to both of them and send them away. "I think we'd better start again, don't you? It's not every day I get a chance to show my breeding." He grinned at her, full power, to show he meant it. Another disaster. She reacted as if he'd kicked her in the face.

"There's no reason why you should automatically approve Rob's choice of a wife," she said coolly.

"You're not his wife *yet*!" It was pure reflex, but the virulence of it rocked her head back. She was halfway out of her chair when they heard voices on the stairs; Mrs. Silver's cackling cockatoo chuckle and Rob's answering boom. Nicky sat down again mechanically. For a moment they stared at one another uncomfortably. Curzon leaned toward her.

"Nicky . . ."

She touched a finger to her lips. He got up to go to the door, then looked back at her. He saw bewilderment in her face, uncertainty; then she gave him a frightened smile, and he nodded because now they both understood.

AUGUST 10, 1942

The house in Eisenhowerplatz, as the American ETOUSA staff had rechristened Grosvenor Square, was crawling with staff colonels. Curzon and Menzies were led upstairs. A welcoming colonel handed them over to an Intelligence colonel who led them through to an anteroom colonel who made them sign a book marked "Allied Commander-in-Chief—Received."

Eisenhower was at a desk backing onto a window overlooking the square. He sprang to his feet at once and came around the desk, hand outstretched. "Stuart. Glad you could come." Curzon was introduced and they settled into sybaritically comfortable leather chairs. Ike—the cartoonist's dream; a three-quarter moon with a half-moon grin—kept the social proprieties to a minimum. He pointed to a large map of North Africa covering one wall of the room.

"Let's get down to business. There's the problem." His finger performed an arc to follow the Moroccan coastal bulge. "Operation Torch. Optimum landing period, late October, but we'll be lucky to make it by early November. You know the proposal: we have four clear objectives—Casablanca, Oran, Algiers, and the Bone area. That means our air cover has to be centred on land-based aircraft in Gibraltar, and *that* limits the distance we can safely proceed into the Mediterranean. Gib is the focal point. I don't have to spell out the hazards. Troop carrying, supply, and protection will call for 110 troop and cargo ships and two hundred battle craft. In the build-up stages we can't afford to telegraph intentions to the German High Command. On the other hand, there's nothing to prevent their agents in Portugal, Spain, and Gibraltar from seeing those ships and reporting activities on the Rock. So—" He gave them the famous grin. "What do we do about it?"

Menzies was quite imperturbable. "I think we can keep them happy. No problem about the spies in Gib. Leave them to us. The rest . . ." He glanced up again at the map. "There'll be German naval and air reconnaissance so there's

342

no point in pretending that what they can photograph isn't there. We have to persuade them to accept our version of *why* they're there. The solution is a deception exercise; a fairly massive one."

Eisenhower wrinkled his nose; a show of disappointment. "Explain."

"We can't conceal an invasion, but we *can* point the Germans in the wrong direction. I suggest we lead them to believe the attack will come at Dakar on the Atlantic coast of French Africa."

Eisenhower squinted at the map. "That might make sense to a command planner at Wiesbaden I guess," he said doubtfully. "But a gossip campaign isn't going to persuade Hitler to move a task force."

Menzies shot a meaningful glance at Curzon. "Agreed. We can sow the seed pretty widely—in southern France, North Africa, Lisbon, Madrid—and specifically through our own double agent system in northern Europe. But there'll have to be a clincher."

"That's a neat way of putting it," observed Ike dryly.

"There's only one man Berlin would expect to come by information this sensitive. One man they'd be prepared to believe without question. He's German; seeded here in 1939. He's under control but he doesn't know it. I've gone to a lot of trouble to convince him he's a free agent. As far as Berlin's concerned, his record's unparalleled. Canaris thinks he's the best. Hitler personally awarded him an Iron Cross. He'll pass the word to Hamburg: a landing at Dakar, all the rest."

Ike gazed at him incisively. "There are three or four hundred thousand lives on the line if you're wrong, Stuart," he said heavily.

"I'm aware of that."

Ike stared at the map for a long time. "All right. We'll look into it. I'll arrange a formal meeting for you with my Intelligence people. If they agree . . ." He left the rest unsaid.

Curzon waited until they were in the car. "Was that wise?"

"I told you, didn't I, Paul? Patience." He seemed very pleased with himself.

"You're hanging *everything* on Price?"

Menzies tapped his driver on the shoulder. "Margaretta Terrace, Robertson."

And for the next twenty minutes, as they worked their way through the midday traffic toward Chelsea, he steadfastly refused to say another word.

The Pepperpot was a shadow of its former glory. Mrs. Plum had flown the hen coop without notice the previous November, taking two of her brood with her. Pepper insisted she had been lured away by the Ministry of Food and the offer of a job at an outpost near her home in Paddington, but Price didn't believe a word of it. Pepper's three University College recruits had disappeared a week later and, just before Christmas, Archie Bassingthwaite moved his Research and Records operation back into the fourth floor to make way for an influx of Home Security clerks on the third. Central Government Research and Audit Service (Cabinet Office) was a wasteland, and the implication that all therein were doomed was blatantly obvious.

The lack of subtlety annoyed Tom Price. Pepper openly flaunted the fact that he was gainfully employed elewhere, yet he took it for granted that his former deputy would suppress any urge to ask at what and why. Work papers still arrived on Price's desk—a trickle now; nothing like the flood of early 1941—and he dutifully gutted them before passing them on to Archie, but he had reduced his Hamburg transmissions to two a week. What little he sent was dross, and painfully inadequate dross at that. Yet, astonishingly, there was no sign of his losing the confidence of either London or Hamburg, and that was a comfort in many ways. Marriage had brought its own very particular headaches.

The back yard shed in Elm Place had become a dangerously insecure radio shack; Sally was one of life's compulsive hoverers. In the first week of blissful wedlock she had disturbed him twice just as he was about to make his call sign. Checks and balances. He'd invented a passion for woodwork—the shed was equipped with a bench and a vise—and he now had the Wehrmacht set neatly housed in the old Phillips radio from Middlemass House. The radio actually worked, thanks to Boyd's advice, and he made a point of switching it on as soon as he withdrew there after supper. But he continued to exercise great caution; a young wife was ill equipped to appreciate the charms of drills, planes, and spokeshaves when they appeared to be competing with her own.

He prepared for the effort of lunch. It was dangerous, stupidly dangerous, but he had brought it on himself. His order to Boyd on the conventional box-to-box call last Friday had been to inform him immediately the moment Geordie's information came through. Boyd had reported success last night and nominated a rendezvous. Time: twelve thirty today. Place, the cafe at the corner of Euston Road and Birkenhead Street.

He slipped out the back entrance into Queen Square, cut through the gardens to Marchmont Street, then a quick left across the crescent of Cartwright Gardens into Burton Street and Flaxman Terrace. All back streets, all residential. Quiet. He stepped into a tobacconist's on the corner of Euston Road and checked his rear through a display window while a flurry of customers were being served. All clear.

Boyd was at a corner table, back to the door. Price took the chair behind him and ordered a powdered egg omelet and a mug of tea. The cafe was full; the clientele was still composed mainly of porters and greasers from King's Cross station, but the third full year of war had rendered a significant cosmetic change. The porters were women in turbanned head-scarfs and coveralls neatly home-tailored to achieve a more seemly fit. Their chatter was comfortingly noisy.

"Quickly, Boyd. I don't have much time," Price said over his shoulder.

Boyd leaned back until their heads touched. "Geordie called. His sister's fiancé, the lieutenant—all shore leaves canceled from 2400 hours August 18 to 2400 hours on the twentieth. The sweeper groups at Aberdeen will be at sea the whole time, night and day. Fishing fleet's confined to harbor under police supervision."

"And that's all?"

He could sense Boyd's disappointment. "The orders are the same right down to the Tyne, he said. He's pretty sure of that."

Price turned away as his omelet was brought to the table. He picked at it with no great enthusiasm. Behind him, Boyd remained stiff with anticipation for several minutes, then relaxed enough to continue his assault on bread-filled sausages and chips. Price finally gave up on the omelet, drank half his tea, and leaned into Boyd's chair.

"Are you lecturing tonight?"

Boyd swallowed a mouthful of chips. "Absolutely."

"What about tomorrow?"

"Tonight's the last of the summer term. Why?"

Price considered carefully before putting his thoughts into words. "Your parents are still living in Kent, are they?"

"That's right, old man. About five miles this side of Southend."

"Near the Essex border."

"Well, sort of, yes."

Well outside the regular Essex transmission area, but if Hamburg was sweeping Boyd's wave band . . .

"Would they think it unusual if you went down and stayed the night?"

"My room's always ready. Mum says . . ."

"Wait." Price slipped the used bus ticket from his pocket and quickly read what he'd written on the back. He had encoded: "British assault planned Dieppe, Varengeville, Pourville, Puys areas . . ." He penciled in "August 18 to 20." The rest could stand: "No further details available. Gimlet via Sibling emergency site to Hotbed. Out." He folded it and slipped it back between the chairs into Boyd's hand.

"Now listen carefully, Boyd. When you leave here I want you to make a call from a public telephone, but not from any of the boxes on your list. Understand?"

"Right you are, old man. Who to?"

"You told me once about a friend of yours, one of the Party workers on your team at Highgate. A solicitor's clerk. He used to borrow your motorbike from time to time."

"Oh, Bertie, you mean. Bertie Summers."

"That's the one. I want you to call him after lunch. Tell him you finished lecturing at Broxbourne on Friday night and left your briefcase at the Institute. You must have it back but you can't go yourself. Ask him if he'll go out there on your bike tomorrow morning and get it back for you."

"But—"

"You'll leave the briefcase there tonight, of course. Let him have your key—and perhaps a note in case he runs into a caretaker. Tomorrow morning, make sure he leaves your flat at least an hour before you do. Tell him to wear your leather coat, your gauntlets, and your helmet and goggles.''

Boyd was lost. "Look, old man, he's in an office, right? Solicitor's clerk. He can't just walk out and . . ."

Price slipped out his wallet and took five one-pound notes from it. He smuggled them to Boyd. "Will that do it?"

Boyd gulped. "Oh, he'll do it for that."

Price half turned in his chair. "The object, Boyd, is to persuade anyone who might be watching your flat that Bertie Summers is you."

"Someone's watching my flat?"

"In *case* someone's watching your flat. Just a precaution, Boyd. There's no cause for alarm. Now—give him an hour to get on the road, then leave your place by the back way, take a bus, and get to a station. Take the train to Southend, then a local bus to your parents' house. Tomorrow night, you'll transmit the code block I've just given you. Carry the wireless set in a suitcase or a stout bag. You'll send at your usual transmission time, repeating the message three times with a break of five minutes between each send. Wait fifteen minutes and repeat again three times."

"From our house?"

"From somewhere nearby. Off the beaten track, lonely. A wood or the corner of a field."

Boyd digested this in prickly silence.

"Must be pretty important, this one. To make you change the site and everything."

"You'll never send anything more important, Boyd."

"Geordie's thing?"

"Geordie's thing."

Boyd turned his head. His eyes twinkled. "Worth a promotion, is it?"

It was the first joke Price had ever heard him make.

Margaretta Terrace was an elegant little backwater between King's Road and the Thames, a terrace of identical miniature mansions in perfect scale. Frank Loughran was waiting for them in his car at the gate. They went in together. The drawing room was on the first floor, and it occurred to Curzon as they sat down that if Menzies didn't actually own the house it had been designed to match his tastes and temperament to perfection: underplayed, discreet, colorless. Loughran looked painfully out of place.

"I thought we'd be more comfortable here." Menzies stood in front of the fireplace. "What I have to tell you now is absolutely confidential. Under no circumstancess will you discuss it with anyone else or"—he swung on Curzon—"with each other, except in my presence. Is that understood?"

They nodded. A tall stained mahogany case clock in one corner chimed the half hour.

"Are you both familiar with the Radio Security Service tracker station at Maldon in Essex?"

They both nodded again.

"On the night of July 2 last year, a little after 2100 hours, the duty operator at Maldon began a conventional sweep through the shortwave bands. It's a thankless job and rather hit-or-miss, so each station gears its sweep in sequence with the rest. No two stations sweeping the same band at the same time, in other words. You follow me?"

Only too well, said Loughran's slouched shoulders.

"The Maldon man hit on a Morse send almost right away. In code and only the tail end, but it was enough. He got his fix. Luckily he was a patient sort of chap. He stuck to the vector and kept combing through. Twenty minutes later he got another send. Also coded, naturally." Menzies stretched his arms stiffly down his back, parade-ground style. "Another man might have given up, called in his superior, and moved on to the next band, but this chap stuck it out. Twenty-five minutes later he got a third signal, repeated three times like the second. He got it down easily. Interesting thing, each of the three separate signal groups emanated from different sites. When Maldon set up a triangulation later, they worked out a distance of between three and eight miles between each transmission site. But"—he showed his teeth in wolfish good humor—"it was the same signature each time."

"Known?" Loughran interposed.

"Not known. Well, you both know the safety-net system. The band was monitored on a three-way sweep from then on. Nothing for days; then, on July 6, Maldon picked up a Hamburg incoming. Short, repeated three times." He looked hard at Curzon. "By which time, of course GC and CS had deciphered the first three messages. The Hamburg incoming matched the code form. Head of Five was informed and we met." He rocked gently back and forth, toe to heel. "The Essex sender was code-lined Sibling. His send of July 2 was an appeal, with a lot of tradescript thrown in, for recognition as a subagent. The Hamburg incoming was an agreement that he was so recognized. Things moved quickly after that. Sibling made another transmission, from Site One, on July 8. It alerted Hamburg to prepare for a pickup at sea, two miles outside the War Channel off the Scottish coast. Documents, we assumed, in a marker buoy equipped with a radio-interrupter."

"And?" Curzon craned forward in his chair.

"Oh, the drop was made all right. A fishing boat out of Peterhead. Young man called George McNeil; crew of two."

"You had it fished out," Loughran guessed.

"And replaced. An MTB stood off till McNeil went inshore of the Channel, then hooked it aboard. I was standing by in London. So was Palmer and a couple of his cipher men, but as it turned out I didn't need them. The captain radioed the style codes of thirty Admiralty Ops Room message sheets he'd found in the container. I called them out on the phone to DNI. They were progress reports on Atlantic convoys."

"Shit," Loughran breathed.

"We decided to leave them intact and the captain put the buoy overboard again. It was picked up by an E-boat at one thirty."

"You let it go?"

"We let it go. It was pretty clear the information would be out of date before Hamburg got round to deciphering, so apart from revamping our own weekly code there was no pressing reason *not* to let it go. On the other hand, I wanted Hamburg and Sibling, not to mention the fisherman, to think they'd got away with it. Quite apart from anything else, we had to find the source at Admiralty Operations."

Curzon's mouth was bone dry. He knew where it was all leading.

"It took a couple of days. A man . . ."—Menzies paused for effect, his eye on Curzon—"called Donald White. A chief petty officer."

"White?" Loughran's teeth met with an audible click.

"We allowed him to run. He was taking fifth-copy tear sheets; the ones sent to the writer responsible for keeping the

Ops Room log. The writer handed back each sheet to his CPO, whose job was to destroy them. White was his CPO.''

''Shit,'' Loughran hissed again.

Curzon started to interrupt, but Menzies silenced him with a gesture. ''We live and learn. However—Sibling was identified after his second send on July 8. Five put watchers on all three of the Essex transmission sites. Sibling turned up at Site Two and we followed him to London. His name is Boyd Corrie. Know him?''

They shook their heads.

''Schoolteacher. Highgate. Registered conscientious objector, member of the Communist Party, cell leader, quite active. In February he'd given up his work on the Highgate Shelter Committee, wriggled out of his duties as a school firewatcher on medical grounds, and volunteered as a lecturer on the evening institute circuit in Hertfordshire. All in the course of a few days. He had a motorcycle and the lecturing qualified him for a petrol ration. He appears to have built his shortwave set himself. George McNeil is also a Party member. Before the conduit opened for business, McNeil met Corrie at his flat in Highgate. It was quite a party. There were six other guests. They stayed from midmorning till well after midnight on July 12, two days before McNeil took the first container to sea.''

''Did you nab them?'' Curzon instantly regretted asking the question.

Menzies clicked his tongue. ''For what reason? No, we let them run. At Admiralty, we performed a few sleight-of-hand tricks to pass White material that wouldn't do Hamburg a great deal of good. It wasn't duff by any means; it simply pointed them down blind alleys. We followed the conduit each time a drop was made—from White to the Peterhead pickup—but surveillance was quite academic by then. We were providing the input, monitoring Corrie's sends, supervising the handover of documents. Root and branch.''

''What about these other young Bolshies? The ones who met at Corrie's flat?'' Loughran was far too absorbed to remember the courtesies of rank.

''Corrie chose them rather well. They're all members of something called the People's Vigilance Committee, all conscientious objectors, all engaged in war work of one kind or another. Docks, railways, munitions factories.''

''How old are these little shits?'' Loughran exploded.

"Average age about twenty-three, I'd say."

"Rule bloody Britannia!"

Menzies studied him with distaste. "You're both aware of the abrupt termination of the White element."

The White *element*. Curzon conjured a fleeting image of pink bloomers on the drying-rack suspended from Alice Petrie's terminal U-bolt. He said softly, "*You* suppressed that," but it wasn't a question.

"It was necessary."

"Why?" Loughran wanted it in plain English.

"Alice Petrie did *not* commit suicide. That must be clear even to you, from what little you learned." A patronizing smile flickered and died. "She couldn't have climbed to a point high enough to hang herself. Everything about it was suspect. She was strangled, the rope was knotted round her neck and her body hoisted to the ceiling. Too far. By some-one who needed to make it look like suicide but overlooked detail. He was in a panic, naturally."

"Are we talking about Donald White?" demanded Loughran.

"We found Donald White's blood all over the carpet in the living room. He was stabbed with a pair of scissors."

"You found *his* body, too?"

"No." Menzies' self-confidence waned slightly. "We never found him."

"So you had him *posted*. Simplest way out." Loughran studied his toecaps intently. "So who killed the Petrie woman?"

"Price," Curzon said dully. "It was Price."

Loughran grinned with feline satisfaction. *I told you so.*

"Who else?" Menzies watched him closely.

Loughran raised a hand. "Let's get back to Boyd Corrie."

"Very well. Corrie turned up as Sibling to ask Hamburg for recognition as a subagent. He transmitted that request on behalf of his controller. When his six Bolshies began servic-ing him with production figures, troop movements and so on, he transmitted on behalf of his controller. When Corrie passed Donald White's tear sheets to McNeil, he was acting on the orders—"

"Of his controller," Loughran finished testily. "What controller?"

"Price," Curzon said again.

Loughran looked from one to the other, first in disbelief, then dismay. "This started last *July*?"

"That's right."

"Around the time you scaled down the Pepperpot? Pulled off Price's surveillance?" He glanced at Curzon. "Sent *him* scooting three thousand miles away to Washington?"

It was Curzon's turn to ask why.

Menzies took a chair and for a moment sat, hands on knees, contemplating the empty grate of the Adam fireplace. "Price broke all his own rules, perhaps even his own behavior pattern, when he killed Alice Petrie and Donald White. I imagine White was becoming rather difficult to handle by September. He'd had medical treatment for several weeks for an ulcer; he was ready to break. I imagine there was a scuffle, Price stabbed him, killed him. Naturally he couldn't leave the woman—her sexual predilections had led Price to White in the first place, I suspect, so in a way he'd used her already without turning a hair. Killing her was logical. It preserved the security of the Boyd Corrie network, his own neck, his future."

"And you had no surveillance on him at the time," Curzon said with cold emphasis.

"No, not on Price. That was unfortunate, but there were other considerations. When I uncovered the Corrie conduit, I called off all existing cover. It made a great deal of sense. First, Price had obviously abandoned any hope of operating effectively through the Pepperpot system, which meant he knew he was being manipulated."

"How?"

"Bad management." Menzies sprawled in his chair. "I can't be sure, of course, but my guess is he actually saw that old man fall under the bus on the day he first contacted Owens."

"He *knew* two years ago?" Loughran's mouth gaped.

Menzies avoided answering the questions directly. "So, when Corrie surfaced last July I decided formal cover was a waste of money and effort. Price had tied up a whole machine and still made fools of us. The answer was to cover him through his subagents—Corrie, McNeil, White, and the others—because without them he couldn't function. In his own right he simply wasn't worth covering. I was proved right."

"And getting me out of the way was critical to the equation, was it?" Curzon almost choked on his rage. "Why couldn't you tell me that? . . ."

"I wanted Price isolated," Menzies cut in. "Professionally and personally—and don't underestimate the relevance of his personal needs. There was greater potential in Price than ever and I had no intention of being deprived of it. I held you in reserve. That's why I encouraged you to write to him; why I ordered you to establish contact again."

Loughran was scowling over his own calculations. "So Corrie transmitted material picked up by his Bolshies from the Essex transmission sites. And this McNeil bastard ran the drops on Donald White's material. Okay—have they ever tried to evade surveillance? I mean, do they know, any of them, that they're being watched?"

Menzies shifted uncomfortably. "We controlled White's paperwork. We feed each member of Corrie's group. We monitor Corrie's sends. We supply every bit of material McNeil drops. It runs smoothly."

Curzon leaned forward on his knees. "If Price knew we were on to him when Evans-Wyke was killed in July 1940, a whole year passed before he used Corrie for the first time. A year in which we took it for granted he suspected nothing."

Menzies jaw hardened. "What's your point?"

"If he could establish one network we knew nothing about, he could have established two."

"Or three," added Loughran malevolently.

"I'm satisfied he hasn't. Completely satisfied."

Curzon shrugged resignedly. "And now you're going to use the Corrie conduit for the Dakar deception."

Loughran threw him a puzzled stare.

Menzies nodded slowly. "It's what I've nursed him for, protected him for. Surely you can see why. If the Pepperpot fed Price something as big as this, he'd ignore it—or find some way of conveying the opinion that it was a plant. If he picks it up through Corrie's Bolshie network he'll accept it one hundred percent. He always has."

Curzon and Loughran exchanged glances. The expression on each of their faces said the same thing: Prove it!

Curzon stiffened. "If he knows about the Pepperpot set-up, he knew about the surveillance we ran on him up to last summer."

"Of course."

"Then he's not stupid enough to think *I'm* just someone he met by accident on the boat coming over."

Menzies couldn't resist a smile. "No, he's not stupid. I'm sure he's suspected you for years. Perhaps from the beginning."

"Then that's it. I'm no use to you."

"You're more use now, my dear Paul, than you ever were. I *want* him to suspect you. I want him to worry about you. Continuously. In fact, I'm counting on it. The more time you spend with him the more convinced he'll be that we're concerned. And if we're concerned, there'll be little doubt in his mind that his operation's successful. We'd naturally check on him if we thought high grade intelligence was getting out of the country, and he knows it. The great virtue, seen from his point of view, is that we're using *you* to spy on him. He's got the measure of you after all, hasn't he?"

Price sensed there was something in the wind the moment he let himself in. His shouted "I'm home!" raised a storm of muffled giggling from the living room, and when he put his head around the door Dinah and Sally, already in stitches, clung to each other for support. He hung up his coat and went in.

"Tell me, you foam-flecked pint-puller," gagged Tommy Handley from the radio, "what's the difference between Mussolini's braces and two-and-a-half hundredweight of nutty slack?"

"A large whiskey and soda," intoned Colonel Chinstrap.

"A large whiskey and soda?"

"I don't mind if I do."

"Oh, turn that off, Diny." Sally's face was crimson, but not entirely with mirth. Price bent to kiss her.

"What's the joke?" he inquired innocently and Dinah went into convulsions again. He eyed her sternly but it had no effect. She gulped at the sight of him and doubled over the back of a chair in an advanced state of hysterical collapse.

"If you could . . . see your . . . *face*!" she spluttered.

Price turned for enlightenment to Sally, but she thrust her knuckles into her mouth to choke back her own laughter. The crimson in her cheeks deepened to bright scarlet.

"Will someone please . . ." he began, half smiling.

Dinah hurled herself at his chest and threw her arms around his neck. "We're going to have a baby, soppy!" she yelled. "A *baby*!"

*   *   *

Later in the evening he went to the shed to prepare for the next night's transmission. He'd made quite a comfortable little den out of it in the past few weeks: the radio, an embroidered tablecloth over the window, an old easy chair, a blanket over the door to keep out drafts, a standard lamp in one corner. Too comfortable.

It was becoming a habit. There was something uniquely pleasing about working with wood; odors, textures, angles, curves. A release of the mind as much as an exercise for the hands. And, to his surprise, he was becoming remarkably good at it. An untapped wellspring, he mused, as he sanded the pinky-beige cylinder of the roller towel he'd determined to finish that night. He held his creation close to the light and ran his fingers along its silken finish. Dinah was right; what was he doing messing with roller towels when he could be building a crib.

He'd had to wait till after supper to snatch a word with Sally alone. "When?"

"End of December, beginning of January."

"Why didn't you tell me before?" Counting back—that first time?

"I had to be sure."

He didn't go into that. "Can you feel it?"

"I can feel something."

Rioting in his head. He grabbed her in a bearhug, remembered the embryo growing inside her and recoiled. As he cradled her head on his shoulder, her heart pounding against his, he felt the first wave of remorse. December! Then Boyd would have to be terminated immediately; Geordie, Simmons and Co. In spite of all his sworn promises, he'd not made one single positive move to put an end to it. He would have to do something soon—in a week, two at most. Wrap them up and go to Curzon. "Nothing has to change, Paul. I'll carry on transmitting, anything you want."

Then why not tell him now? Tell him about Boyd, the others?

He laid the smooth wood of the roller along his cheek. No, he couldn't do that. The Dieppe product was on its way and to stop it now might alert Hamburg, expose his own position, endanger Sally and the baby. No, this one had to go through. The last lap, the final reckoning.

And tomorrow night he'd start work on the crib.

* * *

Paul Curzon was halfway up the first flight when the light clicked on and Mrs. Silver appeared at the door of her flat. "It *is* him. Mr. Curzon, I've got your young lady in here. Been waiting hours, she has."

Nicola Stacey came from behind. Uniform, shoulder bag, gas mask case, hat in hand. Hair glowing like molten gold under the hall light. He mumbled something and led her upstairs.

The flat was in its usual chaotic state but she didn't seem to notice. She wouldn't sit down, so he retreated to the kitchen to make some tea and listened to the living room boards creak as she moved from picture to picture, mantelpiece to desk, bookcase to chiffonier. He sneaked a glance around the door at one point to see what she was doing and their eyes met. She made a dismissive shrug and turned away quickly. When he brought in the tray and set it down on a small table in front of the empty grate she sat down.

"Shall I?"

He nodded. Her hands were long and fine: the nails clipped to Navy regulation length but lightly polished. He remembered how precise her movements had been at their first meeting. They were no longer precise. The cup rattled treacherously in its saucer as she handed it to him.

"I thought you'd used up all your leave."

"I came down this morning. I'm on temporary detachment."

"In London?" His pulse throbbed in his throat.

"At the Admiralty." She brought the cup to her lips but her hand shook so much she was forced to lower it to the saucer. "I'll be here for two or three months at least."

"Oh, good."

The cup was rattling persistently; she put it down. Her hands came together in her lap, the left uppermost. Rob's ring glittered there, sapphire on silver.

"I had to talk to you."

"Yes?" He saw it coming. A clouding of the green eyes, but with resolution, not dismay; a tightening of the chin. Summoning up the blood.

"I can't marry Rob." Her head lifted and she searched his face; an appeal for help.

He returned a coward's look of incomprehension. "You mean till after the war."

"I mean we shan't be getting married."

He hung his head. "You don't owe me any explanations. It's between you and him."

"No, it's not." So softly he almost missed it. "It's between you and me. Isn't it?"

He sat back in the chair, met her gaze. *Say* it! He thought of Rob and there was nothing to say.

"I can't be in London and not see you." She was twisting the ring around her finger. "And I'll want to go on seeing you, I know that. You feel the same. It's all right—you don't have to say anything."

He did. "We don't have to do anything of the sort. *I* don't anyway. You're my brother's—"

"I've written to him." The ring was still turning but now at the very tip of her finger. "On the train, coming down. I posted it as soon as I got here."

"Why?"

"You know why. I said . . ." She lowered her eyes. "I said if we were going to wait, we should be free to . . . reconsider."

"He'll tell you not to be a damned fool. Or post the banns right away. He won't let you go."

"He will. You don't know him as well as I do. He'll understand."

"And while he's trying to work it out, you and I—reconsider, do we?"

His face was burning. He knew what it must have taken out of her to say it—do it—but he couldn't help her. *Dear Rob: I thought I'd let you know that Nicky and I . . .*

"I have no illusions, Paul. If you feel you can't hurt him—won't—I'll understand."

"You're damned right I won't!"

She flinched but didn't look up. "Then I lost both of you. I knew that might happen when I wrote the letter."

"Then why write it, for God's sake? And why come here?"

"Because I couldn't go on as if nothing had changed. I wanted you to know . . . I feel as you do."

He shook his head into his cupped hands.

She smiled—a tight, hard hopeless constriction of the mouth. "I'm not sure what I thought was going to happen next. I didn't expect you to do anything. I thought I'd wait till he wrote back and . . ."

"Then we write a joint communiqué, do we? 'With reference to yours of even date.' "

For a moment she was still, the ring held in the fingertips of her right hand; then she slipped it in her pocket and stood up. "Well, I suppose there's nothing more to say, is there? I should've known better. I won't bother you again." She collected her hat, shouldered her bag and gas mask case, eyed him silently for a moment, then made for the door. He didn't get up. She stopped, hesitated.

"Can you tell he how to get to Dolphin Square? I've got quarters there, but I don't know . . ."

He got up slowly, swallowing anguish and shame and self-disgust. She raised her face to his as he loomed over her. Her lips parted. He touched a finger to them. They closed, pressing his skin.

"I'll drive you there," he said gruffly.

"Just this once?"

He let his finger travel along her nose to her cheek, then down the line of her jaw until it supported her chin.

"Just this once," he lied.

AUGUST 21, 1942

The papers made it sound like a return to the age of chivalry: glory, honor, the ring of steel and the sound of trumpets. No casualty figures, of course. Even the Air Intelligence statistics—91 Luftwaffe aircraft shot down to 98 of ours— seemed to imply that the British planes had been unpiloted and crewless at the time. "No blood on the breakfast table": Lord Beaverbrook's fundamental law of readership appeal.

The *Daily Telegraph*'s front page summary—released a day late to allow Combined Operations and the Ministry of Information to get their stories straight—fairly glowed with self-satisfaction.

"Landings with tanks were successfully made on the six selected beaches, despite the fact that the already strong

German defenses had recently been reinforced. Two enemy batteries were destroyed. We lost the destroyer *Berkely*. The Germans had to bring up air reinforcements from France, Holland, and Belgium. Canadian troops with tanks forced the defenses of Dieppe and fought their way into the town. There was fierce fighting around the Casino, an enemy fortress. In addition to the beaches at Dieppe, landings were also made at Varengeville, four and a half miles to the west of Dieppe; at Berneval, four and a half miles to the east; at Pourville, slightly to the west of the harbor; and at Puys, on the eastern outskirts of the town. Operations were supported with a bombardment of the town by an attendant destroyer flotilla which, from a mile range, poured in hundreds of shells.''

They were calling it "a reconnaissance in force," and Mountbatten's headquarters announced in a communiqué that "as a combined operation, the raid was a successful demonstration of coordination of all three services."

Elsewhere on the front page was a sustained hosanna for the RAF's role in it, a generous genuflection to the part played by the American air units and the US Ranger squad, and an account of "bewilderment" in Germany at the Allies' remarkable achievement—"although Axis propaganda under the guidance of Goebbels naturally proclaims that the raid was a Second Front which completely failed."

Curzon dropped the paper on his desk and picked up the "doom sheet" from the Cabinet Intelligence Committee, an "intermediate evaluation of losses sustained." A final accounting would take a week or ten days; the messier cases were taking a long time to die. The Canadians, who provided the bulk of the shock troops, had sent 4,963 men ashore. The total number of casualties recorded was 3,367.

So what went wrong? Why had the defenses "recently been reinforced?" An idea snapped him upright in his chair but as quickly deflated him. If Menzies was to be believed, Price and the Corrie network had been under surveillance all along, so their hands were clean. Unless one of them, Corrie most likely, had been able to slip under the net and make a transmission undetected. And if he had done it once, he might have managed it before. Often. Back to Loughran's culpability theory: Price was Menzies' private disaster area.

He took up the paper again and caught the headline, "Lovat's men carried out toughest job yet''; an on-the-spot account by

A. B. Austin, the single newsman taken on the raid. "We landed west of Dieppe at dawn. The British Commando troops to whom I was attached—"

More bloody do-or-die. He threw the paper aside. Five hours later he was to remember that thought, that gesture, with a riveting exactness that twisted in his gut like a knife.

It was four o'clock, dark, raining hard, a spate of water threshing through the gutter outside his window, Nicky on his mind. The phone rang and it was her voice.

"For God's sake, Nicky!" He cupped the phone. "I thought I told you never to ring me here—"

"Except in emergencies," she cut in, icily. Rob, he thought. Oh Christ, she's got a letter from Rob at last.

"What is it?"

"I've just had a call from a friend in Combined Ops. She said—Rob was at Dieppe with Four Commando."

More bloody do-or-die. The shock caught him full in the stomach. "Has he—?" Don't say it! Don't!

"He died in hospital last night."

AUGUST 22, 1942

The American senior officer was a brigadier general in his mid-fifties; silver-haired, patrician, and disconcertingly gentle of manner. His parchment cheeks, transparently white hands, and dark eyes belonged to an academic; in fact, Regius Morrison had, only a year before, been the vice-president of a celebrated Wall Street brokerage house with substantial interests in the European market. As he joked in his deceptively mild drawl, he now numbered many of his oldest clients among his enemies.

His juniors, a half dozen majors and colonels, had come to the table at the house in Eisenhowerplatz with bulging file cases. Prominent among the documents they sorted into neat piles around their blotters were the CIC and Combined Operations reports on Wednesday's Dieppe fiasco.

Morrison directed an apologetic half-smile down the table

at Menzies who faced him at the far end. "Perhaps you'd care to open, Stuart."

Menzies' gaze flickered suspiciously over the bronzed faces of the juniors, then back along the stacked papers in front of them. "If you've all read the proposition . . ."

Heads nodded. Curzon saw the clipping from the *Daily Telegraph* article he'd read the day before pinned to a file in front of the American sitting at his left; Rob's face seemed to stare up at him accusingly from the polished table. He blotted it out.

"Thank you, Stuart," General Morrison said softly. "That'll save time. Points, then. You want to lead off, Bob?"

The major sitting opposite Curzon was in his mid-thirties and taller than Curzon by a head. A one-time Washington lawyer, he'd been told.

"Sir, I don't want to labor the point . . ."—a quick glance at Menzies, followed by a reprise of his general's apologetic smile—"but the man who'll fly out to Gibraltar next month to command Operation Torch is an American general. The landing force, give or take support and reserve units, will be American. The outcome—good or bad—will be an American outcome. General Menzies, here, holds the ace in the hole. The only criticism I have of the whole deception plan is . . ." He relayed the bad news directly to Morrison. "We have a material right to say how that card should be played."

"Right," muttered a down-table acolyte.

"Anyone else?" the general asked quickly as Menzies' shoulders squared.

A crop-haired colonel in Marine Corps green said, without looking at anyone, "That's unanimous, general."

"Stuart?" Regius Morrison deferred politely but Menzies, poised for the attack, withdrew at the last moment to the back of his chair. He raised a fan of fingers dismissively.

"So—let's take a look at the objections." The general produced a fine calfskin case and selected a cigar. He lit it and they all watched him. "A US operation with US resources, US goals, and US necks on the line." He brushed away the smoke clouds. "If you'll forgive the over-simplification, Stuart. Now I can appreciate your point of view. Price is yours, you know him, you run him, you have to protect your investment."

"That's right."

"But"—Morrison seemed genuinely distressed to have to

say it—"there are precedents, Stuart. Our Ambassador Winant has been in on the ground floor of Torch from Stage One—at Mr. Anthony Eden's insistence. American diplomats handled negotiations with the French community in North Africa and laid the groundwork for an appreciation of French-African reaction to an invasion. OSS are deeply involved. The concept for Torch was ours. I'd say precedent was clear-cut. We have"—he chose the words carefully—"inalienable rights here."

"Sir?" The Marine colonel, eyebrows raised for permission to speak. Morrison nodded. "With respect to General Menzies . . ." They waited breathlessly for the telegraphed punch. "Dieppe is in the mind of everyone at this table I guess. Someone has to say it." He fixed on Curzon, eyes narrowed. "A lot of men died, a lot of mistakes were made. War Department opinion of the British handling of the war so far . . ." He cut out diplomatically and began again. "If Torch goes under we're two, three years behind schedule right off. Rommel can hold North Africa against the British. That's proved. If we don't break him, he's there for good. Okay—the Dakar deception plan could work. This guy Price may be solid gold, and I guess we all agree SIS does a great job. But we equipped this game and we're playing it. We want to keep an eye on the ball." He looked both ways along the table. "We have to be in on the Price play from beginning to end—and that includes passing information, surveillance and . . . liability."

It struck Curzon at once that the Marine had been delegated the role of Attila the Hun by Morrison. A look at Menzies' face told him his opinion was shared.

"You put me in an invidious position, brigadier," Menzies said at last.

Regius Morrison nodded understandingly. "In your shoes, I'd feel the same, Stuart."

"Any mistakes"—Menzies scrutinized all of them in turn—"by your people or mine and Price will drop out. The slightest hint of interference . . ."

"Agreed." Morrison was prepared to be generous in victory. "We take a back seat, Stuart. You drive."

"And background?" prompted someone contritely.

"Who he is, what he was, his record under your control, his private life if any and how you operate him," put in the

Marine colonel. He engaged Menzies' hard bright gaze. "In case of mistakes, sir."

"Ike's faith in you . . ." added Regius Morrison humbly, "is blue chip. No question. My job is to honor that faith." He ran a paternal glance over his crew. "It'll be a privilege to serve under your command."

AUGUST 23, 1942

For three nights in succession, Rob had died ten times an hour in Curzon's dreams, each death more bloody than the last. They were on a beach and Rob would stretch out a hand. "Paul! Please!" Curzon would run away, hands to his ears, into the cleansing sea but he could not help looking back. And each time, Rob metamorphosed like melting butter until he was a limbless obscenity, sobbing helplessly. And somehow he was six years old again.

Nicky's nightmares were, if anything, even worse. That morning she'd woken at his side in screaming hysterics. He'd slapped her hard across the face then spent an hour nursing her in his arms, but he was no comfort to her. She flinched at his touch, lay stiff and unyielding, heard nothing he said.

All they had left in common were the statistics of their affair. Thirteen days together, thirteen nights. He'd made love to her the first time on the night he brought her back from Dolphin Square with her suitcase, and for the last time on the night Rob lay dying in a Dover hospital. What made matters worse was that she wanted to leave and he wanted her to go and neither could bring themselves to say it.

Tom Price was the last man on earth he wanted to deal with today. He'd avoided him since the talk with Menzies in Margaretta Terrace and the reason, he was prepared to admit to himself, was pathetically naive: Tom Price *knew*. Just that. Knew he was probably with British Intelligence, knew he was a liar, a poseur, a fraud.

But Menzies had insisted; out of the blue, a telephone call that had wrenched Curzon from Nicky. Priority. No explanation. They left the house in Elm Place and strolled to the Queen's

Elm, Price effervescently buoyant, full of plans. And halfway to the pub he announced blithely, "We're—I mean, Sally and I—we're going to have a baby."

Curzon got out the expected response but he didn't know how. His instinctive reaction was a towering, overwhelming fury; blind, suffocating. He survived the next few minutes only because Price's elation had blinded him, too. "We've penciled you in as godfather. Best friend's responsibility, Sally says, so you're elected again. I suppose we'll have to ask Pepper, too, but I'll hang fire on that till—"

Curzon hid his face in his tankard, gulping the thin beer too fast, drowning the fires in him. Blotting out Price's happiness. God damn him, didn't he *understand*? He *wasn't* Tom Price. He wasn't just another taxpayer with a loving wife. He was a spy, a killer; a double murderer who'd trailed his victims, squeezed them dry, and dispatched them without batting an eye. He had no "best friend" and he knew it. Good Christ, how far could he take the deception? If it was still a deception. Perhaps he was mad; so deep in the character he couldn't climb out.

His rage surfaced before he could check it. He didn't know what Price was saying at the time, didn't care. "My brother's dead. He was killed at Dieppe," he blurted savagely.

Price had his tankard poised at his lips. He stopped drinking, his mouth full, and beer coursed freely down his chin to his tie. He swallowed hard and dropped the tankard on the bar. "Oh, my dear God!"

"He ran over a mine. He died in hospital after they got him home." His feeling of triumph, if that was what he'd had in mind, seemed suddenly cheap. Unconsciously he reached for Price's arm, steadying him. "I'm sorry. I shouldn't have—"

Tom Price's eyes filled with tears. He closed them very tightly. "Oh, God, Paul. Oh, Holy God."

SEPTEMBER 16, 1942

Regius Morrison folded himself neatly into the overstuffed chair on the visitor's side of his desk and closed his eyes. "We're committed to the deception as a whole, Bob. You know that."

The Washington lawyer drummed an insistent tattoo on his briefcase with the backs of his fingers. "But we have the right to challenge basic assumptions, sir—to my way of thinking."

"Challenge assumptions—or challenge General Menzies? Discretion, Bob, huh? Let's hear it."

"I'm not challenging Menzies or anything in the Price file, sir. Not factually. I'm talking about interpretation: what Price is, how well or badly he functions on the ground, why certain decisions were made when he first came over in '39. I'm saying maybe the British interpretation was off-target from day one, that's all."

"That's all!" Morrison chuckled. "You have any support for that or are we talking theories?"

"I've had—discussions, sir," the major said guardedly.

"British source?"

"Yes, sir."

"Who?"

"He'd—ah—prefer to keep his head below the snowline, sir. You know what it's like over here—step out of the pecking order and you're liable to get your head sliced off at the knees. He's vulnerable."

Morrison opened one baby blue eye. "I'm on your side, Bob. Name?"

"Frank Loughran. He's over at Five's BIa section and—"

"I know who he is. Ran Price when Five took him over from Menzies. Runs the double stable. You backing his judgment against Menzies'?"

The young major took a firmer grip on his briefcase. "Facts first, sir. From the day he came over, no one, but no

365

one, gave Price credit for being anything but a third-rate amateur. Even when he set up the Corrie network.''

"Because Menzies had him under control from beginning to end, Bob. The man admitted his mistake but he had Corrie corraled from the first transmit. You arguing that?''

"No, sir. The Corrie network he had taped.''

"Meaning?''

"Suppose Price didn't stop at Corrie? Suppose he set up a second conduit, even a third? Suppose he wasn't as ineffectual as they thought? He hogtied Donald White, remember. That was a class operation. And fixing White and the Petrie woman was pretty cold-blooded, any way you look at it.''

"*Bob.*'' The brigadier's pained smile was paternal. "All in the file, son. All in the file.''

"Right, sir. The *fact*, not the interpretation. Take this Evans-Wyke guy. Nobody even suggested Price saw him die till Corrie came on the scene a year later. At the time they just *assumed* Price hadn't seen the accident. Basic assumptions, sir. But there's more. There was a big flap on over at Five a few weeks back. Corrie took off on his motorbike one morning, heading for Broxbourne. There was a car on his tail but when they got to the school, they jumped a mile. Guy on the motorbike wasn't Corrie; some clerk name of Summers wearing Corrie's clothes. Five shoots a man over to Corrie's apartment and he's gone—missing a day and a night. Explanation was that he went to stay with his parents; it's in the file. Loughran has a hunch about that.''

"And that is?''

"It happened a few days ahead of the Dieppe landing, sir. The raid was a catastrophe because the krauts had new defensive positions in place that weren't there three days before. They knew it was coming.'' The lawyer tapped his long fingers on the briefcase. "Basic assumption, sir. Basic.''

Morrison made a cathedral of fingers under his nose. "Where are we going with this, Bob? Are you making a recommendation?''

"Yes, sir.'' He fixed on FDR's portrait behind Morrison's desk. "Loughran has a German double working out of his stable who could put over the Dakar deception and make it stick. Name of Wulf Schmidt. Hamburg thinks he's the bees knees; top agent, first class record. He can do it and we can control him all the way, no fuss. That's point one.''

''And?''

''The British'll hold out for using Price. Okay—I suggest we run our own round-the-clock surveillance on him.''

''Behind Menzies' back?''

''Temporarily, sir.'' He took courage from the word. ''If Price is clean—no second or third network, no cut-out operations, no back-up we don't know about—fine. At least *we'll* know for sure, one way or the other. If not—'' He shrugged eloquently, ''we pull him in; Corrie, McNeil, the whole bunch; and use Schmidt instead. Insurance, sir.''

Morrison stretched languidly, arms high, legs straight. He opened his eyes wide. ''Insurance, huh?'' He levered himself to his feet. ''All right, Bob. I'll buy that.''

Curzon didn't recognize the handwriting at first. He opened the letter in the hall.

''Dear Paul; Will you please send my clothes over to Dolphin Square. There's not much, I know, but I can't easily replace them. Pack them in my suitcase and put it in a cab. The porter will take care of it. I've written to your mother to say I'm going back to Fort William. I don't want to lie more than I have already so I didn't tell her I'd asked for a transfer.

''I don't know what else to say. You haven't written or called since the funeral so I assume you feel the same.

''Some things just aren't supposed to happen and it's dangerous to try. I made it happen and you, who never wanted it, suffered the consequences. After the funeral and that awful scene with your father, I wanted to die. I can't face your parents again without telling them the truth. And I'll never forgive myself. I love you. Nicky.''

He became aware that Mrs. Silver was watching him from her door along the passage. ''Bad news, dear?'' she asked anxiously.

''Nothing I didn't already know, Mrs. Silver,'' he said heavily. He took the rest of the letters upstairs.

It had been only three weeks ago, two days after his confrontation with Tom Price in the Queen's Elm. The funeral of Robert Granger Curzon in the village where he'd grown and matured. Nicky refused to go; she wouldn't, *couldn't*. For three days they had barely spoken to one another, yet she'd stayed on at his flat, done her job at the Admiralty during the day, cooked meals. The night before Curzon was due to go down to Norfolk by train, she capitulated. She *would* go, but alone, by another train. She didn't want them to be seen together.

The funeral was a disaster. It was the custom at Great Westring Church—medieval, in the vicar's opinion, with sinister pagan overtones—that the sexton who tolled the knell and the gravedigger who prepared the ground should see the face of the corpse they were to inter. But Rob arrived from Dover in a stitched canvas shroud and a papier-mâché box enclosed in a crate, and the imbalance of his body was so apparent when the undertaker removed the canvased corpse from the train that he strongly advised the vicar to avoid further desecration.

The whole village turned out, as much, Curzon suspected, from curiosity as anything else, although Rob had been well-liked and respected. The Bart and Eleanora were both in wheelchairs at the church, and Nicky stood between them, holding their hands. She and Curzon had studiously avoided meeting before the cortège left the house, but they both knew their private agony would begin with a vengeance when the mourners returned to the Hall. Still, neither of them could have foreseen the horrific course it would take.

Fifty or sixty people gathered in the library for the inevitable buffet lunch: the lord lieutenant and his wife, county councillors, a throng of landed gentry and farmers, the village elders, two subalterns from Four Commando who had been with Rob at Dieppe, a few of his school friends. And when they were safely locked in, the Bart launched into his speech. He had lost weight, lost much of the fire that had kept him doggedly alive, but his anger was a life force in itself. He began with a valedictory for Rob—a general's passionate soliloquy to a fallen soldier rather than a father's homily to his son. At length he turned to Nicky, "a fellow officer and a brave one, whose courage now will be tested as my son's courage was tested; a woman of quiet strength who loved him selflessly and was to have married him; who will now be our child, Eleanora's and mine."

Nicky and Eleanora were moved to tears, but the Bart had not finished. He swung his chair around and raised a shaking hand to point across the room at Paul. "Today"—his voice trembled with the effort of control—"I buried two sons, not one. *This* is my dead son Paul. He is about to leave." The silence that fell on the room was like a pall of toxic gas. No one moved or spoke; not even Eleanora, who seemed not to have heard. In the two letters she had subsequently written him, she'd maintained a stoic pretense that nothing untoward had been said.

Curzon left the house without a word.

Two hours after he got back to London, Nicky telephoned from a callbox in Great Westring village. The Bart had used his influence to extend her forty-eight-hour pass to a full week's leave and she was to stay at the Hall. "I don't think I can stand it." She was weeping. "He calls me daughter all the time. They won't stop talking about Rob."

She'd never called again or come to the flat. He'd packed her few clothes and toiletries in the small suitcase and left it under the living room window. He had neither written nor attempted to contact her.

Tomorrow, he'd send the case round to Dolphin Square by car. No letter. She was right: some things just weren't supposed to happen.

OCTOBER 24, 1942

"I'm sorry, Boyd, but that's quite impossible."

"But it's urgent, old man. You'll want to see it right away. Honestly."

An ambulance roared by along Old Brompton Road and Price caught his breath, covered the receiver, and pushed open the door to watch it. Its tail lights disappeared at speed toward South Kensington and he breathed a sigh of relief. Not Sally then. For a moment . . . He went back inside. Boyd was piping in panic at the other end.

"Calm down, Boyd. What exactly have you got?"

"Jack Simmons came up specially by train from Southampton this afternoon. He wouldn't trust the post."

"Is he with you now?"

"No, he had to get back for his next shift."

"Where are you now?"

"Albany Road. Just across from Regent's Park. Why?"

370

"You have your motorbike?"

"Yes."

It was a bizarre idea, but no less secure for that. "Meet me in fifteen minutes at the Brompton Oratory. St. Joseph's Chapel. It's the second on your left as you go in."

Price sat bowed in the little school chair with the papers on his lap, the four candles on the offertory frame throwing just enough dancing yellow light to permit him to read. Boyd, at Price's insistence, had slipped into the confessional box out of harm's way, but the squeak of the chair inside proclaimed his discomfort only too plainly.

Price completed his second reading and sandwiched the handwritten pages back into the *Financial Times*. He pushed the newspaper into Boyd's dispatch bag and propped it against the chair in front of him. The facts were clear enough: a succession of convoys from British ports were mounting a massive buildup at Gibraltar. At a time and date unstated, British and American naval escort craft would meet a massed convoy of troopships, support and supply vessels fifty miles west of the Gibraltar Strait and shadow them south to a position five miles off Dakar, in French West Africa. Position papers detailed convoy formation sequences, escort patrol patterns, communication codes, U-boat hunting procedures, operating speeds "over the ground," and umbrella air-cover missions to be flown from Gibraltar. Jack Simmons's accompanying note pointed out that, for obvious reasons, he had not dared steal the original documents; the copies dispatched "for information" to FOIC Southampton by the Director of Naval Operations at Portsmouth had been available to him for no more than a few minutes each day for the past week. On grounds of urgency alone, he'd given up hope of copying a complete set. "I hope I haven't left it too late," he added in a postscript.

More creaks emanated from Boyd's impatient roost in the confessional.

Practicalities. No Director of Naval Operations worthy of the rank would permit circulation of secret material "for information" to home-based fleet officers *months* before an invasion. On the other hand, convoy dispatchers would require basic guideline material at least three to four weeks in advance. If Simmons had spent a week copying it, the timetable was now probably measurable in terms of two to three weeks at most. So: there were convoys, their destination was Gibraltar, they would in due course assemble under battleship cover and steam to a position off Dakar. Strategically, an Allied landing at that point made sense. Further north, American and British troops would have the Algerian-based Vichy French forces to contend with and their cooperation could by no means be guaranteed. By entering through the back door, the element of surprise would assure the Allied task force a head start. More to the point, Rommel's Afrika Korps would be caught off guard. A simultaneous attack: at Dakar, behind his back, and by the British forces facing him across the El Alamein line.

His duty was clear: order Boyd to dispatch Jack Simmons's written sheets at once to Geordie McNeil; encode a message for Boyd to transmit to Hamburg setting the date and time of pickup. Again, at no stage would he be personally involved; in a physical sense he would be outside it. How could it possibly compromise his decision to go to Curzon and make his peace? Another postponement, yes, but no more than a week or two.

Boyd had had enough. He pushed the half doors of the confessional wide and stepped out. Even by candlelight Price could see marbles of sweat glistening on his face. "Sorry, old man. Can't stand being shut up. Have you read it?" He took the chair alongside and toweled his face with his handkerchief.

"Yes, Boyd. I've read it."

He closed his eyes and saw Major Nikolaus Ritter on the day of their parting—camel's hair coat draped across his shoulders, tufted hat turned up piratically at one side—a swaggering image of the man of destiny. "Sommer, we're bound together by fate, you and I. You feel this, I can sense it. The fall of London will be signaled to the Fuehrer personally in Berlin. On his birthday, Sommer. Three words. The Shining Day." *The Shining Day.*

"Well, old man? I mean . . ." Boyd looked nervously over his shoulder. "I left the bike in the courtyard. A bit dicey, this time of night."

But there was another consideration now, the child, whose birthday would be the real Shining Day.

"Look—I don't want to seem pushy, old man. . . ."

He looked at Boyd Corrie blankly. "What do you think, Boyd?"

"Me?"

"You."

"Well, I think . . ." He tugged nervously at the loose folds of skin at his throat. "I say we get the whole kit and caboodle on its way. I can transmit the pickup details day after tomorrow. By that time Geordie'll have this lot"—he tapped the dispatch bag protectively—"and I can confirm date and time. No other way of doing it, is there, old man? Too much to transmit."

"And what are we telling them, Boyd?"

The handkerchief blossomed from Boyd's jacket pocket and he mopped industriously at his face and throat. "Absolutely everything, old man. *Le tout ensemble*. I don't quite see what you're getting at."

"When, Boyd? We have everything but a date. Tomorrow? Next month? Next year? How long does it take to mount an invasion? Do you know?"

"Well . . ."

Price smiled wearily. "Neither do I, Boyd." He felt weak, unequal to the challenge. "Post it to McNeil first thing tomorrow morning. Make your transmission in the usual way, 2100 hours the day after tomorrow. Here . . ." He took out his notebook and pencil, tore out a page, rested it on the open checkbook, and wrote a single code block. "We'll arrange the pickup for the twenty-ninth. Usual time, one hour GMT."

Boyd's relief was radiant. "I told Jack Simmons to call me Monday night. I'll ask him—"

"*Tell* him. The date of the Dakar landing—anything he can learn that pins it down."

Boyd got up briskly and shouldered his dispatch bag. "You can count on me, old man. You know that." His wide brown choirboy eyes shone with sincerity and once again Price felt a sharp stab of genuine regret.

"Get on with it, Boyd," he said harshly.

He bent over the bed in the dark, judged from the depth of her breathing that she was asleep, and straightened up. Before he could move away, she whispered, "You were a long time."

He perched beside her, his hand reaching automatically

for the swell of sheet and blanket over her belly. "I thought you'd be asleep."

"He won't let me."

"I'll have a word with him, shall I?"

Her hand found his. "Why did you have to go out?"

"I had to meet someone."

"Who?"

It was unlike her to nag, but it was hardly surprising. She had been confined to bed for three weeks with dangerously high blood pressure and little to do but read, knit, and worry herself to distraction.

"Work," he said evenly.

She hesitated. "You don't mind my asking?"

"Don't be silly. I'd tell you if I could, you know that. It's just that there are some things I can't discuss even with you. You know why."

No reply.

He said gently, "You mustn't let it get you down."

Her hand tightened on his. "Wouldn't it get you down, lying here for another two months?" Her skin was burning.

He kissed her. "Who was the one who said it was all worthwhile?"

"And who agreed with me? *You* don't have to lie here."

He stood up and stripped off his coat and jacket. "I'll make you a cup of tea." The healing balm. The cure-all. She never refused.

"No! Don't go. Come to bed, Tom. Please."

She fell asleep in the crook of his arm.

OCTOBER 27, 1942

The comfortless poverty of the Buildings was unchanged. Carbolic soap smells rose from the stone floors, generations of institutional dust from the matting on the stairs; the passage of feet sounded furtive. The whole place bore the taint of withdrawal and deprivation. But Menzies was a different man in these surroundings, at one with them. They colored his style, absorbed his personality.

Curzon watched the minute hand on the wall clock shiver into place; a quarter to midnight.

"The drop's timed for one A.M. on the twenty-ninth. Corrie transmitted from Site Two this evening. Hamburg agreed to make the rendezvous."

"Price swallowed it, then." Curzon felt curiously cheated. He had never really believed Gimlet would be fooled by the material slipped under Jack Simmons's eager nose at Southampton.

"He couldn't ignore it."

"No."

An uneasy silence settled between them. Menzies looked at him questioningly. "Well—out with it."

"I don't like it."

"You've made that plain enough," Menzies said dryly.

"I haven't changed my mind. The Simmons material was too complete. It won't fool Price for a minute."

"It *has* fooled him. It's on its way. Out of his hands, now."

"Unless he chose to let it go because he realizes we planted it on him. Suppose he has another conduit in operation. He simply has to tell Hamburg, 'Ignore the pickup product.' For all we know he's been doing that for years with the Pepperpot take."

"There's no evidence to support that. None at all."

"And nothing to disprove it, either." He wondered how he could put it, how to soften the blow. "Loughran saw a report last month on the Corrie surveillance."

"Oh?"

"There was a meeting between Price and Corrie on August 10," he said. "Next day, Corrie left his digs at nine in the morning, got on his motorbike and drove to Broxbourne, to the evening institute. The tail followed him."

Menzies brows came down in a straight hard line.

"It wasn't Corrie." Curzon plowed on. "The tail didn't get a look at his face till he got to the institute. He called Five straight away and they whipped someone else up to Corrie's place, but he'd gone. Corrie turned up next day. They still don't know where he went or why."

Menzies made light of it. "Corrie went home to visit his parents. The man who went to Broxbourne was Albert Summers, a friend of his, a solicitor's clerk. He went to fetch

Corrie's briefcase." He smiled contemptuously. "If Loughran has nothing better to do than embroider fantasies . . ."

"Corrie could have taken his wireless set. He could have contacted someone else, another of Price's conduits. But whether he did or didn't doesn't matter—he *might* have. He was free."

"And all of this, I take it, springs from your new evaluation of Price's personality?"

"He *is* different. He knows about me and he doesn't care. Nothing worries him. He's too damned controlled, confident. He knows what he's up against and it doesn't matter a damn to him."

"So?"

"So he's prepared for everything. The Dakar deception's a classic case in point, in my view. He'll string us along until we think it's a *fait accompli*, then he'll push through a message to expose it as a plant."

"And you really believe I'd leave that to chance?"

Curzon opened his mouth to reply but shut it again.

Menzies studied him coolly. "All right. Let's examine the wider picture. The Americans have spread the word across North Africa—bazaar talk, gossip. SOE are dropping hints in France and Belgium. Berlin are at this moment sitting on a corpse we floated ashore at Cadiz: the body of a British courier carrying top secret documents on the Dakar invasion to the governor of Gibraltar. Lisbon and Geneva are geared to add their two cents' worth in the next few days. Do you at least concede the German High Command might feel there's something in the wind?"

"That's not the point."

"The *point* is that Berlin have a choice to make. To view Dakar as a practical threat or as a deception designed to take pressure off Montgomery at Alamein. Without Price it's either or both. *With* him, it's a fact. His information is all Canaris needs."

"And all Canaris needs to abort it is a prearranged cancellation signal from Price. How do you know he hasn't already slipped that into Simmon's material?"

"Because we intercept it before it leaves the post office at Aberdeen. We always have. It reaches McNeil in precisely the condition we want. Nothing's left to chance."

"The drop's a chance. At least take McNeil out of circulation and let the Navy handle it. Who's to know?"

"And jeopardize the last link in a perfectly coordinated handover? McNeil always calls Corrie the day after a drop to confirm it went off without snags. If he doesn't make that call, Corrie will alert Price at once."

"Then get the Navy to lift the buoy after McNeil's dropped it. A last-minute check."

Menzies shook his head firmly. "We could afford to do that first time around. The system hadn't been proved; the E-boat hung back. But I won't take responsibility for last-minute tinkering with something as important as this. There's no need. We know McNeil has the material Price sent. We know it's not been tampered with. That's good enough for me."

"And what about *after* the drop?"

Menzies yawned and got to his feet. "That's tomorrow's problem, Paul. I suggest we sleep on it."

OCTOBER 28, 1942

The northeaster was piling up twelve- and fifteen-foot waves under a sky so low there was no telling where earth ended and heaven began. Rain rattled like shot on *Dolores*'s tiny wheelhouse windows and tore at Geordie McNeil's hands as he checked the warp and the circular weight in the stern locker. The little boat balked and groaned as the seaway hammered her head on and the decks streamed. Geordie went down on hands and knees and scuttled forward to the wheelhouse. He reached round Iain's legs and touched the container wrapped in oilskins in its locker. All secure. And damn glad he'd be to put it over the side.

"I'm away forward!" he roared in Iain's ear and the older man thumbed his understanding but didn't look round. *Dolores* roared with eager life, but only her manic shuddering beneath their feet told them she was responding; the bellow of her old Thorneycroft engine was lost to the howl of the wind and the monstrous suck and thunder of the sea. Iain brought her another point onto the wind and Geordie immersed himself in a calculation of how much they were losing against wind and tide. There were no books, no instruments to solve the equation for him—only the abstract guidance system composed of touch and smell and sensation. There would be no seeing the marker buoys on the way out through the cormorant gizzard tonight.

He clambered over the useless nets and wedged his body into the bow, his booted feet braced hard against the samson posts, his hands bound like steel clamps on the rail. *Dolores* crested a roller and pitched into the trough as if she meant to dive to the ends of the earth, but at the last moment she caught her foot in the next rise and reared to the sky. Five feet short of the summit, she dove again; the wavetop swamped Geordie and boomed over the wheelhouse.

He should have said no. There was duty and there was insanity and only a landsman or a loon would see the two as inseparable. Not this one, he'd said emphatically when Geordie went down to his little house to pick him up. Not for another run out to the Channel; not for another night tossing like a cork in the devil's washtub; not for more crazy games of hide and seek and no fish. There had been no pretending to Jock the last four times out. No pretending to Iain either, although Iain was different. Iain came. But this run must be the last of the winter. Besides, there were bills to be accounted for: warps and weights and canister buoys and twelve nights of empty nets. Boyd had never let him down yet; the wireless interrupter gadgets had arrived every time, on the dot. But like Jock, a man had to know where and when to draw the line.

He ducked his head into his shoulders as another rogue crumpled like a sagging mountain and hissed inboard to break on the wheelhouse. *Dolores* corkscrewed wildly, dived, rose again; and at the top, Geordie instinctively flung out his right arm. He'd seen nothing, but judgment had little to do with what a man could see. He could *feel* that break channel, smell it. Iain brought *Dolores* hard astarboard and, when the seaway began lifting her dead ahull, Geordie motioned full ahead and Iain set her barreling eastward.

Easier now. He pushed the rim of his sou'wester out of his eyes. Nothing to see; every marker buoy in the gizzard might

have blown off-station for all he knew. Black on black. Feel
her through; nothing else for it. A wing and a prayer.

Thirty minutes to the drop point, five to float the container,
five to pick up the leeway she'd lost, then back through the
gizzard and home on the back of the wind. If she—

Dolores met it on the rise, halfway up the loins of a
looming crest. Her foot banged hard on something and the
shockwave came up through the samson posts and through
Geordie's booted feet and legs and trunk. He heard a great
rasping metallic moan as an object scraped the port side of
her keel, and for a moment he thought she'd bottomed out on
a reef or a wreck. Then she bucked and dived; and in the
slough of the trough she blew apart like a paper bag.

OCTOBER 29, 1942

For some people, disaster is a balm; the initial shock is no
less of a jolt but a certain misty drowsiness quickly settles on
it, enhancing the pain to a comforting throb of relief, as if the
system were saying: It's happened, and it could have been
worse.

Regius Morrison embodied the type. He took the news of
the McNeil fiasco with a fixed and weary smile, hands plaited
securely on his blotter where they could do no harm, eyes
half closed; and—Curzon was sure he hadn't misinterpreted
it—a little shrug of resignation. His God-given cynicism had
not let him down. The three members of his staff present in
the room when Curzon related the facts—or the few scraps
of intuition masquerading as facts—sank into profound reflection that fell a long mile short of despair.

It should have aroused Curzon's suspicions but didn't; he
was too numbed by the catastrophe to register the reactions of
others. Indirectly he had Frank Loughran to thank for reviv-
ing his professional instincts. In mid-afternoon, he had learned
that Loughran was to be called to the top table at the express
wish of the Americans. Friends in need, said Morrison, explaining why he thought "Frank should sit in on the resuscita-
tion exercise." Just how important Frank was to them had not

been articulated. But the next few hours told Curzon all, and more, than he needed to know. In the evening, Morrison convened a post mortem at his office in Eisenhowerplatz. By then, as the Marine colonel put it, the shit had hit the fan and everyone knew it. Menzies had spent four hours with Winston Churchill, there had been placatory calls to Washington, and new lines of demarcation had been drawn.

Brigadier General Morrison was at his conciliatory best.

"I'm taking my share of responsibility for this, Stuart." He waved an insistent hand as if he thought Menzies was about to protest such Christian charity. "No, sir, my entire share. Question now is whether McNeil hit a mine as your Admiralty people suggest or whether Price somehow got to his boat?"

Menzies' eyes widened. "A bomb you mean?"

"A device of some kind. Why not? If he had any doubts about the material he was passing, maybe that'd strike him as the best way out of the whole mess." He turned to Curzon. "You have any thoughts on that, Paul?"

Curzon stole a glance at Menzies to test the water and decided it was the wrong moment for confession. He stuck to facts. "As far as we know, McNeil was right on the War Channel when the boat blew up. We can't be certain until the Navy get a couple of divers down. It could have been Price, sir, but I doubt it, personally."

Morrison nodded. "You're the expert on Price, Paul. I'll take your word for it. Let's leave that aside. Next point: we have to face the fact, like it or not, that Price is out of this particular game. Corrie's going to get no call from McNeil and he'll run screaming to Price. You want to take it from there, Bob?"

The Washington lawyer opened a folded paper under his hand, unconsciously cupping his fingers around it to shield the contents. "We spent the afternoon with BIa section, sir." He met Menzies' stare for a split second. "They're prepared to use one of their doubles, Wulf Schmidt, to run a shortened version of the Dakar deception. He'll have to transmit by wireless, naturally, so we've dummied up a message in two parts. The first part is general—a kind of taster. That goes out tonight. The second brings in specifics—dates, volume of shipping, possible beachheads, that kind of thing. He sends that forty-eight hours later."

"The Schmidt option was always in the background, you'll admit that, Stuart. His credentials with Hamburg are top hole." The general's lapse into stage English didn't embarrass him. "He'll do the job. Next point." He selected a cigar from his case and clipped the end. "What do we do now about Price?"

"You arrest him. That's obvious."

You arrest him. Curzon noted the transfer of power.

Regius Morrison spent a good minute applying flame to his Havana leaf. When it was fully lit, he nodded down the table at the bronzed Marine colonel.

"Sir." The officer had a jaw like a rock, deeply incised at the center. "We don't go along with the Admiralty opinion that McNeil hit a mine out there in the North Sea."

"Initially," purred Morrison. "We need proof, Stuart."

"Right. Proof. We've had our own surveillance on Price for a coupla weeks"—the bombshell brought two scarlet smudges of rage to Menzies' cheeks, but the colonel was not looking his way—"and the picture we get doesn't make too much sense when we compare it with the one coming out of your file."

"A matter of interpretation, maybe." Morrison tactfully cushioned the blow.

"Maybe. The supposition is that Price came over here in '39, walked into the trap you set for him, swallowed the whole Pepperpot play hook, line, and sinker and ran the way you pushed him. Well, sir—there are people on your own side don't think that's the way it went. They figure Price is one hell of a smart cookie. You used him and he used you right back. Take, for example—"

"There's no point in covering old ground, Sam," Morrison said gently. "Keep it current."

"Our opinion," the colonel went on brutally, "is that Price has been running another conduit. Maybe two or three."

Menzies sat motionless. Curzon felt the blood rise to his face.

"We have to accept that. Period. The Corrie-Simmons-McNeil conduit wasn't the only one." The colonel corrected himself quickly. "*Isn't* the only one. Now this is our problem: If Price blew McNeil's boat out of the water, he knows the material on Dakar's a phony. If he didn't, Corrie's gonna tell him tonight or tomorrow that the material didn't get through because McNeil hasn't checked back with him. Either way, Price has to make a move. *Our* guess is he planned all along to sabotage that boat and pass something else on to Hamburg. Via his emergency conduit.''

''And you also have an idea what that something is?'' Menzies inquired mockingly.

The colonel placed his hands flat on the table. ''The chances are he knows about the real landing.''

''But only possibly.'' Morrison qualified the claim with vigor.

''Our position is this.'' The colonel squared his great shoulders. ''With Price, anything's possible. So arresting him is no answer. He'll be expecting that, sure as you're born. Our guess is he's got a drop system organized. Maybe a message already in the pipeline, ready to go.''

Menzies came forward in his chair. ''Are you seriously asking me to believe—''

''I'm asking you to accept that Price may have information and a means of passing it, Stuart. That's all.'' Morrison's tone was uncharacteristically sharp. ''The simple fact is, we can't read him any better than you can—but we can benefit from past mistakes. The biggest of which was taking him for granted. All I know is I have to block every exit. That's what we're talking about here—exits. If he suspects the Dakar deception was a plant, how can he get word out? If he knows—by any stretch of the imagination—what the real plan is, how can he get word out? Not through his own transmitter. We agree about that. Not through Corrie; he's finished. So, he's got an emergency on his hands and for emergencies there are standard procedures, options he's maybe had worked out for years. My guess is he's got a backup man, a guy he probably never meets face to face and never talks to. But they'll have an arrangement, a weekly street pass, say, a certain place at a certain time: over the counter of a store, or at a newsstand, or in the subway. Whatever. And how Price *behaves* on that weekly pass determines the backup man's next move. Pull Price in, arrest him, and he misses that pass. That could be enough to send the contact to a prearranged drop. Price may have a message sitting there right now. *Exits*, Stuart.'' He polished his diplomat's all-weather smile. ''Arrest him and we put Hamburg on the alert.

Whistles blowing all over Europe. No, sir. We play it his way. We'll be one step ahead and one step behind everywhere he goes. If he sets one foot out of line . . ." He slashed the air with his Havana. "Price and his backup man. Take one, take both."

NOVEMBER 2, 1942

By eight o'clock the fog was so thick he could barely see the outline of the shed from the back door. He went upstairs to tell Sally he had to go out for an hour and left Dinah to prepare her supper. In the street he lost his bearings in the first twenty yards and walked headlong into a privet hedge. After that he kept close to the curb, tapping at it with his umbrella like a blind man.

The fog was all he'd needed to persuade him to go; a terrifying commentary on his wretched ambivalence. Fog = invisibility = proceed. If it had been a fine night he would have stayed at home.

His decision not to contact Boyd Corrie three nights ago had been arrived at just as arbitrarily. No objective analysis of pros and cons involved—he'd simply allowed himself the easy way out. Sally had been in pain when the time came to walk down to the telephone booth, and he'd persuaded himself he couldn't leave her. By now Corrie probably had panicked. Hopefully, he'd found the courage to call Geordie McNeil and Simmons and Co. and told them to lie low.

Irrational. Criminally stupid. But the truth was that Thomas Arthur Leslie Price had given up the unequal struggle of trying to impose his will on Wilhelm Sommer. The impulse to withdraw was increasingly stronger than the instinct to act. Yet what he was doing now was a bizarre mixture of withdrawal and action, camouflage and aggression. At best he had been stung into it by doubt.

He walked with some force into a lamp standard and the shock momentarily robbed him of the will to go on. He stood stock still for a few seconds, waiting for his heart to settle before going on.

Everything had sprung from Boyd, even this half-hearted step into the dark. No more Boyd, he'd told himself last night, and, in a fever of distraction, had begun searching his cache under the floor of the shed for any clues he might have overlooked to his association with the Corrie network. There were none, of course; his practice had always been to burn everything, even the rough coded scrawls in his notebook. Having found nothing he sat in the gloom and flagellated his memory for forgotten errors, unfinished business, as if his life depended on it; and out of a gray corner had crawled Boyd's apology of last October. His failure; a groveling admission of defeat cloaked in righteous indignation. His young lions of the People's Vigilance Committee had been unable to produce any verifiable data on the members of the Pepper Circle, other than what anyone could read for themselves in Who's Who or Debrett's Peerage. For the simple reason, puffed Boyd, that not one of them had ever applied for or been granted Party membership. "If they don't belong, they can't be a threat, can they?"

He'd sat for another hour in the shed, dissecting it, the two parts of him: Thomas Price, the pedant who refused to accept unresolved issues, and Wilhelm Sommer, who craved peace at any cost. Sommer wanted to go at once to Paul Curzon and make that peace; Price insisted that no peace could be bought so cheaply. Curzon would be made more malleable if Tom Price brought him real dividends immediately—like the Pepper letters, the albums, evidence of the existence of an active, powerful wedge driving deep into British political life. And Pepper, after all, was in Bristol this week. The flat in Queen's Gate was empty. Steal the letters. *The letters*.

And tonight there had been fog.

Pepper's flat smelled of jasmine, a sharp exotic perfume so pervasive he dared not turn on the lights until he'd ferreted it out. He ran it to ground in the bathroom: an open tub of blue-green brilliantine in an advanced stage of liquefaction. He relaxed. His nerves were in shreds.

He retreated to the drawing room and made an immediate search of the rolltop desk and sideboard, but there was nothing he hadn't found on his earlier visit. He took the bundled letters and the album into the dining room, then began a systematic reconnaissance of the entire flat: lifting carpets;

swinging aside pictures; delving into ornamental jugs and the profusion of plant pots; opening teapots, biscuit tins, suitcases in the bedroom wardrobe; sifting through piled shirts and underwear, suits and shoes. He had no idea what he expected to find.

At the end of it he returned to the dining room empty-handed and perched on the table to sort the letters, but his eye was caught by the wall of bookshelves to one side of the chimneypiece and he went to look at them. He began at the top and worked down, but Pepper plainly did not use his books as hiding places. The bottom shelf was taller than those above it—designed for art books, a collection of heavyweight historical volumes, phone directories, atlases. And another album? He pulled out the leather spine; it was not a book, but a stiff morocco case with a buttoned flap. He opened it.

The photographs, matt-finished eight-by-ten prints, clattered into the grate. He shuffled them together and took them to the table. There was a covering note: "There may come a day when the propaganda value of these pictures will prove to be worth a thousand times the effort I put into acquiring them. We now know that Reinhard Heydrich's execution by the Czech resistance groups on May 27 this year was planned and orchestrated by SOE. These pictures were taken by a Gestapo photographer between May 31 and the night of June 8. In that period, 10,000 hostages were executed by SS Einsatzgruppen in retribution for Heydrich's assassination; many of them individually and at random, but in the main in groups. The flash pictures herein were taken at Lidice, the village where Heydrich's assassins were parachuted in by the RAF at the conclusion of their training in Scotland. They tell their own story. As the group's senior historian and the man most likely to record the matter at the appropriate time, I think it best you retain them." The note was unsigned, but the hand was unmistakably Julian's. He checked one of the letters to confirm it.

One picture showed two SS men, grotesque by firelight and flashgun, holding babies head down in a cattle trough. Another was of ten shirtsleeved civilians, pitching forward as smoke puffed from the barrels of an SS firing squad. A third revealed a great fire—a barn or a shed; just visible behind the shooting flame curtain were the silhouettes of heads and arms. There were several studies of hundreds of distracted women, drawn up in line beside a train of gaping cattle cars.

His mouth was dry, his tongue stuck to his teeth.

In the name of retribution?

He flicked through the pictures again and suddenly stopped. It was a hanging. A young woman, dark, pretty, her wailing somehow transformed by the camera into innocent laughter; a civilian in the foreground—her father? husband?—being restrained by an SS trooper. And behind the young woman, adjusting the noose at her throat, consumed by his work but not so intently that he could not spare the camera a flashing smile, a young officer with the lightning forks of the SS on his lapels and the SD diamond of the Sicherheitsdienst at his cuff. He was hauntingly handsome: blond, snap-jawed, keen-eyed; strength and purpose radiated from him and the life force glowed. He was doing his duty and he knew it was holy. He looked no older than the pathetic young woman, but Price knew his age to the very minute of his birth. Willy Sommer, son of Wilhelm and Else, brother of Kurt, officer of the Reich, had barely changed at all in three years.

Brigadier General Regius Morrison raised the morocco case above the desk and dropped it with clattering emphasis on the leatherbound picture album. The bundled letters, returned minutes earlier from the photographic laboratory upstairs, sat accusingly at Menzies' elbow.

Menzies had responded with remarkable alacrity to the summons to Eisenhowerplatz; his readiness to accommodate the Americans at any time was openly grudging and at four in the morning particularly so, but he'd arrived a half hour ahead of Curzon. So had Frank Loughran, who now sat comfortably in a deep chair with a large bourbon in his fist and an expression of wooden inscrutability on his face.

Morrison tapped each one of his trophies in turn: the album, the morocco case, the bundled letters in their tray, the envelope containing the Lidice pictures. His recital of Price's visit to Pepper's flat had occupied a good half hour of their time; he was an accomplished raconteur and he gave himself to it with disagreeable relish.

When he finished, Loughran—paying the piper, Curzon decided darkly—came in on cue. "What the hell did he want these for?"

Menzies fixed Morrison icily. "Or *did* he want them? He left them, you say, on a table where Pepper would have found them the moment he walked in the door. Why? In fact, why go there at all?"

Morrison inclined his head; a grandee's eloquent bow. "That's the real question, Stuart. Why go at all? It was obviously important to him. He waited for the right conditions—fog you could cut holes in. He took one hell of a risk; and when he left—he ran out of there like a bat out of hell, my people tell me—he made no attempt to cover his tracks."

"Panic," Curzon put in.

The general shook his head. "There was no one else in the flat. And *nothing* else. We turned the place inside out. Just the letters, the albums, and the Lidice pictures."

"*That's* something," Loughran said quickly. "What's Pepper doing with classified MI5 property? Is he cleared for that kind of material?"

"No." Curzon fingered the evidence; the pictures were in a stiffened buff envelope. "Was there anything to explain what they were? As internal memo? A note?"

"Nothing." Morrison drew deeply on his cigar. "May I offer a hypothesis, Stuart?"

His courtesy was contagious. Menzies ducked his head.

"Pepper's in Bristol this week. We know that and we've checked his movements tonight. He hasn't left his hotel. But Price didn't *force* an entry; he had keys." Curzon and Menzies exchanged bewildered glances. "I'm suggesting Pepper gave him the keys and told him what to look for. Maybe these . . ." He touched the Lidice envelope. "Or any of this stuff. Or all of it. Or something else. I'm not saying I know why, but it certainly had one powerful effect on Price."

"If this is leading up to the proposition that Pepper is Price's backup man . . . ." began Curzon.

"Hypothesis, Paul," Morrison chided him gently. "Just a hypothesis. Look at the facts. Pepper can deny any suggestion of collusion. He has an alibi; he was out of town. He can deny the Lidice pictures were ever in his hands. Price took them there."

"He can't deny what's in the letters," Loughran drawled. "What *is* in them?"

"I don't know yet, Frank. First priority was to photograph everything; every letter, every page of the album. We've been doing that upstairs for the past three hours." He fingered the separate envelopes of prints and negatives. "First thing in the morning we'll take the letters apart line by line; run Pepper through the meat grinder and—"

"No!" Menzies slapped a protective hand on the letter tray. "Pepper's a British national and a government servant with high security clearance. If there's any doubt about his fitness, the responsibility is ours."

"Except where it affects Torch," snapped Morrison.

"Five are better equipped to answer that question than you are. I'll call them in myself." His hand stayed firmly on the bundled letters.

Morrison made the gracious gesture in time to avert friction. "Fine. Stuart. Division of labor. Makes sense. The fact is, though, we've got another problem. A time problem. Six days to Torch. Loughran, here, confirms that Schmidt's completed his transmission on the Dakar deception. We're on our way. But I want to know why Price made this trip to Queen's Gate tonight, and I want to know fast. If you want my opinion, he went there for one reason and one reason only: to pick up information Pepper left for him before he went to Bristol day before yesterday."

"Then what the hell's all *this* for?" Loughran said with a wave at the trophies.

"As I said, Frank, I don't pretend to know. But it stands to reason that if Price left them behind where Pepper could find them, he has nothing to fear from Pepper. He's not that dumb."

"What's your point, brigadier?" Menzies cut in.

"Investigating Pepper isn't enough, Stuart. I want him out of harm's way. Keep him in Bristol on some excuse; send him someplace else—anything. But keep him tied up and under surveillance."

"Very well." Menzies' face was devoid of expression.

"After that, I want freedom to act." The cigar trailed smoke in a wide arc across the table.

"What kind of freedom?"

"I want the Corrie network pulled in, Stuart. All of them. Then I want Cabinet support for a police action: full power to detain and question any and every contact Price makes in the next six days." He smiled weakly. "Now that's liable to cause a lot of friction, Stuart, and you'll have to take the flak, but short of arresting Price it's the only way to contain him. Agreed?''

Menzies nodded stiffly. "Anything else?''

"I'd also like Paul, here, to sit in on our surveillance effort. He knows Price better than anyone. He can read between the lines.''

"Yes.''

"Good.'' The general smiled engagingly and pushed back his chair. "I'd say that's about as much as we can do tonight. You'll send me a copy of Five's report on Pepper when you get it?'' -

Menzies shot to his feet abruptly. He piled the letter tray on the album and both on the buff envelope containing the Lidice pictures. "I'll take charge of these. I'll also take the photo copies you've made, if you please, brigadier,'' he said crisply, holding out his hand.

Morrison slid a bulky white envelope across the table. Menzies pointed to its twin pinned under the general's forearm.

"And the negatives, please. *All* of them.''

Morrison parted with the last vestiges of his night's work. The pained smile on his worn face conveyed plainly his belief that there was no trust left in the world.

"Can I drop you off somewhere?''

"Ebury Street, if you're going that way.''

"Get in.''

Curzon settled himself beside Menzies and the car surged out of Grosvenor Square toward Oxford Street. Menzies pointedly closed the glass partition to cut off the driver.

"I talked with the prime minister this evening,'' he said shortly. "He's concerned.''

Curzon rolled his eyes in the dark. Concerned!

"He sent a personal message to British army headquarters in Cairo this morning. Montgomery's planning to break through the Alamein line before the Americans go ashore at Casablanca. The prime minister's calling for a major British effort. We have to go at least halfway to meeting Eisenhower's advance.''

"Neck or nothing?''

"Churchill expects more. He's asked to be informed personally when Monty has taken twenty thousand prisoners. At least twenty thousand. When he gets that message he intends

ringing the church bells across the country for the first time
since the outbreak of war.''

''Politics.''

''That's not your concern. But Price is. Torch is. If Eisenhower fails, Montgomery fails. I have no intention of letting
that happen. You'll give Morrison all the cooperation he
needs. To the hilt.''

Curzon turned to look at him, searching the pale outlines of
his face. ''Morrison won't recognize limits,'' he said tactfully.

''Then neither will you.''

NOVEMBER 3, 1942

Death is not a closing of the eyes but an opening, not the
final decay but a renewal, not the departure of life but a
resurgence of hope.

The rubric ran through his head like a half-forgotten tune of
which only the chorus remained. It started up from the bottom
of the well of memory until, at last, he recalled the source.
The voice speaking it was his mother's. An afternoon by the
fire in the Dortmunderstrasse; she languorous on a couch,
reading a passage from Dickens, he cross-legged on the floor,
reciting it back to improve his English. Why must Tiny Tim
die, Mama? And her answer, quoted from another book or a
prayer or an invocation or a text learned at her own mother's
knee. *Death is not a closing of the eyes.* . . .

He turned on the pillow to look at the bedside clock. Eight
thirty. Almost at once there was a banging on the wall from
the next room—Sally trying to rouse him, knowing he was
late. He swung his feet to the floor and struck the wall with
his knuckles in an answering tattoo. He was drained of strength,
the will to move.

''Are you all right, Tom?'' she called out.

''Yes. I . . . overslept.''

He bathed and shaved mechanically and went in to see her.
Dinah's bed was far too narrow for her, but Dr. Welsh now
insisted she sleep alone and they were both far too concerned
for the baby to ignore his advice. She'd refused to deprive

him of their own bed and the result was that neither of them slept much. He propped her up on her pillows, kissed her, and opened the curtains. The sunshine was dazzling. A *resurgence of hope* . . . When Dinah came up with Sally's breakfast tray, he went downstairs and hurriedly swallowed a cup of coffee and the remains of Dinah's toast.

He put on his coat and dug into the pockets for his gloves; his fingers closed on a scrap of paper. He brought it out and scanned the first line: "There may come a day when the propaganda value of these pictures will prove to be worth a thousand times the effort I put into acquiring them. . . ."

He reached the kitchen sink as the nausea broke over his tongue and coughed out a wracking stream of coffee-sodden toast. When it stopped, he couldn't see for tears. He set a match to Julian's letter, then washed his face, cleaned up the mess, dried himself. He left the house without shouting his usual good-bys. No stomach for good-bys today.

He couldn't face the underground; he needed air, exercise, time to reflect. No—time to reason. Willy was not his son. Not *that* Willy: a hangman who could smile at a camera and kill without remorse. Not *his* Willy.

Habit, stronger than intention, drew him to the shop in Fulham Road where he bought his morning newspaper and tobacco, and he listened politely to Mrs. Pittuck's vicious attack on a government which, only this morning, had sent her husband his call-up papers. A man of forty-three! And they'd already taken her son and daughter. He turned to leave and walked blindly into a man standing literally at his shoulder. The shop had been empty when he entered and the stranger must have come in without triggering the warning bell. He apologized and went out into the street.

He stopped ten yards from the telephone box near the junction with Brompton Road and momentarily toyed with the idea of calling Archie Bassingthwaite at the Pepperpot to make an excuse for not coming in; but before he could act on it a large man brushed rudely past him and slipped into the box. He shrugged. There was no point in retreating now. He must make contact with Paul Curzon today, arrange a meeting— tonight if possible. He could be a free man before the sun rose again. He crossed to the Victoria and Albert Museum to catch a bus.

* * *

The first arrest was made at 9:12 behind the counter of H. M. Pittuck & Son, news agent and tobacconist, in the Fulham Road. Ivy Pittuck, forty-two, married, was invited to assist the security police in their inquiries and was instantly deprived of the right of protest. She was taken to a police station in Lucan Place.

At 9:42 Corporal David Robertson of the King's Own Scottish Borderers was hauled from his seat on the top deck of an omnibus in High Holborn. He was taken to Snow Hill police station by two men with American accents claiming to be plainclothes policemen and locked in a cell "pending interrogation." His kitbag and battle packs were searched, and his commanding officer at Caterham, Yorkshire, was advised not to expect his return to barracks for at least forty-eight hours.

John Edward Cutler, fifty-nine, a widower, tenant of a shop in Kingsway trading in ironmongery, tools, and carpentry materials, found himself at Snow Hill fifteen minutes later.

The arrests were to continue throughout the day.

At 1:45 Albert Basford, twenty-seven, a window cleaner with a medical discharge from the Manchester Regiment, was in the process of finishing his packed lunch on a bench in the central gardens of Russell Square when he was asked to accompany two slab-faced giants built like wrestlers. When he objected, they proved his judgment of their profession to be not altogether off the mark.

At 1:50, Lilian Montagu, seventy-two, a flower seller plying her meager trade at the entrance to Great Ormond Street Children's Hospital, was summarily charged with obstruction of the public footway and removed. In the course of being bundled into a waiting car, she fell heavily and struck her head on the curb. She was taken to Moorfields Eye Hospital, treated for a badly cut brow, and put to bed in a single room. A guard was mounted in the corridor outside.

At 5:23, Roderick "Nipper" Coates, sixty-seven, an evening newspaper seller whose all-weather pitch was tucked away snugly behind the wall where Sicilian Avenue joins the busy artery of Southampton Row, was unceremoniously deprived of his freedom and led to a plain green Vauxhall van. His unsold papers, his blackboard contents bill, his money satchel and blanket-covered folding chair were searched minutely on the way to Snow Hill. Nothing was found, but he joined Corporal Robertson and Mr. Cutler in the cells to "await interrogation."

Not one of the detainees—all of whom protested their innocence—connected their arrest with their unwitting proximity to a fair-haired man in a dark raglan coat and trilby; not even Mrs. Pittuck, the only one to know Price by name, who had sold him his *Daily Telegraph* and an ounce of Cut Golden Bar tobacco less than thirty seconds before the hooligans laid hands on her.

Stuart Menzies nudged the bound letters, the albums, the photographic negatives, the separate prints and the Lidice pictures into neat formation across his desk. Julian Mountford watched the performance with amused tolerance, his long body perfectly at ease on the uncomfortable visitor's chair, a cigarette trailing indolently from the thumb and forefinger of his right hand.

Menzies put an end to his fiddling and reached for his paper knife. "Good of you to come, Julian."

The cigarette danced deprecatingly. "Always a pleasure, Stuart. It must be a year. More. You look well." The stockade of primrose teeth, bold and unnaturally uniform, made a brief appearance.

"Yes. I had a word this morning with the head of Five and—"

"Pressing, he said. Pity. We could have done it over lunch. Overdue."

Menzies' knife bounced lightly on the piled letters. "You have access to the Price operation, of course."

Mountford nodded lazily. "Peripherally. Through JIC, in general terms, BIa at operational level. I can't pretend to be an insider, of course."

"And Pepper. You're quite close in at t' at level. The Pepperpot subsidiary interests; Russian liaiso, , that sort of thing."

The primrose smile spread extravagantly. "If I didn't know you better, old chap, I'd say you were having me on. No?"

"Humor me."

"Oh dear. Very well. As a member of the Inter-Service

Steering Group I'm quite *close in*, as you choose to put it. Russia, yes. I hold the liaison brief for JIC to the Cabinet Intelligence Committee, so I have access to Price. I represent Five on the Foreign Office political review board, which puts Pepper under my nose several times a week. *Stuart!*'' The long hands cupped in civilized appeal.

Menzies began stripping an elastic band from a bunch of handwritten sheets. ''You also know Pepper on a non-active basis.'' He didn't look up.

''If you mean by non-active—''

''He's a personal friend.''

Julian Mountford lay his head back on the chair and chuckled softly. ''If one claimed friendship with every chap one rubbed shoulders with at Cambridge—''

''Not a friend, then?''

''We were dons together several light-years ago.'' He closed one eye. ''Do I take it this sacrament has the blessing of our mutual friend? From top to bottom? No holds barred?'' He sucked deeply at his cigarette.

''Head of Five knows exactly why I called you in. I have his full sanction. If you'd care to call him—'' He touched the telephone.

Mountford waived the privilege airily. ''In that case, my dear chap, why didn't you say so?'' He folded one leg over the other. ''Let's get down to it, shall we?''

''You know Pepper.''

''Cambridge, 1919 to 1923. He was my tutor at that time, of course. He was still in situ when I went back in 1928 as a Fellow.''

''You knew he was a fellow-traveler?''

Julian sighed. ''Stuart, let's not waste time, what do you say? Skip the stuff you've already seen in my file. Keep to what you don't know.''

Menzies fingered the loose pages in his hands. ''Pepper ran a Communist study group. You joined—May 1920. From 1928 you yourself functioned as an occasional lecturer.''

''Conversations. Hardly lectures.''

Menzies turned to a marked page in one of the albums. ''You saw a lot of him. Traveled quite a bit—Paris, Prague, Cairo, Belgrade, Rome—''

''With Vernon Kell's blessing. I began reporting to Five on

the Pepper Group in May 1920. Precisely why I joined. It's all in black and white.''

''But your reports on him don't—''

''Kell told me once they were faint with damned praise. Well, they were. Pepper's an armchair ideologue, Stuart. An intellectual mouse. Most of them were; still are. He was a raddled pacifist from his student days—when the first war came along and he volunteered like a shot. Admiralty Room 40 staff, as you know. Yes, I traveled with him and quite a few others. In the line of duty, if the word's appropriate.''

''Your signature was on his last security clearance, I see. February 1938.''

''I was on the screening committee, yes. So, if memory serves, were you. Old chap. No?''

Menzies eyed him sharply, his face taut; then his mouth rucked at one corner and he smiled. ''All right, Julian. Point taken. I had to be—satisfied.'' He related the events of the night before. Mountford sat with his eyes shut, the cigarette adding more nicotine to the chocolate layer on his forefinger. When Menzies finished, he lit a fresh cigarette from the old.

''What exactly am I supposed to say? My mistake?''

''*Do*, not say. He's your man, your province.'' He dangled the handwritten pages he had set aside between finger and thumb. ''You wrote these?''

Mountford slipped a pair of gold-rimmed half glasses from his pocket, propped them on his nose and peered closely. ''Oh yes. Now perhaps you begin to see what I mean. What kind of conspirator keeps incriminating correspondence in his bottom drawer. Really, Stuart!''

''And these?'' Menzies opened the album at a page and held it up. Mountford ran his eye over three pictures of Pepper and himself in hiking shorts and winced delicately.

''Awfully gauche.''

''The American opinion would have been a little more reactionary,'' Menzies retorted dryly. ''If I'd given them a chance to check them out. Pepper cavorting across half the world with pink-kneed agitators and queers. You—a British security officer—carrying his bag. For God's sake, man, didn't it occur to you Pepper was keeping all this on record?''

Julian shrugged. ''My role was to watch them. It had to be done from the inside. It paid dividends. There were bound to be—anomalies.''

Menzies hunched forward. "We don't have room for anomalies. Not now. Our only priority is the Dakar deception. Nothing else. Price is my responsibility. Pepper yours. I want him kept out of London, pegged down, till it's all over. And I want you to take personal control. Drop everything else."

"Defrock him, you mean?"

"Do whatever you like after Torch."

"And—ah—if I find I've been wrong all these years?"

"Arrest him. Put him away."

Julian sniffed. "That might not accord with current thinking, old chap. Five's view, generally speaking, is to let 'em run. Harness them. Better the devil you know, etcetera."

Menzies got to his feet. "Your province, as I said." He pushed the pile of letters and envelopes across his desk. "You'll need these later on. Just let me know from time to time what you turn up."

Mountford rose, swung a briefcase from the floor and packed the evidence inside. He forced the clasp shut and locked it. He held out his hand and they shook.

"We must have lunch, old chap."

"If you're buying."

"Pleasure," Julian pulled on his coat, turned at the door. "I take it our American friends are taking very good care of Price? Day and night?"

"He's being well looked after."

"Good." He looked down at his case, tapped the bulge vaguely. "I certainly hope so."

The corridor outside Menzies' office was empty, but Julian Mountford strode to the staircase with briefcase and umbrella swinging jauntily, a half smile on his face, as if he were playing to an invisible audience. He handed in his pass to the Marine watch in the lobby with the same air of quiet amusement and stepped outside, breathing luxuriously as he came into the air.

He was halfway across St. James's Park, out of sight of the loungers by the lake, before he allowed the pose to drop like an unwanted glove. The smile slid away, the bulging case dragged his shoulders into an old man's hump, and he stopped by a bench, set down his burden and lit a cigarette. His hands shook and he studied them seriously, as if he expected the tremors to worsen. For a moment he looked about him, taking in the scud of low cloud, the cut of the wind through naked trees, the scurrying lunchtime crowds in The Mall. He shook his head slowly, as if surfacing from a dream, picked up the case again and set out for Queen Anne's Gate.

Price suddenly found himself in Elm Place and came down to earth with a jolt. Wool-gathering, Pepper called it. Self-hypnosis. He mustn't let Sally see him like this. But the small fears crowded back, gray shadow-spiders in dark corners, spinning veils of insecurity. He had called Curzon's home and office numbers eight times during the day without success. In a sudden rush of inspiration he'd searched for and found in the Norfolk directory a number for Curzon, Lt. Gen. Sir Martin, Bart. A servant had told him "Mr. Paul" lived in London and rang off.

He *had* to reach him. To have come this far . . .

He let himself in and Dinah, hearing his key in the lock, rushed from the kitchen.

"Ask me what happened today. Go on. Ask me." She pirouetted in front of him on her toes, grinning hugely.

He realized how little thought he'd given to her in the past few months. Always himself, Sally, and the baby. "All right. What happened today?"

"I got a job!" She took his hands and danced him around the tiny front room. "I got a job. I got a *job!*"

"Where?" He achieved the precise degree of surprise she expected, but his heart sank. He didn't want Sally left alone all day; not at this stage of her confinement.

"Guess!" She whirled him again and he began to feel dizzy.

He pulled his hands free and took off his coat. "Where, idiot?"

"Hamilton's. The shop on the corner near the hospital. You know, the clock shop."

"Doing what?" He remembered the place: a gloomy den lined with grandfather clocks and French ormolu.

"Selling—and things. Mr. John's going to teach me all about clocks. How they work and how to mend them and how to tell how old they are. All that. He says I'll be an expert before I'm twenty."

"You will, will you? And what's he paying you?"

"Three and six a week for a start. Four and six when I'm seventeen, and then he says we'll see as we go along."

He couldn't spoil her moment. He gave her a hug. "I think I'll start making plans to retire, then." He jerked his head upward. "Has the doctor arrived?"

"He's coming at nine o'clock, the nurse said. You'd better go up and report for duty. I'll make the tea."

He swung a hand at her bottom and went upstairs.

The rain came at last in a cannonade of thunder, slashing the roofs of buses and cars in St. James's Street, filling the gutters. Homegoing workers caught unprepared raced for the shelter of doorways and awnings and Julian Mountford had to push through a throng of them as he left his club. He smiled faintly at the rain, buttoned his coat collar against the deathly chill and unfurled his umbrella. He threaded through the stationary traffic and gained the far pavement of Piccadilly. A porter was preparing to lock the gates of the Burlington Arcade but he stood aside when the tall man appeared at his shoulder and let him through with an old soldier's cheerful salute.

The watchmaker's shop stood halfway along the arcade behind an elegant bow window, a hangover from another age. It was already locked and shuttered for the night, but Mountford was still several yards from the door when it opened to him. He passed inside.

"Lock it!" he said sharply. Milos obeyed, pulled the blind, and ushered him through a black crepe curtain behind the counter, then drew the curtain and stationed himself at the outer door.

Georgi Torovin offered Julian Mountford no greeting. He stood behind Milos's repair table, his hands dug deep into the pockets of his black coat, square and short and ageless. The brim of his ancient black borsalino kept his face in permanent shadow, a flat unremarkable square like the rest of him, featureless.

"So?"

"Milos told you?"

"We have no—" Torovin groped for the word with thick capable fingers—"no services to meet this case." His accent was Georgian, guttural and unsure, ill at ease with short vowels.

Mountford dabbed rain from his face with a large polka dot handkerchief. "You'll find them," he said shortly.

Torovin's face rose to meet his; the sloe-black eyes taking a brief measure of the Englishman's expression.

"The penalties are high. The motive—"

Mountford threw his Homburg onto the table with sudden petulance. "Motive is irrelevant! I'm in an untenable position. I have to find a way out of it. If you imagine for a moment I intend to stand here discussing *motive* while—"

"You have no right to—" again the search for a word— "expose me, the Embassy. The Ambassador's position is vital here. To embarrass him—"

"Price is more important at this moment than fifty ambassadors. If he survives the next few days I'm finished. My work's finished. Pepper and the whole Whitehall infrastructure is finished. Do I make myself clear?"

Torovin was not impressed by displays of temper. "The embassy cannot be—connected. There must be no measures of force. No weapons."

"How you do it is your affair." Mountford touched the handkerchief to his nose. "Price is the key. Get rid of him. And quickly."

"And if it is undertaken? You will—correct the matter? Pepper? Your group? You can protect them—their position?"

"I can try."

"Try is not enough. For sure or nothing."

"For sure, then." Mountford lit a cigarette with exaggerated slowness.

"The Americans. You say they have this man under guard?"

"Under surveillance. One car posted near his home in Elm Place; four men within immediate reach of the house, two other cars on standby. All three cars are linked by radio. If Price leaves the house, he'll be followed."

Torovin glanced down sightlessly at a miniature tool kit in front of him. "He is guarded, then. At the house."

"You can't do it at the house, no. Outside. In the street, in the open."

"There is no other way? Perhaps it is possible to—"

"No other way," Mountford cut in sharply. "I want

him—'' he heaved up a great breath from deep in his chest. ''Tonight. Get your people in place tonight.''

Torovin did not reply for several minutes. He stood utterly still, seemingly transfixed by Milos's dainty tool kit. He looked up at last and met Mountford's eyes without emotion.

''The blood is yours then, not mine.''

Sally went through a ritual cleansing ceremony before Dr. Welsh called on his twice-weekly visits, a laborious and painful process involving a sponge bath, a change of bed linen and clothes, and at least an hour of cosmetic devotions. Dinah was called in as nurse and moral counselor on these occasions. Price was banished.

He went out to the shed to look at the crib, held it up to the light and examined it for blemishes, inexact cornering, streaks in the varnish. There were none. It was perfect. He'd picked up the wood for next to nothing in a scrap yard, an old Victorian piano case of polished rosewood; the keyboard lid, carefully cut into sections, provided the arched hood and the curved base. He balanced it in his hands. He'd give it to her tonight, he decided. After Dr. Welsh had gone. Before he went out to call Curzon.

Dinah shouted from the back door. ''He's here!'' and he started violently.

''Coming!''

He took the crib into the house and hid it behind the settee in the front room.

Surveillance is a game for dullards and thieves; Curzon hadn't played it in earnest since 1939 and he'd lost the appetite for it. Imagination was the enemy, inventing sound that existed only in the mind, images and flashes of movement that were not there to be seen, sensations of being observed when there was no one there to see.

When the doctor's car arrived, ten minutes late, the two Americans, Peet and Shoeman, crossed from opposite ends of Elm Place to double check it and signal that all was well. They set off again on their independent tours of the block and Curzon tucked himself into a doorway on the corner of Old Church Street, ostensibly, he told himself, to make sure the car they'd left pulled up on the curb there was safe, subconsciously to indulge a temptation to slink back into its warmth for a few minutes. Not that he would; the Americans were impervious to discomfort and he had no intention of admitting weakness himself. He flapped his gloved hands under his arms to draw the circulation and set off to the furthest point of his patrol on the Fulham Road.

Imagination. Rob at his shoulder, matching him pace for pace, puffed out as always in winter in a shaggy old Ulster and shapeless hat, a great scarf at his neck, Wellington boots on his feet, head bent. He never had looked where he was going, always deep in himself, never sharing what he found. *My other dead son.* He shuddered. Nicky was right; some things aren't meant to happen. And some are. Rob was meant to step on a mine. Price was meant to find Sally Logan. Sally was meant to have her baby, a Christmas baby, so Price had told him last week. How much irony did nature have to force down the throat of humankind before it took the lessons to heart?

He turned at the end of his beat. The early evening rain had laid the groundwork and the east wind had done the rest: ice on the pavements now, glittering muffs of hoar frost on hedges and trees, a high clear sky radiant with star clusters. Not a soul moving anywhere. Price wouldn't move, either. Why should he?

Curzon would take the car, if he did, Peet and Shoeman the pavement tail. "Lay back with the car," Peet had warned, as if he'd invented the game. "Don't let him hear it, okay?"

A second car was cruising aimlessly around Thurloe Square, a third was parked in a builder's yard in Drayton Gardens— both were probably scaring the wits out of the local residents. And there would be another five nights of this. Then Torch and it was all over. No one was speculating yet on what would happen to Price after Torch, no one cared to. *Never kill your turkey till you know for sure there's going to be a Thanksgiving Day:* Morrison, the homespun guru of Wall Street. No reason, though, why Paul Curzon should sit out the suspense and wait for the ax to fall on Price's neck. He'd already applied to Menzies for reassignment. Overseas—and the sooner the better.

He shuddered again; an inner cold.

Come on, Rob. Best foot forward.

*   *   *

They stood in a semi-circle around her bed, and she blushed prettily at their approving smiles.

"Healthy as you or I, Price." Dr. Welsh fished his watch from his pocket and took her pulse again to insure that his first two readings hadn't been mistaken. "You'll be fetching and carrying yet awhile, I'm afraid, but you don't mind that, do you?"

Price shook his head at this monstrous inanity.

"Course you don't." He gathered up his instruments and piled them into his bag. "Excellent, my dear. All in order. Unless the little devil's playing games, I think we can safely assume he'll put in an appearance in time for Christmas. Christmas Day as I said, if I know my babies."

"The Shining Day," Wilhelm Sommer murmured unconsciously through Tom Price's lips.

"Eh?" Dr. Welsh beamed to cover his bewilderment at the incurable absurdity of prospective fathers. "Shining Day? Yes, well that's the spirit."

Price saw him out, then took the crib from behind the settee and carried it upstairs. A small performance: backing in through the door, wheeling dramatically, arms outstretched: "Your crib, madam." He set it on the floor by her bed.

She ran her fingers over the silken finish, her lips slightly apart as a child's are at the moment of giving. Then she suddenly snatched her hands to her face and turned into the pillows, her shoulders shaking.

He dropped down beside her, touched her hair. "It's not *that* bad, is it?" He hadn't been prepared for this; should have guessed.

"Oh, Tom—"

He took her in his arms, pulled her hands from her face and kissed her tears, her forehead, her nose, her mouth. He could feel the life force pulsing within her; his life, his force.

"Look. I have to go out for a minute. All right?"

"Where?" Her eyes searched his, frightened little passes of the iris, left and right, cutting into him.

He pulled her close again and kissed her on the mouth, held it till she responded, felt her rear into him. He laid her back on the pillows then and brushed a wisp of hair from her eyes.

"A couple of minutes, honestly. I'll be back before you know I've gone."

Curzon was at the farthest point of his beat, a good hundred yards from the junction with Elm Place, when Price left the house. Peet had gone back to the car to radio a "situation unchanged" report and Shoeman was rounding the corner of Fulham Road to begin another circuit of the block. Caught flat-footed, the Americans confessed later. The departure of the doctor's car had lulled them; they'd loosened up. Curzon's first indication that Price was on the move was the eruptive appearance of Shoeman from Elm Place, running hard, one arm flagging left and right with his pencil torch. Curzon sprinted to meet him.

"He's out! Headed down Onslow Gardens. Jesus Christ, I nearly walked into him! I'll get after him. Tell Peet to back me up. And alert the cars. Now, man, *now*!"

The nearest callbox was the one in Old Brompton Road. He'd used it rather too often in recent weeks to call Boyd, breaking his own most binding rule, but there was no harm in it tonight, nothing to lose. Nearly ten o'clock. Curzon was bound to be home at this hour. Had to be.

He heard the snickering patter of fast-moving feet some distance behind him and swung on his heel, straining his eyes into the darkness, but there was nothing to see and, although he stood immobile for at least a minute, the sound was not repeated. He walked on at a brisker pace, his heart thumping hard. Overreaction; imagining the worst. The thought made him smile grimly. The worst was over.

Well, almost. Curzon would insist on seeing him tonight; his superiors, certainly. An immediate inquisition, hours of it. No, not hours, *days*. Weeks, perhaps; he had no idea what this kind of thing entailed. Whatever they decided, it meant going home to Sally in a few minutes with some excuses for why he was leaving her. No, the worst wasn't over yet. But he could rely on Paul. Paul would make the Lie good.

He turned into Brompton Road, met a stinging breeze head on and gulped at the freezing air. He glanced up at the stars.

He'd never seen them so bright; the Milky Way was like a sapphire stream, brilliant on an eternity of black velvet. Omen?

The cold began to plague his ankle and he surrendered to the limp, letting his foot drag lazily to ease the pain.

A weakness is never remedied by giving in to it—Georg Sessler.

And omens are for children born on Christmas Day.

Curzon eased the Ford into the curb, switched off to reduce the static and pressed the transmit button of the walkie-talkie. "Come in, One."

"This is Lane. We see you, see him. He's alone."

"Two?" Curzon whispered.

"This is Andrews. We're at the junction of Drayton Gardens and Old Brompton Road. No sign. We'd better close in."

"No! You'll stay where you are, both of you. Is that understood?"

"Roger." The replies were simultaneous and noticeably aggrieved.

Curzon pushed open the door. "I'm leaving the car. Stay where you are and don't *budge* till I give the word. I'm taking the radio."

The callbox stood under a leafless beech, fifty yards away on the far side of the road. Price dipped into his coat pocket for the coins he'd put there and glanced quickly along the road in both directions. A few cars were parked in front of the larger houses, but there was no movement, if you discounted the pinhead red, amber, green of the blinkered traffic lights on the corner of Onslow Gardens. He stepped off the curb and somewhere in the dark beyond the callbox a heavy truck, sidelights dimmed, pulled to a squeaking halt. The lights went out but the engine idled on quietly. He withdrew to the pavement and turned away in sudden alarm, not in reaction to the truck but rather to the responsive chord it struck in his head.

Last chance. There was no going back from this call. It wasn't a temporary panacea and there were no guarantees. Probabilities but no guarantees. He gulped again at the cold air and without knowing why turned and began to limp back the way he'd come. No *guarantees*. For Sally, the baby, Dinah. He pulled up short; ahead of him, one on either side of the road, he thought he detected flickers of movement. He waited. Nothing. A long way behind him, the heavy engine ticked over spasmodically, but he couldn't see a shape, even a loom of black against black. Phantoms! Why hesitate now?

Moral objections? Dear God—morality! He had never been Hamburg's pawn; he owed them nothing. The debt was on *their* side, not his: it would never be paid. And as for Karl's notion of patriotism—earth, blood, fire and steel!—it was the currency of the madhouse, a passport to Willy's world of holy extermination, to Else's promised land of perverted truth and unswerving savagery. He owed *them* nothing, either; they'd chosen their course long before Else sold him to Praetorius and if he'd been allowed to stay they would have taken the same road, with or without his blessing. How could he have convinced them that the summits of human perfection lay in the mind, the intellect, not in a social structure laundered of ethnic strains? Or that nobility lay in the soul, not in the colour of hair and eyes.

Where you are, Germany is; but that was true only in the more enduring context of personal integrity, a sense of honor. Where I am, hope is. Life is. In a few weeks a child would be born; its life cycle would begin as Wilhelm Sommer's new life cycle began, in a renewal, a resurgence of hope. Where the *child* is, my Germany is.

Enough. He turned on his heel with sudden resolution and stepped into the road.

The night bombarded him with more phantoms—two shadowy figures following him, one on either side of the road; again the patter of running feet behind him; the sudden energetic growl of the truck ahead—but he closed his mind to them, his eyes fixed on the callbox under the beech, the coins in his hand, the words forming on his lips. "Paul, this is Tom. I want you to—"

Then the thunder of the engine stopped him in his tracks, in the middle of the road. The truck was twenty yards away and bearing down on him remorselessly. The shadows on the pavements materialized as men, running at first, then frozen still. From behind him, a man's scream, "Tom!" and because he knew the voice he snapped his head around to find it, but two outstretched hands, palms flat, caught him full in the back and sent him spinning into the gutter.

His head struck stone and filled with sunburst light but he saw. He saw. The thundering truck struck flesh with a sickening *plap*! of liquid sound and a body flashed through space in a great arc and cracked like whipcord round the trunk of the beech. The truck swerved, steadied itself and raced on to the Onslow Gardens crossing. It seemed to pause, then a shape—smaller; a car?—lifted away from it and crashed down on its side. The tail lights of the truck winked, winked again, and vanished.

He tried to sit up, collapsed on his side. The phantoms, two men, were on hands and knees beside the body under the beech. He heard a car shrieking out of the void, wind rustling in the trees above his head, the sound of his own breathing, and a voice, half-remembered, his *own*, mouthing the only thing that mattered: he turned on his front, forced himself up on elbows and knees, and crawled toward the phonebooth. *Paul, this is Tom*. His bent head bumped against a leg and with an oath the phantom turned and kicked him full in the chest. No pain, but something snapped sharply inside him and the coins leaped from his hand, clinking on stone. *Paul, this is Tom*. He stretched for them and touched a hand, an arm, a shoulder. Another wild kick, in his side, below the ribs. The force of it lifted him and dropped him down. He struck bone and flesh and blood and recoiled, raised his head, touched, looked.

Paul Curzon's wide green eyes stared sightlessly into an eternity of black velvet and the light of a million stars.

At two o'clock in the morning of November 8, 1942, General George Patton sent the first wave of his Operation Torch attack force ashore at Fedala, fifteen miles north of Casablanca.

Four days earlier, after persistent assaults on Rommel's dwindling Afrika Korps, General Bernard Montgomery had breached the El Alamein line and begun the hard drive westward.

Many months were to pass before the desert victory was assured but, in time, Winston Churchill received the message he had longed for. Not twenty thousand but forty thousand prisoners had been taken by the advancing British on the fine spring Sunday morning when, for the first time since war was declared, the church bells of England rang out in every city, town, and hamlet. As the streets of London echoed to a thousand bells, Churchill made this signal to President Franklin Delano Roosevelt:

"Now this is not the end. It is not even the beginning of the end. But it is the end of the beginning."

About the Author

Frank Ross is a pseudonym. THE SHINING DAY is his fourth novel.